THE
*M*ARABOUT's
Secret

Book Two
❦ *of* ❦
The Hussar's Love

KARL MAY

TRANSLATED BY
ROBERT STERMSCHEG

THE MARABOUT'S SECRET

Unabridged translation of the original German text by Karl May (1842-1912).
First published 1883-1885 as *Deutscher Wanderer*, in serial format.

ISBN-10: 1-897373-73-2
ISBN-13: 978-1-897373-73-6

Printed in Canada.

Printed by Word Alive Press
131 Cordite Road, Winnipeg, MB R3W 1S1
www.wordalivepress.ca

WORD ALIVE PRESS
Just Write!

DEDICATION

It goes without saying that this project, as well as the one preceding it, would not have attained this caliber had it not been for the support of my wife, Toni. I truly am blessed.

Acknowledgements

I would especially like to thank my father, John Stermscheg, who instilled within me the desire to explore the works of Karl May.

To Ralf Harder, for making the original text available on the Karl May Gesellschaft (KMG) website.

To Gord and Trish Kell, for their advice and encouragement in the writing process.

I would like to thank my friend, Ethel Beck, for her proofreading and invaluable suggestions. Your hard work eliminated many typos and enhanced the text.

To Annemarie Kramer, for her insight and suggestions.

To my editor, Evan Braun, who continues to surprise me with his skill. Thanks for all your hard work.

To Clint Byars, for all your design work.

To Michael Michalak, who supported me from the early stages.

I would be remiss if I didn't give honour to the One who has given me the talents to be a writer in the first place. My faith in God has kept me humble and given me perseverance in my new career.

To all of you, thank you. Your work and encouragement has not gone unnoticed, and continues to motivate me.

FOREWORD

I believe that we have all appreciated the way gifted authors, such as Alexandre Dumas, James Fenimore Cooper, and Karl May, have opened up a whole new world to our imaginations through their portrayal of life. I have read and re-read many of Karl May's travel narratives and novels, and I can honestly say that I have never tired of them. His prolific writings have taken me from the plains of Europe to the endless sands of the Sahara, even to the Rocky Mountains.

I discovered that there were a number of variations from May's original work, *Die Liebe des Ulanen*, from which this series of books is derived. As I searched further, I realized that the four novels as we know them today (*The Road to Waterloo*, *The Secret of the Marabout*, *The Spy from Ortry*, and *The Gentlemen of Greifenklau*) later stemmed from a series of *Lieferungen*, or consignments in a local newspaper, *der Deutscher Wanderer*. These 108 parts comprised what would later be known as the *Münchmeyer Romane*. They were sold by Karl May to the newspaper and appeared there on a regular basis, running from September 1883 to October 1885.

These stories, which May penned in a style of adventure and intrigue, were well-received by the general public. As previously noted, May started his tale circa 1870, and introduced the reader to the central characters, spanning to the second and third generation. Particularly clever is the way in which May weaved two central and historical figures, Napoleon Bonaparte and Field Marshal von Blücher, into his story. The inclusion of these larger than life men added an additional dimension to the plot, heightening the drama faced by the novel's protagonist, Hugo von Löwenklau. This second book, *The Marabout's Secret*, takes place about 25 years after the conclusion of *The Prussian Lieutenant*, long after the deaths of Field Marshal von Blücher and Napoleon Bonaparte.

As I contemplated this second translation project, I felt that I had attained a considerable amount of experience after writing the first book. Once again, the challenge I faced was in remaining faithful to May's original work while conveying the story in modern English. When you consider that much of this story takes place in Algiers, a country with different customs and languages, the difficulty of translation is all the more apparent. Also, Karl May's novels, brimming with French and Arabic references, were penned in German over a century ago. It was not my intention to critique or edit Karl

May's use of the Arabic; rather, I wanted to convey to the reader what May had written, thereby conveying his knowledge of the language. Furthermore, Karl May adopted his own opinions, right or wrong, based on his knowledge of the Muslim world and its teachings. Of note is a reference in the opening chapter of the third book (previewed in this volume), that a woman has no soul. He goes as far as to include a number of references to the Koran, or Qu'ran, quoting verses to illustrate the richness of this book, and the profound impact it has had over the last few centuries.

I often encountered obscure idioms, such as: "Da steckt er wieder einmal die Teufelsflagge heraus!" Literally translated, this would read as, *There he goes again, flying his devil's flag for all to see!* Being unfamiliar with some of these older expressions, I have checked various sources, including source material on the internet. To my surprise, I often received the answer from an unexpected, yet reliable source: my father. He was quite familiar with them, and after a moment of reflection usually had a quick response.

Karl May's style was to "sandwich" thoughts in the narrative, often ending up with broken-up or run-on sentences. I recognized that, while this was workable in German, it created long and cumbersome passages in English. To render it more fluent and understandable, I've broken up some of the lengthier sentences.

I was also faced with several nameless figures that were often simply referred to as 'he' or 'she'. I felt that giving these anonymous characters names, particularly the French officers in chapter four, would enhance their contribution to conversations, making them more complete and interesting.

The many words of an era that have long ago faded into the mists of time also needed to be resurrected and explained to give them relevance. I hope that their use in this story lend it the authenticity it deserves. See the translation notes for further details.

This second book, *The Marabout's Secret*, brings about an entirely different flavor. It would be fitting for me to briefly explain the marabout's historical significance.

A marabout, Murābit in Arabic, refers to one who lives in a garrison, or one who is cloistered from others. The marabout is an Islamic religious leader, or teacher of their sacred writings, specifically the Koran (or Qu'ran). They predominantly lived in the Western Sahara. Many of the earlier practices of marabouts suggested that they were reclusive in nature, yet allowed pilgrims to approach them so they could impart teaching and purification.

There were, of course, various sects within the Islamic order, with some marabouts traveling around the Sahara, selling relics (trinkets), a practice that was frowned upon by the fundamentalists. They often presided over important ceremonies and festivals. Some were accused of exploiting young students who chose to follow in their path, by appropriating their monies and goods.

The more formal, idealistic marabouts were teachers of the law and embraced the Islamic traditions with religious fervor. They devoted themselves to many hours of prayer and contemplation, imparting their knowledge to the faithful, many of whom traveled on lengthy pilgrimages to meet the devout men. Some of these marabouts were highly esteemed and even elevated to the stature of a caliph, and revered to as holy men.

Robert Stermscheg
June 2008

TABLE OF CONTENTS

"*If it be a sin to covet honor,*
I am the most offending soul."

-William Shakespeare

CHAPTER ONE
Countess Rallion

During the first half of the nineteenth century, few Europeans managed to visit the infamous Timbuktu.[1.1] Countless researchers and scientists would have gladly given half their wealth to be able to reach the small city on the border of the Sahara and Sudan. Only a lucky few ever succeeded in the attempt, some of whom went at it alone, while others participated in larger, better equipped expeditions, choosing to approach it from the north or the west.

To the north, the desert posed a number of dangers in the form of pervasive robbers who lived in the shadow of the Atlas Mountains. The elusive Tuareg[1.2] tribes that dwelt in the innermost region were unfriendly to the looks of curious Europeans and posed no less of a threat. To the south lived the followers of Islam, a group that already held a seasoned mistrust of any newcomer. The Muslims, acutely aware of their penchant for proselytizing heathens, steadfastly resisted any attempts toward religious conversion.

In 1848, the Berlin Society for Exploration, having been entrusted with the commission of exploring the vast Sahara, came up with plans for a thorough expedition into the desert and, if the conditions proved suitable, a further push toward Timbuktu, though not at the expense of the team's safety. The society made inquiries to secure the most capable, enterprising, and knowledgeable team of adventurers they could find with scientific backgrounds.

The unanimous decision was to select First Lieutenant von Löwenklau for the task of leading the expedition. The young officer enthusiastically jumped at the opportunity, though his parents were forced to overcome their natural reservations over sending their son on such a perilous journey. After all, Gebhard was the only child of Cavalry Master Hugo von Löwenklau and his wife Margot (née Richemonte). The young man's special benefactor and godfather remained none other than the irrepressible Field Marshall von Blücher himself.

Gebhard, the spitting image of his father, had barely reached young adulthood when news reached the Löwenklau family that the Baroness de Sainte-Marie had died and had providently made him the sole heir of the Jeannette estate. The story of the Sainte-Marie family had unfolded tragically.

Baron Roman, having disregarded his mother's objections to marrying Berta Marmont, had fallen out of grace with the baroness. Consequently, he had been forced to leave the estate and relocate to Berlin with his new wife.

Shortly after his wedding, Hugo von Löwenklau had moved to his own estate at Breitenheim, accompanied by his new bride. Occupied with his new business holdings, he was unaware when the young baron's marriage to Berta began to dissolve. He received a letter from Roman outlining how Berta had fled in the company of Captain Albin Richemonte, and that he was pursuing them both. After all this time, it seemed Richemonte hadn't gone far after all. He might have exercised his own revenge on the Löwenklaus had it not been for Berta's intervention.

Some time later, Madame Richemonte received a letter from the Baroness de Sainte-Marie, describing how she had not only lost her son's heart but his mental faculties as well. She learned that Berta had been killed in Marseille, at the hands of her own son.

Since that time, Baron de Sainte-Marie and Captain Richemonte had disappeared without a trace. Richemonte, implicated as an accomplice in Baron de Reillac's murder, had ultimately been discharged from the army for undisclosed reasons.

Choosing to focus on the present and prepare themselves for the future, Hugo and Margot von Löwenklau had decided to distance themselves from the past as much as possible. It was Hugo's wish that his son enlist in the military, resulting in Gebhard's enrolment in the officer's academy. The young man excelled in his studies and distinguished himself among his peers. Only one other cadet, Kunz von Goldberg, proved to be his equal and their common interests formed the foundation of a lasting friendship.

Young people often dream of the future and the promise of accomplishments, and these two friends were no exception. Determined not to fall behind their peers, both men fulfilled the necessary military requirements and received their commissions as officers. After the initial service, Kunz von Goldberg was seconded to the Paris legation. He had already been residing in Paris for several years when Gebhard von Löwenklau received the invitation to lead the expedition to Timbuktu.

Gebhard requested a short holiday so he could make the necessary preparations for such a lengthy trip. There was much to accomplish. He had to procure maps and check the availability of instruments and other scientific items, many of which were only available in Paris. It was thus decided to make the French capital the meeting place for the expedition participants.

Having concluded his business in Berlin, Gebhard took his leave and traveled to Paris. Upon arrival, his first order of business was to surprise his good friend Kunz with a visit. As they greeted each other warmly, Kunz was the first to speak.

"What a surprise to find you in Paris!" he exclaimed. "Are you here on leave?"

"Yes, a holiday that will take me into the Sahara."

"The Sahara? You intend to travel to the desert?"

"Travel to it, yes," Gebhard began, "but my plan is to march right through."

"Gebhard, don't talk in riddles."

"It's really quite simple. I've been fortunate enough to be included in an expedition to Timbuktu."

"All the way to Timbuktu? It sounds like a dream, almost impossible to believe."

"That's how it seemed to me when I accepted."

"Tell me all about this expedition," Kunz encouraged. "How did you manage to take part in it? Who are the participants and what goals have you set?"

Kunz listened in amazement as his friend launched into the story. When Gebhard finished, he heartily shook his hand.

"I congratulate you," he said. "My God! Gebhard, I'm so glad that finally one of us can follow that boyhood dream we had so long ago. You'll see the vastness of the Sahara firsthand!"

"No doubt," Gebhard replied, seemingly in jest. "Not only firsthand, my friend, I'll be up to my elbows in sand while you continue to study and expand your influence in Parisian society. You'll revel in the finer things while I roast under relentless heat. When I return, you'll have been promoted to the rank of major while I'll have been converted to a *Moor*."[1.3]

"Despite all those refinements, I wish we could trade places. What an adventure awaits you, my friend. You'll live with the Bedouins, fight with the Tuareg, and shoot hyenas, jackals, and maybe even tangle with a lion. Heavens, a lioness! Somehow, that reminds me of Hedwig."

"Hedwig?" asked Gebhard. "Hyenas, jackals, lions, a lioness, and lastly... Hedwig. Together, they seem to form a progression toward wild ferocity."

"Hmm, you're not that far off. Hedwig isn't tame at all."

"Ah!" Gebhard laughed. "Is this Hedwig perchance a wild and unfettered tigress? Perhaps she should be confined to a zoo! Or a menagerie."

Although Kunz shook his head, he cast his friend a glance that conveyed a hint of the mysterious. "No, my friend. Hedwig is a wonderful being who unfortunately possesses a measure of the untamable. She isn't confined to a tiger's cage, but rather to a palace on *Rue de Grenelle*."

"Is she young and beautiful?"

"A beauty whose looks could drive a man to madness."

"Is she rich?"

"Destined to inherit a fortune. She lives with a wealthy aunt."

"*Zounds!* Then take your Hedwig and leave the aunt for me."

Kunz laughed. "With pleasure! Though you might think about Hedwig's younger sister, a far sweeter choice. Together, we could divide the spoils as brothers-in-law!"

"You don't say! So, your Hedwig has a sister? May I solicit you for a description of her outward appearance?"

"Yes, though I wouldn't do it for just anyone."

"Thank you," Gebhard said. "Now then, how old is she?"

"About seventeen."

"And the color of her hair?"

"Blonde."

"Hmm, my favorite color. What about her eyes?"

"Hazel," Kunz said. "They shine like the stars."

"Are they more like a distant planet or a blazing comet?"

"They're so soft and tender, likely to melt your heart at first glance."

"What about her figure?"

"She's slim and, despite her youth, has an appealing shape."

"What's her voice like?"

"Like the golden voice of a nightingale."

Gebhard let out a low whistle. "She sounds almost too good to be true. Does she already have an interested suitor, like your Hedwig?"

"No, not yet."

"How convenient. Tell me, what's her name?"

"Ida."

"That doesn't sound too bad. Does she have any parents?"

"No," Kunz said. "They're both dead."

"Really? She must be nearly ready for marriage."

"Unfortunately not. There is a large obstacle, a *Cerberus*."[1.4]

"Does this obstacle come in the form of an old, rich aunt? We could overpower the dinosaur with a good club," Gebhard suggested. "Or better yet, with our charm, whichever proves more effective."

"I hate to be the bearer of bad news," sighed Kunz mockingly, "but in this instance, you can't wield a weapon. Nor can you rely on your skills as the consummate socialite."

"I believe you," replied Gebhard. "Perhaps I'll have more luck than others."

Kunz's eyes sparkled tenaciously. "I'll endeavor to pray for your success."

"You're too kind," Gebhard said. "Now, here's what you can do for me. Take me with you to *Rue de Grenelle* and facilitate the introduction."

"As long as she doesn't snarl, howl, or bite," Kunz mused.

"Do you think I'm afraid of an old woman? Don't forget, my name is Gebhard and Blücher is my fearless protector. My motto is *Go forward!*" Just then, another thought occurred to him. "You spoke of howling and biting. Where on the rungs of the social ladder might I find this old aunt?"

"She's the Countess of Rallion."

"I take it she's not friendly."

"My friend, she's positively set against anyone of German extraction. What's worse is that she doesn't seem to like any newcomers at all."

"Yet you managed to get close enough to become infatuated with her niece."

"Well, yes," Kunz admitted after a brief hesitation. "I should add that I did so despite a few obstacles."

"What might those be? There's more than just a disagreeable aunt, I presume."

"First, of course, is the aunt. Second, Hedwig herself. The third comes in the form of a bad-tempered nephew, Count Rallion, who's always getting in my way."

"Does the aunt favor him over you?"

Kunz shook his head. "Not in the least. It's as though the old lady has no desire whatsoever in welcoming any suitor for her nieces."

"Stop exaggerating, Kunz," Gebhard jibed. "I wouldn't mind getting to know this family. That's where you come into the picture. Since they're already familiar with your finer qualities, it shouldn't be too difficult for you to introduce me."

"Then you want an introduction?"

"If it's not asking too much."

"How long will you be in Paris?"

"No more than two weeks."

"That's good!" Kunz exclaimed. "You won't have enough time to cause too many problems for me. I'll do my best."

Gebhard narrowed his eyes at his friend. "You think I would cause you some embarrassment?"

"Well, you are taller. And stronger. And have more sex appeal. I have a lot at stake here, my boy!"

"But you forget that I'm also your friend. Don't worry. I'll be gentle and do my best to conform to etiquette. Believe me, you have nothing to worry about. I'm not a fan of boisterous women – you can keep Hedwig all for yourself."

"Heaven knows she's feisty," Kunz said. "Ida on the other hand is quite compliant. I'm convinced you'll be impressed with her, if only you were staying a little longer."

"Two weeks is long enough," Gebhard laughed. "Tell me, does the aunt have a weakness or preference by which we could work our way into her good graces?"

"A weakness?" Kunz asked, thinking about it. At last, he snapped his fingers. "Of course! I nearly forgot. That's what I wanted to talk to you about. Certainly, she has a weakness."

"A weakness for what?"

"Have you ever heard of Gérard?"[1.5]

"Gérard? Which Gérard? The general?"

"No, the famous lion hunter."

"Oh, you mean Gérard from the Sahara," Gebhard said. "His exploits are legendary. Of course I've heard of him!"

"Hedwig and her aunt are infatuated with his adventures."

"There's a curiosity," Gebhard said. "I suppose it's understandable. They are women, after all."

Kunz nodded. "Uncomfortable for me, though," he said, gaining a faraway look. "Especially since I'm no lion tamer."

"Ah! So that's it. Your Hedwig won't settle for anything less than a lion hunter. Have you considered that she's trying to get you all worked up?"

"Possibly."

"In which case, you can count your blessings."

"How come?" asked Kunz, puzzled.

"A girl who's bent on irritating a man, who hasn't done anything to deserve it, is doing it because she's in love with him."

"Do you really think so?"

"I'm convinced of it."

"Dear God! Do you speak from experience?"

"I have plenty of it!" laughed Gebhard sardonically.

"How is that possible? I've always considered you to be an untainted youth."

"Which is exactly what I am. No female has yet tried to corrupt me. How is it that the two ladies are so enraptured with this lion hunter?"

"Two reasons. The aunt reads practically all day—"

"Romance stories?" interrupted Gebhard.

"Far from it! She despises romance novels. She has a great interest in stories about expeditions, though. Hedwig conveys the excitement of the periodicals through her daily reading. Both ladies devour anything about adventure and admire those who play a part in it. Gérard is widely talked about. It's no wonder they both yearn to hear about his escapades."

"All right, that's one reason. What's the other one?"

"It only applies to the aunt. It seems that some time ago she had the opportunity to meet Gérard. She was so enchanted with him that she invited him and his entourage over for the evening. You can imagine what a sacrifice this was on her stingy nature. In doing so, she discovered an uncanny resemblance between Gérard and – hmm, I don't want to be indiscreet."

"Kunz, we're friends!"

"True. Well, she discovered a resemblance between Gérard and a previous suitor that she patronized."

"Really! I'm sure she didn't tell you this herself. How did you manage to find out?"

"My son, who do you take me for?" he asked with mock indignation. "*I am a diplomat!*"

"But still only a lieutenant."

"That may be, but I do mingle in those circles."

"Excellent! Nicely done, oh wise one."

"As such, I've learned how to forge relationships within the ranks, solicit information without being too obvious, and sift through relevant news that others would find cumbersome."

"So, you managed to discover the identity of her previous suitor?"

"Yes, with incomparable cleverness I might add."

"How did you pull that off?"

"I was once in her boudoir—"

"Zounds! As a potential admirer?"

"Not at all, as a reader. Madame showed me the contents of an envelope, mostly pictures of relatives. What caught my eye, however, was the way she examined one, nearly failing to put it down. I looked closer and discovered it to be an older portrait, the image of a handsome man who wasn't a relative at all. After some investigation, I discovered he was her husband's banker. She quickly added that it had been fashioned by an artist, but she was only trying to mitigate her disclosure."

"That was rather skilful of you."

"Thank you. I knew I was on the right track."

"Smart ass. You probably didn't find out the banker's name."

"Of course I did," Kunz grinned.

"Surely not from the old lady herself?"

"Of course not. Who do you take me for? I sought out her niece Ida for clarification."

"Ah, the sensitive and friendly one!" Gebhard couldn't resist adding.

"She recognized it at once and supplied me with a name. He was a Parisian who at one time was with means, but later succumbed to the vices of an opportunist, Baron de Reillac. After that, he sunk into misery and hardship."

"Reillac?" asked Gebhard quickly. "What was the banker's name?"

"Richemonte."

"Really? Richemonte!"

Kunz looked at his friend with apprehension. "You look surprised to hear that name. Why?"

"You still don't realize the significance – it's my mother's family name."

"Now that you mention it, I recall your mother is of French extraction, Kunz said ponderously. "Of course. She was born by that name, Richemonte."

"Whose father was a banker..."

"...and was misled and betrayed by Reillac! You're right! Forgive me, my friend, that it slipped my mind. I didn't realize how closely connected they were."

"There's no need to apologize. I never knew my grandfather. Whether I should hold him in honor isn't clear to me. Do you think it's the same man who was the patron to Countess de Rallion?"

"Certainly! Even though my intention was not to hurt your feelings."

"You didn't in the least, Kunz. My grandmother was his second wife. Perhaps this all occurred prior to the second marriage. It's all very interesting."

"I believe you. Actually, I suspect the whole affair still pains the countess to this day. Not in the same way as when she was younger, but it still influences her! I believe she had, and still does have, the ability to entice a man."

"How fortunate that you didn't know her then."

"Exactly. Now I can take my time to lead her niece astray."

"The untamable one!" Gebhard noted. "I must confess, your revelations about the family are of more than passing interest to me."

"Then let's see if I can introduce you to the family."

"When?"

"Hmm! I suppose you're in a hurry."

"Of course. I'm only in Paris a short time. When is the countess most disposed to receive visitors?"

"In the evening, though I've been known to attend in the afternoon as well. Once you see Hedwig, you'll realize why she's captured my heart. It's fortunate for me that the countess doesn't permit many visitors. Both nieces would have been snapped up long ago."

"Despite the dragon?"

"They would have found a way."

"And now you want to steal one of the nieces. Well, I wish you the best of luck."

"I can't tell you how much I desire to be near her," Kunz admitted. "I couldn't bear for another to sneak past me and capture her heart. Would this evening suit you?"

"I have a commitment, but I should be able to get out of it."

"Six o'clock?"

"Yes. We can meet here at six o'clock."

"That's best. I'll make my way over there in the course of the afternoon to prepare the countess."

Gebhard paused, considering the timing of the introduction. "Wouldn't it be better if you postponed the announcement? She might turn me down and yet be inclined to accept me when you announce me tonight."

"You don't understand her ways, especially her mannerisms. Above all, her will is what counts. Besides, the usual formalities associated with social events are foreign to her. If I were so bold as to bring you along unannounced, I'm convinced she would refuse us both outright."

"Then do what seems best to you. Just don't discuss my family history with her. I would rather initiate that so I can evaluate her response myself."

"Do you really think your grandfather was her acquaintance?"

"Yes. But I have to go now. If I'm to spend the evening with you, I have to rearrange some of my commitments."

They parted company until the evening. All day, Gebhard thought about their conversation. The story which his friend had unraveled affected him more than he had disclosed. He had never been in love. Now that he was about to embark on a dangerous outing, a romantic liaison seemed inappropriate, and yet he had a feeling that the nieces were going to play a significant role in his life.

CHAPTER TWO
The Aristocratic Menagerie

Gebhard, dressed in his best suit, arrived on time at his friend's suite. "You certainly are punctual," commented Kunz. "Ida, the perfect picture of refinement, seems to have drawn your interest."

"Perhaps it was the lure of meeting the dragon," laughed Gebhard. "You're all dressed up and ready to go yourself. Is Hedwig the Untamable to thank for this?"

Kunz looked a little embarrassed. "How would it look if I greeted you in my pajamas?"

"Well, why not?" his friend said with another laugh. "I wouldn't have held it against you. Since you're properly attired, though, I take it as a good sign that we've been granted an audience with the countess."

"Very astute of you," Kunz acknowledged. "You have me alone to thank for arranging this difficult meeting."

"I'm deeply indebted to you." Gebhard's voice dripped with mock irony.

"It might surprise you to learn that I was being serious. The old Madame is no friend of constant companionship. When I informed her of your German background, her forehead wrinkled. When I elaborated that you're an officer in the military, you can imagine how she..."

"...wrinkled her nose," suggested Gebhard, laughing.

"You're not far from the truth," replied Kunz. "Initially, she remarked that she was reluctant to make herself available."

"How is it then that you were able to change her mind?"

"I explained to Madame that I had given you my word you could accompany me tonight. I suppose I must have some standing in her household, since she gave my request some consideration. Otherwise it would have meant little to her if I had to break my word to you. She then resorted to her typical ways, however, by insisting that you would only be received this one time."

"Unbelievable! She doesn't waste any time."

"You had better be on your best behavior."

"Whatever for?"

Kunz sighed. "Then I feel sorry for you, old man."

"I intend to portray myself the way I actually am. Those who want me to come across as pleasing need to show me their hospitality."

"My dear friend," cautioned Kunz. "I can tell you're already thinking like the nomads. You've adopted their mindset."

"And you're a diplomat through and through. Your strategy seems to center on you coming across as amiable. Actually, it seems she's not really interested in exploration, otherwise she would have been more hospitable in receiving me. Doesn't she want to discuss my upcoming trip to Africa?"

"She knows nothing about your trip, Gebhard."

"Hmm, perhaps it was best that you kept it from her. Shall we go, Kunz?"

"Yes, come on, you old desert bandit."

They took a carriage, and a short time later arrived at *Rue de Grenelle*, stopping in front of the residence of the countess. Even though it was a monstrosity of a house, they couldn't find an attendant at the large gate. Few lights were on, making it difficult to see. When they stepped inside, the staircase and foyer were sparsely lit, but at least there was a servant here.

"Is the countess available for a visit?" Kunz inquired.

"She is currently in the drawing room with her two nieces," the servant replied formally.

"Is anyone else with them?"

"Of course!" the man replied, his eyes twinkling with repressed information.

Kunz reached into his pocket and withdrew a coin. "Who else is inside?" he asked, handing it to the porter.

The servant, apparently rarely rewarded by the stingy countess, bowed deeply before replying. "Count Rallion, her nephew, is presently with the ladies, Monsieur."

"Has he been here long?"

"No. He just arrived five minutes ago."

"Please, announce me, as well as First Lieutenant von Löwenklau."

The servant preceded them, complying with their request. The large drawing room, once adorned with elegant and costly furniture, was now no more than a reminder of a past opulent era. An expensive candelabra, normally adorned with six large candles, sat in the middle of a large ornate table holding only two candlesticks. Consequently, they shed little light and encouraged the room's occupants to sit closer to the table. The pronouncement of the newcomers having been made, they pushed their chairs back and rose to greet the two officers. Gebhard's eyes fell on the countess, who was closest to him. Not tall in stature, she made up for it with quick and graceful movements that easily belied her sixty years. Her countenance revealed sharp features and dark, piercing eyes.

Gebhard had to agree with his friend's earlier assessment. He supposed that at one time she must have been attractive, perhaps even beautiful. Some of her beauty still resonated in her features and self-assurance. She was flanked on each side by a lovely girl, both of whom stood out against their aunt's dark gown.

Hedwig the Untamable was dressed in a blue silk gown. Her penetrating glance, the droll dimples, the mocking smile of her lips, and the thrown back head all gave the appearance of a woman who was eager to pick a fight. Yet at the same time, there was also a hint of mysteriousness in her eyes.

Her sister made quite the opposite impression. Ida was dressed in a rose silk gown. Although a year younger than Hedwig, she was more impressively endowed. Her soft hazel eyes, veiled by long eyelashes, were inquiring rather than penetrating like her sister's. Her small, finely shaped head seemed almost too small to support her full-bodied hair. Ida's chin and full, luscious lips were complimented by an exquisite forehead and elegant, curved eyebrows. Her unpretentious beauty was not lost on Gebhard and had a profound effect on him.

The last occupant stepped into the recesses of the shadows, allowing himself to make observations of the strangers while he himself evaded their scrutiny. Count Rallion, the nephew, was approaching thirty years of age. His physique could be described at best as long and thin, culminating in a gaunt, elongated head. His small, irregular face was offset by a rather bushy brow situated over an aquiline nose that resembled a scavenger's beak. The count's small, beady eyes, thin lips, and long neck all added to the impression that anyone desiring to come closer would be kept at bay by the proud demeanor of the bearer.

The two officers, dressed in civilian clothes, bowed deeply before the family.

"Gracious Countess," said Kunz von Goldberg. "I am honored to be able to present to your company my good friend and colleague, First Lieutenant Gebhard von Löwenklau."

The countess stepped forward and surveyed Gebhard with a sort of calculated indifference. "I bid you welcome, First Lieutenant von Goldberg," she commenced. Then, almost reluctantly, she turned to face Gebhard. "Lieutenant von Löwenklau, may I present the two countesses, my nieces, and over there, Count Jules de Rallion, my nephew." Her welcome was clearly meant for Kunz alone, judging from her scant acknowledgment of Gebhard and conditional introduction.

Gebhard bowed. Instead of dismissing the countess' impolite welcome, Löwenklau countered with his own, one that still conveyed a pointed message, though in a less deliberate manner. "I thank you for the introduction, gracious lady," he replied coolly and deliberately. "I only arrived in Paris today and my first obligation was to pay my friend Goldberg a long overdue visit. Since he had committed himself to visiting you tonight, I saw no other means of spending time with him apart from accompanying him." To those present, the rough translation was clear: *I'm not here on your account, but rather for my friend.*

The countess was slightly taken aback by his forward remarks. Ida raised her eyelids as a warning to him. Hedwig tilted her head further back and tapped her fingers together. Count Rallion coughed irritably, and even Kunz felt he should convey a warning to his friend by way of a cautious glance.

"Please take a seat," the countess replied curtly. Turning to Kunz, she added, "So, Monsieur, I take it your friend desired to have your company."

"Of course, Madame," he confirmed, "but not exclusively, as he intimated."

"I will allow that," she said, her tone approaching mockery. "Perhaps he is not as familiar with our French language so as to express himself more eloquently."

The count jumped at the opportunity to vent his frustration. "I find that the Germans as a whole use an inferior form of French. And what about their names? So difficult to pronounce. What was his first name? Gepar—" He broke off the attempt. "It was something ridiculous!"

"You are mistaken, Count," replied Löwenklau evenly. "It is not Gepar, but rather Gebhard. I suspect the real reason our German words cause you to stumble is that you are not as comfortable in the German as I am in your French. I would like to point out to the countess that I have mastered French, so I can present myself as one having been born here. There is nothing deficient or lacking in my understanding of it."

It was as though a bottle of wine had been carelessly knocked over. The Rallions looked at one another with wide, unbelieving eyes. Kunz, trying to appear circumspect, kicked his friend in the shin. Only Ida failed to show her displeasure. She realized Gebhard had been insulted and secretly admired the way in which he had chosen to defend himself.

"Pah!" snorted the count. "Gebhard is still a poor choice for a name. I believe this was Blücher's Christian name."

"I was christened with that name after the famous Field Marshall, yes. He was my father's friend and my godfather," Löwenklau said, smiling.

"What?" the count exclaimed. "Blücher was your godfather?"

"Yes, Monsieur."

"Well then, my only advice to you is not to disclose that little known fact. If you do, forget about being included in Parisian society. Blücher made a huge blunder by failing the French people."

"Are you of the opinion that Napoleon was an angel?" the German asked. "He chastised the world and tried to become its dictator. Since you took it upon yourself to offer me advice, I would like to reciprocate with the same. My mother was born in Paris and loved her country. Therefore, I am not only familiar with her people, but I also respect them. I have been welcomed everywhere I have been introduced. I have been accepted with hospitality and gladness, with the exception of yourselves, where I have been ridiculed for my name and my use of the French language, which I consider to be on par with yours. My coming expedition will take me into the Sahara, where I am convinced that the wild *Tuareg* will bid me welcome once I enter his modest tent with *Habasek ja sihdi*, (welcome oh fine one). Should I tell this untamable nomad that in Paris, the center of culture and innovation, this custom of welcoming strangers has been overlooked?"

Although Löwenklau could have said more, he opted to remain quiet while stillness enveloped those around him. When no one answered, he slowly rose from his chair and continued his discourse.

"My friend had illustrated this family as a fine example of Parisian aristocracy, and I came here as a guest of this fine house, convinced I would find confirmation that the French have embraced the life of a blameless cavalier. Monsieur von Goldberg is a good judge of character, and I'm curious to learn whether or not he came to a hasty conclusion here."

They were all still looking at him. Whether out of astonishment, fright, or anger, it was hard to tell. Before he could turn away, a soft alto voice addressed him. "Pardon me, Lieutenant," Ida said. "Didn't you disclose that your mother was a Parisian?"

"Yes, indeed, dear *Fräulein.*"

"Are you really planning on embarking on a trip into the Sahara?"

"Across the Sahara to Timbuktu. Perhaps even further."

"Your mother must be very courageous in allowing her son to undertake such a dangerous journey. I wish I could personally tell her how much I admire her courage and her faith in God." Ida's voice magically drifted through the vast drawing room, resembling that of an angel. Employing her feminine cleverness, she had successfully broken the tension. She had grasped the vital points which Gebhard had elucidated in his speech to arouse her aunt's curiosity.

Gebhard approached her, extending his hand.

"Mademoiselle," he said. "You have salvaged your nation's honor, whose child I also am. I am grateful for your warm interest in my mother, whom you haven't even met. I intend to take her picture with me into the vast Sahara so that she may encourage me even there. May I introduce you to her by way of this photo? And when I return home, I will tell her of the warm welcome I have received from a fellow Parisian."

Gebhard loosed a small ornate locket from his watch chain, opened it, and handed it to the young countess. Ida took the picture into the light so she could examine the features.

"Oh, Monsieur!" she exclaimed. "What a beautiful lady and what exquisite eyes. Your mother must be very fine. Dear aunt, don't you want to have a look as well?"

Ida handed the locket to her aunt. She was still unsure if she should respond with an angry outburst to Gebhard's chastising or simply have him thrown out. Without realizing it, Madame had the ivory picture in her hand when a knowing recognition struck her. She quickly looked over at Gebhard.

"Is this really your mother's picture, Lieutenant?" she asked, her voice remaining hard and standoffish.

"Yes, Madame," he replied.

"Did she grow up in Paris?"

"Yes."

"What was her family name?"

"Richemonte."

"Richemonte, really?" she mused, her interest piqued. "I know a family by that name. I now recall there was a daughter who I saw quite often. I believe she would roughly have the same lines and features which I see in your mother's portrait. How was your mother's father employed?"

"Originally he was employed in the capacity of a banker, Madame."

The stern expression on the aunt's face softened somewhat, and the slight movement of her hands suggested she was more interested than she let on. "What was his full name?"

"Jean-Pierre Richemonte. Actually, it was *de Richemonte*. However, one of his ancestors omitted the 'de' for some unknown reason."

New life came into the countess' face. Her lines softened considerably and her eyes rested on Gebhard in a manner that could almost have been mistaken as friendly.

"*Mon Dieu!*" she continued. "That must be the man whose family I was acquainted with. Could you relate to me the address where they once lived?"

"Certainly. His business was located on *Rue de Vaugiard*. After his death, my grandmother moved to *Rue d'Ange*. It was there that my father, a Prussian officer at the time, met my mother."

"Did she really love him?" she asked as hardness crept back into her voice. Kunz had correctly characterized her as a hater of the German race.

"Yes, dear lady. She still loves him to this very day."

"But is that appropriate? I mean, she being a French lady."

"Evidently, Madame. It was our Lord Jesus who commanded that we should love one another, regardless of our descent. Was it not our God who instilled in each of our hearts such a mighty love, one which drowns out any prejudice, hate, or trace of racism? Each one of us possesses the same ideal. How fortunate if we choose to follow His leading."

Ida's eyes had a shimmer of light in them that conveyed approval of the way he handled himself. His words had even affected her aunt, whose previously close knit eyebrows relaxed a fraction. Her eyes exhibited distance, as though she were reminiscing about a distant memory the young officer had resurrected through his disclosure.

"You may be right in what you say," she acknowledged haltingly. "I hadn't intended to judge your affairs, considering I may not even be in a position to exercise this right. I am still not clear if you are referring to the same family. Did your mother have any siblings?"

"She had one brother."

"What was his name?"

"Albin Richemonte."

"Really? Do you know of his profession? Was he also a banker?"

"No, Madame. He was an officer, a captain in rank, and attached to the Emperor's old guard."

"Yes, now I recall. Is he still alive?"

"Perhaps. No one knows for sure."

"No one knows? Surely you must be familiar with his whereabouts, Albin being a near relative."

"Not in this case, dear lady."

"Have your parents lost touch with him?"

"They did their best to avoid him altogether. Whenever he succeeded in approaching them, the results were detrimental to them."

She slowly nodded her head, as though recalling certain details. "Yes," she acknowledged. "He was a conniver who played a part in his family's demise. Do you know anything about his affairs?"

"I am certainly acquainted with some details."

"Are you familiar with his accomplice, a man with whom he labored to bring about his parents' and sister's demise?"

"If you are referring to Baron de Reillac, then you can take some comfort in the knowledge that he is dead."

"Really?" she asked, raising an eyebrow. "I suppose the world is spared in dealing with one less demon. How did he die?"

"He was murdered."

"Recently?"

"A long time ago, probably on the same day on which the Battle of Waterloo took place."

"Who was the murderer?"

"His friend and accomplice, Captain Richemonte himself."

"His own friend and companion?" she gasped. "What a despicable deed! You will have to tell us the whole story! But first—" Her voice assumed the same flat frosty tone she had employed earlier. "I have to advise you that the manner and tone in which you conducted your earlier conversation was not very pleasant for the ears of a lady."

The countess glanced at Löwenklau calmly and expectantly, waiting for an apology. He bowed again, continuing with a smile. "Madame, we Germans like to make use of our proverbs. May I illustrate?"

"Which one did you have in mind?"

"What goes around, comes around."

"I'm not fond of this idiom. It only proves that the German is the one who seeks retribution and revenge, while he conveniently lays it at the Frenchman's doorstep."

"Oh, he merely wants to point out the brevity and certainty of life, which I'm sure you're familiar with. A German's character has always seemed to me to be more passive than active. It only changes into retribution, when it's been forced upon him."

"Who drove you to this forced predicament?"

"The answer lies in your own question, gracious lady. Since you imply that I was forced to appropriate a form of defense, the implication is that I was driven to it as a result of being provoked."

"It was certainly no direct attack upon yourself, Monsieur."

"Still, it was full of energy and emotion."

"A small misgiving, one of a social nature, which can occur quite innocently," the countess explained. "Besides, since it was uttered by a lady, it would have seemed prudent to a gentleman to overlook it." Her haughty eyes conveyed both anticipation and challenge.

Gebhard was quite prepared to continue their earlier 'discussion'. Instead, catching the unspoken plea in Ida's beautiful eyes, he was persuaded to continue in a more cheerful direction.

"You are absolutely correct, dear Countess," he continued. "A lady of your standing certainly deserves to be treated in a dignified and respectful manner. If I have encroached on this and my etiquette has been lacking…" He purposely failed to finish his sentence, instead bowing respectfully before her.

The crease on her forehead waned. He had managed to ask for her forgiveness without actually having to do so outright. Nonetheless, she had in effect won a small victory over him. This allowed her to show a milder, compassionate side.

"I had no intention to be cruel, Monsieur von Löwenklau. I wish to extend to you a belated, yet heartfelt welcome." The countess extended her hand in a warm gesture, which was gladly accepted. Gebhard in turn placed a kiss on her outstretched hand.

Hedwig's expression was wide with surprise, as though to say, *That clever German pulled one out of the fire and won!* Ida's face radiated her approval of the way Gebhard had handled himself. The count, however, was far less enthusiastic.

"Dear aunt," he replied sharply from his shadowy refuge, "you seem to have forgotten that you are not the only one here."

With a surprised look, she turned to face her nephew.

"Are you implying..." she started.

"...that several people are present who have been offended."

"Well," she said, "I hadn't considered that. If you feel offended, then that is your concern. However, I reserve the right to speak my mind and govern myself accordingly."

"Still, it must concern you, dear aunt."

"In what way?"

"Only that, as your nephew, I also have the right to determine that which concerns me."

"Certainly, if that nephew were a child, one who requires my intervention. It is because you men are so passionate about your affairs that I felt you would be able to handle it on your own."

"What you're saying is that you welcome this man despite my objection?"

"Naturally, you heard it for yourself."

He stepped out of the shadows. "Then I must assume," he said haughtily, "that my presence here is not particularly welcome. Perhaps even undesirable." He assumed a posture of authority, one bordering on a challenge.

The countess maintained her composure and looked at him in amazement.

"My nephew is always welcome in my home," she said evenly. "There is no reason to refuse him entry. If I choose to admit another, then that is entirely my own affair. My house is my property and I will discourage anyone from telling me how to deal with newcomers."

The count shrugged his shoulders. "Naturally, I defer that honor to you," he replied sarcastically. "Yet let me warn you of those long hours which have yet to come... the ones where you have decided to entertain unaccomplished people whom you'll end up loathing, having relinquished my company in favor of strangers."

The countess tilted her head back in a manner reminiscent of the beautiful Hedwig. "I don't mind that you relinquish the opportunity to spend that time with us. I am not the one who will likely regret it."

"That is obvious to all!" was the cool reply. "Whether on account of a stranger or a newcomer, I am reluctant to give up the enjoyment of your company, which I still prefer. I had no intention of embarrassing you. I merely wanted to caution you about forming relationships that will only end in your disappointment. I trust my cousin Ida is in agreement with me."

"Since I reside with our aunt, I have to abide by her example," the younger sister said slowly and deliberately. "I concur with my aunt's opinion. I haven't been offended by Monsieur von Löwenklau."

The count hadn't expected her contradictory answer. Rather than countering with a deprecating remark, he turned to Hedwig. "What do you think, dear Hedwig?"

Hedwig simply shrugged her shoulders. "Cousin," she began, "I must confess, you are being oversensitive. I am in complete agreement with Ida."

"You think so!" he said angrily. "But there will come a time when you will pay more heed to my views. The time has come for me to take my leave."

He quickly turned around, coming to face Goldberg. "Monsieur," he said. "It must have occurred to you since our first meeting that I haven't enjoyed your visits. And yet you continue to return. I find that most peculiar and impertinent of you."

"Pah!" replied Kunz, slighted. "It must have occurred to you after our first meeting that my subsequent visits were meant for another. That you failed to grasp this simple fact is even more peculiar."

"*Diable!* Are you trying to make fun of me?"

"Not at all. I merely wished to point out that my visits were intended for your aunt, the gracious lady, and not you. Therefore, it's of no consequence to me if you find my visits objectionable. Actually, I should clarify that everything that you've said or meant is entirely inconsequential. Surely, you must have realized by now that your presence doesn't mean anything to me."

"Well, perhaps my presence means something to your friend."

He turned to face Gebhard, who had in the meantime taken a seat at the table. The lieutenant glanced up at him noncommittally, clearly indifferent to the count's rambling.

"Are you an officer, Monsieur Löwenklau?" he inquired.

"Yes, as you have no doubt heard."

"I doubt that."

"Your remark could be construed as an insult."

The count stepped closer. "You're no officer, and no gentleman."

Gebhard turned aside, trying to ignore the obvious provocation, but the count persisted, stepping even closer. "I see you have chosen to ignore my comment. If I have not made myself clear, then let me put it this way: I'm calling you a liar if you claim to be an officer and a gentleman."

Gebhard's eyes flashed momentarily, though he restrained himself. When he spoke, his voice was calm and devoid of animosity. "You will permit me to respond to your accusation tomorrow."

"I don't need to wait for your answer. He who barges in and makes a nuisance of himself cannot be considered an officer and a gentleman."

"Well then, permit me to respond by way of an answer to you tomorrow."

"I don't need to hear it!" the count repeated contemptuously. "You have offended the countess, and now you dare to sit smugly at our table. You're no officer."

"I have already told you that you will receive my response tomorrow," Gebhard said again, this time leaving his chair. He approached the count and stopped within a breath's distance, his penetrating gaze causing the count to wince. "Don't you know what it means when I have already told you to expect my answer tomorrow?"

"I have no idea," replied the count.

"Aren't you an officer?"

"No."

"But you're a nobleman?"

"Of course. I'm Count Jules Rallion."

"Yet you claim to be ignorant of what I meant?"

"I'm still unclear."

"I was convinced that France's nobility was adept in understanding those things which cannot be settled by words alone. I seem to have been misinformed."

Curiosity played across the count's face. Something dawned on him, and he sought to clarify his thought. "You're not suggesting a duel, are you?"

"Well, it occurs to me you seem to be unaware that such matters are not customarily discussed in the presence of ladies."

"That which pertains to me can be readily discussed in front of these ladies. Are you intending to fight over this matter?"

"You will find out soon enough, Count!"

"Fine! Let me make it clear to you that I have no intention of pursuing it with you."

"Why not?"

The count tried to puff himself up, attempting to intimidate Gebhard. "I've been an expert fencer for years. I fear that I would strike you down in no time."

Gebhard could hardly suppress a smile. Pointing to Kunz, he continued. "I assure you, Count, there's no need for you to show me any special treatment. My comrade, Monsieur von Goldberg, will attest to the fact that I am an accomplished fencer, and hence don't require mercy."

The count seemed disappointed. "In that case, I will be forced to shoot you with my pistol."

"That doesn't cause me any concern, Count. I am proficient with firearms as well. I can hit a swallow in flight. But to prove to you that I really am an officer, one who has to hit his mark in battle, I will put a bullet into your head."

This last comment brought the count back to reality. He wasn't sure how to respond, and finally said, a little less sure of himself, "You won't be able to accomplish that. I can guarantee it."

"Why not, Monsieur?"

"Because I have no intention of engaging in a fight with you."

"May I inquire how you came to that singular decision?"

"I don't intend to duel with anyone who's not capable of giving satisfaction."

"Are you inferring that I am one of those?"

"Yes. You've demonstrated by your conduct that you're not capable."

"Ah! Another insult," Gebhard crowed. "Well, now that you've managed to bring this delicate matter out into the open for all to hear, I will give you my decision in their presence. I will settle for an apology, thereby addressing your rude behavior. Monsieur von Goldberg will make himself available as my representative. Punctually, tomorrow morning at nine o'clock, you will find him at your residence to discuss the terms with a representative of your choosing. If you fail to respond, then I assure you I will openly proclaim you a coward, starting right now!"

"You're trying to frighten me," responded Rallion by laughing disdainfully. "I know exactly how to deal with people like you," he hissed. "I will prove it soon enough. Good night, ladies."

He turned on his heel and stalked out of the dark room. As was common with such uncomfortable scenes, a short pause ensued. Faced with embarrassment, the countess sought to mitigate the unpleasant impression left by her nephew.

"Monsieur von Löwenklau," she said, hoping to shift his attention. "You were about to inform us about the demise of Baron de Reillac."

"I am prepared to keep my word," replied Löwenklau. "It is just that I am not sure if murder is a suitable topic of discussion for refined ladies."

"Please, Monsieur, would you be so kind as to indulge us?" Hedwig asked quickly, all the while making herself more comfortable on her settee. "Though murder certainly is horrible, I enjoy a spine-tingling story. I cannot wait for you to begin."

"Well then, Mademoiselle," he said smiling, "I will give it a try. I hope I will not spoil your enjoyment of this tragic tale."

Gebhard related the entire story, which he had heard from his parents. The ladies listened attentively and only interrupted him with the odd exclamation or look of shock. Because his illustration of the events hung in close proximity to that of his family, he was inundated with a flurry of questions. He was a good storyteller and held their rapt attention.

Afterward, his youthful enthusiasm and knowledge of events led to a lively conversation. The nieces listened to his words, recognizing that he hadn't embellished his experiences. Rather, he drew on the wealth of his days in the officers' corps. This appealed to the women. The usually vocal Hedwig listened with interest, forfeiting her brash comments. Ida, usually reserved, appeared contemplative, saying little. But her eyes spoke volumes. Each time her eyes met his, her beautiful, secretive eyelashes lowered, accompanied by a slight redness in her cheeks, something she couldn't see, yet felt in the beating of her heart.

So it was that the two officers, along with Madame Rallion, carried the conversation. She laid her earlier unfriendliness aside, becoming interested in the family connection, thankful that Gebhard had distracted her from the embarrassment of her nephew's thick-headedness.

When Gebhard concluded his dissertation, the countess invited both men to join them for dinner, much to the delight of her nieces. Their aunt seldom invited any gentleman for dinner, an indication of the impression Löwenklau had made on her.

Shortly before supper, the countess excused herself for a few minutes, giving Kunz the opportunity to speak to Hedwig in private. She walked over to the grand piano, seemingly preoccupied with finding a particular piece to play. While she perused the material, she carried on a quiet conversation with Kunz out of earshot of the other two.

"Was your friend serious about his challenge?" she asked.

"Certainly, Mademoiselle."

"Will the duel really take place?"

"I'm convinced of it."

"How uninteresting!"

"Uninteresting?" he asked. "I thought you would enjoy the drama. Do the sordid tales of murder draw your interest more?"

She looked at him sideways. "And you call yourself a good judge of people."

"Aren't I?" he laughed, ignoring her look.

"Just yesterday you claimed that you wanted to get to know me better."

"Of course."

"And that you professed to have more insight."

"That, too."

"But now you claim that I would only be interested in ghoulish, murderous stories."

"I deduced it from your lack of interest in the upcoming duel."

Hedwig shrugged her shoulders, momentarily offering a more revealing view of her bust line. "It depends on the circumstances," she said.

"How so, Mademoiselle?"

"A duel, resulting from one of the parties claiming the other is not an officer – how childish."

"Perhaps you mean because one provoked the other?"

"That might be described as philistine, but not interesting."

"What then would satisfy your demands for an interesting duel?"

"Hmm! There are several ways," she replied, her face becoming contemplative.

"Would you enlighten me about one of these ways?"

"Inquisitive, aren't you? You seem to be ignorant on the subject, so it's up to me to educate you." Hedwig furrowed her brows, trying to project an intellectual air. Instead, he was merely dazzled by her looks. It took self-control for him not to wrap his arms around her.

"I'm at your disposal, Mademoiselle. Please, educate this hapless man."

"Well, it hinges on the object of the conflict. If it's interesting, then so too would be the ensuing duel. Now, Monsieur von Goldberg, find me a fitting example, and not something that is rooted in a childish prank."

"A childish prank?" he asked, leaning over her.

She playfully struck him with her fan. "Germans are nothing but bears, and you especially, you—" She stopped speaking.

"What? What am I supposed to be?"

Hedwig looked at Kunz in feigned apprehension. "You're a clumsy oaf."

He pulled back in mock offence. "Mademoiselle," he said, "you've strayed from our topic."

"Oh no, sir, we're exactly on topic."

"But we were discussing a duel?"

"Yes, a duel."

"You were questioning me about what constitutes an interesting duel?"

"Yes, that very question."

"I don't follow. Or are you implying that only duels with clumsy oafs are exciting?"

"Not at all. I want to explain myself by illustrating with a German word. How would you translate the French word *lourdaud* into German?"

"I would render it as clumsy, or awkward."

"Well then, I would describe a duel between two oafs as clumsy. In other words, not interesting at all. But we weren't speaking about oafs, much less clumsy ones."

"What else then, my grumbling lady?"

"You're quite boring. You can't seem to stay on topic," she said, pretending to be earnest. "Each time we converse, I have to ensure we stay focused."

"Fine," he laughed. "I will do my best to remain on the topic at hand."

"Yes, I adjure you to do your utmost."

"Ah, now I recall. I must plead with you to make allowances for my senile memory—"

"It's not faulty from senility, but rather from lack of use," she interrupted.

"Whatever you say. So, what would be of interest to you?"

"Well, is the word 'lady' sufficient to rouse your curiosity?"

"Out of respect for you, I will allow that."

"And can a lady be interesting?" She looked at him reproachfully. "Of course! Shouldn't a lady be interesting? So unlike a man!"

"Naturally, not in the least!" he mocked. "You infer that a duel is interesting because it likely involves her."

"That's what I meant."

"I would like to qualify that supposition."

"In what way?"

"This may shock you. There are also uninteresting women."

"Hmm, the very idea is completely foreign to me."

"Yet it is true. A duel arising out of ordinary circumstances would be boring."

"This just proves that you're a bear! Give me one example to prove your point!"

"Would you be interested in a duel involving your aunt?"

"Of course!"

"Even if it was on your account?"

"Yes, I would. Definitely."

He smiled and allowed himself a short chuckle. "Ah," he said. "You've just told me what you earlier forbade me to tell!"

"What was that?"

"That you're the interesting lady."

"Thanks for the honor!" she said, striking him with the fan again. "Tell me, is your friend really an accomplished swordsman, or even a fine marksman?"

"He's the best I know of."

"Then my cousin will succumb, because he's not familiar with weapons."

"I was under the impression he wanted to strike him down with a foil."

Hedwig considered that, then shook her head. "I don't think so."

"Or shoot him down."

"He lied to get out of it."

"Didn't he say that he was an accomplished fencer?"

"He was only bragging. Truthfully, he was afraid. The main reason he chose not to pursue a military career is because of his aversion to firearms."

"My friend will settle for an apology. Failing that, he will pursue the duel."

"What if the count refuses?"

"For what reason?"

"Because he's unfamiliar with weapons."

"Then he should be more careful about the way he offends a nobleman. Besides, victory doesn't always belong to the one who's most proficient with weapons."

"Are you suggesting that an inexperienced man could wind up the winner?"

"Quite so, as evidenced by many duels."

"Dear God, what if Monsieur von Löwenklau is injured during the duel?"

To Kunz's surprise, her voice gave away an unusual concern for his friend's well-being. "Are you really that concerned for him?" he asked.

"Quite concerned."

"Really? I envy him."

Hedwig sensed something in his voice. "For what reason?"

"Because you show a degree of concern for him. Who knows if you would show the same affection for me, should I find myself in a similar situation?"

"Do you mean I should worry about you?" she laughed. "For your safety? Not in the least!"

The crease forming on his forehead deepened. "Is that really true?" he inquired.

"Of course!"

"Then I wish you all the best, Countess. I must go!"

Although his intent was to quickly get up, she grabbed him by the hand and held him firmly in place. Though Kunz could have easily freed himself, he didn't want to create a scene.

"Where do you want to go in such a hurry, Monsieur von Goldberg?"

"Away from you!"

"But why?" she teased.

He didn't respond. She still looked at him playfully.

"Could it be because I'm not concerned about your welfare?" she asked.

Still, he failed to respond.

"You're a bear, Monsieur!" she said. "A big bear! Please, tell me what should implore me to show concern for you?"

His eyes, shimmering in a peculiar light, fixed on her. "You're right, Countess," he replied. "What business do you have with a German bear? He has pined for a kind word, even an understanding word, yet all he can do is wait and hope. Should he ever face danger, you haven't the slightest concern for his well-being."

Although he had spoken with exasperation, she responded lightly. "You're absolutely right," she allowed.

"What? Are you so certain?"

"Of course."

"Then let me go. It's time that I left."

"Whatever for?" she asked, still holding onto his arm.

Kunz took her hand in his and pleaded earnestly. "Hedwig, please, don't play games with me. Be serious with me for once: do you hate me?"

"Hate you?" she whispered in surprise. "Of course not!"

"Then why do I matter so little to you?"

"That's not the case. A friend of our household certainly matters to me."

"So, I'm important to you because I'm a friend of the household?"

"Of course."

"Nothing more?"

She lowered her eyes, looking down at an open book. She looked as though she might say something, but instead kept silent.

"Hedwig, please," Kunz pleaded, taking her other hand in his. "I don't like this deathly quiet. Please, give me an answer."

"I'm supposed to demonstrate greater interest in you?"

"Oh, how wonderful that would be!"

"And how would you garner this greater interest from me?"

"How can you ask me that?" he lamented, dropping her hands. "Even still, I want to answer. I suppose that I haven't distinguished myself to merit your devotion. One could commit any number of deeds and still fail to rouse the admiration you hint at. But to hear that you're unconcerned whether or not my life would be in danger is too painful to bear."

"I don't recall saying that."

"Didn't you just tell me that you wouldn't show the least concern for me?"

"Indeed."

"Well, isn't that the clearest sign of indifference?"

"Not at all, Monsieur!"

With that, he dropped his shoulders and gave up trying to follow her reasoning. "Then I don't understand you at all."

"You really are a bear! If the bear fights with a fox or a wolf, there's no need to be concerned about him. It's almost certain that he will prevail."

He shook his head. "You just can't leave jokes alone."

Her eyes widened and her face projected pure solemnity. "Monsieur, I can be serious when the situation calls for it."

"If this really is true, Mademoiselle, then consider my one plea by responding solemnly. Earlier on, why did you say that you had no reason to be concerned for me?"

"Very well, I'll be serious," she replied.

"Can I really believe that?"

She nodded with a friendly smile. "You can believe me," she replied. "I can be serious. Quite serious, especially when it matters."

"If that's true, then would you render me a small favor?"

"Which one?"

"By being serious for a moment."

"Is that really so necessary?"

"Yes. Absolutely."

"All right," she agreed. "Your wish is my command."

"Why did you tell me earlier that you had no concern for my well-being?"

This time she placed her hand on his arm. "I will be serious, and tell you that you're a bear. Consider the words I spoke earlier. Aren't you a logical man?"

He shook his head, still feeling doubtful. "I wish I could understand you."

"Then I'm forced to speak quite plainly. Do you know whom one worries about?"

"Who?" he asked.

"Children, of course."

"Really!"

"Yes, for children, and also for all the careless and irresponsible people in this world. I'm not sure if you agree with me. You see, for those people who can take care of themselves, there's no need to worry."

"How would you respond then to a wife's concern for her husband, one who's involved in a skirmish, or on the battlefield?"

"Is it merely a concern that she feels? Isn't it more a fear of the unknown?"

Kunz nodded thoughtfully. "That may be. So, you're not concerned about someone whom you respect or trust?"

"That's what I said."

"What about someone whom you love?"

"You're being too presumptuous, Monsieur!"

Kunz quickly grabbed her hand, holding her in place. "Please," he continued. "At least tell me if you know of someone whom you love, but aren't concerned about."

Her usual playful smile crossed her lips. "Yes, I know of one," she said sweetly.

Nearly caught off guard, Kunz asked quietly, yet haltingly. "Who is it? May I know?"

"Of course, Monsieur. It's not a secret."

"Well, who is it?"

"Ida, my sister."

"The—!" he erupted. He had come close to cursing, having only managed to withhold the second word. "Dear God! Countess, are you trying to push me to the brink of despair? I assure you, I wasn't thinking of your sister."

She seemed to understand what he was getting at and faced him, once again, seriously. "Ah!" she responded. "Now I realize whom you've been thinking about."

"Thank God!" he exclaimed, venturing forth with new resolve. "So, is there such a person?" he whispered into her ear.

"Yes, Lieutenant," Hedwig answered coyly. She nodded encouragingly, allowing him take the bait.

"Who is it?" he asked quickly.

"My aunt."

The two unexpected syllables were too much for him. He opened his mouth, about to utter a curse, barely checking himself in time. He turned for a second time, again intending to leave. She tried to hold him back, but this time missed him. She deemed what seemed best under the circumstances, and followed him to where Gebhard and Ida were standing. She covered the short distance, and caught up to him just as he approached Gebhard.

"Are you upset with me?" she whispered.

"You know that I am!"

"Did I deserve that?"

"I thought I had found a bright star. Instead I came across a silly girl." His anger got the best of him, allowing for the slip of the tongue.

"My dear sir, this just proves that you really are a bear! I suppose, in your case, a silly girl is quite comparable to a star. I need to point out that I'm upset with you."

"Really? What for?"

"Tell me, is it your intention to get married?"

Kunz was utterly shocked and unprepared for the question. He couldn't come up with a suitable response. "Naturally, I want to get married some day," he sputtered.

"But when?"

Hang it all! he thought. *Why these serious questions all of a sudden?* He decided to get it over with and replied as truthfully as he could. "As soon as my military duty and financial circumstances allow."

"So your plans are tied to your finances and your duty?"

"Unfortunately."

"Oh dear, I feel sorry for the heart that has to calculate its happiness."

"Does this include mine as well?"

She sighed gravely. "Perhaps more than any other."

"More? Perhaps because it works for naught?"

"No, because I wish that it loved without having to work at it."

"I can imagine. Ladies despise everyday responsibilities."

"Not me," Hedwig pointed out. "I consider them a challenge for the intellect."

"Then I plead with you to stand by my side."

"In forging plans?"

"Fine," he said, placing his hand in hers. "Here is my hand. What shall we consider?"

"The demands of your profession and the merits of your circumstances."

"For how long?"

"Until we reach a consensus."

"And what will determine this consensus?"

"There you go again, acting like a bear. One shouldn't grasp at straws with paws."

"Pardon my eagerness, but before we reach our consensus, the wisps of the dream could vanish."

"Or perhaps demonstrate that I'm not some figment," she said. "Rather a rising star."

"Well, certainly not for me!"

"For who then?"

"For others, perhaps."

They stopped walking. "Why would you say such a thing?" she asked.

"Because it's in a garrulous girl's nature."

"Perhaps your girl can transform herself into that star, which for you shines with all its intensity, and yet remains inert for all others. Where is your faith?"

"Dear God! Who can have a measure of trust when there is no foundation to build on?"

She held his hand tightly. "Isn't Hedwig a fine name?" she asked. He looked searchingly into her face as she continued. "Build your future on this one word. I can't make it any clearer than that."

She walked the few steps over to the window where Ida and Gebhard were engrossed in their own conversation, oblivious to anything else around them.

❧✠☙

Earlier, as Hedwig had left the table to select some music, Ida walked toward the window, searching for something in the knitting basket. Finding himself alone at the table, Gebhard rose and followed her. When she heard him approach, she turned around.

"Monsieur," Ida began, "it just occurred to me that I nearly stole something which belongs to you."

He knew exactly what she meant. The countess had returned Gebhard's locket to Ida, who had kept it in her hand. She had playfully attached the locket to her own chain, forgetting to return it to its owner after the count's boisterous departure.

"Yes, a theft," he teased. "A significant theft." He stepped up to the window where, concealed by the curtains, the two remained out of view of Hedwig and Kunz.

"I simply forgot," Ida replied, embarrassed. A slight redness spread across her cheeks. "If my aunt hadn't invited you to dinner, you would have departed without your mother's picture."

"I would have returned to claim it, Mademoiselle," he said, smiling at her. "I was thinking of a different kind of robbery, though."

"A different kind? I had no idea that…" She allowed her voice to trail off softly.

"You have no idea, Countess? To be unassuming is in many cases something to be desired, and I won't interfere."

"Oh no, Monsieur," she replied quickly. "If I have committed an injustice, I want to apologize for it."

"Injustice?" he asked. "Oh no, a thousand times no! Please, Mademoiselle, would you give me your hand?" Trustingly, she extended her right hand. "I have to thank you for coming to my aid," he said, picking up her hand.

"You managed to pull off a small victory, Monsieur von Löw—"

"—yet not without your clever intervention," he interrupted.

"I merely followed my heart. I saw the travesty in my aunt's unfair judgment. You see, she detests the German race and abhors their military prowess. She especially despises their officers."

"Why is that?"

"She is a staunch French lady, adhering to her ideals."

"In your opinion, is that sufficient justification?"

"It's not my opinion, but hers."

"Would you despise someone simply because of their background?"

"No. Never! Earlier you spoke of our Savior and his precepts just as I would have. The voice of the heart is…" She stopped mid-sentence, having ventured too far into a personal area, leaving room for subjectivity. He was still holding her hand in his and she didn't make the least effort to remove it. A slight shiver reverberated through her body as she reacted to the subtle squeeze of his fingers.

"You spoke of the voice of the heart," he prodded. "Please continue, Mademoiselle."

"No, I am afraid I have lost my train of thought," she whispered, quickly trying to change the subject. "You spoke of a serious head wound, which your father just barely survived. Does it still cause him discomfort?"

Gebhard took a moment to adjust to the sudden shift in conversation. "Yes, he is still subjected to the pain once in a while."

"It's such a shame. Your father must be an extraordinary man."

"I'm convinced his fame and accomplishments would have spread had it not been for that nearly fatal blow."

"I feel I already know your parents."

He couldn't hide his surprise. "Really?" he asked.

A slow smile spread across her face. "I don't intend for you to take it literally," she quickly added. "You're a good storyteller. Your depiction of your family was so vivid that I imagined what they might look like. I am afraid I went too far. That is all I meant."

"Are you interested in getting to know them?"

"Yes. Who could look at your mother's picture and not be drawn to her beauty? And the one to whom she entrusted her life must certainly be worthy."

Her words had a reassuring quality to them. *She's fond of my parents*, he thought. *Would it be wrong to pursue the matter further? After all, she respects my father for being worthy of my mother's love. Perhaps my love for her could blossom in the same way.*

"Your father is a brave and daring man," she continued. "I'm convinced that you are the spitting image of him."

"How did you arrive at that?"

"It's no guess," she assured him, "but a certainty. If someone is bold enough to venture into the Sahara, he must then possess considerable courage. In fact, you proved it today in the way you conducted yourself."

"Because of the duel?"

"Oh no! No, my dear Lieutenant, because of my aunt."

"Is she always this intolerant?" he asked jokingly.

"No, not always," she said. "Merely prejudiced. I had that awful feeling she was about to leave the salon, which would have demanded your immediate dismissal. I am not in the least concerned about your upcoming duel."

"Mademoiselle, a confrontation with arms is not to be taken lightly."

"I'm aware of that."

"Injuries occur frequently."

"Unfortunately."

"Even death!"

She nodded in wholehearted agreement. "You are absolutely right! That is why I have never understood why certain classes think that they have to settle their differences in such a vulgar and unfair manner while others resort to kinder and gentler means."

"You may be right. Members of nobility perhaps adhere too much to the precepts of lineage, courtesy, and honor. Please, tell me, how else could I have dealt with your cousin?"

"Unfortunately, you had little choice but to challenge him, so as not to be viewed as a coward. I've heard this is customary in officer's circles."

"It was actually the lesser of the options open to me."

"What else could you have done?"

"If the confrontation had occurred elsewhere, not in the presence of ladies for instance, I would have acted immediately by chastising him right then and there."

"*Mon Dieu!*" she exclaimed. "How fortunate that didn't take place."

"I appreciate that our host exhibited tolerance in light of the unpleasant circumstances. I want to be honest with you and tell you that I admired her composure in dealing with a close family member."

Ida smiled. "There was nothing to admire there." And then, seeking once again to change the subject, she continued. "I heard that you're accomplished in the use of the foil, as well as firearms."

"I only mentioned it because your cousin bragged about giving me a sound thrashing."

"Still, I felt you were speaking the truth. Nonetheless, all your skill and aptitude will be in vain."

"Really? Do you suppose your cousin has an advantage over me?"

She shook her head. "Not in the least. I only meant that the duel will never take place."

"I'm of a different opinion."

"And I speak from experience."

"So, has the count participated in previous duels?"

"Not in a single one! He doesn't avail himself of this form of discipline."

"But you said that you spoke from experience."

"Of course. Although he has been challenged before, he's never accepted."

"But there's no honor in that!"

She contemplated that for a moment. "You're right, of course. He's a complete coward. My aunt views his actions with contempt, and we..." She paused again, hesitating to go on.

"And you, Mademoiselle?"

"I cannot condone it. Nor can I accept it."

"I'm afraid the count left me little choice but to pursue and engage him in a fight."

"I doubt you will succeed in taking it that far."

"Then I won't be able to see you again, Mademoiselle."

"No? Why not?"

"Because I will be forced to do something that will provoke your anger."

Curious, she met his gaze with her wide eyes. "Tell me, what form will this provocation take? Can you tell me?"

"Yes. In fact, I must tell you. Perhaps you have enough influence with your cousin to prevent further harm."

"Monsieur, now you're frightening me."

"You're not as fond of morbid tales as your sister?" he teased, noting one of many differences between the sisters.

"No, not at all. What harm could befall my cousin?"

"If he chooses to sidestep my challenge, I will be forced to discredit him publicly."

"Really?"

"I'm afraid so. If I fail to elicit a response from him, the whole blame falls upon my shoulders."

She shook her head in disapproval. "I don't intend to reproach you for your actions," she said. "However, I do feel sorry for you and your colleagues who adhere to this regimented ideal. I also see that you won't allow yourself to be tainted with the mantle of cowardice. May I know how you plan to chastise the count?"

"I'm afraid I don't yet know myself, Mademoiselle."

"Perhaps you could do so in writing. Or public proclamation?"

"Most likely the latter."

She was silent for a moment, glancing out the window. He was still holding her delicate right hand in his when suddenly she turned to face him, extending her left hand and leaning in.

"Would you render me a favor, and not deviate from its course?"

Gebhard felt a tinge of discomfort. He hoped she hadn't noticed. "I believe I can guess your request," he said. "But I am afraid I won't be able to accommodate you."

"On the contrary. I don't believe you will guess what I wish to propose. In fact, it shouldn't be difficult for you to grant me this kindness, if you were to follow your heart."

Kindness, he mused, considering her choice in words. *Perhaps she means simply more than kindness.* His heart warmed itself to her.

"Do you want to plead for leniency in your cousin's case?" he asked.

"Of course not! How can I ask for something that would damage your reputation?"

"Then please explain yourself, Mademoiselle!"

"It's quite straight forward. I only ask that you conduct yourself in a manner that would not tarnish your mother's respect for you. This is my only plea. I hope you won't chide me for this request."

"I understand you completely," he replied in a singular tone that conveyed both joy and admiration. "How could I be displeased with you? Not at all. I will conduct myself just as you propose. You have given me a gift, both costly and priceless, that I wouldn't exchange for any earthly treasure."

"A priceless gift?" she asked unawares.

"Yes, you have willingly brought me a priceless gift, without realizing it. You have spoken openly and honestly through your plea, Mademoiselle. May I speak frankly with you?"

"Yes, please."

"You have been privileged to see my mother's portrait," he started. "She is the picture of loveliness, but also the picture of tranquility."

"I am convinced of it, Monsieur von Löwenklau."

"My father was an honorable officer, capable, humble, intelligent, and daring in his accomplishments. When my parents met each other for the first time, both had this unique feeling that they belonged together for life. Do you believe that love can appear so quickly? That it can grow in intensity from the outset?"

Embarrassed, she lowered her head. "Perhaps," she replied.

"Do you believe me when I tell you that my father spoke of his love for my mother that very first day?"

"Since you said it, I believe you."

"Would you hold it against him for being so bold?"

"I have no standard by which I could measure such things, Monsieur. But I would think that he who carries a true and unwavering love in his heart must have the conviction to speak it."

"You mean that he would sense he had the freedom to speak to his lover about it?"

"Absolutely," she said. "Wouldn't it make sense for him to find out in that very first hour if his influence or his love had a chance of being returned, or withheld?"

"That implies that the lover is capable of discerning within that first hour the impact of that impression, and recognizing the immeasurable joy of being loved," Gebhard noted. "I should clarify that my mother felt drawn to my father in that very first hour as well. This allowed her to search her own feelings and to decide on an appropriate response."

"Is that not always the case, Monsieur?" she asked.

The simple question raised a storm of feelings within him, causing him to pause before replying. "Yes, I suppose that is so. And now I want to confide in you that I too heard this voice of the heart of which you spoke earlier. It came so suddenly and unexpectedly that I felt as though a mighty beam of light reached into the caverns of the deep, spreading light of hope where there was none."

Gebhard had spoken slowly and intimately. He was still holding her hands, which she hadn't withdrawn. Ida was quiet, though he felt a slight tremor in her hands.

"Aren't you a little curious," he continued, "to know who it was that brought this ray of sunshine into my heart?"

"How could I ask such a thing?" she whispered.

"Of course you can. You're entitled to hear it. May I tell you?"

"Please tell me."

"Let me first confide in you by saying that I also heard this inner voice you mentioned earlier. There's an old adage which tells us that God always sends two souls to earth who belong to each other. They take on human form and live apart from each other for a time. However, when they meet, they recognize each other immediately and remain together for the rest of their lives on this earth."

"What a wonderful story!" she exclaimed softly.

"It crossed my mind the first moment we met," Gebhard admitted. "I felt two eyes probing my inner being, clear and true like I had never felt before. A greeting reached out to me, as though from another world. I had that distinct impression of having found my soul mate. She was beckoning to me. Am I mistaken, Mademoiselle?"

"Is it possible for me to be sure?" she asked, her voice barely audible.

"Yes, I believe you can," he said. "It was, after all, your eyes that gave me such a warm greeting. From that instant, each beat of my heart has become a constant reminder of the question that begs to be answered: is it true that you are my light and my soul?"

"Oh my God!" she whispered. "How can I answer that? What am I supposed to say?"

"Only that which you feel yourself. Nothing else."

"But I can't speak," she said in dull embarrassment. "This is all so sudden. I find myself caught between wanting to reply and afraid to say anything at all."

He saw two teardrops forming in her eyes, a physical confirmation of the unfaltering love he could sense growing between them. He realized immediately how much he meant to her. Not until this moment had he recognized the impact his words had had on this quiet soul. It wasn't pain or sorrow that brought tears to her eyes, but an inward conviction. The drops pearled on her exquisite cheeks, witnesses to her deepest feelings. Gebhard was incredibly happy, still holding her hands in his.

"I'm speaking from the innermost parts of my heart," he said. "If I have offended or embarrassed you in any way, simply tell me, and I will stop. If you have the same compelling belief as I do, then you have given me joy beyond measure. I'm not here to place demands upon you, Ida, save for one thing... that you give me your answer." He sighed, remembering his upcoming expedition to Africa. "I am obligated to keep my word and participate in the expedition. I will carry my mother's portrait and your memory into the Sahara. When I return, I will be in a position to demonstrate to you that I am worthy of your love. Only then will I ask you for an outward sign of your commitment."

"What would this sign be?"

"Your first kiss!"

She withdrew her hands, a move he nearly mistook as a sign that he had offended her. Then he detected the warmth in her eyes.

"You wish to wait such a long time for a single kiss?"

"Yes, of course."

"Then for now, will you be satisfied with the knowledge that I will await your return?"

"Ida, thank you. You have blessed me more than you know, more than any treasure could amount to."

The previously timid girl had instantly changed. Driven by her new love, she surprised him by wrapping her arms around his neck and resting her head on his shoulder. "Here is your treasure," she whispered. "That first kiss, which you won't have to wait all those years for."

Before he could deny himself any longer, he felt her warm lips on his. He wrapped his arms around her, responding to her kiss.

"Is it really true, you wonderful girl?" he asked incredulously. "Do you really love me?"

"Yes, I can't describe it!"

"And you've only known me for these last two hours."

"And yet wasn't it you who told me that love can be so overwhelming, so sudden?"

"Yes, I did say so. I was overtaken with the same feeling, my love."

"The story of the two souls is true."

"Yes, Ida. From now on, we will no longer be two, but function as one."

They stood still, side by side, occupied with their own thoughts. Before they could speak again, their interlude was interrupted as Hedwig and Kunz came up to them.

"Ah," Kunz said good-naturedly. "Are you lost in thought about your expedition?"

"Not really," Gebhard replied. "Why?" He reluctantly turned his attention to his friend, forcing himself to act nonchalantly.

"Well, you're standing with your lady at the open window and appear to be counting the stars. I suspect it would be more interesting and appealing out in the desert. Doesn't Sirius[2.1] appear much larger there than our moon over here?"

"I doubt it. To put your mind at ease, I will give you a detailed account in my first letter."

"I certainly hope so," Kunz said. "However, it seems we won't have any more time to devote to heavenly observations – here comes our gracious host."

The countess walked back into the salon just as a servant announced that dinner was ready. It wasn't until they were all seated at the table that the lady of the house brought forth her favorite topic, namely the gamut of expeditions and excursions into foreign lands of which she was aware. It soon became apparent to Gebhard that, unlike other women of her standing, she was very knowledgeable in the field and had occupied herself in substantially broadening her worldly outlook. He didn't hesitate with his answers, which seemed to put her into the finest of moods. When Gebhard demonstrated his knowledge of Gérard's expeditions, she became particularly enthralled as all of her previous doubts disappeared.

"I was led to believe that the Germans were mostly ignorant of his accomplishments," she stated. "How is it that you are the exception?"

Gebhard was wise enough not to disclose his basic disagreement with her premise. "I became interested in this field as a boy," he said instead, "and sought to grasp some of the knowledge."

"Some?" The single word belied just how impressed with him she actually was. "You have already demonstrated how well acquainted you are with his work. In fact, I believe you know even more than I do. I certainly haven't attained your knowledge of foreign languages. Tell me, do you also speak Arabic? It would be an asset to understand it on your journey through the desert."

"I haven't yet had the opportunity to engross myself with it. However, as soon as I became a member of this expedition, I began my studies. Besides, we have arranged to be accompanied by translators."

"Please, Monsieur, visit me daily! I plan to invite Professor Grenaux over in the near future. He's a teacher in Arabic and may be of great help to you."

He couldn't have asked for a better recommendation. Clearly, he had won the dragon's approval.

"You're one lucky man," Kunz commented as they headed for home. "Who would have predicted that?"

"Certainly not me."

"At first, I thought you had gone mad."

"You mean when I spoke my mind with the countess?"

"Yes! You were more than just bold, Gebhard."

"True, but I achieved precisely what I intended – a lasting impression," laughed Löwenklau.

"But what about this Count Rallion? I don't believe he will make an appearance any time soon."

"I trust that you will represent my interests tomorrow."

"Of course. I'll make the entreaty on your behalf and advise you of the outcome," he said. "What did you think of our host, the countess?"

"I was impressed by her demeanor."

"Yes, well, that's because you were the lucky Hans.[2.2] Just make sure you remain in her good graces! What's your opinion of the nieces?"

"Hmm, they're young."

"What?" asked Kunz incredulously. "Young girls, nothing more? I don't understand you. At first, you craved to meet the family, and now that I have introduced you, you're the picture of indifference."

Löwenklau smiled neutrally. "Well, I'm satisfied with how things turned out," he assured his friend.

"All right! Are you planning on a return visit?"

"Isn't that evident? The countess seemed quite pleased with me."

"What about the nieces? My friend, you must have blood as cold as a fish in your veins. Tell me, which of the two girls do you prefer?"

"Ida. Naturally, you prefer the untamable, right?"

"Of course."

"You sure were musical today."

"Don't make fun of me. We occupied ourselves with operettas."

"Did you perhaps encounter an operetta entitled *The Taming of the Shrew*?"

"It was more like a tragic comedy."

"As long as you managed to subjugate her," Gebhard laughed.

"Possibly. Dear friend, perhaps I've approached Hedwig the wrong way. She's alive and bubbly, coy and full of schemes, whereas I've always behaved a little stiff. Perhaps I've been too serious."

"Yes, that would be a mistake."

"One which I won't repeat!" Kunz assured him. "I see I'll have to change my approach if I want to capture her heart."

With these parting words, the two men went their separate ways, each one occupied with dreams of his lover. The maker of dreams, however, could be mischievous, deciding not to honor either man's requests.

CHAPTER THREE

Mistaken Identity

The following evening, both men presented themselves before the countess at her villa. It was there that they met Professor Grenaux. Both the countess and the professor occupied Löwenklau's time from the outset, leaving him little opportunity to speak alone with Ida. After supper, Hedwig, an accomplished pianist, sat down at the grand piano, intending to play a lengthy Beethoven composition. Gebhard sat down beside Ida and whispered a greeting to her as her sister played, pretending to be merely absorbed in the music.

Her first question to Gebhard concerned her cousin, Count Rallion. "Did your friend keep the appointment?" she asked.

"Yes, he did."

"He was turned away, am I right?"

"No. My friend didn't even meet up with him."

"Did he evade the meeting by going for a lengthy walk?"

"He excused himself by leaving word he had left on a lengthy trip."

"Where did he go?"

"To Geneva," he answered. "Perhaps even further."

"What will you do now?"

"For the moment, nothing. I've learned he plans to be absent for several months. By then, I should be long gone. I'll have to be patient and deal with this situation when I return from my trip."

"And then?" Ida asked.

"I hope you'll give me your advice my love."

"Really? You're going to abide by my wishes?"

"Of course. I'm convinced you wouldn't ask me to do anything that would tarnish my honor. Since last night, we've become as one life, and share one will. Therefore, you have as much to say about it as I do."

She squeezed his hand in gratitude.

❧❈❧

Gebhard visited the countess daily. Although it wasn't what he had initially intended, the aunt came to favor him more and more with each visit. Throughout his time in Paris, he also kept his parents updated via mail, and received timely replies. He was gracious in allowing the countess to read his letters, thereby giving her valuable insight into the affairs of his family, which aroused her interest.

Gebhard's departure date was set for the following week. As usual, he was with the countess in the evening, discussing various elements of the upcoming expedition. Kunz, by now part of the captive audience, resigned himself to listening about the trip with the two nieces.

"Ah!" the countess exclaimed in the middle of the conversation, interrupting him. "Now I remember what I wanted to ask you, Gebhard. Has your parents' latest letter arrived yet?"

"Yes, Madame. It's probably the last one I will receive in Paris."

"It's not personal, is it?"

"No, not at all. May I show it to you?"

"If you would be so kind."

Gebhard passed her the letter. She took out her reading glasses, pulled the table lamp closer, and started to read. The four young people conversed quietly among each other as Gebhard kept a discreet eye on the countess. When she reached a particular place, she glanced sharply in his direction. Although she scrutinized him for a while, he pretended not to notice. The countess, having resumed her reading, continued to the end, though her face had once again taken on its old, hard expression. When she finished, she handed the letter back to him without the usual comments on its contents.

After supper, she approached Gebhard with the news that she had received some new geographical correspondence. She invited him to accompany her into the sitting room. Gebhard hadn't been privileged to see it until now, and so he considered it a great honor. He followed Madame through several adjoining rooms, including her library, which he had been fortunate to visit on several other occasions. She led him through it into her private drawing room, a room that until now had only been described to him by Kunz.

Once her guest was seated, the countess began to pace back and forth, obviously preoccupied with something.

"Young man," she began at last, "if you were expecting to see charts or topographical data, I confess not to be in possession of any."

Gebhard had suspected the ruse, yet he played along by offering a surprised look, as though he didn't have the slightest idea what she was getting at.

"This concerns something that can only be discussed under four eyes," she continued. "It is of considerable importance and I expect you to be forthcoming."

"Dear lady, I trust you know my intentions—"

"That's fine," she interrupted. "However, you haven't been candid with me."

He pretended not to understand.

"May I please see your mother's letter again?" she asked.

"Of course," he said, retrieving it once more. "Here it is."

She took the letter from his hand and unfolded its pages. "Now then," she said. "I'm going to read you a few lines, which I'm sure you're more familiar with than I." She began to read aloud: "I'm most pleased to learn from your last letter that you have been able to find that special someone in my old city of Paris. The mother's heart within me goes out to you and we trust you made a good choice. Rest assured that we want it to be a blessing for you just as much as it was for us, your parents."

Although there was more to it, the countess stopped reading. She handed the letter back and resumed her pacing. "Now, do you understand why I told you earlier that you haven't been honest with me?" she asked.

"Ah! Madame, do you mean because I have failed to share with you that which I earlier disclosed to my parents?"

"Indeed. I realize it would have been presumptuous of me to have asked, but I hoped you would have considered it."

"Please accept my apology. I was negligent!"

"I forgive you, but please, you can be candid with me. I suspect you had left your home country without having chosen a betrothed."

He nodded. "That is the case."

"Are you perhaps in love with a French lady?"

"Yes."

"A Parisian woman?"

"Yes."

"I don't wish to pry into your affairs, but is she at least from a respectable family?"

"Yes, without question."

"Is she of equal social standing?"

"Completely."

"Does she return your affection?"

"In the same way, Madame."

"Then it's not simply a union of convenience."

"No. We truly love one another."

The countess stopped pacing and looked out the window, which she had just opened.

"I envy you," she mused softly. The daylight extenuated her hard features, showing that she was caught up with her emotions.

What thoughts must be flooding through her soul? he thought. She stepped back from the window and approached a desk, removing an envelope from one of its compartments. She produced a color portrait and held it out for Gebhard to see.

"Look at this portrait," she invited. "Do you recognize the man?"

After peering at the image for a few moments, Gebhard guessed who the man was, yet replied guardedly. "I've never seen him before."

"I'm well aware of that," she said. "You see, he is closer to you than you realize."

The countess crossed her arms and stood in front of him, a customary gesture of strong-willed women. "I was once young, like you, and was in love with him. My father was a baron, but his father was a commoner whose forefathers had dispensed with the prefix of 'de'. We weren't permitted to pursue our friendship, which broke my heart. As the years passed, I became the Countess de Rallion, and he too married another. We didn't socialize in the same circles, yet we never forgot one another. He was a banker and eventually became my husband's financial advisor. This gave rise to the opportunity of meeting at social functions and other events. The old love was rekindled, and yet we had to refrain from showing our emotions in public. I have managed to retain just one item from all those years ago – this portrait. It is worth more to me than the many jewels I have in my possession. As life so often dictates, he died before his time, and shortly thereafter, so did my husband. I was rich, yet unhappy.

"Then, an unexpected event occurred. I met a relative of his, who awakened familiar feelings in the heart of this old, spent body. Can you guess who this man was?"

Gebhard was forced to utter a white lie. "I have no idea, Madame."

"No? Not at all?"

"No, Madame."

"He's your relative, dear Lieutenant!"

"Mine?" he asked incredulously.

"Yes, yours! You're looking at the portrait of your grandfather, the banker Richemonte, your mother's father."

"Ah! So this is my grandfather!" he exclaimed.

Although he had guessed it, he had only glanced at the picture in a cursory way. His attention had been directed at the countess. Now, he took the portrait and examined it more closely under the light.

"Yes, take a closer look," she encouraged him. "Though he was a handsome man, he ended his years in misery, as you well know. Then you came along. I have watched you closely and quickly discovered that we share the same interests and passions. No doubt you feel the extent that I probed and checked your qualifications. I decided to grant you my approval and help you attain your aspirations."

"My aspirations?" Gebhard asked, no longer having to feign surprise.

"Yes," she laughed. "Or didn't you think I exerted such influence?"

"Gracious lady, you have already done too much for me."

"Oh, I had plans for more. Much more. But then you've made it impossible for me to complete them."

"In what way, Madame?"

"Well, through your undeclared love."

"My undeclared love?"

"Yes. Let me be candid with you. I was thinking of a betrothal for you."

Gebhard hadn't expected that. He was genuinely stunned by her disclosure. Without realizing it, his jaw had dropped.

"Surprised?" she asked. "It's the absolute truth. You're well aware that I'm sympathetic to those who have chosen to expand their horizons, even traveling to exotic destinations. You have chosen to embark on an expedition to the Sahara, which in itself is an enormous undertaking, requiring various skills and, above all, courage. I can see that you will be a famous man one day. This is what I find so delightful. When you would have returned one day, and received your accolades, I would have favored you with something that I treasure above all."

"What could that be, Madame?" he asked, trying to contain his mounting euphoria.

"A wife."

"Heavens! Whom do you have in mind?"

"I have already told you," the countess said. "The most precious gift which I can give to you – my niece."

"Really?" Gebhard asked, trying to quell his mounting excitement. "I'm speechless. Yet you have two nieces, Madame."

"I was referring to Ida. My quiet, sensible Ida, the one I hold dear to my heart even though I seldom let it show."

Gebhard felt like jumping for joy, scarcely daring to believe what he had just heard. The situation he found himself in was most curious, and he didn't exactly know how to proceed. He managed to compose himself.

"Did I hear you right, Countess? Did you say Ida?"

"Yes. My niece, Ida."

"Are you certain she would have complied?"

"I'm quite certain."

"Have you spoken of your intentions to her?"

"No, not one word. I hoped that in time your hearts would have drawn closer on their own."

"Unfortunately, this is no longer the case," he replied regretfully.

She paused, acknowledging the letter she still held in her hand. "Well, from what you have said, your heart is spoken for."

"Yes, Madame, and Ida's as well."

"What did you say? Is she, too, in love?"

"Yes!"

"With whom?"

"A German officer."

"*Mon Dieu!* You don't mean Lieutenant von Goldberg?"

"Madame, I expect you know Goldberg is one of my friends. I would never betray his confidence."

"Really! It has to be him," she said firmly. "In fact, I think he's still here. We have to see about this right away. Come with me, dear Lieutenant. I need to see…" She was already in such an excited state that she was rushing to leave the room immediately. Gebhard grabbed her hand to calm her down.

"Please Madame," he said quickly. "Stay for a moment. I need to inform you that—"

"I don't want to hear another word. Come with me. Quickly now!"

She pulled her hand back and hurried back to the drawing room. Gebhard followed behind her, imagining the scene that was about to take place. When they arrived in the doorway, the two sisters were sitting with Goldberg at the table, oblivious to the impending storm that was about to unleash its fury in the form of an angry aunt. They stood up in unison, recognizing at once that she was in an unpredictable mood.

"Monsieur von Goldberg," she announced. "I need to speak with you immediately!"

"I am at your service, gracious lady," he replied.

"I expect nothing less from you. Furthermore, I want you to tell me the whole truth!"

"Of course!" Kunz had no idea what she was talking about, certainly not what 'truth' she wanted to elicit from him. Madame stood in front of him, her eyes blazing with hidden significance.

"Monsieur," she continued. "You have seduced a lady!"

Her words struck him like a thunderclap. "Me? A seducer? How can you say that?"

"Yes, you've been quite clever. But I have all the proof I need."

"Proof? What kind of proof?"

"Are you still trying to deceive me? Do you deny that you're in love?"

He stepped back, astonished. "That… I'm in love?" he stuttered. "Me, my dear lady?"

"Yes, you! You're in love, of this I am certain."

"In love with whom, gracious lady?"

"With my niece!"

The accused man stood speechless for a moment, unsure of how to defend himself. He looked demurely into the determined face of the countess, who stood in front of him like a judge bent on ferreting out the truth. As he struggled to come up with an appropriate response, a glimmer of hope came to him in the form of a thought. He recalled how Gebhard had left him alone with the young ladies to confer privately with the countess. They had obviously discussed something important, possibly concerning him. Considering her fiery return, venting questions and seeming too eager to learn of his exploits, it made sense.

"You enlightened Madame about my personal affairs," he said, turning to his friend.

"No one gave you away, Monsieur," the countess replied in Gebhard's place. "However, someone figured it out. Your friend was very discreet. Although he never mentioned your name, I still deduced it was you. Are you going to cling to the role of the innocent man?"

Kunz realized he was trapped. No amount of denial would alleviate his predicament. He resigned himself to what would likely follow. "Madame," he managed. "The voice of the heart speaks its own language. It's often—"

"You can keep those comments to yourself! It would be better to concern yourself with the voice of reason and responsibility. It behooved you to see me first and discuss the matter like a gentleman. That is the least I expected from you, Monsieur von Goldberg."

"Madame, I wasn't convinced yet that Mademoiselle would give her consent."

"Then surely now, you must be clear on that point."

"Well, not entirely!"

"What do you mean by that remark?"

"I'm telling you the truth, Madame!"

"In that case, I will satisfy myself." She approached Ida, continuing her tirade. "Monsieur may still be reluctant to divulge certain details, but I hope that you at least will be honest with me. I trust I mean that much to you. Do you love him?"

Ida was shocked by the intensity of her aunt's anger. With this last question, she had completely lost grip on her composure. Failing to make the distinction between which 'him' she was referring to, she bowed her head and replied fearfully. "Please forgive me, dear aunt."

"I want to know, here and now. Are you in love with him?"

"Yes, dear aunt!"

"Does he love you in return?"

"Yes."

"Did you discuss this between yourselves?"

"Yes."

"When was this?"

"At the end of last week."

"And did he declare his love for you openly?"

"Yes."

The countess, prepared to continue her interrogation, heard loud sobbing behind her. She swiveled on her heel and found that Hedwig was pale as a ghost and holding a handkerchief to her eyes.

"What's wrong with you?" she asked curtly. "Why are you crying?"

"Oh, he's... he's terrible!" she managed to say between sobs.

"Whom do you mean?"

"That liar!"

"I asked you whom you meant?"

"Lieutenant von Goldberg!"

"Why is he a liar?" the countess asked, furrowing her eyebrow.

"Because he also spoke of his love for me, dear aunt."

"Really?" she exclaimed, her anger on the rise again.

"Yes, really!"

"Well, what did you tell him?"

"I... I... I... I...!" she stammered.

"Out with it!" she continued. "I want the truth, the whole truth!"

Goldberg was completely perplexed. Managing to compose himself enough to formulate a few words, he quickly walked over to where the countess was standing.

"Gracious lady," he began. "There must be a mistake!"

"A mistake? Be quiet! Hedwig wouldn't lie to me!"

"Of course not, and that's not what I meant. I'm sure she spoke the truth."

"Well, explain this mistake then."

"I was referring to Mademoiselle Ida."

"Her? I thought you loved her as well?"

"Not at all! I don't understand how she could...?"

"Be quiet!" she interrupted him. "Ida was certainly truthful. She has never lied to me!"

"Even so, she was mistaken tonight."

"Yes, dear aunt," Ida acknowledged, embarrassment reddening her cheeks. "I have made a mistake."

The countess clasped her hands together in confusion. "What?" she cried out. "You made a mistake? Didn't Monsieur von Goldberg just say that he loved you?"

"No."

"But you confirmed it to us just a few moments ago."

"Oh, I thought... Dear God! I thought—" She was too embarrassed to continue, but the countess pressed for an explanation.

"What did you think, Ida? Out with it. I want to get to the bottom of this!"

"I thought you were talking about... someone else."

Finally, it was Madame Rallion's turn to be speechless. She didn't know what to make of this latest news.

"Someone else?" she said at last. "Someone who loves you?"

"Yes."

"Someone whom you truly love?"

"Yes, dear aunt."

"Someone who has spoken of his love to you?"

"Exactly!"

"Could it really be true? My word, how they presume to carry on behind my back! My dear Monsieur von Löwenklau, please forgive me. You must surely see how this gathering has quite unexpectedly transformed itself into a love triangle that I am now obligated to deal with. Would you please excuse us until tomorrow morning?"

Löwenklau bowed politely before answering. "Of course, gracious lady," he said. "Is it your wish that I withdraw?"

"Yes. Under these unusual circumstances, I am afraid so."

"Certainly, if that is what you desire," he said, then added, "even though I feel that my presence could help in clearing up some of this mystery."

"How could your presence enlighten us, Lieutenant?"

"I feel I could give you the necessary explanation. *Quid pro quo*[3.1], you see."

"About what?"

"About this present situation. It is I who is actually this someone else."

"What? The one who loves her?"

"Yes."

"Do you love him, too?" asked Madame, turning to face Ida.

"Thank God, yes!"

Upon hearing these words, Gebhard walked over to Ida and placed his arm around her waist. He tenderly caressed her luxurious hair with his other hand. "Don't be afraid, my love," he reassured her. "Our dear and gracious aunt will forgive your little indiscretion."

Even the most accomplished artist would have had difficulty trying to capture the look on the countess' face. Astonishment, anger, joy, relief, annoyance – each of these emotions played across her face. Yet it was astonishment that gained the upper hand.

"Do you two truly love each other?" she asked.

"Yes, completely, and those two over there as well," replied Löwenklau, pointing toward Hedwig and Kunz.

"I will address those two in a moment. But first, I need to clarify something with you. Didn't you tell me earlier that you loved another?"

"Not at all, Madame. I failed to disclose anyone by name."

"Didn't you tell me that Monsieur von Goldberg was in love with Ida?"

"No. May I remind you that it was you who jumped to that conclusion."

"Dear God!" she cried, flustered. "You're getting me all confused. What then did you actually say?"

"I merely said that I loved a wonderful girl with all my heart. I also added that Ida was in love with a German officer."

"Why did you fail to reveal to me that your lovely girl and Ida were one and the same?"

"May I disclose the whole matter, gracious lady?"

"I would be most pleased to hear your explanation."

"Well," Gebhard began. "I noticed the affection that my friend Goldberg held for Mademoiselle Hedwig, the same affection which was returned to him."

"Did you really observe that? I missed it entirely."

"I suspected they loved each other, even though neither one had been able to elicit the other's affirmation. It reminded me of an impasse that, if left unchecked, could easily derail their love. I realized I needed to employ extraordinary measures to bring this to a successful conclusion. Although I risked much, the results speak for themselves. Monsieur von Goldberg declared his love openly for Mademoiselle Hedwig, and she in turn finally admitted that which she had hidden in her heart. My task has come to a successful end and I beg Madame for a merciful verdict."

The group of four stood perplexed, not quite believing what they had heard.

"What an awful prankster!" Hedwig exclaimed, annoyed at herself for crying over Goldberg's apparent unfaithfulness.

"You schemer," whispered Ida to Gebhard, still unsure what it was he had privately related to her aunt.

As for the aunt, she was completely perturbed over whether she should be angry over the mix-up or just start laughing. On the one hand, she was pleased with herself that her plan had come to fruition. On the other, she was annoyed that Gebhard had set his sights on her niece without her permission.

Kunz took advantage of the quiet moment. "Troublemaker!" he said softly to Gebhard. "What made you think of meddling in my private affair?"

"Those who are unhappy in love complain, but those who are content revel in its tranquility," retorted Löwenklau.

"Have it your way. Tell me, when did you speak to Ida about your intentions?"

"On that first night."

"Don't be ridiculous."

"No, really. It's the truth, isn't it, Ida?"

She nodded her head in agreement.

The countess approached them, wanting to understand more. "Really?" she asked him. "You have known since your first meeting?"

"You will have to ask Ida when you are alone with her. But as for my own feelings, from the first moment I felt we were meant for each other."

"Did you discuss this behind my back?" Her countenance once again conveyed annoyance.

Gebhard, pointing his index finger at her in mock seriousness, replied, "Madame, wasn't this your idea all along? One that you purposed behind our backs?"

The serious expression vanished in an instant, and she started to laugh. "Young people today are incorrigible. Who can see through their craftiness? When you do find one who is truthful and sincere, he does an about-face and comes across as a conniver to a fault. Well, I have to see about some sort of punishment."

Gebhard impulsively reached for her hand, pulling it to his lips. "A thousand pardons, dear lady!" he pleaded. "I informed Ida of my love for her, yet I qualified my remarks. I told her I would openly express it once I returned from my expedition. This is why we chose to remain quiet about our plans. I wanted to earn your respect rather than encroach on your hospitality. If I have offended you by my actions, I pray I will find a measure of your mercy."

When the young couple looked upon the countess, they noticed a softness in her face, a tenderness in her eyes that was foreign even to the nieces. "I forgive you both," she replied emotionally. "May it be as you have intended. Your love will stand the tests before it, and I hope you will be rewarded for your perseverance." Then she turned to Kunz and Hedwig. "Now for these other two. Monsieur von Goldberg, you claim to love my niece, Hedwig. Is this true?"

"With all my heart!" he replied without hesitation.

"And you, Hedwig?"

In an instant, that playful side of hers burst onto her face. "Me? Oh, I... I don't want anything to do with him," she answered, pouting.

"Why not?"

"He called me scatterbrained."

"Well, you do have your silly moments," replied her aunt.

"She promised me," clarified Kunz, "that she would transform her silliness into something heavenly, something that would not only shine in all its splendor, but also remain faithful for all time."

"Is that true, Hedwig?"

She looked embarrassed for the briefest moment. "Yes, dear aunt," she said. "I promised him."

"Do you intend to fulfill your commitment, Monsieur von Goldberg?"

"As God is my witness, Madame," he confirmed.

"Then tell me first, what can you offer to my niece?"

"For now, a heart full of love. I promise that I will endeavor to build a future for her, one that she can be satisfied with."

"Then make sure you stay fixed on this course. Your love will grow therein. It's a shame that you're not pursuing the work of a geographer."

"I believe I can advance in my current position."

"Still, you might consider accompanying Monsieur von Löwenklau. That way, you would become an instant celebrity. Surely you can see that for yourself."

Kunz allowed a smile to creep onto his lips. "Madame may have something there," he said. "As enticing as your suggestion may be, though, I do have my responsibilities to attend to here. I'm convinced I can demonstrate to you that my future will shine as brightly on its own merits, as my friend's. You can place your trust in its fulfillment."

CHAPTER FOUR
The Eye of the French

There are instances in life where significant pauses occur, leading one to believe that the threads of a story have been severed. Life often imitates the natural movement of the ocean. The waves are not tossed about as a result of linear movement in water, but rather because the current continually moves up and down. A singular drop that at one moment may rise in a crescendo of spray, will drop into the depths the next, disappearing from view. Perhaps it will emerge as a single drop, or appear united with many others, finally coming once again to the surface. So it is with the diminishing lives of a nation, or in the case of an individual, who disappears from view only to reappear in a place and time when he is least expected.

Several years had passed since the events in Paris. On this day, a small number of French officers sat together in a coffeehouse in Biskra, smoking, drinking, and of course enveloped in lively conversation. Biskra was a small city in the province of Constantine, in Algiers. It was situated on the busy caravan road, drawing the Berber and Bedouin alike to its nearby markets. They came from the surrounding area for the purpose of dealing and selling local goods.

The coffeehouse, designed to appear European, ended up more closely resembling an Oriental building. It would have looked out of place in a busy Parisian street, but here in Biskra even more so. The structure was erected according to Moorish standards, despite the fact that a few window openings had been constructed in the stone wall, almost as an afterthought. A plain signboard with a French slogan adorned the entrance.

The followers of Mohammed simply spread their carpet on the plain floor and sat cross-legged. To accommodate European tastes, a few rough hewn chairs had been brought in to serve as acceptable seating places for the officers. These gentlemen, however, were not drinking coffee. They rather preferred strong Portuguese wine, and not in small quantities, as was evident by the growing pile of empty bottles. The men were in a gregarious mood and a few were so affected by the wine that it wouldn't have taken much more for them to descend into complete drunkenness.

The innkeeper, who personally served them, wore clothes of local product, but aside from outward appearances, he was a Frenchman. When he was drawn into their conversation, he spoke the dialect usually heard back home in the area of Tours. They pestered him again with question after question, wanting him to join in, but he knew better and merely shook his head.

"How could I know that, Monsieur Brulé?" he replied evenly. "I don't know if he's ever been to Biskra. All I know is that he's never set foot in my little establishment before."

"Are you sure about that?" asked Brulé.

"No, unless he did so without me being aware of it," the innkeeper conceded. "I don't even know him."

"Is he that inconspicuous?"

The man nodded. "Nobody knows him. He could very well be sitting here among us, without anyone being the wiser. General Cavaignac is the only one who knows him."

"This man," said Chirac, one of the other officers, "he only deals with our commander?"

"Who knows?"

"What does he call himself?"

"No one seems to know for sure," the innkeeper said. "It seems that he's not known to us, or to the Bedouins. They have given him a name, which in itself states what they think of him."

"What is that name?" Chirac pursued further.

"*Ain el Fransawi*, which literally means, Eye of the French. Or more correctly, the French spy. Rumors continue to abound... he's here, then he's there! Some describe him as older, while others insist he's younger. In short, very little is known about him. Why don't you ask Cavaignac, the Governor General? He could give you more details if he so chooses."

A man, perhaps in his early thirties and dressed in poor Bedouin attire, sat on a chair at the back of the café listening to the exchange. He was seated in a manner that suggested he was more comfortable on a mat and cushion than on a plain chair. He sported a thin beard, in the custom of many Arabs, and stared ahead with indifference to their conversation, much like a true follower of Mohammed. A coffee cup lay in front of him and a *tschibuk*[4.1] sat comfortably in his hand. He drew the smoke from the pipe and slowly released it through his nostrils.

"Who is that fellow?" asked Brulé.

"I don't know him," replied the innkeeper.

"Is he a Bedouin?"

"Evidently, since he requested the pipe and coffee in Arabic."

"Perhaps he understands our language. It doesn't suit me to have strangers listening in on our musings."

"See if he'll respond in French," suggested Rigeau, another officer.

Brulé complied and turned to face the stranger. "Who are you?" he asked him in French.

"*Tugger* (a merchant)," he replied in the customary curt style of the Arabs.

"What do you trade in?"

"*Fewakih* (in fruits)."

"Where do you come from?"

"Wadi Dscheddi." In Arabic, this referred to the river valley of the small Dscheddi River, which carried water just south of the town.

"Do you understand French?" continued Brulé.

He nodded. "*Kalil* (a little)."

"Where have you heard our language spoken?"

"Algiers."

"Really? The city? You've traveled that far?"

"*Na'm* (yes)."

"Were you there a long time?"

"*La* (no)."

Although the language barrier made it difficult for the Frenchman to understand the Bedouin, the stranger was able to communicate through hand signals more than mere words, encouraging the Frenchman to continue his quest for information.

"Have you ever heard of a certain man known to your people as *Ain el Fransawi*?"

"*Lissa ma* (not yet)!"

"Are you a rich Bedouin?"

"*Ma li scheh* (I don't have much)."

"Poor devil. Here," offered Brulé, "have a glass of wine."

The officer wasn't playing fair. He knew full well that no follower of Mohammed would touch wine, much less from a foreigner. The stranger made a dismissive motion with his hand.

"*Kullu muskürün haram* (foreign drinks are not permitted)," came his labored reply.

"Then leave it be and don't visit places where wine is served! Don't you know your refusal insults us?"

"*La* (no)."

"Then go to hell or join us for a drink. Why should we put up with a big-eared ape like you who sits and listens but keeps to himself?"

The situation could have gone badly for the unfortunate Bedouin had the Frenchman's attention not been diverted by the arrival of the innkeeper's servant just at that moment. The servant was armed with the latest newspapers from Europe. News from Paris, here in the midst of the Atlas Mountains, proved considerably more important than chastising the manners of some unimportant Arab. The Bedouin used the distraction to withdraw quietly.

The periodicals were immediately distributed among the Frenchmen, each man choosing a different section to peruse. They weren't patient enough to finish even a single page before blurting out newsworthy items as they came across them.

"It seems I've found something relevant," noted Brulé. "There's some interesting news about Algiers."

"Really?" asked another. "What does it say about the colony?"

"Even more than we know," said Brulé. "For example, there is another mention of the marabout Hajji Omanah."[4.2]

"What does it say about him?"

"It reads:

> The famous marabout Hajji Omanah's loyalty remains unclear. He has considerable influence among the scattered tribes who dwell in the Aures Mountains, so it would be of great advantage to the ruling body if they knew whether or not he favored their policy. The consensus is that the government authority will send representatives to find out which side he supports, even though he has been known to be standoffish.
>
> "His descent is unclear, yet he wears a green turban, a sign that he is a direct descendant of the prophet Mohammed. His followers claim that he came from the holy area of Arabia to enlighten the masses in the Aures Mountains. It is a curious thing, however, because his facial features point to a European heritage. Furthermore, a strange story has circulated in which a French traveller claims to have seen him up close. He purported to observe a resemblance to an acquaintance from the region of Metz or Sedan. The basis of his assumption lies in the striking similarity of their features, though it is probably nothing more than mere coincidence."

Finishing, the reader looked up from the top of the paper at the other men, who were carefully considering the story.

"Then we're no further ahead in solving the mystery," said Chirac. It was clear from his expression and tone of voice that he was a more seasoned officer than the others. "Isn't it curious how these marabout live, withdrawn and failing to marry? It strikes me that this marabout must have been married at one time."

"It doesn't disqualify him," replied Brulé. "He can still live a solitary life."

"I've heard it's not that solitary," said Chirac. "Apparently, he lives with his son. Is that the life of a recluse?"

"Perhaps not quite. But think of the monks who live their lives cloistered, yet work among other monks. Is that not solitude?"

"Well, certainly a form of solitude, but they're not entirely alone. By the way, the son is almost as revered as the father. What other news did you glean?"

"There's more under the heading 'Timbuktu':

> Two years ago, an expedition was equipped and sent out by the scientific community whose purpose was to explore the expanses of the Sudan. Word has it that the expedition, led by First Lieutenant von Löwenklau, is already on the homeward leg of the journey. A source claims that, aside from the scientific knowledge, they have acquired significant material resources and plan to travel through Insalah, Golea, and Tuggurt."

"Dammit!" called out Rigeau. "That insolent German will probably come as far as Biskra. I know all about their unpleasant ways. Ever since our defeat in 1814, they feel they can look down on us. And that name, Löwenklau... doesn't that sound familiar?"

The resounding consensus from the others at the table was that it wasn't.

"It seems like I've heard it somewhere before," said Chirac. He concentrated, finally nodding in satisfaction. "Ah! Now I have it. Löwenklau was the name given to one of Blücher's favored officers. I believe he was the one who became entangled with the old Captain Richemonte. No doubt you've heard of Richemonte?"

"Is that the same Richemonte who was summarily dismissed after the battle of *Belle Alliance*?" asked Brulé.

"Yes, the one and only. I remember my uncle served with him and consequently related some stories after the fact that weren't too flattering of the captain of the old guard."

"I haven't heard anything about him since," Brulé pointed out. "Perhaps he succumbed to one of life's harsh lessons."

"I doubt that. Even though he was forced to leave France, he probably managed to elude the worst of his predicament. I suppose you're all familiar with the reason that France blockaded Algiers in 1827?"

"Yes," answered Rigeau. "The *Dey*[4.3] of Algiers struck the French consul Deval in the face with a... a fly swatter."

"Well, in a later conversation," explained Chirac, "Deval claimed he had seen Richemonte nearby."

"Did he know him from before?" wondered Rigeau.

57

"Yes. Deval had corresponded with him in Paris on several occasions. It's unlikely he would have mistaken him for someone else."

"Was Richemonte dressed as a *Moor*?"

"Yes, come to think of it."

"Was he wearing a turban?" asked Rigeau.

"*Mais oui*. Just like Deval reported."

"Could he have converted to Islam and become a follower of the prophet?"

"Anything's possible with that dishonest man. Was there anything else mentioned about Algiers?"

"Yes," replied one of the others. "It's reported that the governor general plans to conduct an inspection of the colony... which concerns us directly."

"It stands to reason Cavaignac intends to surprise us with an impromptu visit," Chirac speculated. "He belongs to that group of generals who like to keep their troops on the *qui vive*. He's supposed to arrive within the week, but I'm convinced that he'll—"

He was suddenly interrupted by the sound of the front doors being thrown open. When they turned to see who it was, they found a young and out of breath officer. It was obvious to all that he had run all the way from the barracks.

"What's going on? What news do you bring?" they called out, drowning each other out. The newcomer took a deep breath, grabbing one of their unfinished glasses of wine and draining the contents in one gulp.

"Something important, Messieurs," he said at last.

"Is it good or bad?" asked Chirac.

"Depends on your view point, sir. Cavaignac, the governor general, will be arriving shortly."

"The devil!" said Chirac. "So I was right after all. He hasn't arrived yet?"

"Not personally, no, but one of his adjutants just came into town a few minutes ago. The general is en route from Busada and should appear within the half hour."

"Then we still have a bit of time to sober up," Chirac concluded, reaching for a nearby water glass and emptying its contents in a single backward swig. The others followed his example, then stormed out the door.

Suddenly, the Bedouin man was the only one left, aside from the innkeeper. He had pretended to ignore the Frenchmen's conversation, all the while managing to hear every word. Rising from his chair, he put the pipe on the small table and reached into the folds of his cloak. Only after leaving behind a small silver penny did he venture out into the busy street.

Enterprising merchants sat behind their tables, keeping out of the sun, ready to bargain over their wares. The Bedouin approached one of these men, a long and gaunt man who sat behind a mound of dried dates. He was dressed in the garb of the local villagers. The poor state of his turban told the Bedouin that he was without means. His *burnus*[4.4] was tied together with an old rope made from camel hair.

"They have left," he whispered to the approaching Bedouin. "Did you overhear any of their conversation?" Surprisingly, he spoke fluent French.

"Yes," the Bedouin replied, also in perfect French.

"Who were they talking about, Henri?"

"You!"

"About me?" the merchant asked, surprised. "Hang it all! How did that happen?"

"First they spoke about a certain First Lieutenant von Löwenklau. The conversation drifted to the old regime, and all of a sudden your name came up."

The merchant was approaching sixty years of age, although he could have been older. He was in fact Captain Albin Richemonte, his hair completely covered by a turban. His face was graced with a thick white moustache. At the sound of the Löwenklau name, his upper lip curved up, revealing two rows of yellow teeth reminiscent of a predator baring its fangs.

"Löwenklau? A lieutenant?" he asked. "Is he German?"

"Yes, I think so," replied his cousin.

The old man's face glowed sinisterly. "It can't be him," he said, allowing his head to sink lower. "It must be someone else."

"What makes you say that?" asked Henri.

"Because the man I remember couldn't possibly still be a lieutenant. Thirty years have passed. Who is this Löwenklau they talked about?"

"He's a participant in an expedition sent out from Germany."

"Where does he come from?"

"I don't know."

"Where is he now?"

The Bedouin paused, trying to remember the details of the conversation. "He's on his way back from Timbuktu."

"Ah! This is interesting."

"Very interesting, cousin! What's more, the expedition is well-equipped, transporting costly wares and valuables."

"The devil! How do you know that?"

"The officers talked about it in the café. Besides it was in the newspapers."

The old man's eyes flickered like a wildcat's. "Really? Excellent news! Which route are they taking?"

"They're coming from Insalah and el Golea to Tuggurt."

The old man nearly jumped out of his stool.

"Toward Tuggurt?" he exclaimed. "Then it has to be the same European we heard about from our sources."

The Bedouin nodded in agreement, his face no longer the perfect picture of indifference he had showed the officers in the bar. Suddenly, he was completely animated. "I don't doubt the report," he said.

"When will the expedition pass through Tuggurt?"

"It's still too early to say."

"Does it have an escort?"

"Aside from the camel herders, it's accompanied by about thirty warriors from the *Ibn Batta* tribe."

"Pah! We'll overpower them." Richemonte's thoughts turned again to the mention of his own name in the men's discussion "So, did the officers really speak of me?"

"Yes. They said you were summarily dismissed after the battle of *Belle Alliance*."

"They should all go to hell! What else?"

"Some of them claim to have seen you near the *Dey*, the former governor."

"It's too bad the consul wasn't blind. Unfortunately, he saw me."

"Then the conversation shifted to the French spy," Henri continued. "I guess they didn't realize that you and he are one and the same."

"What did they say?"

"That he's a mystery to them."

"Hopefully I will remain that way for a long time."

"They also spoke of the marabout, Hajji Omanah."

"I suppose he's a mystery to them as well," Richemonte mused.

"Naturally!"

"It is their own fault. They should consider sending more suitable emissaries, ones more adept at obtaining information. Why did the officers leave in such a hurry?"

"They just found out about Cavaignac's impending visit."

"Ah! I thought so. When is he expected?"

"They indicated half an hour," Henri answered. "But that time's nearly up already."

"Then hurry! Walk toward his entourage and let him know that I've arrived."

Henri left quickly without uttering another word. He continued toward the gathering place where the French troops were assembling themselves in preparation for the governor general's arrival. A considerable number of locals had even come together to welcome the famous Cavaignac, who had earned their favor through his many accomplishments.

Henri, still dressed as the Bedouin, had barely joined the ranks of the villagers when he spotted the cavalcade to the west. A few *Turkos*[4.5] led the procession, guiding it into town. Next came the soldiers, the *Chasseurs d'Afrique.*[4,6] The escorts pulled back once they reached the town, allowing the general to lead the column the rest of the way in. In an instant, the drum roll started up and the waiting troops came to attention. The general saluted and rode down their flank. When he reached the end, Cavaignac turned toward the gate, where he was met by the commander of the garrison. He motioned for the commander, a man named Poisson, to join him as the procession filed into the city.

"Are you satisfied with the mood of the villagers?" Cavaignac asked.

"I have no reason to complain, General," said Poisson.

"As long as you follow my precepts, you won't have any. The Bedouins consider any form of kindness a sign of weakness. We have to show them grit and fortitude; they will respect this. What news do you have of the tribes in the mountainous regions?"

"They fail to come near the towns."

"Did you offer the ornate *burnus* to each one?"

"Certainly."

The French government had presented each sheik with a costly *burnus*. However, accepting such a gift didn't come without a price. The sheiks realized that in doing so, they would be obligated to support the interests of France in their country.

"Did they refuse them outright?"

"No," the commander said. "They're much too clever for that."

"What do you mean?"

"I sent out messengers, but they reported only finding remnants of their camps. The tribe seemed to have moved on without the slightest indication they were leaving."

"Even worse," Cavaignac said "It's as though a bullet was fired into loose ground. The result is completely useless – a waste of a good bullet – whereas a well-placed shot can break apart the strongest rock. Perhaps we should consider..."

The general trailed off thoughtfully, his eye catching the sight of the Bedouin man standing by the side of the road. Cavaignac brought his horse to a halt and looked down at him. His usually serious countenance turned to one of gratification.

"Ah! There you are!" he said with satisfaction.

Richemonte's cousin placed his hand across his chest, bowing respectfully. "*Allah jikun ma'ak* (God be with you)!"

"Are you alone?"

"*La* (no)."

"Is your relative with you?" the general asked.

Henri nodded. "*Na'm* (yes)."

"Where is he?"

"*Hunik, filsuk* (at the market)."

"He is dealing in fruits, then?"

"*Na'm* (yes)."

Cavaignac paused, then asked, "Are they good?"

The question carried a two-fold meaning, neither of which Henri missed. He smiled understandingly. "*S'lon daiman* (as always)," he replied.

"Then he can bring me some of his wares. I'm sure he'll be able to find out where I'm lodging." With that, the general nodded in a gesture of goodwill and rode on. The commander of the garrison watched Cavaignac move on, surprised that the general knew any residents of Biskra, let alone a lowly Bedouin.

"Do you know this man, General?" he asked, catching up.

"Yes," Cavaignac answered curtly.

"I have not seen him before," said Poisson.

"I have often seen him. He deals in fruits and I became acquainted with him in Bildah." Seeking to change the subject, he added, "Where should I spend the night?"

"It would be an honor to me if you would reside at my quarters."

"That's fine. I accept your hospitality. Now, when this Bedouin man's relative shows up, don't detain him unnecessarily. Admit him right away."

"How will we recognize him?"

"By his large grey moustache, and by his name... he's the *fakihadschi*[4.7] Malek Omar."

While the general continued to the commander's house, Henri made his way back toward the market, where the old man was waiting for him.

"Well?" Richemonte asked with anticipation.

"I spoke with the governor. He asked me if you were here."

"He must have suspected I was. Go on."

"I advised him of your presence and he instructed that you pay him a visit."

"Where is he staying?"

"I don't know."

"Go and find out while I wait here."

Henri left once again, leaving the old man to his fruit stand. His cousin returned after a short interval and informed him of the general's lodgings.

Richemonte filled a hand-woven basket with an assortment of fruits and dates from his stand and proceeded alone to the commander's house. His bearing was one of a carefree Arab, moving through the town as though at home in it.

When he arrived at the gate, a sentry stepped out to ask him his business.

"Where do you think you're going?" he was asked.

"*Fil seri' asker*," the supposed merchant replied.

"What is that gibberish? Speak French, man!"

"Ge-ne-ral!" Richemonte said slowly, feigning difficulty.

"Do you mean General Cavaignac?" To this, Richemonte nodded. "Who are you?"

"*Fakihadschi* Malek Omar."

"More Arabic!" the sentry exclaimed. Then, recognizing something in the unfamiliar words, he paused. "That does somewhat sound like the name we were told to listen for. You can pass." He motioned for Richemonte to enter.

Richemonte walked in, and after going through a dark, narrow hallway, ended up in an open portico. He met an ordinance officer there who repeated the same questions. When he was satisfied, he led the fruit merchant to a large sitting room. Richemonte found the general present, relaxing on a divan. When the governor recognized the newcomer, he rose from his comfortable place and approached Richemonte. When they spoke now, Richemonte's merchant guise slipped away and he conducted himself in French.

"Ah, timely as always!" Cavaignac said. "You must have surmised that my duties would lead me to Biskra."

"Yes, General."

"Did you meet up with my messenger?"

"Yes, four days ago. He caught up with me at Wadi Hobla and I left right away to meet up with you."

"Do you have any news?"

"Not much," Richemonte admitted. "The *Beni Hassan* tribe is making preparations to resist your attempt to conform them."

"Really! Where are they currently located?"

"To the south of Biskra."

"How many men do they have?"

"If they can assemble all of their small factions into one, they could gather several thousand men."

"Hmm!" Cavaignac mumbled thoughtfully. "That's a considerable number, more than I hoped. This could prove to be a prickly situation. Who's stirring them up?"

"The marabout Hajji Omanah, I suspect."

"Has he adopted a contentious position toward us?"

Richemonte nodded. "It would seem so. However, I doubt if they can amass all those numbers right away. Some of the smaller groups have wandered further south, while some have moved into Tunisian territory."

"I can take some comfort in that," the general said. "We have deployed most of our resources in the north and west. It would be impossible to send a large contingent to the south as well. Are your sources still trustworthy?"

Richemonte shrugged his shoulders. "So long as I pay them well," he replied.

The general smiled, not missing the underlying point. "You imply that you have depleted your purse."

"Exactly, General."

"Well, rest assured, I will replenish your pocketbook. I know the value of a good scout. In fact, I find myself in the position of offering you an opportunity to earn a considerable bonus."

That caught Richemonte's attention. "I am at your disposal."

"It concerns the marabout."

"I guessed as much."

"Then your insight hasn't betrayed you. If he is an actual threat, I need to find out once and for all what he represents to our regime."

"I was under the impression that you had figured him out by now," Richemonte said with a knowing smile, ever the careful spy.

"Unfortunately not," Cavaignac admitted. "The men I assigned to the task proved incompetent. As a result, I learned little. Which is why I come to you now and prevail upon your expertise. Are you confident you can locate this marabout and extract information?"

A dubious expression crossed Richemonte's face. "That would be difficult indeed!"

"Yes, I can imagine."

"Especially dangerous for me personally."

"Dangerous? Are you intending to exaggerate the task to make more money? You are a crafty one, my friend."

"I don't exaggerate the truth," replied Richemonte, feigning offence.

"Tell me, how could a visit to this marabout prove dangerous? You portray yourself as a good Muslim, and thousands of such followers of Islam visit the devout man without threat of danger."

"That may be. But consider that I have been dubbed the French Informant, or the Eye of the French. The marabout is more than a passively devout man. Just as I desire to look into his affairs, he longs to capture the French spy. The smallest slip on my part could prove costly, ensuring my discovery and eventual demise."

The general wasn't moved. "Then make sure you're careful."

"It looks easier than it actually is."

"In other words, you're not willing to assume the risk."

"On the contrary. I just need to satisfy myself of the compensation."

"Just as I thought! What do you require in exchange for reliable information concerning his views about us?"

"Aside from the usual expenses, five thousand francs."

Cavaignac rose from the divan and began pacing back and forth, deep in contemplation. After a few moments of consideration, he came to a stop in front of the spy.

"That is a considerable sum," said the governor. "However, I am prepared to furnish you the large reward after you accomplish your task. Are you familiar with the marabout's location?"

"Yes," Richemonte revealed. "Even though I have never traveled there."

"Have you ever seen him?"

"No. As you well know, I've been occupied in Algiers and Morocco."

"Of course," Cavaignac said with a nod. "You have completed your assignments there to my satisfaction. I am therefore reassured that you will be successful in this one as well. Are you prepared for your trip?"

"I have all that I require, notwithstanding the money."

"Here is the purse with the agreed upon amount," the general said. He removed an ordinary-looking purse from his pocket and handed it to Richemonte. The contents had a metallic sound, momentarily satisfying him. "It should cover your initial expenses. As for the bonus money..." He paused. "Well, that you will have to earn."

"I am convinced that I will."

"When do you anticipate getting under way?"

"Today, General."

"Very well. When can I expect your good news to reach me in Constantinople?"

"That is unclear," Richemonte said. "I hope to have favorable results in about two weeks."

"I'm a little uncomfortable waiting that long."

Richemonte merely shrugged, then moved on to the next order of business. "Do you have any other assignments for me?"

"Of course," the general said. "You mentioned that the *Beni Hassan* are about to take up arms against us. Did you observe signs to that effect?"

"Yes. I spoke with a few sheiks about this very problem."

"Are you well acquainted with them?"

"Not only am I their friend, but they consider me a guest."

Cavaignac was clearly impressed. "What lie did you tell them about where you came from?"

"I simply told them I came from an oasis in the east," Richemonte said with a smile, "and that I was searching the Western Sahara for a man with whom I have a blood feud. It was the only way I could explain my personal situation without invoking too much scrutiny."

"You convinced them?"

"Yes. With these tribes, nothing counts more than revenge or a blood feud."

"That's good. I would prefer for you to spend as much time with them as possible. That way I could depend on your observations of events as they occur."

"Don't worry, General. A revolt doesn't materialize overnight. The preparation for such a vast undertaking can take weeks, perhaps even months. I'm convinced that I'll be on my way back well before any sort of firm decision has been made."

"Are you saying that nothing important will happen within the next two weeks?" Cavaignac asked.

"Not even during the next month."

"That's a relief," the general said. "Well, good luck on your trip. I will look forward to our meeting in Constantinople. Is there anything else you need to tell me about?"

"No."

The general paused, keeping an appraising eye on Richemonte. "There is, however, one more matter that I would like to address."

"I'm listening."

"Are you prepared to be as forthright as you have been up to now?"

"Of course."

Something about the spy's demeanor caught Cavaignac's attention, something that seemed to convey the merest hint of mistrust. "Does that apply to any subject?"

"To any subject that concerns our arrangement," Richemonte replied carefully.

"I see you insist on qualifying your response. Which subjects then are you referring to?"

"My personal considerations, naturally."

"Those are the ones that interest me. How long have you served France's interests here in Algiers?"

"Since 1830."

"Was it always in your capacity as a spy?"

"Mostly."

"Were any of your associates or employers aware of your true identity?"

"Not one."

Cavaignac leaned closer, his eyes probing Richemonte's face. "Why do you feel it necessary to be so secretive?"

"Partly it's in my nature. It's also for my own well-being."

"Why haven't you considered placing your trust in me?"

"I do trust you, General," Richemonte replied. "Otherwise I wouldn't be working for you. However, in this one instance, I'm obligated to keep a confidence, one which I cannot divulge."

"I suppose I have to respect your personal affairs, even though I prefer to deal with confidants whose circumstances are familiar to me. At least you could enlighten me on this matter: were you born in France?"

"Certainly. I am a subject of France."

"Under what circumstances did you leave?"

"I would rather not answer that question."

The general's countenance darkened. "I believe you are going a little too far with all this secrecy," he said, a little displeased. "It seems to me that you were forced to leave France."

"Not at all. I left on my own terms."

"Hmm. The tone of your voice implies you are being truthful. I will honor your request by not prying into your earlier affairs. Still, I wish there was something I could do for you. Do you have any relatives back home?"

"No," Richemonte said. "At least, not close relatives."

"Is it still necessary to conceal the fact that the fruit merchant Malek Omar and the Eye of the French are one and the same?"

"Yes, and it's to your advantage that it remains that way. If the truth were to become public, my future efforts would be thwarted."

"All right then! You have enveloped yourself in an impenetrable secret, and are forcing me to respect it," the general said begrudgingly. "This is the reason why you shouldn't expect me to be forthcoming. Trust begets trust. You pretend to be a friend to the Bedouins, just as you pretend with me. Yet who are you siding with?"

"Naturally, toward you and my countrymen, General!"

Richemonte's words were spoken convincingly, and yet the spy thought he could detect mistrust in the general's earlier words. His moustache rose, revealing his yellow teeth.

"I hope so for your sake," replied Cavaignac. "Anything to the contrary would end in your demise. Watch yourself, my friend."

The sunburned cheeks of the former captain of the old guard reddened in anger. He shot an unguarded and venomous look at the general. "How could you come to the point of mistrusting me now, General? Have you ever found me untrustworthy?"

"Oh, you are much too careful for that. I'm telling you here and now that I have been more upfront with you than you have been with me. It occurs to me that your service to France has not been quite as explicit as you pretend, but rather reserved. Even the cleverest, most cautious man will eventually expose himself if he is not being entirely honest," Cavaignac observed. "I get the impression that you offer your services to the highest bidder and clearly France is richer than any Bedouin sheik. If the reverse were true, how would you handle yourself?"

"I would still serve France!" replied Richemonte.

"Really?"

"I am prepared to die for my country."

"Well, don't be too hasty there. It certainly is an honor to die for one's country. It is, however, far more advantageous to live for your country. I trust I can depend on you in every situation." The general began to turn away from Richemonte. Remembering a final point of interest, he looked back. "Just one more thing. What is your companion's name?"

"Ben Ali."

"Which means as much as Ali's son. But he's not your son, is he?"

"No."

"Is he your relative?"

Richemonte inclined his head. "Yes. He is my cousin."

"Is he also a Frenchman?"

"Yes."

"Is he forced to remain secretive regarding his situation?"

"Yes, just like me."

"Most peculiar!" Cavaignac exclaimed. "Well, I'm not going to force you to reveal your private life. If you serve me well, you may count it as an advantage, but if I catch you in treachery, you can count on my harshness and justice. I expect to find you in Constantinople soon. *Adieu!*"

Richemonte, seemingly ignoring the reproach, made a deep bow and left. Cavaignac watched him leave, rubbing his chin thoughtfully as the old man stepped out of the room. *I'm sure I've seen that face before!* he mused. *It doesn't bear the usual trustworthy lines. I remember my childhood in Paris... my parents lived in the city and an officer lived across from us on Rue d'Ange. His mannerisms were similar to this man's, in that he often stood at the window and ground his teeth. He occupied half of the first floor, while his mother and sister occupied the other. Unfortunately, I can't recall his name. I don't trust this spy and I have to be more careful.*

Cavaignac's memory, although coming short of recalling the captain's name, was entirely correct.

CHAPTER FIVE

Richemonte Forges New Plans

Richemonte left the house annoyed and tried to compose himself. However, when he returned to his companion, he allowed himself to blow off some steam.

"Your face has lost its luster," his cousin quipped when Richemonte came into view of the stand.

"For a damn good reason!" he replied irritated. He dumped the basket of fruit back onto its original pile as his cousin watched.

"Such carelessness," the younger man remarked.

"What do you mean?"

"The fact that you brought back the basket. His men will assume you paid him a visit for another reason."

"I know. There was no time to worry about the dates."

"Was there that much to discuss?"

"Of course," Richemonte said. "One thing is clear. From this day forward, I will despise General Cavaignac."

The cousin was taken aback by the vehemence of the old man's statement. "That's news to me. What happened?"

"He insulted me," hissed Richemonte, baring his teeth threateningly. "And not just in a small way."

"How did he do that?"

"He doesn't trust me."

"Ah!"

"He told me he's concerned that I serve just one master. Namely, the one who pays the best."

His cousin snickered before replying. "Is he wrong to think that of you?"

"No! But he doesn't have to tell me to my face."

"Well, this general is no fool. Are you allowing his views to taint our plans?"

"Of course not!" grumbled the old man. He dropped his chin in frustration, allowing it to rest in his hands. He stared pensively ahead, as though contemplating something. "I've had nothing but bad luck. I've strived in vain for years to better my situation."

"That pretty much sums up your life."

"Be quiet!" he snapped. "I had a career, even honor. Then came that damned Löwenklau. There was a treasure worth millions – and again that Löwenklau got in my way. They stripped me of my honor and I had to leave France. Ever since then, I've had just one thought, to become rich above all else. I wanted to return to France a rich man! In doing so, I would regain my honor. I served the *Dey*, I worked for the English, then the French... Hell, I even worked for the Bedouins! What did it get me? Nothing! Nothing at all. I sent for you, hoping you could support my plans. I gave it considerable effort, but the pursuit of riches is fleeting. Nothing wants to work out for me. The general offered me a lousy five thousand francs. What use is that?"

"Five thousand francs? What for?"

"I'm supposed to locate and pump the old marabout for information."

"What are you going to do?"

"What choice do I have?" Richemonte asked rhetorically. "Could I possibly earn such a large sum serving the Bedouins?"

"Why not?" asked Henri slowly.

The old man was overcome with despair, yet he looked to Henri for a moment before shrugging his shoulders. "What of it? Where could a *Kabyle* or a *Tuareg* come up with that kind of money? Even if they had such a large sum, what service could I possibly render for them?"

"For a man like you, that shouldn't be too hard to figure out."

"Are you pretending to be smarter than I?"

"No. But, just maybe, I think I have something this time."

"Well, let's hear it."

"Are you wondering where a simple Bedouin might get his hands on riches?" his cousin asked. "Arrange a deal with one and he will gladly share with you in the spoils."

"You must be dreaming!"

"Believe me, I'm wide awake. Didn't you just mention this Löwenklau fellow, the one whom I've heard so much about?" he asked. "Do you suppose there could be many by that name back in Germany?"

Richemonte shrugged at that. "No, I wouldn't think so."

"Well, it stands to reason that the one you know so well is probably closely related to this one who is traveling back from Timbuktu."

"Perhaps! Ah! Now I see what you have in mind."

"What do you see, cousin?"

"Are you implying that I take my revenge on the old Löwenklau by incapacitating the young one and relieving him of his rich 'burden'?"

"Of course."

The old man smiled wickedly. "That is a great idea! It will make me feel better and make me a rich man. If only we can carry it out."

"Why shouldn't we be able to accomplish it?"

"To begin with, this Löwenklau is accompanied by at least thirty warriors of the *Ibn Batta* tribe, while I count only the two of us!"

Henri good-naturedly placed his hand on Richemonte's shoulder. "Cousin," he said, "aren't you forgetting something? All this time, we've been dealing with the *Beni Hassan*. Yet you overlook such an important point. There's a blood feud between the two factions."

Enchanted with the revelation, Richemonte jumped out of his seat excitedly. Anyone watching would have considered the move peculiar for the Bedouin character he had worked so hard to create for himself. "Heavens!" he exclaimed. "I hadn't considered that. Now I realize what a good teacher I've been to you for you to come up with such a brilliant idea. We haven't a moment to lose. We need to depart right away."

"Where to?"

"We need to visit our benefactors, the *Beni Hassan*."

"I thought you had to pay the marabout a visit first?"

"Later," Richemonte said dismissively. "There's time for that."

"What about our dates?"

"We need to get rid of them. Over there," he said, pointing to an old *Tagir* (merchant) who was sitting under his covering. "I'm sure he will take them off our hands if I make it worth his while. Let me go fetch him."

Richemonte quickly walked across the courtyard, an act that was normally against traditional Muslim customs. He returned shortly, accompanied by the eager merchant. They quickly settled their deal and the *Tagir* happily returned to his place in the market with his bargain. Having settled the matter, Richemonte was eager to get moving.

"Did the general provide you with an advance?" asked his cousin.

"Yes."

"How much did he give you?"

"I haven't had the time to count it."

"Then have a quick look."

"Why?"

"Because I need my share now. I need to purchase a few items."

The old man shook his head. "There's no time for that now. Surely you have everything you need for the trip."

"Yes, I have all that, but I don't have a pipe, or slippers, or rings, or a sunshade."

"Are you crazy? What do you need all that stuff for?"

"Need, you ask?" he asked incredulously. "The pipe is for Sheik Menalek, and the slippers, rings, and sunshade are for his daughter, Liama."

"Are you really that interested in her?"

"I want her for my own," replied his cousin with such conviction that any rebuttal would have fallen on deaf ears. Richemonte withdrew his moneybag and counted out some coins.

"Here, take it," he said, not too pleased. "Two-thirds for me and one-third for you."

"Fine. Are you coming as well?"

"Yes," Richemonte said. "But I'm not going to wait all day for you."

They walked into a nearby bazaar, where Henri had no difficulty finding the desired items. He purchased an exquisite pipe for the sheik. For Liama, he found wrist and ankle bracelets made of genuine silver, a pair of blue satin slippers, and a silk sunshade.

Cradling the new purchases, the two men wandered out of town.

❧✠☙

They walked along the west side of Wadi Biskra on their way out of town. As Biskra disappeared into the distance behind them, both men made their way toward a nearby terebinth brush. As they worked their way deeper into the brush, they suddenly heard the snorting of horses ahead. They followed the sound, coming at last upon two concealed, saddled horses.

"What luck! They're still here," the younger man said.

"Of course they're here. Who would have come across them?" Richemonte replied disdainfully.

"Perhaps thieving *Tuaregs*?"

"They have no idea we concealed our horses here."

"Perhaps predators, then?"

"There aren't any lions or panthers in the area, either. Even if one were to come this way, they only leave their lair at night to hunt." Looking both ways quickly to make sure they were alone, Richemonte reached to the rear of one of the saddles and pulled out an attached sack. "Let's change our clothes."

He opened his sack and removed the fine clothes and quality weapons hidden inside. In a matter of a few short minutes, their old garments were removed and rolled up into bundles. Donning new clothes, and transformed into affluent Bedouin, the two spies reaffixed their bundles to the saddles.

They led their horses out of the underbrush. Once clear of the brush, they mounted their animals and rode in a southerly direction toward Uinasch. If they were seeking to find the marabout, this was clearly an out of the way route. The two men, comfortable in their new style of dress, found time now to continue their previous discussion, far from prying ears.

"Listen, cousin," started the younger one, "do you feel we can persuade the *Beni Hassan* to hold up the German and his entourage?"

"I'm convinced of it," Richemonte answered. "All we have to do is convince them that he's an unbeliever, a Frenchman. They're on poor terms with the French. Besides, we'll inform them that they're being escorted by warriors from the *Ibn Batta* tribe. Don't worry, I'll handle it."

"Will they leave the riches for us?"

"I hope so. We have to play our hand skillfully, though. If they refuse, we'll have to be more insistent."

"Insistent? You mean to force them?"

"See, now it's my turn to show you up," laughed Richemonte. "If necessary, I will force their hand by involving the French troops."

"How will you do that?"

"I merely convince my good friend Cavaignac that it's in his best interest. Then I will claim the treasure as my property."

"Will the French agree to your plans?"

The old man shrugged. "Certainly. I've already discussed it with the general. He thinks the *Beni Hassan* are on the verge of assembling themselves, perhaps for an uprising."

"That's fine, but—"

"But what?"

"What about my plans for Liama?"

"Dammit man! I don't understand you. This Bedouin girl has turned your head around."

"Can you blame me? She's as beautiful as an angel."

"Pah! I'm not going to argue about her beauty. In France, breeding and culture are just as important."

"What sort of a cultured French lady would ever marry a spy?"

Richemonte frowned at his younger cousin. "Poor choice of words! Does this enlightened woman know anything about your past schemes?"

"She could find out."

"Don't be so naive. When we return to France, it will be as refined, rich gentlemen. It will diminish our past blunders."

"Fine, that's your view. But this girl means more to me than all the riches I could dream of possessing."

The old man's moustache lifted awkwardly, his displeasure obvious. "You're incorrigible! Before you make too many plans, answer me one question: is she in love with you?"

"I don't know."

"Have you spoken to her about your aspirations?"

"No, not yet."

"Really? Rather then dealing with certainty, you're grasping at straws."

"Why shouldn't an ordinary Bedouin girl fall in love with a Frenchman?"

"Right!" laughed Richemonte. "Do you think all you have to do is approach her and hold out your hand? What about her father? What will the sheik say about a foreigner who's interested in his daughter?"

"He'll give his consent when she returns my affection."

"Hold it," Richemonte said. "A stranger can only marry the sheik's daughter if he becomes a member of the tribe."

"Fine. Then I'll become a Bedouin."

"Hang it all! I'm starting to see how this so-called love can disrupt your rational thoughts. Careful, or else it could even enslave you."

"Haven't you ever loved anyone, cousin?"

"Of course I have."

"Really?" exclaimed his cousin, surprised. "You've never mentioned it before."

"It wasn't necessary. I have loved. And just for the record, I'm still in love."

"Whom do you love?" asked a surprised Henri.

"Me!" he crowed. "Now you know the truth. This is the only sensible way to love. By the way, I would quickly curb this extravagance of yours if I didn't think it would fit my plans."

"I believe you. An egotist like you does nothing without finding an advantage in it. What plans are you referring to?"

"You know that I've portrayed myself as your father to the *Beni Hassan*. If my son were to attain the status of becoming the sheik's son, I could stand to gain considerable influence. The tribe, when fully assembled, can wield as many as three thousand men. You see then how we could exert significant power over the entire region."

"You're right. That's why I thought of Löwenklau."

"In what way?"

"If the sheik becomes my father-in-law, he won't object if I divide the treasure this German officer carries with him."

"Divide? Hmm!" the old man mumbled into his beard. "According to our current agreement, I get two-thirds."

"I know, but this is different. Our arrangement only concerns profit from scouting activity."

"Really?" Richemonte asked. "And I suppose you think you're entitled to half?"

The younger cousin's eyes hardened. "I not only think it, I demand it!"

"Fine. Then the buried strong box in the Ardennes is also an exception. I will recover it myself, without your help."

"You don't even know where it's buried."

"Don't worry," Richemonte assured him. "I'll find it."

"Are you actually thinking of going back to France?"

The old man smiled. "Why not? As soon as I'm wealthy, there won't be any reason not to."

CHAPTER SIX

The Lion's Roar

A flatland stretched from the north to the south, encompassing a vast area and linking two caravan roads. The westward road connected Uinasch with el Baadsch and the eastward one ran from Tahir Rafsa to Um el Thiur. The northern stretch of land was broken up by the Dscheddi valley, and to the south was Wadi Itel, providing proof to the claim that these parts of the desert weren't completely arid. El Thiur, which in Arabic meant *mother of birds* was further proof that where there are birds, there must also be brush, undergrowth, or trees. In fact, there was more grazing land in this part of the country than actual desert.

A tribe of the *Beni Hassan*, under the rule of Sheik Menalek, had set up camp in the flat plain to let their herds pasture. The plain was not particularly rich in vegetation, but yielded enough accessible grass for their vast herds. The white tents of the Bedouin were nestled in the expansive meadow. Their horses moved about freely, the cattle grazed at their leisure, and the camels and sheep lay out in the open grassland contently chewing their cud. Shepherds watched over their charges from a distance, mindful of any cattle that may have strayed too far. Young Bedouins raced back and forth on new horses, eager to hone their Arabian horsemanship. Others were content to rest in front of their tents with a good pipe, watching over their women and children, who busied themselves in their work, walking about with their faces uncovered, unashamed and unafraid. These nomadic Bedouin women were unaccustomed to covering their faces, the most noble and visible part of their womanhood, unlike their counterparts who resided in cities.

A rider appeared in the west. Wherever he had come from, his steed had obviously covered a lot of ground; the rider had difficulty keeping up a slow trot. He was a young man, barely twenty years old, as evidenced by the slight fuzz which covered his upper lip. He wore the white duffle coat of the Bedouins and his head was shielded from the strong rays of the sun by a bright colored scarf. His saddle and bridle were distinctly Arabic, but his weapons were foreign. He carried a double-barreled rifle, which he cradled in front of him. Two pistol butts poked out of his saddle bags, which on closer inspection seemed to be genuine *Kuchenreutersche*.[6.1] But despite his weaponry, the young rider was not European, but a Bedouin. His carefree glances spoke volumes about him. His gaze conveyed the joy of a man returning home from an extended absence, rekindling the memory of viewing the same serene countryside of youth.

The shepherds kept their eyes on him for some time as he approached the camp. When he coaxed his horse into one final gallop, he reigned in and stopped at the last minute in front of the furthest shepherd from camp.

"*Mubarek* (blessed be your day)," he greeted.

"*Ne harak saaide* (may your day be blessed)," replied the shepherd as he examined the rider more closely. "*Allah il Allah!* Saadi, is that you? I almost didn't recognize you."

Saadi smiled at the shepherd. "Has time changed my appearance so much?"

"No. I suppose my eyes were struck with a momentary blindness."

"How are the sons of the *Beni Hassan?*"

"They serve Allah, who looks on them with favor."

"What about the daughters of the tribe?"

"Allah favors them with beauty of the body and soul."

"What about your flocks and cattle?"

"Allah nourishes them, so that they increase daily."

"Is the sheik in the village?"

The shepherd nodded. "He sits in front of his tent, contemplating his blessings."

"How about my brother, Abu Hassan. Is he doing well?"

"Allah has granted him a long life of happiness."

Saadi turned to look toward the camp. "Well, I should go see if he greets me, his brother, with joy."

He prodded his horse into another gallop and rode on through the roaming cattle. He didn't stop until he was in front of Sheik Menalek's tent. Just as the shepherd had told him, Menalek was sitting by the tent flap. He looked up, noticing Saadi's approach. As Saadi dismounted to greet the older man, the leader of the *Beni Hessan's* face hardened. The tension between them was almost palpable.

"*Allah jinn ma'ak* (God be with you)," Saadi announced.

"*Ruhr ill dschehennun*[6.2] (Go to hell)!"

The newcomer lifted his head proudly. "What did you say?" he asked.

"Go to hell!" repeated the sheik.

Saadi's eyes flamed up. "Because you are older than me," he began calmly, "I will forgive the outburst!"

"I don't need your forgiveness."

Just as the young man's mind was formulating a sharp response, the tent flap was pulled aside, revealing a woman inside. She was such a picture of loveliness that Saadi's words evaporated on sight. Menalek kept his eyes focused on Saadi, unaware that his daughter had appeared behind him. The young man's eyes, however, were fixed upon the object of his affection.

She was at most seventeen years old, yet her womanhood was evident at first glance. Her features were soft and melancholy, common traits among Persian women of high standing. Her large, dark eyes held within them an earnestness that hinted at youthful maturity beyond her years. Her magnificent black hair hung in thick tresses, adorned with golden threads. Her forehead and neck were covered alternately with silver and gold pieces.

The young maiden wore red silky slacks and her ivory-colored feet were hidden in slippers of the same color. Her upper body was covered by a sleeveless blue jacket that was also embroidered with gold threads. Her fully developed bust was barely concealed by a white blouse, its long sleeves just covering her exquisite arms. This magical creature wore gold and silver bracelets on her ankles, completing the ensemble.

When she first noticed the young man, her cheeks reddened and she placed her index finger to her lips in a pleading gesture. She immediately disappeared behind the veil of her tent. Her father, still preoccupied with Saadi, failed to notice her appearance or her sudden departure.

The young man, immediately grasping the meaning behind her plea, suppressed a bitter retort and chose instead to reply in a milder tone. "Forgive me," he said to Menalek. "You are right. It is disrespectful of me to presume that you require forgiveness."

With that, he grabbed the reins of his horse and led the animal past most of the nearby tents, only stopping again once he reached one that was small and ordinary in contrast to the others. The horse's hoof-beats no doubt alerted the occupant, who threw back the covering of the tent. A Bedouin emerged who, judging from his facial characteristics, was closely related to the newcomer.

"Abu Hassan!" Saadi called.

"Saadi!" exclaimed his brother, Abu Hassan.

Saadi slid down from his horse and stepped toward his brother. The two young men embraced each other warmly.

Before they separated, the tent flap was moved once more and a woman peered out at the newcomer. Her plain attire in no way diminished her own loveliness. She waited for an opportune moment, when the two men had parted, and beamed with delight at her brother-in-law, extending her hand to him in hospitality.

"Come in," she greeted. "You are most welcome here!"

"Allah be praised!" sighed Saadi. "Finally I see some real hospitality."

"My brother, were you not welcomed by others?" Abu asked, his tone instantly turning serious.

"Yes, the sheik."

His brother allowed himself a soft sigh. "You have to forgive him. He's displeased with you."

"How come?"

"Because you chose to depart our village and live with the *giaurs*[6.3] (infidels)."

"Has Allah ever forbidden us to associate with them?" Saadi challenged.

"No, but our sheik hates the French."

"I've never left to serve the French, and you know that."

"Wasn't the Englishman also an infidel?"

"True," Saadi admitted, "but as I recall he was the sheik's guest."

Abu nodded. "You're right, but his hatred runs deeper than that. He's upset because his daughter refuses to forget you."

"Allah alone is master over our fate, certainly not a mere man. May I enter your tent, my brother?"

"Come in! That which is mine is yours... we are as one."

The two men vanished behind the covering of the tent. Without a word from Abu, his wife removed the belongings and saddle from Saadi's horse. She gave it a light slap, letting it know it was free to roam the grassland. She then turned and entered the tent, ready to serve her husband and their newest guest.

⤖

A short time later, Liama left her tent and walked absentmindedly among the cattle. She stopped from time to time to look about. She then turned and walked purposely toward the nearby ravine that stretched down to the valley. Taking one last look around, she vanished through the ravine's entrance.

Soon after, both brothers emerged from Abu's tent. Saadi looked down the long line of tents until he found the one he was searching for: the sheik's tent. He was nowhere to be seen and Saadi guessed he had withdrawn inside. The two brothers walked down the line, stopping frequently for Saadi to greet old friends and acquaintances.

Having fulfilled his obligations, his mind wandered back to Liama. He recalled how he had committed himself to her, and her alone, declaring that her love was worth more than all the cattle and possessions of the entire tribe. He made his way through the brush, climbing lower into the ravine, unaware that he was following in Liama's own steps. He remembered this ravine well and the last time he had spoken to Liama. He looked for the familiar place, and as he parted the last bushes, he shouted with joy. He found himself standing before the one he thought so much about.

"Liama!" he exclaimed loudly, trying at the same time to curb his excitement. She immediately blushed.

"Saadi," she managed to whisper.

He took her hands into his. "Why did you come here?" he asked.

She lowered her dark eyes without saying a word.

"Liama, why did you come here?" he repeated.

"I've been here often," she said. "Why did you come here on the first day of your return?"

"Because this is where we first met."

He could barely contain his longing for her. Since he had last laid eyes on her, she had blossomed into a beautiful young woman.

"I thought you had forgotten this place," she said.

"Never. As long as Allah gives me breath, I will not forget. Tell me, how often do you come here?"

"I come here daily."

He bent down to look into her wonderful eyes. "Because you enjoy the solitude?" he asked softly.

"No. Because of a memory."

"Were you reminiscing about someone?"

She hesitated with her answer. Saadi put his arm around her, pulling her closer.

"Please tell me, Liama! Who were you thinking about?"

She lifted her long eyelashes. "About you," she replied.

"Really? You haven't forgotten about me?"

"Never."

"Me, the poor nomad? You are the daughter of a rich sheik!"

"Allah decides whom he will bless with riches."

"Yes, you're right! I am rich," he said, "rich in my unending love for you, the most beautiful daughter in all the camps in the desert. Do you remember what we promised each other when we last parted?"

She didn't respond audibly, choosing instead to slowly nod her head.

"Please tell me!" he asked her.

"You tell me!"

"We promised each other to remain faithful for life. I have kept my oath. Have you, my dear Liama?"

"I have as well," she confirmed.

"I thank you from the bottom of my heart, you, the delight of my heart." He pulled her closer and kissed her full, red lips. Liama didn't resist. In fact, Saadi felt her respond. "What will your father say?"

"Allah will guide his will."

"Yes, Allah is all powerful," Saadi said reverently. "Do you condemn me for my actions, for journeying with the Englishman?"

"No..."

He felt she had been about to say his name when she trailed off. "Don't stop!" he pleaded. "Say it."

Liama placed her head on his shoulders and her cheeks flushed. "My Saadi," she whispered.

"Thank you, my love!" he replied, nearly overwhelmed at his newfound happiness. "Should I speak to your father?"

"Yes."

"Should I disclose to him that you decided to become mine?"

"Yes, tell him."

He paused, looking deep into her eyes. "I've been absent for two years. Was there no one else who desired to have you for his own?"

"There were a number of suitors."

"What was the sheik's response to them?"

"They were all too poor in his eyes."

"I'm even poorer than they. I don't even own a lamb to prepare for a meal should I receive company."

Sensing his disappointment, she cast her previous inhibitions aside and wrapped her arms around him.

"No, you are rich," she said. "The daughter of Sheik Menalek loves only you, and furthermore has promised to become your wife."

"Will you keep your word?"

"Yes. Only death could separate us."

"Then swear it."

"I swear it by Allah and the prophets."

"I thank you. You're sweeter than the music of heaven and purer than the beings in it," he intoned. The more he thought about the other suitors, the more he couldn't resist asking of them further. "Who were the men that came to rob you from your father?"

"One was the son of a sheik from the *Merasig* tribe. Another was an old emir from the *Ualad Sliman*. Then came a sheik from the *Beni Hamsenad*. Lastly, two foreign Arabs came from the Far East, a father and son who were in pursuit of a blood feud. The son pursued me, not openly, so I was always on my guard."

"Where are they now?"

"I don't know," she admitted. "They will likely return soon."

"Who told you that?"

"The son. His name is Ben Ali."

"What is his father's name?"

"Malek Omar."

Saadi couldn't hide his confusion at the men's names, and yet there was something about them that was vaguely familiar. He couldn't quite place the memory. "How can this descendant of Islam call himself the son of Ali, when his father is called Malek Omar? Is he young?"

"He's a little older than you."

"Is he handsome?"

"I wouldn't say he was unattractive," Liama answered coyly.

"Is he courageous?"

"Not that I could see."

"Is he rich?"

"Both men always had gold pieces with them."

Then, Saadi snapped his fingers, remembering where he had heard the name before. "Malek Omar! Of course. I remember meeting a man by that name. He was a fruit merchant, a *fakihadschi*. I often saw him enter and leave the governor's house in Biskra." He frowned. "But it must be a different man. Has his son ever proclaimed his love for you?"

"No. But even though he remained silent, his eyes spoke volumes."

"Don't worry. From now on, no one will pursue you. Tomorrow, I will speak to your father and he will have to listen to me."

"Why wait for tomorrow when we can talk now?" asked a nearby voice.

Both spun around at the angry words to see who had interrupted them, only to find the sheik himself standing there. His face was marked with rage and his eyes glittered with disapproval.

"*Giaur* (infidel)!" he said, spitting out the word.

This single word, meant to humiliate Saadi, was the greatest insult a fellow Muslim could hurl at another. The reproach stung more than a thousand other words could have combined.

Saadi stepped back, gripping the hilt of his knife. "What did you call me?" he thundered.

"*Giaur* (infidel)!" repeated the sheik. "Unbeliever!"

Saadi removed his knife from its sheath, but Liama intervened before he could act. "Stop!" she called out fearfully. "Put your knife away. He's my father."

Her admonition was just enough to bring him back to his senses.

"I will listen to you, Liama," he said. "But you must leave. I couldn't bear for you to listen to what is to come. That which is directed at me, I can forgive, but what is overheard by another, I cannot ignore. I would have to avenge the insult."

"No, stay here!" Menalek ordered his daughter. "I want you to witness how I deal with French collaborators."

Unsure of whether to stay or go, she hesitated. In one respect, she knew Saadi was right, but she was concerned about what might occur if she left her father alone with Saadi. Her betrothed seemed to read her thoughts.

"Go, Liama!" he pleaded. "I love you. I promise I won't do anything that would upset you."

She glanced deeply into his trustworthy face. "I believe you," she said. "I will go, my love."

"No, you're staying!" the sheik demanded. He reached for her garment, but she dodged his grasp and vanished behind the bushes. "Dammit! She ignores her father now, and even listens to outsiders. By God! I intend to hold a strict examination of you both. But first," he said, turning his attention to Saadi, "I will strike you down."

He raised his fist, just as Saadi confronted him.

"Sheik Menalek," he began, "are you a child or a man? Didn't the prophet teach us, *Women and children are enslaved by anger, but a man understands how to conquer it*? Listen to me. I gave Liama my word that I wouldn't do anything to distress her, but if you assault me, you will end up a dead man."

Menalek let his hand sink to his side. He knew Saadi well enough to know this was no bluff. "Are you threatening me?"

"No. However, you place yourself in danger by threatening me. Now, speak and tell me what you have to say. I will listen quietly and then give you my response."

The sheik's eyes were filled with malevolence. "Why are you pursuing my daughter?" he asked.

"I love her," was Saadi's simple reply.

"What about her? Does she have anything to say about it?"

"She loves me, too."

"You have deceived her. Who are you, and what have you accomplished in your short life?"

"I am a free warrior, proud to belong to the *Beni Hassan*. Are you worth more?"

"I am the sheik of this tribe."

"Who elevated you to this position?" Saadi challenged. "It wasn't you. Our wise elders appointed you as our leader, and they can remove you just as quickly."

"Why don't you count my cattle and my herds? What do you possess? Nothing!"

Saadi straightened himself to his full height. "I have Allah!" he stated proudly. "That is enough."

"Don't boast of our God. You have lost your faith in Allah on account of choosing to live with the French infidels."

"Weren't those same infidels your guests?"

"The Qu'ran doesn't forbid it."

"Likewise, the Qu'ran doesn't forbid me to associate with them."

"Yes," Menalek agreed, "but you chose to follow their faith and become like them."

"Who told you that?"

"No one. I can see it plainly enough. Had you remained a follower of the Prophet, you would at least respect the will of a father. It's plain to me that you intend to rob me of my child."

"Not at all. Rather than rob you, I want to give you a son," Saadi said. "Namely, me."

"I don't want you. You're a disgrace to the *Beni Hassan*."

"Sheik, stop trying to provoke me with insults. My knife would have finished you off a long time ago had I not given Liama my word."

"Your knife? Ah! You don't even have the nerve to settle this as a man. You're nothing but a coward."

Saadi's cheeks paled. Out of his love for his betrothed, he mustered every ounce of strength to keep himself from retaliating. "What have I ever done to you to deserve this treatment?" he asked. "I love your daughter and I offer you my respect. Instead of welcoming me, you come at me with insults. For anyone else, this would have been a fatal mistake. Should I take the life of the sheik and leave the tribe without its leader and a daughter fatherless? Should I pursue a feud with your relatives, all because I am powerless to resist a love which was placed in my heart by Allah himself?"

The sheik shook his head with contempt. "Since you're a coward, you won't be blamed for any blood feud," he replied. "I notice that you carry weapons like the infidels. They're not dangerous to me. You don't even know how to use them."

"You're mistaken," Saadi cautioned him. "I have dispatched the mighty lion and shot the deceptive panther with them."

"Don't lie. I can imagine you taking part in a hunt with a hundred unbelievers for a lowly hyena, which you now claim to be a fierce panther. The infidels do nothing but boast of their accomplishments, something you obviously learned from them."

"Don't you remember the Englishman?" the young man asked. "The one who stayed with you as your guest? I sojourned with him. I saw him go out alone to hunt lions, not with huge companies."

"He must have lied to you. I don't trust him. Any sane Bedouin knows that you need at least fifty capable warriors to kill a lion."

"No, Sheik, he didn't lie. I saw for myself when he shot the lion. I was fortunate to be with him, and I managed to shoot the lioness."

Menalek scoffed. "You're worse than the Englishman. If one of our men leaves to settle a blood feud, he does so out of duty and for his honor. But if one of our young men leaves our camp only to visit the places where unbelievers reside, he deserves nothing but shame."

"I left our band for a short time because I was poor."

"Oh, Allah! Did you want to earn money from the infidels?"

"Yes."

"You, a free Arab?"

"Yes, I."

"Did you allow yourself to be employed by that Englishman?"

"Yes, but I was not his servant. I was his guide and protector. I showed him the ways and the vastness of the desert. I acquainted him with the camps of our friends. Is that what you call shameful?"

The sheik nodded. "Of course it is. He paid you for it, didn't he?"

"I didn't receive any wages. I neither expected nor demanded any payment. I went with him to travel our vast land and learn about other peoples. He offered me a gift in return for my friendship. Is it disgraceful to accept a gift?"

Menalek couldn't refute this last answer. Instead, in a mocking tone, he asked the young man a simple question. "Was it a generous gift?"

"I am satisfied with it," replied Saadi, reserved.

"What did he give you?"

"He gave me gold. The Englishman was fond of me and was a rich man. With his gift, I can now establish my own tent."

"Well, go ahead and prepare your tent. Even find yourself a wife! Just leave my daughter alone. If I find you with her even for one minute, I will see to it that you are horsewhipped the way slaves are disciplined at the Sultan's bidding."

"I'm warning you, Sheik Menalek. If you dare reach your hand out to me, I will be forced to kill you."

"I'm not afraid of you. You're nothing but a coward."

"Your words are those of an unwise man. Learn from me, a young man who knows how to control his temper. Allah may be merciful and all-knowing, but his patience has its limits. Take heed. That's why I'm leaving without retaliating for your insults. Foremost on my mind is Liama, your precious daughter."

Saadi turned and started to walk away.

"Coward!" yelled the sheik after him.

Menalek had offended him to the depths of his soul. Outwardly, he remained calm, but his inner spirit seethed with rage. Because he loved Liama so much, he managed to find an inner resolve to overcome the spiteful accusations of the sheik. How his soul had longed to see his homeland. Yet since his return to his people, he had found only hate instead of love, disrespect instead of high esteem.

As he walked away from the ravine, the brush through which he crossed consisted of wild thorny acacia trees and mimosa bushes.[6.4] He barely noticed the way the prickles and thorns scraped at his arms. As he walked through them, his only thought was to calm himself. Continuing deeper into the brush, the gorge expanded wider in front of him and the grade receded as it bottomed out. The sandy floor became rocky, intermingled with large, broken-up pieces of fallen rock from the steep ravine walls.

Something about one of the rocks caught Saadi's eye. The rock surface bore strange marks, as though a rake had been scraped across it. Saadi, aware of the approaching darkness, bent down and looked closer at the markings.

"Allah!" he breathed aloud. "The stalker of our herds!" Drawing on his recent experience, he recognized the markings as those belonging to a fearsome lion. The king of the animal kingdom wasn't a stranger to this part of the desert.

Saadi bent over to examine the markings more carefully. *They're very recent,* he contemplated. *The lion must have been here earlier today. He was probably hungry, and so sharpened his claws on these rocks. Surely he will come out tonight and be on the prowl, looking to rob us of our cattle.*

He decided to follow the lion's trail further, but quickly discovered that it meandered back and forth. It seemed that the animal was unclear which path to take.

Perhaps he hasn't found a suitable lair yet and is still looking, pondered Saadi. *The lion was here just this morning and likely only arrived very recently. There is only one set of tracks. Evidently, he left his mate and young ones to reconnoiter the area. He will probably collect them once he's realized there is plenty of bounty to be had.*

The young man demonstrated a certain amount of insight and skill that he had learned during his travels. The Englishman, whose guide and companion he had been on his last journey, had taught him much about the habits of prowling lions. The Englishman had been no amateur hunter.

Should I follow these tracks? Saadi thought to himself. *No, I better not. Except for my knife, I don't have any weapons on me and night is approaching fast. The lord with the thick mane[6.5] conceals himself during the day, yet he will surely return at night. If he came across me now, I would be no match for him, rather easy prey. I have to go back to camp and warn the others so that we can prepare ourselves if he should pay us a visit tonight.*

He quickly climbed out of the ravine and made his way back to the camp. Although he knew its location, he could barely make it out in the fading light of dusk. In the Sahara, nightfall approached quickly. As Saadi came closer to the camp, he spotted the flickers of tiny fires, the first indication that women were preparing their evening meals. He felt it was his duty to advise the sheik first, since he himself didn't have the authority to call for a meeting of the elders.

A fire burned out front as Menalek sat outside his tent. He was observing his wife and daughter, as they prepared kuskus.[6.6] When the older man spotted Saadi's approach, his hand instinctively reached for the hilt of his dagger. His only conclusion was that Saadi had come to avenge himself.

"What do you want?" he asked threateningly. "Get away from me!"

Mother and daughter caught the menacing words and braced themselves for what was about to transpire between the two men.

"You have no right to dismiss me," Saadi calmly replied. "You are the sheik, and I have to speak to you."

"Do you have business with the sheik, or with Menalek?" he demanded.

"I have come to speak to the sheik."

"Then speak your mind, so long as it's not offensive to the women."

Saadi glanced at Liama and her mother, then returned his gaze to the sheik and continued. "They can remain," he said. "Call for the men of our village, so we can inform them of important news. The *lord of the earthquake* will soon be coming to our camp, hoping to steal cattle."

"You're out of your mind!"

"I have seen his tracks."

"Where did you see them?"

"At the bottom of the ravine."

"You were dreaming of the cat that you hunted with the infidels," Menalek said, scoffing.

"I know how to distinguish the tracks of a cat from those of a lion."

"Love has deceived your eyes. Go to your brother's tent and have a good rest. Tomorrow you will come back to your senses."

"Your hate is directed at me," Saadi said slowly, "but that's no excuse for you to relinquish your responsibility. Whenever news of an approaching lion reaches the sheik's ears, he must assemble the men."

"Are you threatening me?"

"No. But if you fail to perform your duty, I will blow the horn myself."

Saadi pointed to the large steer horn that was suspended from a hook at the tent's entrance. Its primary use was to alert the men that an assembly was about to take place.

"Just try it!" the sheik said, spitting out the words.

Despite the threat, Saadi stepped closer. In the same instant, Menalek drew his knife. "Get back! If anyone approaches without permission, I have the right to strike him down."

Saadi stopped. "I'm not afraid of your knife. However, I respect the rules of our elders. I will not violate your tent, but I implore you to reconsider and call for a meeting."

"I'm not about to call for the men of this village to burden them with your lies."

"You're a free Arab and have the right to exercise your will," the young man said. "I have the same right. If it doesn't suit you to perform your duty, I know what I have to do. Pay attention!"

He put two fingers in his mouth and released a shrill whistling sound that pierced through the early evening. It was the only means left to Saadi – the alarm of the *Beni Hassan*.

"What are you doing?" Menalek asked, now somewhat subdued.

"I'm calling for the *dschemma* to warn them about the lion. Furthermore, I plan to ask them how they intend to deal with a sheik who fails to exercise his authority concerning those who have been entrusted into his care."

The sheik didn't have to have the *dschemma* explained to him. He was quite familiar with it, an assembly of the tribe's wise men. Matters of importance were dealt with through the meeting. Most importantly, the *dschemma* possessed the authority to remove a sheik from power.

"You're forcing my hand!" the sheik shouted angrily. "Have it your way, but remember that I reserve the right to avenge myself."

"I'm not afraid of you, especially when it concerns my responsibility," replied Saadi calmly.

By this time, Saadi's shrill whistle had alerted all men who were within hearing range. Many men were standing in front of their tents, awaiting a second signal that would reveal to them the location of the gathering. Menalek had no choice but to blow the horn. No sooner had the tone sounded than they rushed to the sheik's tent. The women and children remained behind, knowing full well that they weren't permitted to take part in the deliberations. Even Liama and her mother had to withdraw from their presence.

A large circle was formed, into which the sheik entered.

"Listen, you men of the *Beni Hassan*," he addressed them. He then pointed to Saadi and continued. "This defector, who has journeyed in the company of infidels, has forced me to call an assembly. He claims that tonight, the *lord of the tremor* will pay us a visit. Can you believe this nonsense?"

"No, it can't be true!" blurted a young man's voice.

"I, too, consider it far-fetched," replied the sheik. "I ask for your understanding, since I was compelled to summon you against my better judgment."

"Listen to me, men," came the voice of an old and respected man, an elder of the tribe. "Since when is it the custom among us to listen to the opinions of the young and inexperienced before those of the elders? Since when do we so easily dismiss a warning, though improbable, by calling it far-fetched or untrue? We have been fortunate, not having lost a single sheep or other animal. Why shouldn't Allah allow the *lord of the earthquake* to cross our path? I ask that Saadi be allowed to speak to us and tell us what he saw."

The old man's persona and dignity carried so much influence over those who were assembled that not even the sheik thought about contradicting him. The lack of responses from the men confirmed that they were in agreement with the old man. Saadi took this as a good sign and stepped forward.

"That which I declared to the sheik is the truth, not a fabrication," he began. "Late in the afternoon, I went for a walk and came down into the ravine, which follows the Itel valley. I saw strange tracks. They were unmistakable, and belonged to a mature lion, probably an older animal."

"Are you that familiar with the tracks of a lion?" asked the concerned elder.

"Yes. When I rode with the Englishman, he showed me how to distinguish the tracks of various predators."

"If the *lord of the quake* was in the valley, he would have wreaked havoc on our herds long ago," another man commented.

"He only came here last night."

"How do you know that?"

"The tracks meander here and then there," Saadi explained. "It seemed to me that he was searching for a lair. I found a large stone where he sharpened his claws. He has to be hungry and ready to embark on a prowl."

The elder cleared his throat, satisfied with Saadi's report. "I'm convinced you speak the truth. Let's deliberate what we should do – just remember that the old men will speak and the young ones will keep quiet."

The discussion was very short. All the men gave credence to Saadi's report. Only one man downplayed it, the sheik. They resolved to light fires around the perimeter of the camp and keep their herds as close as possible. Should a predator actually appear, they would allow it to claim only one victim. In the morning, the men would gather and collectively pursue their new enemy.

Most Arab tribes performed poorly in that capacity. They would only attack the animal during the day, having attained a considerable superiority in numbers, and never at night. Their strategy would be to shoot at the lion or panther, inflicting as many wounds as possible, even if they were mostly superficial, until the animal finally collapsed from blood loss. Unfortunately, this often happened only after a number of warriors had been attacked or killed.

Saadi was still perceived as a young man and didn't want to push his luck by joining the elders' discussion. He had already done his duty and was rewarded by being listened to.

"Well, the *dschemma* has made a decision, and you men can do as you please!" said the sheik. "I still don't think there's any danger and thus have no reason to worry about my herds. Besides, even if by sheer chance a predator came along, we know that they never go on a hunt before midnight."

With respect to his last comment, several men nodded in agreement. Saadi, however, was of another opinion, and felt he needed to say something.

"Honored elders," he began humbly. "Even though I am still young, permit me to voice my concern."

"Speak, my son," encouraged the oldest of the elders.

"I have already told you that, in all likelihood, the lion has just recently arrived in the ravine. He must be hungry from his journey. He has sharpened his claws, and he's impatient for a kill. I consider it possible that he may strike before midnight."

"Your words are well considered," the oldest man said. "However, we should still have warning either way, since lions customarily announce their arrival with a mighty roar."

"You are correct," replied Saadi. "Yet I have learned that old, experienced predators can be as cunning and silent as the panther. They only announce their presence after the kill. Besides, I don't believe he will approach our camp from the flatland. Rather, he will come up from the ravine, which emerges not far from here. If that's the case, it will be too late for us to adequately prepare ourselves."

"What you say sounds prudent," said the elder. "We will move our herds right away and position them in such a way that the camp stands between them and the ravine."

The men left in a hurry, in order to arrange for this contingency. Only the sheik resisted the entreaties of his friends to move his animals to a safer location. It was clear that he didn't want to give any credit to Saadi.

After the meeting, Saadi rejoined his brother in his tent, where they consumed a simple meal. Since Abu was poor and possessed only a few animals, it wasn't difficult to coral them close to the tent and out of imminent danger. Instead of returning to the tent, though, Saadi reached for his double-barreled rifle and carefully examined the ammunition. As he turned to leave, his brother approached him.

"Where are you going?" Abu asked concernedly.

"I'm going to check on the herds."

"Why are you worried about them? You place yourself in danger needlessly."

"Calm yourself, my brother," he said, not wanting to alarm him. "There's no real danger for me."

He left the tent and purposely walked toward the area where the sheik's animals were situated. Saadi inhaled the soft evening breeze that emanated from the ravine. He was convinced the lion would approach the herds from the gorge, and intended to wait for him. The sheik had insulted him by calling him a coward, a title that didn't sit well with him, and he intended to disprove it. He lay down in the grass among the animals, and steeled himself to wait for what might come.

Fires burned all around the camp, nourished by branches from nearby acacia trees. The entire area was lit up as Saadi laid in wait. The minutes seemed to drag by at a snail's pace.

Suddenly, a figure approached the animals from camp. After scrutinizing the man's outline, Saadi recognized the sheik. As Saadi listened in, Menalek issued a few instructions to the hands who were watching his herds. Then, to everyone's surprise, the sheik turned and walked purposely toward the ravine, blatantly ignoring Saadi's warning. He stopped in the vicinity of the ravine opening. From his hiding place in the grass, Saadi judged the time to be less than an hour before midnight.

Menalek's light-colored *burnus* was clearly visible from afar. He ignored frantic calls from his wife and daughter, letting their calls dissipate in the stillness of the night. Although he was barely twenty paces from Saadi, he couldn't see the young man. Saadi had removed his *burnus*, opting to wear a darker, more practical coat.

"Oh Allah!" Liama called out to her father. "Please come back. The lion could come at any time."

"Be quiet!" he yelled. "There aren't any cats around here."

In that very instant, it seemed as though the ground were about to burst. A deep throated growl, reminiscent of a rolling thunder, erupted directly in front of the sheik. The noise quickly subsided into a moan, and Saadi thought it sounded like the entire herd lay at death's door. Fear gripped everyone who was nearby, both men and beast alike.

Menalek failed to move a muscle, acting like he was tied to a tree. Filled with terror and wonder, he watched as the lion emerged from the underbrush exactly where Saadi had suspected it would come, not skulking, but proudly and majestically moving toward them. The lion was large and powerful, truly worthy of being called the *lord of the jungle*. The flickering flames of the nearby fires exaggerated the animal's size, leaving the impression that he was the size of an ox.

The lion proudly shook his mane and lowered his head. When he spotted the unmovable sheik, he let out a second roar, the tone of which seemed to penetrate to the bone and marrow. Menalek's soul shook. The roar also extinguished any remnant of resistance within his body. The lion was in no hurry and for a few seconds seemed to evaluate the brightly lit figure in front of him. Instantly, the beast ducked down, ready to lunge at the sheik who was not thirty paces from him. The leader of the *Beni Hassan* had perhaps two seconds, at most three, to live. The reality of his predicament, though still binding him to the spot, loosed his tongue.

"*Ma una meded* (Help me)!" he feebly called out.

Just then, a voice called out to him seemingly out of nowhere. "Now we can both attest to the fact there are cats around here," it said.

Then a shot rang out, followed by a horrible roar. Immediately, a second shot tore through the air and struck the lion. In the same moment, the sheik was thrown to the ground by an immense force, losing consciousness.

He awoke a short while later, lying in the tall grass where he had fallen, surprised to see so many other people nearby, some holding torches in their hands. His wife and daughter were beside him, their concern for him written on their anxious faces.

"What happened? Where am I?" he asked.

"You're with us, father," replied Liama. "Praise be to Allah that you're alive! He rescued you just in time, before the *lord of the thunder* ripped you apart. Are you injured?"

"I don't think so. Where's the lion?"

He concentrated hard, trying to remember what had happened. Liama pointed behind him.

"There he lies," said his daughter. "Can you get up and have a look?"

Menalek managed to sit up and survey the scene. Just a few paces away from him lay the mighty ruler of the desert, defeated and motionless. Saadi was kneeling next to the lion, prepared to start shaving away the lion's fur. The sheik stared at the animal in wonder.

"Who shot it?" he asked.

"It was Saadi," replied Liama.

"Saadi?!" exclaimed the sheik. He tried to get up, and this time succeeded. He walked gingerly over to the young man and, with a look of foreboding, glanced at the dreadful animal. "Saadi," he stammered. "You... you saved me from this beast?"

"Yes, it was me," he answered. "Allah is good and merciful. It was his will that I intercede and protect you. He alone is worthy of all praise, not me."

"How could this have happened?"

"I knew that the lion would come," the young man said. "I also realized your cattle would be easy prey. I made my way to the ravine, intending to confront him. I lay down in the field to await his approach when suddenly you appeared to check on your herd, and that was when he came at you. You cried for help and I fired my first shot. My bullet grazed his massive forehead, but failed to enter into his eye the way I planned. He leaped at you, but in the midst of his jump, my second bullet struck him in the heart. Even though the force of his jump knocked you over, he didn't injure you. The *mighty king of beasts* lies dead before your feet, while you live. Praise be to Allah!"

The sheik was utterly speechless as a thousand feelings tried to overwhelm him at once. He recalled the moment of danger. In his mind's eye, he saw the large, yellow eyes of the predator in front of him. He heard the terrifying force of his powerful bellow. While remembering how the lion tensed his muscles for a leap, he was powerless to stop his body from shaking. Menalek closed his eyes and once again composed himself. He turned to face Saadi, extending his hand.

"You saved me from certain death," he acknowledged. "You are wiser than I, and Allah has given you a brave heart that doesn't tremble in the face of danger. Will you forget that I have insulted you?"

The young man's eyes lit up with joy.

"All that has been said earlier between us, I will put behind me, as if it never happened," he said. "You are the sheik, and I am not going to be angry with you."

"Then come to me as soon as you have removed the lion's skin." Menalek took his wife's hand, then his daughter's, and strolled with them back toward his tent.

"Can you still hate your savior?" his wife dared to ask him.

"I've found a new respect for him," he replied. "He has demonstrated that a young man can occasionally shame an older one." With that, the sheik acknowledged his shortcoming without letting the reprimand drive him to bitterness. He was a proud, but sensible man.

Most of the villagers remained behind to admire the extraordinary size of the lion. Saadi explained to them that this was clearly one of the "loners", an animal that even avoids its own kind, living in enmity with other lions and their packs.

"Such predators as these," he began, "are often referred to as hermits. They present themselves as especially dangerous because of their experience, cunning, and resourcefulness."

After the excitement had ended, Saadi was escorted back to camp with well wishes and the highest honors. He gave his sister-in-law charge of the lion's coat, which she would later prepare. When this was taken care of, he proceeded to the sheik's tent. Naturally, this time he was welcomed in a much better fashion. He was allowed to sit in the place of honor next to the sheik. Not only did he receive rich tobacco and a fine pipe, he was personally served by Liama, a task she performed with pleasure. The two men smoked a long time without uttering a word.

At last, the sheik laid his pipe aside. "Saadi, you courageous son of the *Beni Hassan*," he began, "you preserved my life as I stood on the brink of death. Do you love Liama, my daughter?"

Saadi recognized the sheik's benevolent mood and also laid his pipe aside. "I love her with all my heart," he replied. "My life belongs to you and Allah."

The sheik turned toward his daughter. "Liama, the apple of my eye, is your soul bound to this courageous young man?"

"Yes, father," she confirmed. "Allah has given him my heart. I am powerless to withstand his will."

"Then may he be your master and you be his wife, as long as Allah grants you life," he said, intertwining their hands. "May my blessing be a comfort to you and signify a long life for you both."

They knelt in front of the sheik as he blessed them. His wife, crying out of happiness, also laid her hands on them.

"Now, you are husband and wife," Menalek proclaimed. "We will celebrate your marriage at the coming of the new moon, even to the far reaches of our pasture lands. From now on, Saadi will live with me in my tent. Liama is my child and he is my son. All that I have will be treated as his property. Allah's will shall come to pass."

The sheik retired to the rear of his tent, allowing the two lovers to bask in their newfound happiness under the stars.

CHAPTER SEVEN
The Beni Hassan

Three men rode into camp the following morning, long before most of the inhabitants had risen. They were completely covered in trail dust, looking as though they had traveled a great distance.

They wearily dismounted in front of the sheik's tent. Menalek was quickly alerted by their arrival and came out from behind the front flap. His brows furrowed as he scrutinized the newcomers.

"Who are you?" he asked curtly.

"We are *Tuaregs*," one of them replied proudly.

The *Tuaregs* were comprised of many factions and were generally people of the deep desert. Although darker in complexion than the *Moors*, they were commonly regarded as robbers and vagabonds.

"What business do you have with the *Beni Hassan*?"

"Are you Sheik Menalek?"

"I am he."

"We are looking for two men, both residing in your camp under your protection."

"Who are they?"

"They are father and son," one of the visitors said. "They came from the east and arrived in this area to settle a blood feud."

"What are their names?"

"Malek Omar and Ben Ali."

The sheik paused, remembering the names. "I know of them."

"Where are they?"

"They rode away without revealing their destination."

"Are they likely to return?"

"They said they would."

"Do you know when?"

Menalek shook his head. "No, I don't."

"They told us that we should wait for them here. Will you permit us to await their arrival as guests of your village?"

The sheik mulled that over for a few moments. "I'm willing to grant you this request," he said at last, "providing you are their friends."

The newcomer smiled. "We are friends, yes."

"They are our guests, and friends of my guests are also my friends. Come inside, and I will arrange for you and your companions to receive salt and bread. Then rest for a while. I can tell you've traveled a long way."

"We've ridden several days and nights to bring your guests important news."

The three men removed their saddles and allowed their horses to graze nearby. They followed the sheik into his tent.

They weren't in the tent for long when two more riders approached the camp from the north. It was Richemonte and his cousin Henri. Just like the three men before them, they stopped in front of Menalek's tent. As before, the sheik came out to greet them. He told them that three *Tuaregs* had arrived ahead of them with important news.

"Where are they?" Richemonte asked.

"In my tent."

"Inform their leader that we wish to speak to him," he replied.

The two disguised Frenchmen dismounted just as the *Tuareg* who had spoken with the sheik earlier came out of the tent. He was led by Richemonte a short distance from the row of tents to allow for uninterrupted conversation.

As they walked, they encountered Saadi, who was out walking in the field with Liama, inspecting the sheik's herds. As the men passed by him, his attention strayed toward them and his eyes met Richemonte's. A momentary recognition crossed each man's face, yet the group continued on their way. Saadi returned to the camp, finding the sheik in front of his tent.

"Who were those men?" he asked.

"Two Arabs from the east," Menalek replied. "They're my guests. The others are *Tuaregs* who have just arrived for an important meeting."

"Who is the guest with the grey beard?"

"He calls himself Malek Omar."

Saadi's mind returned to the conversation he'd had with Liama the day before. He recalled how she had described the younger suitor, referring to him as Ben Ali.

"I've seen that man, this Malek Omar."

"You know him?" asked the sheik in amazement. "How could you know him if you've never traveled to any of the eastern oases?"

"I've seen him in Algiers," was his firm reply.

"You must be mistaken. He's never been to Algiers."

"I'm not wrong," Saadi insisted. "He's Malek Omar, the fruit merchant."

"My son, your eyes are playing tricks on you."

"No, my eyes haven't betrayed me. I've seen this man a few times in the house of the governor general. Do you really think I could be mistaken about a face like that?"

The sheik couldn't deny that. "You have a point," he mused, rubbing his beard thoughtfully.

"What do you think of their dialect?"

"I've heard a few different languages and dialects, but theirs is unknown to me. They must stem from a remote oasis or some foreign land."

"Could it be that they speak our language, but with a slight French accent?"

A fleeting twitch crossed the sheik's face in recognition. "*Allah akbar* (God is great)! You may be right, Saadi!"

"Are they here to settle a blood feud?"

"Yes," Menalek said. "That's what they told me at first."

"Think about how curious a situation this is, Sheik! I've lived among the French, and quickly learned of their treacherous ways. These men came from the east, yet they fail to reveal their origin. They are on a quest to resolve their blood feud, but they never talk about it. They deal with *Tuaregs*, who count for little more than robbers and murderers. Their speech is similar to the French. The father calls himself Malek Omar, and his son goes by the name Ben Ali. Wouldn't he be called Ben Malek Omar if he were truly the son of the other? I have seen this fruit merchant in Algiers, and yet he told you he has never been there. Lies and deception cling to these two. I'm telling you, they are not who they claim to be."

"You're right, my son," the sheik replied, his eyes searching for the three departed men. "Why would they lie to me? Who could they really be?"

Saadi gave the matter some thought. "Have you heard about a secretive man called the French Informant?"

"Yes. He's a spy, gathering information for the French."

"No one seems to know him or where he came from. Yet when I consider all that I know, my thoughts keep returning to the fruit merchant, Malek Omar."

The sheik was stunned. "*Allah il Allah!*" he called out. "My son, guard your thoughts."

"Perhaps I'm not far from the truth."

"You can't be serious. Do you really think that they are one and the same person?"

"It's possible," he said. "Even likely, but I can't prove it just yet."

"He's still my guest. Woe to him if he lied, for then he would have to die."

"Perhaps we can uncover his secret. Let's test him."

"Test him? How do you propose to do that?"

"I will speak to him," Saadi suggested, "and tell him that I've seen him in Algiers."

"What sort of a test is that?"

"If he's truthful, he will admit that he's visited the city. If he lies, we will know his heart is set against us."

"That still won't be enough to be certain."

"No, but at least we will know that he's not to be trusted."

"Your words are prudent and wise, my son," agreed the sheik. "Stay with me and you will be a witness to the things they speak of. Did you stay in Algiers a long time?"

"I was there several months."

"Did you become acquainted with the French language?"

"Yes."

"Do you remember any of it?"

Saadi nodded knowingly. "I remember many words, and some phrases."

"Then speak a few words to these men when they least expect it. Perhaps we will catch them off guard and they will revert to their language."

The young man agreed to the plan.

☙✠❧

In the meantime, the three men who had garnered so much interest walked toward the entrance of the ravine. They came to the vicinity where the lion had been killed the night before. The cadaver had been burned by the villagers, leaving no trace of its remains. They sat down on some nearby stones, confident that no one would overhear their conversation.

"How long have you been in the camp?" Richemonte asked, breaking the silence.

"Only a short time," the *Tuareg* replied.

"And what news do you bring?"

"That which you asked for."

"Have you seen the traveller who came from Timbuktu?"

"I saw him," the man said. "We accompanied his caravan for two days."

"Have you learned anything worthwhile?"

"We learned much!"

Richemonte's eyes glinted with anticipation. "Tell us everything."

"We came across the caravan about two days before we reached Insalah. We were well-received. The expedition's leader comes from a distant northern land. He's a foreigner, a *Nemtse*."

"Were you able to find out his name?"

"Yes. It's a name that only a barbarian or unbeliever would carry. I've tried to speak it, but my tongue gets twisted. It sounds like Lo-we-kau—"

"Do you mean Löwenklau?" Richemonte asked.

"Your tongue is more pliable than mine. Yes, that's how his name sounded."

100

"Is he accompanied by many people?"

"He commands a head guide, who's in charge of fifteen men. He also employs thirty warriors from the *Ibn Batta* tribe to safeguard his belongings."

"What sort of belongings are his camels carrying?"

"Many have crates with plants, animal skins, and books. There are jars and bottles with all sorts of worms and insects. A number of camels were laden with costly items that are profitable only to the French, not the *Tuaregs*."

"When will the caravan reach Tuggurt?"

"In about two weeks."

"Can you keep an eye on it there?"

The *Tuareg* man hesitated. "What will you give us?" he asked.

"What do you want for your efforts?"

"I'll have to talk it over with my companions."

"Go ahead. You can find us here in two weeks and inform us when the caravan departs Tuggurt."

"Then we won't find rest here. We'll have to ride toward Rhadames to meet it. Can we obtain fresh horses?"

Richemonte nodded. "You can exchange them. I'll assist you with the arrangements. For now, you can return to the sheik's tent and get some rest. I need to speak to my son."

The *Tuareg*, satisfied with the news, turned and walked back to the camp, leaving the supposed father and son to begin conversing in French.

"Are you aware that I almost lost my composure a few minutes ago?" asked Richemonte.

"What about?" his cousin asked.

"Henri, did you notice the young man we encountered on our way here?"

"Yes."

"I've seen him before," Richemonte revealed. "And I fear he recognized me, too."

"Really? Where did you see him?"

"In Algiers. He was the English consul's companion. He probably saw me when I visited the governor."

Henri lowered his head. "That's a damn shame."

"Yes, but it's too late now."

"Still, it's not that serious."

"That's where I disagree with you. What if the fellow starts to talk about my presence in Algiers?"

"Does it really matter? Just admit that you've been there before."

"What reason could I give?"

"The blood feud! Couldn't we say that we were searching for our enemy in Algiers?"

"Perhaps," Richemonte allowed, considering it. "But you forget I've already told the sheik that I've never been to Algiers."

"Dammit!"

"I'll have no choice but to deny it."

"Under the circumstances, that would seem to be the best choice. I doubt it will be enough to stir up any mistrust. Who knows? Maybe he didn't recognize you after all."

"I'm afraid he did, judging by the way he reacted. I saw it in his eyes."

"Well, perhaps he just made a mistake," Henri said optimistically. "People look alike, don't they? It occurs to me that should the sheik suspect something, he'll think twice about supporting our little attack on the caravan."

"That would be a blow to our plans."

"What would we do, in that case?"

"We'd have to rely on the support of the *Tuaregs*. They would have to gather a larger number of men. I'm sure they would be prepared to do so."

"Then these robbers would take everything for themselves and leave nothing for us."

"Don't worry about that," Richemonte assured him. "Much of the goods on those camels are unsuitable for them, and therefore more profitable for us. Let's go find the sheik. I need to know whether or not we've been found out."

As they headed back, Richemonte's cousin noticed Liama standing nearby, occupied with a young camel foal.

"Look over there!" he said, pointing to the young girl. "The sheik's daughter."

"Yes, it looks like her."

"I have to speak with her. I may not get another opportunity."

"Hold it!" Richemonte scolded, quickly losing patience for the younger man. "Not now. There will be time for that later."

But Richemonte's words failed to hold Henri back. While he headed for her, Albin uttered a curse into his beard and decided to walk back alone. Henri approached the beautiful girl, his eyes burning with desire.

"*Sallam aaleïkum* (peace be with you)!" he greeted.

"*Aaleïkum sallam*," she replied automatically, turning to the newcomer. When she recognized Ben Ali however, her smile faded somewhat, clearly not an indication that she was pleased to see him.

"The daughter of the *Beni Hassan* is as beautiful as ever," he said.

"The man from the east flatters a simple girl, just as before," she replied.

"Isn't it the truth?"

"You don't have to say it."

"Why not?" he asked. "Doesn't it please you, to know that you're beautiful?"

"Allah gives the maidens beauty, and he can take it back. It belongs to him alone, not to us."

Henri said nothing for a moment, stepping closer to her. "You're right. So long as one is blessed with it, she should be grateful and rejoice. Don't you know what luck beauty can bring?"

"What?" she asked indifferently.

"Beauty brings about love."

"A love nourished and sustained through beauty is not to be desired."

"Why not?"

"Love can only find its fulfillment in the desires of the heart."

He smiled, clapping his hands together. "Bravo! You're right again. Tell me, do you have a pure heart?"

"Who can tell if one's heart is pure? Who can judge his or her own heart? Only Allah can search the recesses of the heart."

"Your words speak wisdom, like those of a marabout. If you can't gauge the worth of a soul, you can still try to measure the voice of the heart. Tell me, Liama, is your heart still free?"

"What do you mean by free? Can a heart become enslaved?"

"Yes, a slave to love."

"Then I would detest this love," she said. "Only a tyrant possesses slaves."

"And yet, love is a tyrant. She dominates the heart completely. My heart is enslaved to love."

"I feel sorry for you," she replied coldly.

"Yes, by all means, pity me. But redeem me instead with your mercy."

Henri stepped toward her, intending to place his arm around her, but she evaded his advance.

"I don't understand you," she said. "How could I help you?"

"Simple. By acknowledging my love for you. Yes, Liama, I can't hold it back any longer. I'm in love with you. I think about you day and night, and I won't find happiness without you. Tell me that you love me, too."

His eyes glowed with burning passion, but his words had barely escaped his lips when she responded with a cold, "No."

"No?" he asked. "Why not?"

"I don't know. Only Allah can answer that."

Henri bit his lip uncertainly. He hadn't expected such a direct answer. He, the educated Frenchman, a member and citizen of the mighty French nation, had been spurned by a simple Arab girl. He didn't think such a thing was possible.

"Am I that unattractive?" he asked.

"No," she replied, smiling.

"Am I too old?"

"No."

"Am I too poor?"

"I have no idea what your wealth amounts to."

"Are you perhaps in love with someone else?"

She stood up straight, surveying him with a proud look. "How dare you affront the sheik's daughter with such a question?" she demanded. "Am I your servant, that I'm obligated to answer you?"

He groaned inwardly. She became even more beautiful when she was indignant. His eyes nearly swallowed her whole. His passion weighed heavily on his beating heart, as though he had lost his breath after a long footrace.

"No, you don't have to answer me," he managed to say. "I only ask you for one answer."

"You don't have permission. You're too bold."

"Really?" he persisted. "Are you in love?"

"That's none of your concern."

"On the contrary. I've told you that I love you. Each of my breaths belongs to you. All my thoughts are fixed upon you. Liama, you should... you must love me. You should become my wife! I'll fight for you, and I'm telling you now that I'm going to possess you!"

He grabbed her hands before she could sidestep him.

"Leave me alone!" she cried.

"No, I can't leave you!" he insisted. "My love for you commands me to secure your love."

She tried to free her hands, but he held on tightly.

❦✠❧

Standing outside the sheik's tent, Saadi was still airing his concerns about the motives of the mysterious Malek Omar when the *Tuareg* man emerged from the ravine and headed back to camp. A short time later, just behind him, the other two men followed. Saadi noticed how the younger of the two abruptly changed direction, heading toward the camels where Liama was watching over them. He seemed to be purposely steering for her.

"He's going toward her!" Saadi said, his eyebrows furrowing.

"To Liama?" asked the sheik. "What does he want with her?"

"Didn't Liama tell you?"

Menalek narrowed his eyes. "No."

"He's been following her. It's more than a passing interest."

"And she's told you about it?"

"Yes."

"He should watch himself! He's a stranger who's temporarily a guest in our village. If he breaches our hospitality by insulting my child, my knife will quickly find his heart." He meant to say more, but he was interrupted by Saadi.

"Look!" the young man shouted. "He's talking to her. Come with me!"

Saadi took the sheik's hand and pulled him along. They navigated their way through the tents and made their way into the meadow. The grazing animals provided ample cover, allowing them to approach undetected. A large transport camel stood nearby, nourishing itself on the plentiful grass.

By now, the conversation between Liama and the suitor was becoming increasingly loud. Obviously, he was behaving a bit too friendly for Saadi's tastes.

"Conceal yourself behind this animal," Saadi instructed.

"How come?" asked the sheik.

"I want to address him in French. Perhaps he'll reply in the same tongue, but he might not if he sees you. The sand will dampen your steps."

The sheik nodded in agreement, and scampered after Saadi with an agility no one would have attributed to him, the large and serious Muslim leader. Saadi moved cautiously toward the camel, appearing suddenly behind Henri.

"I demand you leave me at once!" Liama pleaded. She tried pushing Henri away, but he dug his heels into the ground.

"Leave you? Oh no, a thousand times no!" he countered, pulling her closer to him against her will. In his rapture, he had forgotten where he was, which was out in the open plain, visible to all. His passion for Liama blinded him to everything around them.

He failed to notice the approach of two men who had come up behind him. Liama, however, noticed their approach, the momentary flash in her eyes eluding him.

"Should I call for help?" she asked.

"Go ahead!" he replied. "It won't do you any good, for this very hour I intend to ask your father for your hand."

A loud voice, spoken in French, came from someone behind him, interrupting his thoughts. "What are you doing with her?"

Henri spun around and recognized Saadi standing behind him.

"What concern is it of yours?" he replied, the words carelessly falling out of his mouth in French.

"More than you might think."

"*Mille tonnerre*, what do you mean by that?"

The sheik emerged from behind the camel and looked at Henri in surprise.

"Allah is great!" Menalek said. "I see you're familiar with the language of the French."

Henri immediately realized his mistake, but composed himself again instantly and pointed to Saadi. "This one as well," he said accusingly.

"I knew that he spoke French, but not you. What are you doing here?"

At this point, the Frenchman reluctantly let go of the girl's hands. "I was speaking to your daughter, Sheik."

"Your manner in speaking to her is deplorable," Menalek replied, none too pleased. He inadvertently gripped his dagger's hilt.

"But I haven't molested her," evaded the Frenchman.

"What? I saw how she struggled in your grasp!"

Henri's mind raced to find a way to downplay his actions. "Every girl is shy when the subject of love arises. Sheik Menalek, I plead with you to hear me out before you jump to a hasty conclusion. Let's go to your tent. I have important things to discuss with you."

"What about?" he replied curtly.

"Concerning your daughter, Liama."

"Well, she's here and so am I. Speak! There's no need for us to go to my tent. I can understand you just as well out here."

Henri hadn't expected him to accept his offer so openly, and what was worse was that the sheik's mood was not favorable at all. He was out in the open, unable to count on the support of his cousin, who was waiting for him back at camp.

He pointed at Saadi. "What about this man?" he asked.

"I permit him to be present," the sheik replied. "Speak, I am listening."

Henri saw no other means of stalling the sheik. "I... I... I love your daughter," he stammered.

The sheik nodded somberly, without replying.

"I hope that you won't forbid my love for her."

"How can I forbid such a thing?"

"Then I ask that you make her my wife."

Proudly, the sheik threw his head back in laughter. "You're a man of few words, Ben Ali. I am Menalek, the Sheik of the *Beni Hassan*. These are my herds," he said, gesturing widely to encompass the animals surrounding them. "Who are you and where are your herds?"

The Frenchman was clearly out of his element, not having prepared himself for such an encounter. He failed to hide the awkwardness of his plight. Not having Richemonte to rely on, he couldn't divulge much information.

"I'm rich!" he improvised, the words blurting out without much thought.

"Prove it!"

"Speak to my father. He will verify it."

"I don't know anything about him."

"He will tell you who we are and what we possess."

"Will he enlighten me in the French language?" the sheik asked, his question dripping with spite.

"He doesn't understand French," Henri lied. "He's a Bedouin like you."

"Yet you understand it."

"Only a few words, that I managed to pick up here and there."

"Have you spoken to Liama of your love for her?"

"Yes."

"I'm curious," Menalek said thoughtfully. "What was her reply?"

The Frenchman hesitated. He was too embarrassed.

"Does she love you?" the sheik persisted.

"I don't know," lied Henri again.

"You're a liar! You know full well that she doesn't love you. Surely she has told you that her love belongs to another."

"To whom?" he asked haughtily.

Menalek pointed to Saadi. "To this man," he said with conviction. "She loves him and I have already determined their future. You're too late. I don't want to see you near Liama again. Saadi killed a mighty lion yesterday, so he's likely to make short work of you as well if you dare to affront his betrothed again. Is there anything else you need to talk to me about?"

The Frenchman turned pale. Jealousy gripped his innermost being. He shot a venomous look at his rival. "Who is he?" he asked disdainfully.

"His name is Saadi, an accomplished warrior and skilled hunter."

"Fine!" Henri said indignantly. "You asked me if there was anything else? Not now, Sheik, but there will be later."

He turned around and walked back toward camp.

"Allah be merciful!" exclaimed Liama once Henri had disappeared from view. "He will avenge himself."

"Avenge himself? That puny man?" asked her father contemptuously. "I'm not afraid of him. How could he possibly avenge himself when he needs us to attack the French caravan? He needs our help, not the other way around. Come with me, Saadi, my son. We need to find out what this father and son are planning to do with the *Tuaregs*."

As they walked back to the sheik's tent, Menalek took the opportunity to ask the younger man about the French words spoken by Henri. Saadi explained their meaning.

"Is it possible he only understands a few words?" asked the sheik.

"No. Only someone familiar with the language could have responded the way he did."

"So you're convinced he's not a Bedouin, but in fact an outsider, even an infidel?"

"I'm sure of it. He speaks our language just like the French officers do in Algiers."

"Then we must be cautious," Menalek warned. "If he really is a spy, it could benefit him if we were to attack the caravan. But it would lead to destruction for us! He would take the spoils for himself while we leave ourselves vulnerable to the governor's anger. We can't leave ourselves open to attack."

The two Bedouins returned just as Henri was seating himself next to Malek Omar. He hadn't yet had the opportunity to explain his predicament, which made him understandably nervous. The fruit merchant and his 'son' picked up their pipes without showing any mistrust. While they waited, the sheik's wife prepared a simple breakfast meal outside the tent.

When it was ready, the guests consumed their food while Saadi and the sheik stood by. Contrary to their usual custom of hospitality, not partaking in the meal with the guests was a clear message that they didn't trust them.

Richemonte certainly noticed and decided to comment on the slight. "Why are you not eating with us, oh Sheik?"

"I don't usually eat breakfast," he replied.

"I seem to recall seeing you eat some food the other morning."

"I seldom do so," the sheik said curtly.

When each man had finished his portion and wiped the excess fat from their fingers on his *burnus*, Richemonte felt it was time to bring up their business interests.

"I understand that your tribe lives in enmity with the *Ibn Batta*," he started.

"That is so," the sheik replied. "We are in a blood feud. They killed two of our men."

"Would you kill an *Ibn Batta* warrior if you encountered him?"

"Yes," Menalek confirmed. "He would be killed."

"Would you be pleased if I delivered any of your enemies into your hands?"

"I would welcome such news."

"Well, I'm here to tell you that this will soon happen."

This piqued Menalek's curiosity. "When?"

"In two weeks' time."

"Where will this take place?"

"On the road to Tuggurt. I have information that a French caravan from Timbuktu is on the way there."

"What business do I have with the French?"

"Thirty warriors from the *Ibn Batta* accompany them."

"Then I have no quarrel with them," the sheik said coldly.

Richemonte was taken aback.

"I'm not interested in those men," Menalek clarified.

"Why not those men?"

"Because they are working for the French."

"But they are still your blood enemies."

"True," Menalek agreed. "However, the French would avenge them."

Richemonte was perplexed, not sure where he stood with the sheik. "Are you afraid of the French troops?" he sneered.

"I'm not afraid of them, but I have a deep respect for them."

"I thought you hated them."

"Yes, but my desire is to live in peace with them whenever possible."

"How is it that you've changed your mind so quickly, Sheik Menalek?"

"I haven't changed my mind," Menalek said. "My position has always been to consider that which most benefits my tribe rather than risking harm to my people."

"Harm?" Richemonte asked incredulously. "I seriously doubt that. I can assure you that a great reward awaits you."

"What reward do you have in mind?"

"The caravan is considerable, laden with a quantity of commodities, even treasure."

"As far as I'm concerned, the caravan can span the breadth of the Sahara."

"Many camels, horses, and weapons would be yours. I'm satisfied to take only the leftovers."

"Only the leftovers?" asked the sheik ironically.

"Yes, only the remnants, which would easily be outweighed by your booty."

Menalek shook his head, disinterested. "I'm not interested in camels, horses, and other property that belong to the French. Besides, I happen to know that you're leading me on."

"Me?" Richemonte asked, feigning astonishment. "What do you mean?"

"Just that I suspect you're not being forthright with me."

"How come?"

"Because you yourself deal with the French."

"May Allah guard your mind," said Richemonte, not wanting to confront the sheik. "When have I ever dealt with the French?"

"In a nearby city," Menalek said. "Algiers."

"Really? I've never been there."

"Yet you've been seen there."

Richemonte hesitated. "Who would claim such a thing?"

"I do, and here is Saadi, my daughter's betrothed," the sheik said, pointing out the young man. "He saw you in Algiers."

Richemonte, who had long ago mastered his facial expressions, couldn't help but show genuine surprise when he looked at Saadi. "You've seen me in Algiers?" he asked.

"Yes."

"Then your eyes have deceived you."

"My eyes have never misled me. I saw you there."

"Where was that?"

"You were visiting with the governor general," Saadi explained. "I even know your name."

"Allah protect you. Of course you know my name. Anyone here knows me. No doubt you've heard it. My name is Malek Omar."

Saadi nodded solemnly. "Yes, Malek Omar, the *fakihadschi*, the fruit merchant."

"I don't understand. I don't know any *fakihadschi*. I've never been a fruit merchant."

The sheik expressed his mounting impatience by interrupting the little *téte à téte* between Saadi and Malek Omar. "No doubt you've heard about a man who we refer to as the French spy."

"Yes."

"Have you seen him?"

"No."

"Surely you've laid eyes on him."

"*Allah il Allah!* Where could I have seen this secretive man?"

"Everywhere that you've been, he's been there. All you have to do is look in a mirror, and you'll see his reflection."

The sheik's plan was to dupe him into making an admission, but Richemonte possessed enough wherewithal to elude the trap without giving himself away.

"Once again, I don't understand," responded Richemonte. "You speak in riddles which I cannot solve. Can you be plainer?"

"Let me speak clearly. Malek Omar, you are the French spy!"

Despite the implication, Richemonte played his role perfectly. He would have fooled even the surest man into doubting himself.

"Have you lost your mind, Sheik Menalek?" the Frenchman asked. "Are you trying to insult me? Are you intending to heap reproach on yourself by calling a true follower of the Prophet a 'French spy'? Don't you know me better than that?"

"No, I don't know you! You've never told me where you come from."

In the moment, Richemonte realized that it was time to add some details to his story in order to satisfy the sheik's trust. "My home is situated in Sella, to the north of the Harudsch Mountains."

"Does Ben Ali come from there as well?"

"Yes, he's my son."

"Do any French soldiers reside there?"

"No."

"Have you ever dealt with the French?"

"Never!" he denied. "I swear it by Allah and all the prophets."

"And yet you speak their language."

Richemonte felt the sheik was grasping at straws, and failed to grasp the implication. "How could you believe such a thing? I don't understand a single word of this."

"Not even your son, Ben Ali?"

"No, neither does he."

The old captain was so preoccupied with coming across as convincing that he failed to notice the sideways glances from his cousin.

"Has he ever had dealings with the French?" Menalek pushed further.

"Never, just like me."

"*Allah il Allah!* You're nothing but an unbeliever, an infidel!" the sheik suddenly yelled.

"What! An unbeliever?" Richemonte said, raising his voice. "Curb your tongue, Sheik Menalek. If you weren't my host, I would have replied with a well-placed thrust of my knife into your chest."

"You're a *giaur!*"

"Prove it!"

"You swear by Allah and the prophets, and yet you don't speak the truth. Only an infidel would be that reckless. One who doesn't believe in Allah and despises the Prophet!"

"Your reproach is ill-considered. How can you imply that I'm lying? Show me one lie that has passed my lips!"

"You just told us that your son is unfamiliar with the French language."

"It's the truth."

"No, you insult me with your lies! I myself have heard him speak French this very day."

At last, Richemonte shot a glance at his cousin. Only now did he notice Henri's frantic attempts to alert him by rapidly blinking his eyes. It suddenly dawned on the old man that his cousin had been careless.

"What, you heard it for yourself? Where?"

"Outside, near the tents," Menalek said. "He was with my daughter when it came out."

"If he resorted to strange words, then it wasn't French," Richemonte adlibbed. "Probably some other tongue. He understands Turkish, for instance."

"It wasn't Turkish. Saadi also heard him. He understands French and spoke to your son in the same language."

"He's a liar!" Richemonte replied in anger, trying to disguise his growing fear. But no sooner had the words left his lips than Saadi reacted. He pulled his knife out of his sheath, jumped up, and would have vaulted himself at the Frenchman had the sheik not grabbed him by the tunic.

"Stop! I order you to put your dagger away!" the sheik uttered more as a plea than a command. "This man is still a guest in my camp and has partaken in a meal with me. He is under my protection."

Menalek turned to face Richemonte. "You claim that your home lies to the north of the Herudsch Mountains, at Sella. Do you speak their language?"

Richemonte was now fully committed. "Yes," was his forced reply.

"I disagree with you. I know the people of Sella. I have been there, as well as in Fugha, during my first pilgrimage. I'm familiar with their dialect, yet you speak our language with an accent much like the French. You speak nothing but lies. This man is not even your son!" the sheik said, gesturing at Ben Ali.

"Prove me wrong!"

"His name should stem from yours. If he were your son, his name would be Ben Malek Omar."

"I named him after his grandfather, Ali."

Menalek scoffed. "That can't be true. In that case, he would be called Ben Malek Omar Ibn Ali. Your words betray you. You still don't understand our customs. This man, who you claim is your son, has broken our custom by insulting my daughter, Liama. He forced himself on her and she struggled to free herself. No true follower of the Prophet, no noble Bedouin, would even contemplate such a thing. You're nothing but French spies who've come to persuade me to commit a crime against my own people. I can no longer be your host," the sheik said, imperiously rising from his mat. "You're safe as long as you vacate my tent immediately. If you fail to heed my warning and linger around our camp, I will see to it that you are dealt with without mercy."

Both Frenchmen, deeply offended, rose from their mats. "Are you serious?" asked Richemonte, still bewildered. It had all happened so quickly. He couldn't understand what had come over the sheik. His moustache lifted awkwardly and his teeth ground like a predator's, a sure sign that he was inwardly agitated.

"I'm deadly serious."

"Do you realize that you've disgraced us?"

"Yes. You deserve no less."

Out of options, Richemonte turned toward the flap. "Then we will leave. You've brought a stain on the *Beni Hassan*, one you won't be able to eradicate. You've dishonored and insulted those to whom you've extended protection and hospitality. You'll reap dire consequences for this."

"I scorn your threats."

"What about the three *Tuareg* warriors?"

"They're your friends and likely spies as well. They can leave."

The three men rose from their mats. "Are you telling us to leave as well?" asked the leader of the *Tuaregs*.

"Yes. Had you openly come to me, rather than with these spies, I would have bid you welcome. Now you share their fate."

The dark-skinned leader looked down on the sheik contemptuously. "Do you realize that what you're doing is worse than death?"

"I know it," the sheik replied.

"You've become the enemy of all *Tuaregs*," he cursed. "Your tribe will vanish from the face of the earth. Death will swallow you up, along with all your sons, daughters, and children's children."

In the echoing silence that followed this proclamation, the five banished men left the confines of the tent and climbed onto their horses.

"Where to?" Henri asked his cousin quietly.

"First, we'll head east," Richemonte said, "so these men don't realize our actual goal."

Although their horses were still tired from their previous trip, they were now forced to gallop around the ravine and head eastward along the Itel River. After a few hours of hard riding, they reached the shores of the Schott Melrir.[7.1]

Richemonte reined in his horse and dismounted, while the others followed suit.

"Now we can talk," he said to his cousin. "Follow me."

Henri followed while the *Tuaregs* plopped themselves down on the ground, looking on with indifference.

"What did you get yourself into?" Richemonte asked, somewhat irritated. "I don't understand any of what just happened back there. Did you forget yourself and speak French to the sheik?"

"Unfortunately, yes," Henri admitted sheepishly.

"Idiot! How careless of you. How could you have forgotten?"

"It could have happened to either of us."

"All right, tell me then."

"I was speaking to Liama—"

The mention of the young girl's name caused Richemonte to roll his eyes. "Then this insanity is of your own making," he said, unaware of the prophetic significance of his words. "I called you back, but you wouldn't listen. Did you share your plans with her?"

"Yes."

"And what did she say?"

Henri responded with a curse. "She... Ah! She doesn't want me."

"I thought as much. What was the reason?"

"A valid one. It turns out she's already spoken for."

"Damn! To whom?"

"To that Saadi," Henri said disdainfully, "who the devil seems to adore."

"Hmm. He's the one who saw me in Algiers."

"He's the one who tricked me into speaking French!"

"Really? How did he manage that?"

"Oh, the fellow was quite clever. I was about to put my arms around the girl when someone behind me called out in French, 'What are you doing?' I responded involuntarily in French as well."

"That was clever of him," Richemonte said, "and you fell for it." Richemonte then tore a strip off his young companion with a few well-chosen words. Strangely, Henri listened without objection until he was finished. "Now what do we do?"

"I want revenge!" Henri hissed.

"Naturally. But how?"

"I'll abduct the girl."

"Leave her alone. Why get involved with her after all of this?"

"I want to marry her."

Richemonte let out a long, weary sigh. "Don't be ridiculous."

"No, I'm serious. I must have her, and I'll find a way to get her. As for Saadi, he'll not only lose her, he'll forfeit his life."

"Of course. Actually, I don't object to you claiming her as your own. She's beautiful and you're infatuated with her. Lovers can remain enveloped in their pursuit until they've been satisfied, usually by getting their way. But to go as far as marrying her, that's crazy."

"Let's not argue over it," a determined Henri replied. "We can sort it out later."

"True! The most important thing is not to waste any more time. We have to come up with a suitable plan, and then avenge ourselves."

"Yes, and at the same time avail ourselves of the German's wealth."

Richemonte shrugged. "Naturally! I think we can make use of the *Tuaregs* for both."

"How so?"

"They could plunder the German's caravan."

"You think you could talk them into it?"

"Sure."

"But that's only one part of it," Henri reminded him. "What about the second part, our revenge?"

"It's closely tied to the first one. The *Tuaregs* will overthrow the caravan, but we'll place the blame on the *Beni Hassan*."

"Donner and Doria!"[7.2] he exclaimed. "That could work."

"Of course, it'll work," Richemonte said. "It's relatively simple. Cavaignac will learn of the ambush and be forced to punish Menalek. I'll ensure that we are appointed as scouts and land the opportunity to lead the soldiers on a mission of reprisal. I'll convince them to allow me to negotiate with the *Beni Hassan*. That way, we'll force the sheik to deliver Liama into your hands."

"Of course, and we'll be assured of our success!" his cousin replied triumphantly. "Let's speak to the *Tuaregs*."

"Patience!" Richemonte cautioned. "We still have two weeks before it's time to act. This gives us plenty of time to carry out the governor's assignment."

"You mean in regards to the marabout?"

"Yes. We'll have to find him."

Henri looked out into the distance. "How far is it?"

"We'll probably require a full five days. After all, our horses are nearly worn out."

"Hmm, five days there and five days back," the cousin mused, working it out in his head. "That leaves us just four days to spare."

"Perhaps we can do it in even less time. It all depends on whether luck favors us or not." He stifled a yawn. "Now go and have a rest. I'll deal with the *Tuaregs* and send them on their way."

While Richemonte walked over to speak to the dark sons of the desert, his relative stretched out in the sand, reflecting on the events of the last few hours. His inner being churned with feelings of love, hate, and most of all revenge. He burned with a restless passion for the beautiful *Moor* daughter, nearly to the point of becoming unhinged. His desire to possess her nearly drove him to madness. Perhaps his physical being wasn't capable of withstanding the brutal punishment so often meted out by the Sahara. His mind wasn't able to repel the flood of emotions. The passion won over his thoughts to the point that he was continuously fixated on her.

Naturally, his hate and resentment for the one who had usurped his place as her lover only grew. Henri's thoughts moved to one of elation when he considered how and when he would remove all obstacles in his way. He pondered and plotted while lying in the sand, unaffected by the old man's negotiations with the *Tuaregs*. He was completely immersed in his thoughts when Richemonte summoned him back to the present.

"Get up!" Richemonte called. "We're finished."

Henri arose, finding that the *Tuaregs* were already on their mounts, ready to depart.

"*Sallam* (peace)!" they said quickly.

"*Sallam!*" he replied mechanically.

Within moments, the three men departed on their steeds, heading south.

"Are we leaving right away?" Henri asked.

"Of course!"

"Did you reach an agreement with them?"

"Completely," Richemonte said, giving Henri the notion that he had attained everything he'd set out to accomplish.

"What did you work out?"

"They'll ride toward the Ben Abbu oasis and gather as many *Tuaregs* as they deem necessary for the attack. They'll follow the caravan, naturally at a distance, through Rhadames and Tuggurt, until they reach the pasture lands of the *Beni Hassan*, where the raid will take place."

"Are we going to take part?"

"Of course."

"What will we get?"

"Six camel-laden cargoes," Richemonte said with a smile. "All of our choosing."

"Isn't that too little?"

"Ah! Think again. We'll select the best ones and leave the rest for the *Tuaregs*. Besides that, they insisted on all the weapons and animals. The main thing for them is getting revenge on the *Beni Hassan*."

"Will the governor actually believe they are responsible?"

"Leave that to me!" Richemonte said. "Now, mount up! We have a long way to ride, and it's possible we were followed."

They rode away a few minutes later, heading north, the opposite direction the *Tuaregs* had taken.

CHAPTER EIGHT
The Dying Marabout

The heights of the Aures Mountains stretched southeast from the el Arab valley, sinking gradually into flatland. The mountains were characterized by deep, jagged crevasses that defined the face of the peaks, making them virtually inaccessible. The mighty lion and black panther roamed the ravines and outcroppings. The cry of the hyena and the howl of jackals pierced the night. It was a rarity to find any semblance of human activity, so were those who dared to venture into the harsh wilderness.

There was just one exception. If one were to climb from the valley of the Mahana, one would reach the foothills and come up to a ridge that rises prominently like a huge mount from a massive range. The traveller would find a thick forest that lent it a gloomy, dreary atmosphere, and beyond it a peculiar structure situated near the peak. Detached from the surrounding darkness, this whitewashed hut, small and seemingly insignificant, stood out prominently from the forest green.

The pious marabout Hajji Omanah lived in these humble surroundings, the subject of thousands of pilgrimages whose visits culminated a journey of faith. The faithful one would leave encouraged and enlightened, knowing his prayers were heard and that he had remained obedient to Allah's precepts. The followers of the Prophet would wait for the moment when the marabout would leave the small hut to bless the faithful with his hands.

Unfortunately, this was no longer the case. His son now appeared in his place, bringing the blessings of his father who was no longer able to leave the small hut. No one seemed to know where the marabout came from, and what he previously called himself. Here he was known as the Hajji Omanah, and in turn his son was called Ben Hajji Omanah, or son of the pilgrim of Mecca.

Five days after leaving the camp of the *Beni Hassan*, Richemonte and Henri arrived at the foot of the mountain on horseback. Instead of stopping to rest, they located a copse of bushes and led their horses as far into it as possible. They didn't want to be overheard, and so carried on a quiet conversation in whispers and gestures.

"Are you sure our horses will be safe here?" Henri asked.

"Of course."

"What if someone should come in here?"

"Come in here?" Richemonte asked mockingly. "Who would think of looking for horses in this thick underbrush? Besides, the time of the pilgrim treks is long past. Grab your weapons and follow me!"

"How do we climb up there?"

"There's no specific route. It'll take us several hours to reach the summit."

"But it'll be night by then."

"That was my plan all along."

His cousin looked at him questioningly. "What business do we have up there at night? Will he be available for us to speak to him then?"

"What? Do you want an audience with him? What are you thinking? Why would I want to speak with him?"

"What else then? How else will you find out what we want to know?"

"Idiot!" Richemonte said. "Your love for that Bedouin girl has really clouded your judgment. The marabout lives alone with his son in that lonesome hut. They're not going to sit there stupefied! They talk with each other. They no doubt speak of current events, and perhaps even about their past. The one who's able to overhear that kind of conversation gleans much. When would be the best time to accomplish this?"

"In the evening, when it's dark," the younger man admitted.

"Exactly! It seems that you've finally caught on. Tie up your horse, but make sure you give it enough freedom to munch on the nearby leaves."

Once their horses were secure, the two men began to make their way up the mountain. Only the local Bedouins were familiar with the small, concealed path that wound its way up. Because Richemonte and his cousin were ignorant of this path and without a guide, they were forced to make their way through thick brush and climb over countless broken rocks. They started their arduous climb in the middle of the afternoon, arriving at the top just as the sun was setting in the west.

They stopped inside the tree line to avoid detection. They noted a clearing in front of them that contained a small structure, presumably the marabout's hut. Now that they were in closer proximity, they could see that it was assembled out of stones and covered with lime. The sun's burning rays reflected off the walls, shining far into the surrounding area.

"Do you think he'll be at home?" the cousin whispered.

"Of course! Don't you remember what we overheard in Saribut Ahmed, how he no longer leaves the confines of the hut?"

"I was referring to his son," Henri said in defense.

"That's different. We'll have to wait of course."

The two men didn't have to wait for long. A man soon approached the hut from another direction, coming out of a clump of trees and walking toward the hut. His face was darkly tanned, and to an astute observer he appeared to be near thirty years of age. He wore a *burnus* made out of camel hair and had it tied with a coarse belt. He wore a green turban on his head, a privilege reserved only for a descendant of the Prophet. There was no sign of weapons and a variety of small sacks hung from his belt.

When he noticed the receding sun, he stopped walking. The young man faced eastward toward Mecca, kneeled, and proclaimed his evening prayers in a loud voice. Suddenly, a second voice joined his from inside of the hut, accompanying the first, albeit weakly and subdued. When he finished, he arose and walked toward the hut, disappearing inside.

The interior decor went beyond plain; it was impoverished. The rock floor was covered with a layer of moss just wide enough to accommodate sleeping arrangements for two people. A worn book, a copy of the Qu'ran in Arabic, lay open in a wall cavity. Several pots and assorted jars sat in a corner, containing herbs and plaster for the preparation of salves and ointments. A person lay on the moss, wrapped in a similar camel hair coat. Barely visible within the coat, and covered by a green turban, was a long, gaunt face that would have been more fitting for a dead man than a living one.

"*Sallam!*" the young man greeted.

"*Sallam*," the old man replied from his mossy lair.

"Did Allah give his blessing?"

"Yes, Father. The sick man will recover."

"Praise be to God! He gives joy to the suffering and hope to the penitent." The old man had spoken slowly and nearly in a whisper. It was obvious that speaking posed some difficulty for him. His breathing was rapid and labored, suggesting that he was very sick, perhaps even to the point of death.

The young man opened the small sacks and removed a number of tiny boxes and containers, which he placed among the pots and pans. The old man watched him silently while his deep-seated eyes regarded him with a steadfast love.

"My son, were you able to accomplish anything worthwhile today?" he asked.

"Unfortunately not, my father," came the reply. "Perhaps I've caused something adverse instead."

"May Allah protect you! Evil is like a predator that one unknowingly nurses from his youth. Later it consumes its own master."

"I was reluctant to do it, but I blame my decision on overhearing the French tongue."

"The French language? Explain yourself."

"I was caring for a sick man, and went to Wadi Sofama," the marabout's son explained. "Along the way, I was searching for herbs with certain healing properties when I suddenly heard human voices."

"In the Sofama Forest, where the panther roams?"

"Yes. Those two men were strangers to the area and probably had no idea the panther was on the prowl. They spoke to each other in French."

The old man's expression became more animated. "French?" he asked. "How were they attired?"

"Just like Bedouins. Their horses were near them. Both sat at the base of a tree. I was close enough to them to hear every word."

"My son, did you eavesdrop on them?"

"Yes, Father."

"That is not becoming of a follower of the Prophet."

"Perhaps you'll forgive my indiscretion once you've heard my report."

"Then give it."

"The two men spoke about our friends, the *Beni Hassan*," his son replied.

"Under what circumstances?" the marabout asked.

"They referred to them in a hostile manner. They cursed our friends. One of them was old and had a large, grey beard. The second man was younger, about my age. I gathered from their whispers that they had at one time been guests of the Bedouin tribe, but were later driven away as suspected spies. The younger of the two appears to be infatuated with the sheik's daughter, even though she's betrothed to marry Saadi."

"Saadi?" interjected the marabout. "Do you mean Hassan the Magician's brother? He's the bravest and most cunning young man among his people."

The son paused to show his agreement with a nod, then continued. "Next, they spoke of a certain German traveller who's on his way from Timbuktu in a caravan, laden with all sorts of riches. They are planning to ambush the caravan with the help of the *Tuaregs*."

"Oh Allah! A German? Did they mention him by name?"

"Yes, they called him Löwenklau."

"Löwenklau," he repeated slowly, the word escaping his heaving chest with a gasp.

"Are you sure you heard it right?"

"Yes, Father. I made a mental note of it."

"Were you able to find out his position or title?"

"Yes, an officer. A first lieutenant."

"And they plan to ambush him?"

"Yes. They intend to ambush and plunder the caravan."

"Did you hear where this is to take place?"

"On the grasslands belonging to the *Beni Hassan*, so the blame will fall at their feet."

The marabout's eyes widened. "What a devilish scheme! My son, how fortunate that you overheard their plans. It was Allah himself who guided your steps, so you could prevent this sinister and bloody deed. Hurry now, run to our neighbor and obtain a fast horse. Then ride out to Sheik Menalek and tell him all that you've heard. You must compel him in the name of the righteous and all-powerful God to ride out with his warriors and meet this Löwenklau. My son, the sheik must protect him!"

"Father, how could I possibly leave you now? You're sick."

The marabout smiled peacefully. "Allah will protect me."

"You can't even get up."

"Allah will enable me."

"You could die in the meantime."

"Allah will meet my needs. Hurry, my son."

"Perhaps there is still time, Father. According to their words, both men planned to reach the *Tuareg* in nine days."

"God is merciful. That is enough time," the marabout said. "Are you sure that's what they said?"

"Yes. They spoke of a two-week period and that they've only been underway for five days."

"Where were they going?"

"I wasn't able to hear that much. They didn't talk about it."

"We don't have to concern ourselves about that. It's comforting to know that the ambush will take place later."

The old man discarded his hermit's cloak, revealing two thin, nearly fleshless arms. The turban had fallen off, bringing a gaunt and hairless head to the forefront that closely resembled a skull often used in anatomical lectures.

His son bowed, lowering himself to his bedside. "You're very weak, Father," he said with concern. "Shall I fetch some water to refresh you?"

"No. I no longer require an earthly tonic. Oh Allah, I thank you that there is still time to avert this tragedy. You've allowed me to die in the arms of my son."

"Father, don't say that!" his son said.

"Please, be quiet," pleaded the old man. "I will go to God from whence I came. I'm leaving the earth, this land of misery, error, and sin, fleeing instead toward the fulfillment of purity and bliss. Has the sun already set?"

His son quickly walked to the entrance and looked out. "No, Father," he replied. "The last rays are still visible."

"Then carry me outside. I want to see the fading daylight as it gives way to the advent of the first stars. My departure from here will be like an ascent on the other side of this beautiful, yet deceptive world."

His son hurried to prepare a bed of moss outside the hut. When it was ready, he wrapped his strong arms around his father and carried him outside, placing him tenderly on the makeshift bed so he could lean with his back against the wall of the hut. From where he now sat, his father could see the golden light giving way to the approaching dusk.

The marabout's eyes consumed the fleeting colors of the sinking sun. "My son," he said. "Earlier, I heard you recite the Muslim's evening prayer. Do you still remember the Christian songs I taught you?"

"Yes."

"Even the evensong, which speaks of the setting sun and the rising stars?"

"I remember it."

"Pray it for me, would you?"

They both folded their hands. His son kneeled beside him and prayed in a loud voice. It was truly remarkable to witness the prayer of a Christian song in the midst of a Muslim land and in the presence of a devout marabout.

> *"Who am I? No more than dust, and a sinner;*
> *Yet the Father of all children,*
> *You pardon even me.*
> *When quietly weeping tears*
> *Announce their repentance,*
> *Then I will hear your mercy!"*

When his son finished speaking, the old marabout lowered his head and replied with an amen, sighing deeply. His son remained on his knees. A deep, somber stillness rested on this lonely, out of the way place. The light of day faded quickly as the sky rapidly embraced night.

The two eavesdroppers remained concealed under the trees. They had no idea that they had been overheard by the marabout's son at the oasis.

"That must be the old devout man," whispered Henri, as the son carried his father out of the hut, propping him up against the wall.

"Evidently," Richemonte replied. "Look at the old buzzard. It seems that his Muslim belief doesn't quite ring true. Listen, I think they're praying!"

At that moment, the marabout's son kneeled and prayed the old song.

"Heavens!" Richemonte said. "They're praying in French! It sounds as if it's part of a hymn, like those sung in churches back home. Isn't that something?"

"Unbelievable! If we're quiet, we'll be in a position to pick up some extraordinary things. Is it possible that these hooded Muslims were actually born in France?"

"It wouldn't surprise me in the least," Richemonte said. His eyes turning to the setting sun, he grew restless. "The sun is going down. It'll be completely dark in a few minutes. If we carefully make our way to the other side of the hut, we should be able to hear everything."

"What if we're discovered?"

"What's the harm in that? Are you afraid of that skeleton of a marabout, or the one kneeling and blabbering prayers?"

"Neither."

"Well then, we're two men, the likes of which could take on a hundred like them. Now, we can sneak over to the far side if we keep to the bush's edge. I need to find out as much as I can about this pious marabout, and I have a feeling we've arrived at just the right time."

They snuck along the edge of the forest to the rear of the hut. The quickly approaching nightfall suited their plan, shrouding them in darkness while they reached their goal undetected. Minute by minute, the darkness cast deeper shadows, finally giving way to the first light of the stars. After the prayer, father and son remained quiet, preoccupied with their own thoughts.

At last, the marabout slowly lifted his head, looking at his son. "The sun's rays radiated wonderfully before departing for the night. How I long for the last rays of my life to end in the same way." Yet it was not meant to be. "I've collapsed like a plant riddled with worms."

"Please, Father, spare yourself," his son pleaded.

The marabout ignored his plea and continued. "Yes, worms... worms of reproach and regret. My son, there is a burden heavier and more cumbersome than any other. It's called guilt."

"You've never carried this burden, Father."

"Oh, is that what you think? How wrong you are!" the marabout said. "Only repentance can possibly minimize the load. How I've regretted my actions. The Christian faith teaches that he who acknowledges his sins will be forgiven. I have no intention of carrying my sins into the afterlife. I want to reveal and confess them to you, my son."

"Dear father, your words are tearing my heart apart."

"And yet you will have to endure this bitter draft, out of love for me." The old man beckoned his son with a bony finger. "Come closer, my son. Sit by my side and listen to what I have to tell you. Perhaps your heart will move you to forgiveness."

"Oh Allah! What could I possibly forgive you for, Father?"

"There is much, my son, for I have also sinned against you. Come and listen to your dying father. You will have an opportunity to look into his soul and learn secret things that, until now, have been kept from you."

Unbeknownst to them, the two French scoundrels heard every word.

"What do you think we will hear?" Henri whispered.

"Quiet!" Richemonte whispered back. "I don't want to miss a single word. Listen, he's starting to speak!"

In the meantime, the dying marabout had retrieved a small packet from the folds of his cloak. He handed it to his son. "Open it," he encouraged him.

"What's inside, Father?"

"A costly possession," he said, "and one that belongs to you."

His son removed the wrapping and unfolded several old and worn papers. There was just enough remaining light for him to make out the words. "Oh Allah," he marveled. "These are words from the French language."

"Yes," replied his father. "It's time for you to find out why I've chosen to be your teacher in all things the French are proficient in. We call them unbelievers and infidels, yet they are more clever and wiser than most Muslims, who despise them. Read the papers, my son. They will disclose a great secret to you."

His son obeyed. He unfolded the first document. It contained a state seal with an official signature. He read the contents, then looked inquiringly at his father.

"Dear Father," he said, "this is the birth certificate belonging to a child, now a man, Arthur de Sainte-Marie."

"Yes," agreed the old man, nodding.

"It says that his father is the Baron Roman de Sainte-Marie from the castle Jeannette."

"Yes, my son."

"Father, where is this castle located?"

"In beautiful France, in the vicinity of Sedan."

The son could hardly believe what he was reading. "This Baron de Sainte-Marie stems from nobility. From what I read, the boy's mother, Berta Marmont, had a plain name. Was she a commoner?"

"Yes. She was raised by an innkeeper in a tavern."

"I've heard that only people of equal standing wed within these French circles."

"That is generally the case," the marabout admitted. "However, there are exceptions. Look at the last document."

His son complied and read it. "It concerns the same boy," he said. "It's his baptismal certificate. He was baptized in Berlin a few weeks after his birth, as was witnessed by three members of the Löwenklau family. Ah, Father! That is the same name as the lieutenant whom they plan to ambush."

"Apparently. Now, read the rest."

His son read on, examining the rest of the documents. "Here is Roman de Sainte-Marie's birth certificate, and here is the marriage certificate, confirming his marriage to Berta Marmont. There are a few passes and notarized letters."

"Exactly. As for you, my son, do you have any idea how closely this concerns you?"

"Me? What possible connection could this have with me? I've never visited Berlin, or this castle Jeannette."

"Still, you've been to both of these places."

"I have?" his son asked, looking bewildered.

"Yes, you yourself. Of course, you were much too young to remember any of it. Why don't you calculate this boy's age?"

The young man once again examined the document, and considered. "Exactly my age," he said at last. "Twenty-nine years according to the French calendar."

The old man stared ahead pensively. "Yes, twenty-nine years," he said at last. "What a long, long time! How dark and threatening are the shadows that emerge from the abyss of time gone by and sent to unnerve me. Oh, my God, can you forgive me? Can I separate myself from the past, with the realization that my God has indeed forgiven me, the repentance justified by his son's death on the cross?"

An awkward pause ensued, which his son ended. "Allah forgives all sinners on account of the Prophet and the holy caliphs."

The old man slowly shook his head. "I renounce the merits of the Prophet and the caliphs," replied his father. "They were merely human. Christ, however, is God incarnate, from eternity to eternity."

Startled, his son looked at him. "What did you say, Father?" he asked. "You are recognized as a holy man among the faithful, yet you distance yourself and criticize the Prophet?"

"My son, it's time that I inform you of something important. I'm not a Muslim, but a Christian."

"*Allah il Allah!*"

"Yes, it's true. You're one as well."

"Me?" asked his son, moving back.

"Yes. You were baptized as a Christian, even though you weren't confirmed. I have never allowed you to take part in a ceremony where you left your faith to embrace the precepts of Islam. I've taught you about the Christian faith, as well as the beliefs of Mohammed. You pray the verses of the Qu'ran, and you adhere to their precepts and obligations. But despite that, you pray in the way Christians do, and sing their songs. According to the baptism, you're a Christian. With respect to your life and convictions, you're neither a Muslim nor a Christian, but a pious man who serves his creator without asking if he should refer to him as God or Allah."

His son remained silent for some time, more surprised than dismayed. "Father, why did you choose today to reveal this to me?"

"I thought I had more time. But now, I feel death encroaching on me. You need to learn everything I had kept from you."

His son noticed how draining this ordeal was on his father. "Spare yourself, Father," he said. "God will not allow me to endure this agony by taking you so quickly."

"He who senses that the angel of death is near can also hear the rustling of wings. He shouldn't tarry in bringing his earthly accounts in order. My son, can't you guess why that former boy is now exactly the same age as you?"

"How could I possibly know?"

"Then let me explain it to you," the marabout began. Then, with his eyes focused intently on his son's face, he said, "You are that boy!"

"I am?" called out his son. "Who am I supposed to be?"

"The boy, the one who was baptized in Berlin with the name Arthur de Sainte-Marie."

"*Allah akbar* (God is great)! How can I be that boy?"

"Because I am your father."

"Yes, you're my father. You've been a loyal and trustworthy father for all of my life."

"It's with deep regret that I now tell you that my youthful sins have affected your life as well. I am that baron you read about, Roman de Sainte-Marie."

His son clapped his hands together in wonder. "Unbelievable! Is it really true, Father?"

"One doesn't jest about such things when one's life is nearing its end."

"Then you're not an Arab from the *Shammar* tribe?"

"No."

"Are you a Frenchman?"

"Yes."

"Is that innkeeper's daughter my mother?"

"Yes."

"Oh, Father, quickly tell me! Is she still alive?"

The old man slowly, almost painfully shook his head. "No, she's no longer alive. She died a long time ago."

"Why did Allah call her home? How happy I would have been to see my mother's face!"

"Yes, you would have been happy. She was a gentle and honest soul, which makes my guilt all the more severe. You see, it was I who... ohh!" stammered the marabout. He hesitated, gripping his bare head with his hands.

"Go on, tell me more, Father," his son implored him.

"I want to continue, yet it's so difficult, my son. Arthur, this is your real name. The bible speaks of a place where the fire burns without extinguishing and the worm eats, though never dies!" With his hands he pointed toward his head and heart. "All the pilgrims, including you, considered me to be a pious man, a follower of Allah and the Prophet," he continued. "Yet I was formerly a totally different man. I was a... thief. Worse, I was... I was a murderer."

This last revelation came out of his mouth only after considerable effort. The son, Arthur, looked into his father's diminishing strength with even deeper concern. He gripped his hand to comfort him.

"You must be mistaken. My father simply cannot be a murderer and a thief."

"And yet, I was one!" the old man replied. "Do you know who I murdered, Arthur?"

"No, how could I know such a thing?" he asked timidly.

"I murdered the one who you wish you could have seen. Namely – oh, how terrible to be reminded of the act... it's so difficult for me to say it – your mother."

"Allah!" Arthur found himself nearly speechless. "Are you saying that you murdered my mother? Your own wife?"

"Yes," the marabout moaned. "Berta, my love from long ago, my wife!"

Arthur couldn't contain himself and jumped up. "Tell me that you did it by accident, Father!"

"Oh, if only I could say that."

"Dear God! Did you do it on purpose?"

"Yes, on purpose. But it wasn't premeditated. I did it out of anger."

His son breathed a sigh of relief. "Praise be to Allah," he said. "At least it happened in a fit of rage. Our Prophet tells us that we aren't treated as harshly if our sins are committed in anger."

"That which the Prophet says doesn't comfort me. The strong, Almighty God of the Christians will hold me accountable!"

Arthur took his father's hand into his. "Father, haven't you taught how this mighty God is also called a God of love, mercy, and grace? Didn't you tell me how the angels in heaven rejoice over one sinner who repents rather than over ninety-nine righteous ones?"

"Yes, my son, that's true. It has been my only comfort in life, and it's now my only consolation in death."

"Cling to courage, Father! Trust in me and tell me what's troubling you. Perhaps it will ease your burden and free your heart."

"Yes, I want to. I've already told you so much, and yet there is more to confess. Perhaps you will forgive me, and through your forgiveness I can take a measure of hope with me that the eternal Judge will have mercy on my soul."

"Then speak, Father!"

The marabout hesitated, wrestling with one of the most difficult decisions of his long life. "I want to tell you. I must tell you! Put my head higher on the moss and come closer so you will hear it all. It's as though the vampires of hell are buffeting me about the head. I'm ashamed of what you will learn in the next few moments, and yet you, my son, shall be my judge. Oh,

God in heaven, show your mercy, so that my son will have compassion and allow me to proceed into eternity!"

Arthur fulfilled that wish. He made him more comfortable on the moss and moved closer to his father.

❧✠❧

Dusk gave way to the darkness of the night, engulfing the flatland and creeping up the mountainside. A refreshing breeze wafted from the nearby trees and at times intermingled with the rising aroma of the desert.

A long pause lingered between the two pious men. It was difficult for the marabout to begin his disclosure. It was no different for his son, who was anxious, afraid to learn something he might not want to know. He had felt privileged to regard his father as a marabout, and he was about to learn that his father was not only an ordinary sinful man, but in fact a venal malefactor.

The two eavesdroppers had until now caught every word. As the other two had stopped to reflect, the younger cousin nudged Richemonte and used the interlude in conversation to ask a few questions.

"Did you hear that?" he whispered.

"Yes," confirmed the old spy.

"He's not a marabout after all... not even a Muslim, but a Christian."

"A thief!" said Richemonte condescendingly.

"Even a murderer!"

Richemonte looked at his younger cousin grimly. "I've known it for some time."

"What? You knew about it?" asked Henri, surprised.

"Of course."

"Are you familiar with the marabout?"

"Only too well, cousin."

"Then why did you embark on this cumbersome journey to elicit information from him?"

"I had no idea at the time that this pious Hajji Omanah is actually an old acquaintance," Richemonte said.

"An old acquaintance? Did you know him in France?"

"Yes. He's from Sedan, actually Raucourt."

"Does he know you as well?"

Richemonte nodded. "Quite well, I should think. It's possible he'll reveal some things about me."

"That would be very interesting."

"Perhaps, but it wouldn't suit me."

"Really?"

Richemonte turned to Henri. "Can I depend on your discretion?"

"Why not? Are you having second thoughts about my loyalty?"

"Maybe. You've never been that dependable. Need I remind you that you're under my authority?"

"Oho!" replied the young man a little too loudly, offended by the criticism.

"Not so loud!" chided Richemonte. "Keep your voice down. I don't want them knowing about our presence. Besides, I just wanted to warn you."

"Warn me? About what?"

"You might hear certain questionable things about me in the next few minutes."

"There must be some juicy stories about you!"

"Be quiet! I trust you'll keep them to yourself and carry them to your deathbed. If I hear anything to the contrary, I know how to deal with you. It's not a joking matter for me!"

Henri looked at his cousin quizzically. "Really? Are you threatening me?"

"Take it any way you want! Actually, I'm prepared to reward your discretion."

"In what way?"

"You'll find out later."

"When?"

"Maybe even today," he said. "I've been thinking up a formidable plan, one that has lain dormant for a long time but that has awakened in me just now. While you were still a boy, I had great things in store for you. Unfortunately, I couldn't bring them to pass. Perhaps I can now accomplish that which was impossible back then."

"You're making me curious."

"Just be patient! Listen, I hear him coughing. I think he's going to start again. Be quiet!"

The marabout took a deep breath and cleared his throat, finally ready to continue.

"Do you remember what I taught you about Napoleon?" he began.

"Yes," replied Arthur. "He's even revered by the Arabs and addressed by them as *sultan el kebir*, the great sultan."

"Yes, he was a great leader," the marabout agreed. "And yet mortal. His body is wasting away on a fortified island in the middle of the ocean as we speak, where they beat him into submission like a blacksmith forges iron in his smithy. They do it because they're afraid of his influence."

"I've heard that he hasn't died, but is still alive."

"A farcical tale," the dying man grunted. "His earthly body has died a long time ago. However, his spirit lives on and is poised to rise up at the appropriate time, thwarting all who opposed him. I never supported Bonaparte. In fact, I worked against him. Yet despite all my effort, it brought me no reward. I've ended up a poor pilgrim without a home."

"Were you forced to flee, Father?"

"Yes."

"Did they drive you from our country?"

"They? If only I could blame the authorities. It was all my own doing. I had to flee and hide myself. Listen to me, my son!" He closed his tired eyes for a brief moment, as though he intended to mentally visualize the past. "I was a young, rich, nobleman, full of hope for the future. A rewarding, successful life was within my grasp. My name was Roman de Sainte-Marie and I held the title of baron. I had a warm, loving mother and possessed an easygoing temperament and character that didn't have the time or the opportunity to get grounded in life. Somehow, I convinced myself that I was the most humble man, the most handsome cavalier, one without reproach on the face of the earth." He took a deep breath and continued. "Look at me now! A walking skeleton and a past filled with disappointment, self-deception, and regret."

"Don't speak like that, Father!" his son pleaded. "Tell your story as if you were relating it to a stranger."

"I'll give it a try and do as you ask. Tell me, my son, have you ever loved?"

"Loved someone?" Arthur asked, astonished.

"Yes. Perhaps I've failed to notice if you were fond of a Bedouin's daughter from one of the tribes we've associated with. I've certainly never asked you."

"My heart has only belonged to you."

"You've never desired to hold a girl, to have a woman and marry?"

The young man shook his head. "Never."

"Then it'll be difficult for you to understand and comprehend what I'm about to say. Love can be so powerful that only a few have the willpower to withstand its effects. It flows over its victims in cold blood, desiring to govern those feelings. There's a segment of the populace whose shameful ways are to treat the pursuit of women like a sport. Thousands of young men take up the challenge to lead pretty, blameless young women astray. They pretend to care for them, and even tell them they love them, only to desert them once they've worn down their resistance."

"Is that how some Christians pursue women?"

"Yes."

"God will punish them."

"Indeed," the marabout agreed. "Just like he punished me."

"Really? You were one of those men?"

"Yes. I knew many young girls whose love I sought to ensnare. The last one among them was Berta Marmont, who eventually became your mother."

"Didn't she become your wife?"

"Yes, although it wasn't my intention to marry her. I only played with her emotions, like a womanizer amuses himself with his unsuspecting, trusting victims. Berta was chaste and full of goodness. I wasn't able to count her as

130

one of those I could dismiss shortly after meeting her. This prickled my ego. I actually convinced myself that I passionately loved her and sought to possess her at any cost."

"As your wife?"

"Yes, as my wife."

"Was she in agreement?" the son asked.

"I didn't propose right away. My mother was noble and proud. She noticed my interest in the pretty girl, albeit a commoner, and forbade me any further involvement with her."

"Were you obedient?"

"My son, a mother's deepest plea is no match for such an infatuation. I made up my mind to marry Berta secretly."

"Really! Did you carry out your plan?"

"Not right away," the marabout said. "An incident occurred along the way that nearly derailed my plans. A distant relative came for a visit. She was accompanied by her beautiful daughter, whose looks captured my every thought, such that I forgot about poor Berta."

"What was this girl's name?"

"Margot Richemonte. I was captivated by her beauty and charm, and from that moment on I sought for a way to possess her."

"Was she as honorable as Berta?"

The marabout closed his eyes for a moment and fondly recollected the young lady. "Yes. She was proud, noble, and pure as a rose that has never been touched by human hands. Unfortunately, I discovered shortly after her arrival that my love for her was hopeless."

"Was she reluctant to return your affections?"

"She was already engaged to someone else."

"*Allah il Allah!* To whom?"

"To a fine German officer. He had come to France with the sole purpose of spying on the emperor, the *sultan el kebir*."

"An enemy of the state!"

"True, but not our enemy. You see, my mother was German by birth, and I was never taught to hate the German people."

"But surely you hated this German officer," the old man's son guessed.

"No. I wanted to, but I couldn't bring myself to do it. He was a decent man, worthy of my respect."

"What was his name?"

"Hugo von Löwenklau."

"Löwenklau? That's the same name as the lieutenant's who is to be ambushed!"

The marabout nodded. "Yes. He had come to Jeannette to visit his betrothed. Strangely enough, the emperor also arrived that very same day.

When he laid his eyes on Margot, he became infatuated with her completely. He pursued her, and even tried to possess her, but the two lovers fled."

"She must have been just as chaste and noble as you said."

"Indeed. She also had a brother, who was everything that she wasn't. He pursued the two lovers in order to bring them back to the emperor, but he wasn't successful. Even though he discovered their whereabouts, Napoleon had already been defeated at the Battle of Waterloo and been forced to withdraw. Bonaparte eventually surrendered and was banished by the English to St. Helena Island in the Atlantic."

"What happened to Margot and Löwenklau?"

The old man considered that for a moment. "In an effort to rescue Margot from French brigands, he became entangled in a fight, leaving him wounded and near death. You see, he received a devastating saber strike to his head, a blow that would have proved fatal for many. Miraculously, he survived, but his recovery took several months. Eventually he moved with Margot to Berlin, where they were married."

"Was he granted permission, since he was still serving as an officer?"

"Yes. Unfortunately, he decided to resign his commission."

The son was surprised. "Really! At such a young age?"

"Apparently the young officer had no choice. The near fatal blow had injured his brain, the consequence of which was a peculiar memory loss. Although he regained his mental faculties, he wasn't able to recall those fateful hours prior to his injury. He deemed it possible that his memory could later be compromised, and perhaps even affect his military decisions. Therefore, Löwenklau reluctantly took his leave from his regiment and retired. Because he had served his fatherland with such distinction, he was rewarded for his efforts with land holdings. Coupled with his officer's pension, he now found himself in a good financial position, allowing him to pursue other ventures."

"What about you, Father? You had also been enraptured by Margot."

"I was young and carefree, yes. Even flippant. At first I thought I would die if I had to relinquish Margot to anyone. But after she married, it wasn't all that difficult for me to accept the inevitable. I simply returned to my former lover."

"To Berta Marmont?"

"Yes," the marabout answered. "I became obstinate and swore to myself that I wouldn't give up on her, even though my mother pressured me to back off from my pursuit. She reminded me of her previous edict, but it fell on deaf ears. I had worked myself into a stubborn state, refusing to bow to any of her demands."

"Did she recant her position?" the young man asked, still full of questions.

"No. In fact, she arranged for Berta to disappear. This one act affected me so deeply that I left reason and gratitude behind, deciding to embark on a journey to appease my frustrations."

"*Allah il Allah!* All alone, without your lover?"

"Yes, without her. Then later, I managed to find her trail and pursue her."

"You said she was poor. What about you, Father?"

His father closed his eyes, as though tired from the stars' glow. He opened them after a while, with confession on his lips. "No, my son. I was rich because I had become a thief!"

His son's face visibly paled at the remark. Nevertheless, he kept his hand on his father's arm. "Did you resort to taking someone's property?"

"Yes. My mother's."

Arthur let out a long sigh. "*Allah kerihm!* I'm relieved. Your mother's possessions are also yours. You didn't do anything illegal."

"I know. But my mother's belongings weren't actually mine. I had gathered all available cash on hand and left. I then traveled to Paris, where I tendered checks on my mother's accounts, receiving monies that weren't rightfully mine. I even stole her costly family jewels, the greatest visible expression of our wealth. I had left... as a thief."

"What did your mother do?"

"At first, she didn't do anything. She didn't even send out emissaries to find me. She allowed me to keep all that I had plundered from her. But once she found out what had become of me, she made it very clear that she no longer considered me her son and never wanted to see me again."

"My poor, poor father. Did this curse find its fulfillment?"

"Yes, my son. I never saw her again," he said haltingly.

His son perceived how deeply this decision had affected him. "Did you ever ask her for mercy? Did you ever apologize for your actions?"

"I tried several times."

"Without success?"

"She wouldn't receive me," he said sadly. "I brought her the greatest portion back, but she turned me away. She refused to see me and didn't want to accept my reparations, even though I had left Berta."

"Really? You didn't remain together?"

"No. She gave birth to our son in Berlin. Margot and her husband were the godparents. I had arranged for a picture to be taken and sent it to my mother, but she returned my letter unopened. My exasperation turned to bitterness and eventually I allowed it to transfer onto my wife. Your birth had not only cost me my relationship with my mother, but your mother struggled with sickness constantly and eventually lost her beauty. The end result was that I ceased to love your mother."

"My poor, poor mother!"

"Yes, poor Berta! It wasn't long before I hated her. I laid all the blame at her feet. I came to loathe and neglect her. But I didn't stop there. I criticized your mother for all the things that had negatively affected me, making her more unhappy with each passing day. Then, one evening, I came home and found that she had left me."

"Allah! Where had she gone?"

"For a long time, I had no idea."

"Was she alone?" Arthur asked.

"No. She had taken you with her."

"Ah! She cared about me more than you did!"

The marabout's eyes were profoundly sad to hear his son's accusation. "No, my son. Even though I was cruel toward her, my life revolved around you. You were my likeness. I couldn't go on without you, and I had to find you."

"Did she return to her home country?"

"Yes, just as I had surmised."

"Did you pursue her?"

"Yes. That's when I discovered I wasn't mistaken. I found her trail, along with that of another person, one I hadn't anticipated."

"Who was it?" asked Arthur quickly.

"Captain Richemonte. The same person who had attempted to facilitate a union between Margot and the emperor. I asked myself, how did he find her? What were his plans with her?"

"Did you find out?"

"Yes, the first part. But not the second."

"Did you find them together?"

"Yes. For some inexplicable reason, which I've never learned, Richemonte was forced out of the officer's corps. In any case, he traveled to Germany, perhaps to avenge himself on Löwenklau. Instead, having found no opportunity, he spotted Berta on the street. He knew her from Jeannette, and it would have been relatively easy for him to learn of her unhappiness. Persuading her to leave me wouldn't have taken much effort. He managed to bring her as far as Marseille, where he promised to find her employment. By the time I arrived, both had been there for two days."

"So you tracked them down," Arthur mused. "Did you confront them?"

"Yes."

"What did the captain say?"

"He had gone out, leaving Berta alone at the inn."

"Were they living together?"

"No. She could never have become another man's lover. She had left me, no longer wanting to remain in our marriage, but she had only followed him because of his promise to find her a position with relatives. That's all."

"I take it he had relatives in Marseille."

"Actually, not as far as I knew," the marabout revealed. "He must have concocted a devilish scheme that somehow made it worth his while to carry off a mother and child. Although I did everything possible to learn his reasons, I was never able to find out."

Arthur couldn't help but ask the next question that burned on his mind. "How did my mother react to seeing you again?"

"She was frightened, of course," he said. "But she quickly composed herself. I pleaded with her to return home with me, but she refused me outright. I resorted to threats, but that didn't help either. Finally, I demanded that she hand over my child. She told me that she would rather die than be separated from you." The marabout stopped momentarily, overcome with guilt. "The words drive the pain further into my soul," he said at last.

"If she died, then she's in heaven and she would have forgiven you a long time ago, my dear Father."

"Yes, she died a long time ago," the old man said, sadness evident in his voice.

"When did she die?"

"That very night."

"The night you found her in Marseille?"

"Yes. Whether by threats or pleas, I couldn't get her to hand you over to me. When I tried to do it by force, she became like a lioness protecting her young. She grabbed a sharp knife from a nearby table and threatened to stab me. I laughed at her words, completely ignorant of a mother's protective nature. I grabbed her anyway, in an effort to throw her to the side, but she only resisted more. We struggled and fought. Because her strength was no match for mine, she used the knife, somehow cutting my arm open."

"What a woman!"

A tiny smile nearly appeared at the edge of the old man's mouth amid the grief and regret. "Yes, what a mother! I was already in a belligerent state for not getting my way. Her resistance and the subsequent injury she inflicted on me caused me to redouble my efforts. She tried to strike a second time, but I grabbed the knife out of her hand. By this time, I was incensed, overcome with anger. I struck back in one swift motion. She collapsed to the floor in a subdued cry, never to get up again. I had stabbed her in the heart."

"Oh, *Allah il Allah!* You murdered her!"

"Yes, my son, I was, and still am, her murderer," said the old man in resignation. He paused, not wanting to continue as regret filled his heart. Stillness came over both men.

At last, Arthur broke the silence. "What happened then, Father?" he asked, wanting to know the rest of the story.

"At first, I didn't even think," the marabout replied. "I just stared absentmindedly and in horror at the corpse of the one whom I had so dearly loved. The fear of discovery and of losing you brought me back to reality. I had to act quickly."

"Didn't the other guests hear the commotion?"

"I don't think so. As lively as our argument was, we had spoken in subdued tones, so as not to wake you. The fight had played out in eerie silence."

Arthur hung his head. "Then you managed to get away."

"I quickly removed my coat and bandaged the wound with my handkerchief. I took you out of the crib and put your little coat on you. Then I locked the door, taking you with me."

"Why did you do that?"

"I wanted to leave the impression that Berta had gone to bed for the night. This way, neither Richemonte nor the inn's servants would bother her until the morning, and I would have a good head start."

"Dear God! Mother lay there, bleeding, with no hope of escaping a slow and awful death."

"My son, she was mortally wounded. I had examined her, and she was dead."

"But wouldn't Richemonte learn upon his return that a stranger had visited her?" Arthur wondered. "Surely it would have awakened his curiosity."

"No one had seen me. I managed to get in and out without detection."

That, at least, seemed to bring the son some comfort. "I can at least be grateful that you got away. To lose one's mother is horrible enough, but to also lose one's father to the authorities would have been unbearable. I would have been an orphan."

"True enough. And I would have faced the fate reserved for those who murder their spouse. I would have been sentenced for a long time."

"You said you were bleeding, Father. You must have been covered in blood. How did you manage to escape?"

"To begin with, I needed to reach my hotel room without being seen. I had a brigand's luck. The entire affair went off without a hitch. You were so quiet and still throughout the ordeal that you fell asleep in my arms. I didn't have to worry about being betrayed by an infant's crying."

"What happened then?"

"As luck would have it, I remembered a shipmaster who was staying at the same hotel. He came from a place called Ajaccio, and was planning to return there that same night. I quickly ascertained that he was willing to take on another passenger, which was especially helpful since I would have needed travel documents and adequate money if I had been on my own. Naturally, I washed up and changed my clothes. While you were sleeping, I carried you on board the ship, concealed within my travel case. We arrived at Ajaccio the following day, where I finally felt safe again."

Arthur paused in his questions before continuing again. "My father, you managed to get away, but could you flee from yourself?"

"My son, I'll speak about that later."

"What could they have said the following morning when they discovered my mother's body?"

"I journeyed to Sicily at the first opportunity. There I later learned that the hotel staff had discovered Berta's corpse during the night. Her blood had leaked through the floorboards and dripped through the ceiling of the floor below. The authorities quickly discovered that she had been stabbed and her son was missing. Not a single item in the room was missing, which ruled out robbery. Since it was well-known that she had fled from her husband, the subsequent investigation went in my direction. When they learned I had been pursuing her, there was no longer any doubt that I was responsible. As a result, it became impossible for me to return to my homeland."

Speaking was becoming more and more difficult for the marabout. He was exhausted and had to pause. His son was quiet, filled with a deep sadness over the tragic tale he had been told. The sadness of the son was no less that the grief of the father.

At last the old man resumed his confession. "Therefore, my son," he continued, "the thief turned into a murderer, becoming a homeless nomad, whose deeds followed him from place to place. I discovered that the police had learned of my flight to Ajaccio, and were now looking for me there. Where could I find some peace and solitude? I decided to travel to Egypt. I wasn't there for long when news reached me that they were searching for me in Sicily. It was just a matter of time before they learned of my flight to Egypt.

"My only hope for evading capture was to temporarily separate myself from you. Somehow I had to convince those around me that you were a Muslim child. To make the deception convincing, I was forced to circumcise you. Fearing discovery, I performed the necessary procedure myself. Once the wound had healed, I took you to a local orphanage, one which had ties to a well-respected mosque in Cairo. I left you at the gate and waited until one of the occupants found you, ensuring that they would take you into their care. I then departed, taking a boat upstream on the Nile, even across into Nubia, where I remained for two years. In the space of those two years, I learned to speak Arabic, becoming so proficient that I considered myself as having been born there. I soon realized that my best chance was to disguise myself, and so I made myself out to be a genuine Arab, a believer and a follower of the Prophet. I conformed my outward appearance to that of the local faithful, thus avoiding detection as an outsider."

Hearing the news caused a memory to slide into place in Arthur's head. "Father, I remember being in a large courtyard, enclosed by a high wall. There were many other boys, all of us being looked after by old men with long beards."

"Yes, that was the orphanage next to the mosque," the marabout confirmed.

"I eventually returned to Cairo and visited the home. I told them that I was an honorable man, desiring to adopt a child. In return for a donation, I was given the opportunity of selecting one of the children. I recognized you immediately, and even received the garment you had worn when they first found you. I remember buying it from a local merchant in a narrow alley in Cairo. Because it was the time of the annual pilgrimage to Mecca, I chose to accompany the pilgrims, deciding to live my life for you. The best way to accomplish this was for me to be perceived as a true Muslim."

"I think I know the rest, Father. You took me to Mecca."

The marabout nodded sagely. "We remained there for five years, where I immersed myself in the study of Islam. But I longed to find a place closer to home, where it was possible to glean some news from the old country, so I left Arabia and came back to Egypt."

"And then you came through the desert to Tunisia, and later to Algiers."

"Yes, that's what I did. I carried an Arabic name in Mecca. The sheriff had drafted a new identity and certificate based on it. I carried portions of the Qu'ran around my neck and a flask of holy water from the holy spring at Zemzen on my belt. I possessed many relics, which I had obtained in Mecca, and some in Medina. I counted myself as a pious Hajji. No one would have suspected that I wasn't who I pretended to be, that I was a fugitive from justice. Grief and remorse had mellowed my disposition, while the sun had given me a dark tan, making me indistinguishable from the other men. I even wore the green turban reserved for those who were direct descendants of the Prophet. Naturally, I could only do this in Algiers, not in Mecca. Had my mother, or Margot, or even Richemonte himself encountered me, none would have recognized me."

"Was it your intention to live in seclusion from the start?"

"My desire was to be your father and teacher at the same time. I wanted you to embrace all the qualities of a good temperament and explore the inherent rewards of character, which had been lacking in my youth. I dreamed of a son who would one day attain greatness. This dream vanished into obscurity not quickly and suddenly, but slowly, barely noticeably, and yet more firm with each passing day. You see, I had attended a university at home and occupied myself with the discipline of medicine. Many plants and herbs containing healing properties grow on these surrounding hills. I gathered them and sought to explore their medicinal properties. Soon I was heralded as a benefactor by the local tribes. Could I have chosen a better destiny?"

"No, my father!"

"You're right, and I'm grateful to you. I built this hut and remained the person I had become. You were to become my successor. No one was supposed to find out my true identity... or yours."

Arthur looked at his father with a combination of wonderment and confusion. "And yet, you chose to reveal it to me now."

"My son, a man's thoughts and decisions can be equated to a single strand of hair that has fallen to the ground. The smallest breeze can propel it to go many leagues. In all likelihood, the hair would not have intended to travel so far. I was your father and protector, but now my time has come to depart while you alone remain behind. Who are you to honor and who will love you? You'll stand firm under the banner of Islam, highly respected, yet your heart will fail to find fulfillment. I alone have dragged you through this hot desert, which has often proved a cold, spiritual wasteland. I have robbed you from the savior and carried you far from civilization. I must now send you back from whence you once came."

"Father, I will never leave you!" the young man protested.

"My son, my life here has come to an end. I will return to dust in just a short time. My blessing and my spirit will remain with you. And now, Arthur, you've heard my confession. Your father lies near you, his soul painfully aware of the long and bitter road it has taken to find repentance. His heart cries out for words of forgiveness. Above us, God's stars shine in all their glory, proclaiming His love and mercy. I've disclosed my works, such as they are, to you. You can condemn me, or forgive me, as the Almighty gives you guidance in this hour, my last one on this earth."

The old man sighed and drew a labored breath. "This last discussion and revelation has worn me out, and I look forward to my heavenly rest. I can already feel the coldness in my limbs. I fear that my ears will quickly lose their hearing, not able to receive your condemnation or mercy."

He stretched out his legs and folded his hands, awaiting the condemning or comforting words of his son. Arthur was deeply moved and cried out with grief, wrapping his arms around his dying father.

"My father, oh my father!" he called out. "If God will truly take you from me, if we truly must part, then I'm grateful for your thousand fold love and for your faithful care! I wish I could die with you!"

"I don't want to hear your platitudes!" replied the old man. "I want to hear your verdict!"

"God is love, my father. He doesn't condemn you. Instead, he has forgiven you."

"What about you, Arthur?"

"Me, too. With regards to your parting, my pain is unspeakable. Yet my desire, my plea, to remove all blame from you is a thousand times greater. You may leave this world in peace, knowing that no reproach from me awaits you in heaven."

A soothing sigh escaped the marabout's lips. The stars gave off just enough light to reveal a contented, blissful smile spreading across his entire face.

"Thank you, my son, thank you!" he said slowly and with effort. "I can now die peacefully, knowing that I have at last found mercy. Later, my son, I want you to dig under my mossy bed. You'll find the old garment you wore in Marseille. You will also find my credentials, which will legitimize your claim, along with jewels and the rest of the money I stole from my mother. Take them back with you to Jeannette and see if you can find grace there, just as I experienced with you."

His son held him in a tight embrace. He kissed him on his pale and already cold mouth, asking him under flowing tears, "Is it true, is it really true that you have to die?"

"Yes, my son, my dear son. When I'm dead, carry me into the hut and mortar the entrance shut. Just leave an opening facing east, so that a glimmer of light can fall on my grave each day, signifying a life that received so little light in its course."

Arthur nodded, fighting back tears. "I'll do it. Yes, my father, I will do it."

"Now, my child, a final wish... I can barely speak. Earlier you prayed a beautiful song. Pray it again, the song... the song of my life and death."

"Yes, Father, my loyal father!"

"Prop me up once more, so that... I can overlook... the starry sky... once more."

With a heavy heart and flowing tears, Arthur fulfilled his father's last request. He knelt down and folded the man's hands. He suppressed his own sobs and prayed with a loud, shaky voice:

> *"Covered with your blessing*
> *I long for the repentance*
> *Your name be praised.*
> *My life and my end are yours.*
> *Into your hands, Father,*
> *I commit my spirit."*

His words resounded high into the crowns of the trees and a long way down the mountainside. It was a Christian death prayer in the midst of an Islamic land.

"Amen," came a whisper from the old man's dry lips. And then he was still. Arthur didn't move. He waited for his father to call him, to offer even one final word, but he waited in vain. He finally rose to his feet and approached his father. He knelt down next to him.

"Father, dear father," he said.

There was no answer.

"Are you sleeping?"

Still, no answer. He took his father's hands into his own. There was a remnant of warmth in them that quickly dissipated.

"Dear God, is he really dead?"

The two eavesdroppers heard a silent rustling of clothes as the marabout's son felt for a heartbeat, needing to convince himself that this was indeed his father's eternal slumber.

"Allah! Merciful one!" he cried, trying to suppress his sobs. "He is dead. Be merciful to him up in heaven, and also with me down here in my loneliness."

He then held his father one last time, and then it was quiet. A slight rustling passed through the trees, as though a long lost soul was parting the tree branches in preparation for an eternal journey home.

CHAPTER NINE

A Baron Returns

Richemonte nudged his companion. "Let's go!" he whispered to him.

"Where are we going?"

"Just follow me. But quietly, so he won't hear us."

The two men crept from the rear of the hut, keeping under the cover of the trees while moving toward the edge of the clearing. When they reached the fringe of the tree line, the former captain grabbed his cousin's hand and pulled him further into the dark forest.

"Well!" he said, finally coming to a stop. "We're far enough away that he won't be able to hear us. It was grueling to stay motionless so long. I don't think I could have lasted another five minutes."

"Neither could I," replied his cousin.

"Did you catch their conversation?"

"Yes, every word."

"What do you have to say about it?"

"Unbelievable! Damn, who could have imagined that?"

"Hmm! You know, I had an idea what he was about to reveal when he started his little confession."

"Really?" Henri asked. "But is it true?"

"Yes, all of it."

"The emperor was really in love with your sister?"

"He was nearly delirious."

"And she took off?"

"Unfortunately. Thanks to that damned Löwenklau!"

"What a blunder on her part. Did you pursue them?"

"Naturally."

"Without Napoleon's permission?"

"On the contrary, by his express order," Richemonte corrected. "If he had only been victorious in the Battle of Waterloo, he would have become lord of the whole affair and ruler over all Europe. Margot would have slipped into the role of a *maintenon* or *pompadour*,[9.1] and I... Damnation! What opportunities lay before me! The things I could have become!"

"Were you really forced to leave the army?" his cousin inquired.

"That's none of your business. Whether you believe it or not, it makes no difference to me."

"Did you actually dare to travel to Germany, even as far as Berlin?"

"Of course! I had nothing left in France. I would have liked to exchange a few pleasantries with that Löwenklau, but Satan always seemed to get in the way. That's when I discovered that simpleton Sainte-Marie with his over inflated ego and his plain wife, his *dulcinea*, Berta Marmont. He was a welcome sight!"

"What do you mean? Was it because he had money?"

"It was more than just money. It would have all become mine anyway," Richemonte noted. "First, I cast my eye on his child."

"His little boy? I don't understand. The money and jewels should have been a thousand times more appealing."

"There you go again," Richemonte mocked. "It just proves what a simpleton you are."

Henri rolled his eyes. "Pah! It doesn't take much brains to realize you should have gone for the man's riches instead of saddling yourself with the boy. Children demand endless care and provide little reward in the end."

"Hmm, suit yourself then."

"Was this Berta willing to go with you?"

"It didn't take much to persuade her. She despised her husband and was already looking for a way to get out of the relationship so she could remove the child from his negative influence. It certainly was a big blow to my plans when I discovered her dead body, and the toddler missing."

"Tell me, cousin, what plans did you have for the little one?"

"Can't you guess?" encouraged Richemonte.

"How can I?"

"Yes," the former captain laughed into his beard. "This Richemonte has concocted plans not just anyone can follow, much less duplicate. Let me help you. Who do you suppose was the child's father?"

"The Baron de Sainte-Marie, of course."

"Right. And who was the child?"

"Hmm!" mumbled his cousin, dumbfounded by the question. "His son, naturally."

"Very astute of you. Do you know what a legacy is?"

"A possession," Henri began, "usually land that is passed down from one family member to another without it having to be sold."

"Yes. French law dictates that the one who inherits can't be passed over, even if the original heir has lost favor with the authority. Do you understand the implication?"

"Not really."

"Then I lament your limited insight. The boy was clearly his father's rightful heir."

"That's true."

"Quite so. He's the heir, even today."

Henri's eyes widened as he finally began putting the pieces together. "This Bedouin hermit? He's now the heir to all of the baron's holdings in France?"

"Yes."

"*Mille tonnerre!* A rich Bedouin just over there, and here I stand, a civilized and cultured man, with little to drink and not much food to sustain me."

"It's your own fault," chided his older cousin.

"Why do you say that?"

"You could change your circumstances."

"You're out of your mind, cousin. How could I possibly change them now?"

"Oh! Quite easily!"

"You'll have to explain it to me. After all, I'm not opposed to a change in my present circumstances, as long as I'm better off in the end."

"Then listen. A well-placed shot, a measured thrust of a knife, is all that's required."

"You're talking in riddles."

"For you, every well-conceived plan and brilliantly devised scheme is a mystery. Can't you guess what I had in mind for the baron's little brat?"

"Go on."

"Have you ever thought about what my intentions were for you when you were young?"

"No," Henri said vaguely. "I was too little to give it much thought. I was probably still in diapers."

"You were a toddler, approaching two years of age."

"Still, I was too young to ponder such weighty matters."

Richemonte looked at the halfwit disdainfully. "Then ask yourself now."

"Stop leading me around and just give me the answer."

"Because of your lack of insight, that's all I can do. Pay attention! Even back then, you had no father or mother."

"Unfortunately! I was reared by an older cousin, Brigitte, who was more concerned with dishing out punishment than my upbringing," Henri said, remembering the woman who had raised him. "Now I'm privileged to have a new tutor. You."

"Clearly your manners have improved, though I haven't seen too many results yet," Richemonte observed. "I approached that former cousin and talked her into letting me take charge of you."

"She was eager to accept, something she later confided in me."

"Indeed, I told her I was prepared to adopt you. She would have been free of the burden."

Henri grimaced, again remembering the past. "Sadly, nothing changed. You didn't come back. How come? I've often asked you for a full explanation, but you've never given me one."

"I've had my reasons. However, now I can fill you in."

"Go on then! I'm as curious as ever about your secretive past."

"As you probably know, both parties stand to gain from the adoption process."

"What do you mean by that?" asked Henri.

"What belongs to one, belongs to the other."

"Go on."

"And what one inherits, of course, benefits the other."

"Of course."

"Well, I desired to become your adopted father so as to profit from things that would come to pass for you."

"*Parbleu!*" the young man exclaimed. "You're carrying on as if I'm about to inherit a dukedom."

"Not exactly a duke's inheritance."

"Well, maybe a count's holdings?"

"No, not that, but you're on the right track."

"Do you mean a baron's title?"

Richemonte shrugged. "Well, it's feasible."

"You're living in a fantasy world!" he said, dismissing the suggestion with a flip of his hand.

"Pah! I always know what's possible and attainable. And now, after all these years, I'm willing to confide my original plan to you. I trust I can do so without your criticism. Do you catch my drift?"

"If it concerns a baron's inheritance, I know how to keep quiet," he said mockingly.

"I don't like the tone of your voice. It doesn't suit me," the old captain chided. "Listen up. My plan was to find suitable employment for Berta, as you've already heard."

"For the benefit of her and the child?"

"No. In any event, she would have started to work, which meant she would have had to leave her child in care."

"Would she have agreed?"

"I'm sure I could have persuaded her. Naturally, she would have placed her son with someone trustworthy. Can you guess who I had in mind?"

"I've no idea, cousin."

"Your old cousin Brigitte," Richemonte revealed. "Who else?"

"*Parbleu!* With her? Why with that old woman?"

"To begin with, Berta would not be coming back."

"Really? Why wouldn't she come back for her child?"

"Do I have to explain down to the smallest detail? Her disappearance would have been my own doing, which needn't concern you now. With Berta out of the way, I would have arranged for her offspring to disappear as well."

"But for what purpose, cousin?"

"Simpleton! Naturally, you would have appeared in the child's place. All the papers were in hand. I would have dared anyone to contest that you weren't the rightful heir."

The 'simpleton' let out a quiet, cunning whistle. "Impressive! Was that your plan?" he asked, his admiration evident in his voice. "The neighbors could have verified it, since they knew me and the old cousin."

"Everything else would have fit into place. As far as they knew, I had adopted a Baron de Sainte-Marie. The adoption would have been recognized in France, but would have been more problematic anywhere else."

"Heavens! What a scheme! Too bad it went awry."

"Berta's untimely, but very public death upset my plans, not to mention the boy's disappearance."

"But why did you still adopt me?"

"You are in effect both my cousin and like my own son. I suppose I still had hope of carrying it out one day, but it all hinged on catching that fellow and his twerp."

"Why did he have to get away? I could have been a baron!"

"Look! What was impossible then could still become reality today."

"Ah! If only that were possible!" Henri replied excitedly.

"Why shouldn't it be possible?"

"Everything went wrong. I don't see how it could happen now."

"There you go again, playing the simpleton. Didn't I just tell you that a shot or a quick thrust of a blade is all that is required?" Richemonte asked, sowing the seed of thought on fertile soil.

"*Mille tonnerre!*" his cousin uttered. "Now I'm beginning to get your drift."

"I can only hope so. The young baron has to disappear without a trace, just like before. All it takes is one bullet."

"That's true!"

"All the papers are in hand still."

"Indeed! The birth certificate, the baptismal certificate, various identity papers belonging to the father, the money... and, of course, the family jewels."

"That's proof enough. You're nearly the same age. You've lived in the desert, you speak Arabic, and now you're familiar with your father's, the Baron de Sainte-Marie's, mysterious past."

Henri was speechless and yet his brain churned. Richemonte was clever enough not to interrupt him at such a crucial moment as this. He knew his cousin only too well. The planted 'seed' would grow to fruition with incredible speed. He knew he was right, because Henri replied after only a short pause.

"I'm going to take care of the 'hindrance' in the hut," Henri decided. "However, I'm not sure I'll be able to convince the authorities back home of my legitimacy."

"Pah! I'll be with you every step of the way."

"Can I really depend on you, old man?"

"Of course! I should point out, though, that I wouldn't labor unless there was a suitable reward waiting for me."

"That's understandable. So, do you think it'll work?"

"Quite easily," Richemonte assured him. "But we have to act quickly. Did you overhear the part about Löwenklau?"

"Yes. How did they know about him?"

The old man paused. "Perhaps the young one overheard us in the brush."

"It's possible."

"And another thing. It's quite likely he'll depart right away to warn Löwenklau and the *Beni Hassan*."

"Dammit! That would ruin everything."

"Not only that, consider if he were to leave the old man and gather up his belongings while we waste our time debating details."

"Yes, cousin, we need to act now!"

"Well then, let's move."

"Hold it," said Henri. "Just one more thing!"

"Now what?"

"I'm telling you right now that I'm not taking part in this unless you concede one condition?"

"What is it?"

"It concerns Liama."

"What! That girl again?" asked Richemonte irritated. "What could you possibly want with her now? The circumstances have changed considerably in our favor in these last two hours."

"Maybe, but my love for her hasn't changed."

"You couldn't possibly make her your baroness!"

"Why not?"

"It's a ludicrous idea, the biggest nonsense I've ever heard."

"I'm not going to budge on this," he said obstinately.

"Listen, cousin, come to your senses," Richemonte urged. "There's a baronet waiting for you."

"And you, cousin, have you forgotten my feelings for her? I'm in love with Liama and I must have her."

"Take her as a lover, for all I care," Richemonte said dismissively.

"No, I want her to become my wife."

"But that's impossible! How can you appear before the authorities as a claimant, and then, after you've been legitimized, purpose to marry a Bedouin girl?"

"That won't be necessary. I'll marry her over here."

"Have you forgotten that she knows you as my son, Ben Ali? The young Sainte-Marie must appear as the former Ben Hajji Omanah."

"Why?" he asked stubbornly.

"Because the old man most likely used that name in his papers."

"Then I'll assume that name."

"If only it were that simple. The girl will surely divulge your previous name."

"Once we're married, she'll learn to abide by my instructions."

Richemonte realized that this was not the time to dissuade Henri from his plan. There would be plenty of time later to persuade him of his folly in marrying a Bedouin girl. What was most important now was to act quickly. After a moment of contemplation, he backed off. "He who doesn't follow advice has no reason to complain later," he said simply. "Have your way. Just keep in mind that if things don't work out as you envision, don't lay the blame at my door. Now, let's go and find this marabout's son."

Richemonte was about to leave when his cousin grabbed him by his arm.

"Umm… who will then…?" his cousin stammered.

"Who will what?" asked the already irritated Richemonte.

"Well, who's going to help the young man to disappear? Me or you?"

"You, of course!"

"Why me? You're a much better shot," he evaded.

"That may be, but I'm not going to take the chestnuts out of the fire for another, burning my fingers in the process."

"For another? This 'another', as you call him, is your own flesh and blood. Your adopted son even!"

"I wouldn't do it for ten of you."

"Yet you stand to enjoy the same benefits."

"That remains to be seen," Richemonte pointed out. "I was prepared to kill him back then. Now that the circumstances have changed, I'm no longer going to stick my neck out."

"How come?"

"Because of your Liama."

"Because of her?" Henri asked. "I don't understand you."

"It's easy to explain. She knows you're not the marabout's son. She could divulge everything and, in such a case, I certainly don't want to be saddled with the accusation of murder."

"Is that all?" he asked, relieved. "Fine, I'll take the shot. I'll do anything for the girl. She won't betray us."

Richemonte snickered to himself. He had never intended to carry the burden of the son's murder. He was much more interested in having control over the soon to be made Baron de Sainte-Marie. By intimidating Henri into action, controlling him would soon be feasible. After all, the best way to curb a murderer was through threats of exposure. "Let's go then. Did you check the ammunition?"

"Of course."

They crept quietly through the trees until they reached the clearing again. Richemonte ducked down and crawled the rest of the way toward the hut, followed by his cousin. Halfway to their goal, they halted, spotting a dim light inside the small building.

"That's good news," whispered Richemonte. "He'll be busy inside and won't pay attention to anything else. We can walk the rest of the way."

"Yes, but he's got a light."

"Even better. He'll present an easier, clearer target for you. Let's have a little fun by surprising him. I'm sure he'll have a fright when he's faced with two unexpected visitors at night."

"Wait! What if he has weapons on him?"

"Coward! A marabout with weapons? Absurd."

"There could be some on hand, from his previous life."

"In that case, just make sure you're faster than him. Come on!"

They carefully crept closer to the wall. The body of the marabout was still leaning on the far side of the entrance. They gingerly walked around the corpse and ended up in front of the entrance which had no door, lending them a good overview of the inside of the hut.

A small, round clay pot, apparently containing a fatty substance, lay on the floor. It sustained the lit wick and gave off just enough light to distinguish the inside of the hut. The young marabout had shoved the bed to one side and was occupied with unearthing the ground with a tool reminiscent of a spade. He was too preoccupied in his task to notice their entrance, but spun around at the sound of the stranger's words.

"*Mesalcheer* (good evening)," Richemonte started.

The young man faced the two armed Bedouins. Though frightened at first, Arthur quickly composed himself.

"*Allah jumessik* (what do you want)?" he asked evenly.

"We've come to speak with you," replied Richemonte.

"Come closer."

As the two men entered, the old man pointed to the freshly dug hole. "What are you doing here?" he asked bluntly.

"I'm digging the grave for the dead man whose body lies propped up outside the door."

"Who is he?"

"My father, the pious marabout Hajji Omanah."

"You're lying," Richemonte accused.

"You're mistaken," he said, shocked. "I'm not lying."

"And yet you're not speaking the whole truth."

Arthur narrowed his eyes at the two intruders. "Who are you? You are strangers, and therefore I will forgive your words. A man from any of the nearby villages would speak differently. It doesn't seem reasonable to assume a man is lying, having only just met him. The corpse of the marabout honors this place, but your speech desecrates and dishonors him."

Although he had spoken solemnly and without fear, Richemonte continued in his offensive manner. "As I've said, you're lying! I know the man whose body lies outside this hut."

"If you profess to know him better than I, whose son I am, then tell me."

"Naturally, he's now no more than dust of the earth. But previously he was called Baron Roman de Sainte-Marie," Richemonte replied, returning to his native French.

"Allah!" exclaimed the frightened young man.

"He murdered his own wife!"

Arthur's eyes opened wide in horror.

"He stole from his own mother."

"Who are you?" asked the bewildered young man.

"I'm the one he talked about earlier."

"Ah! So you dared to spy on us!"

"Yes. Do you recall the name Richemonte?"

"Was it the name of the French captain?"

"Yes. I am he."

"God protect me!"

"Go ahead and call on your God," interrupted Henri. "But Allah won't listen to the pleas of an unfaithful Muslim."

With a lightning-like movement, he produced a pistol, aimed at the young man's head, and fired. The thunderous report echoed far into the night. Mortally wounded, Arthur de Sainte-Marie collapsed to the ground, the bullet having penetrated his skull.

The captain bent down and examined the wound. "Excellent. Well done, my boy!" he praised Henri. "The bullet lodged itself deep into his brain. He died instantly and didn't suffer. Fitting isn't it, that he would end up dying next to the holy man?"

The murderer, however, turned aside timidly. He didn't dare look at the corpse, much less examine his own handiwork. Instead, he avoided the victim altogether. "Are you satisfied?" he said, feeling he should say something.

"Yes."

"Now, you move him outside."

"Why me?"

"I don't want to look at him," replied Henri, trying to shake the image. "That bloody wound, the convulsive clenched hands, and those lifeless, horrible eyes!"

"Don't be such a coward! We'll both move him outside, so we can finish the work he started. Grab a hold of him!"

"No," Henri protested. "You do it!"

"Suit yourself! I'm not afraid of him. I'm not the one who shot him. I'm not tainted by his blood."

The words struck Henri like a thunder clap. "What do you mean about not being tainted?" he asked, becoming subdued. "Didn't you arrange the entire matter?"

"Pah! Since when do you have to do another man's bidding? If I had suggested that you fire a bullet into your own head, would you have done it? Each man carries the responsibility for his own actions. The final decision on any course of action rests solely on the individual, regardless of outside influence. I don't want you to bring it up again, inferring I had somehow compelled you to pull the trigger, thereby killing the marabout's son."

Richemonte grabbed the corpse by the arms and dragged it outside, dropping it near the door. He returned inside and examined the freshly dug hole.

"Why do you still have the pistol in your hand?" he admonished Henri. "No doubt the bloody smell has brought you out of your senses. Here, my boy, start digging!"

His cousin complied without argument. He stuck the spent pistol in his pocket and grabbed the discarded spade. He had been digging for only a short time when the spade struck something solid.

"This must be it," he said in monotone.

"Then clear away the earth!" Richemonte commanded. "I'm curious to see what we've found."

Henri obeyed, finding the neck of a vase like pot with a clay lid. The older cousin, having carefully removed the lid, found a thick bundle inside. Richemonte examined the contents with the aid of the lamp.

"They are documents belonging to the old sinner," he elaborated. "It's a detailed account of his departure from Jeannette, his pursuit of the girl, and her resultant murder. It describes his exodus to Egypt and details his life until a few years before his death."

He also found a woolen cloth underneath the bundle. When they opened it, both men shouted, pleasantly surprised. They were admiring an exquisite array of jewelry, adorned with pearls and precious stones. Beneath it, they located a large number of English guineas.

"Damn! This is more than I had hoped for," said an elated Richemonte.

"What a treasure," agreed his cousin, eyeing the contents with greedy, shimmering eyes. He wanted to take hold of the riches, but was pushed back by Richemonte's hand.

"Hold it, my boy!" he admonished. "They're not yours yet!"

"What! Am I not Ben Hajji Omanah, now Baron de Sainte-Marie?"

"No, not yet. All that is yet to come."

"Then all of this will become my property!"

"Naturally! But until such time, I'm holding onto it, purely for safekeeping," Richemonte said. "I know you only too well. As soon as you come into possession of some money, you'll be powerless to stop from spending it. You're capable of giving all this stuff to your fabled Liama for just one kiss."

"I'm not that crazy!"

"Caution begets caution! I'll allow you to sit beside me while we count the gold coins, but we're not taking a single one with us. I received an advance in Biskra that should be sufficient to carry us through."

"What are we going to do with the treasure?"

Richemonte looked down at the gold, then back to his ward. "We'll bury it for the time being, until we've dispensed with Löwenklau. Then we'll return for it and travel to France to see if circumstances have changed for us."

"Shouldn't we secure the entrance, cousin?"

"What for?"

"It's still possible that someone might come here during the night."

"Pah! Who would come here at this hour? Besides, we have the finest honor guards lying outside. They'll keep a good watch and are sure to keep anyone away. Now come here, my boy. Let's evaluate our new fortune."

First, they assessed the jewelry items. There was quite an assortment of settings and precious stones, representing a substantial worth. They carefully rewrapped the jewels and turned their attention to the English gold pieces. They counted roughly three thousand.

"That pious marabout really was a crook," mused Richemonte. "Modesty certainly wasn't one of his earlier traits, as we can gather by these stolen items. So much the better for us, his grateful heirs. He can rest with Allah and make a peaceful transition to the afterlife."

"It's puzzling to me," Henri commented, "that his mother never bothered to reconcile with her family."

"Puzzling? Not really," Richemonte said. "It only proves that she possessed too much pride. Her sense of honor allowed her to disassociate herself from her son. Lastly, she was rich enough to bear the loss of her family jewels. You can see how it's now worth your while to become the Baron de Sainte-Marie."

"Could the old lady still be alive?"

"Who can tell? Women often lead robust lives. But in all likelihood, she's passed away some time ago. She wasn't that young, even back then."

"Where shall we bury this treasure? Up here, near the hut?"

"No, I have a better place in mind. It'll be more secure down the mountain, in the brush."

"What should we do with the corpses?"

"For Allah's sake, the marabout can remain where he is. We'll prop him up inside the hut after we've filled in the hole. We'll have to bury the other one somewhere else, some place where he'll never be discovered."

"At least until such time that I've taken his place and the body has decayed," Henri added. "Let's get to work before the lamp goes out. I don't care to stay here in the dark."

"Right. Let's fill the hole."

They went to work and quickly filled in the cavity. They trampled the earth down, covering the floor with the original moss. Richemonte dragged the marabout's body inside, laying him on the simple bed.

"There!" he said. "We're not going to mortar the entrance shut, as he wanted. He desired to have a solitary sunbeam, but we're Christians and we'll allow him more."

"What about his son?"

"We'll have to leave him until morning. It's impossible to finish burying him in the darkness."

"Where should we wait?"

"Somewhere under the trees. I couldn't possibly sleep now."

"Are we taking the treasure with us?" Henri asked.

"Yes, even though it's safe here with the bodies." Just then, Richemonte paused, as though an idea had struck him. "Heavens, I nearly forgot the central thing."

"What's that?"

"The documents the young marabout pocketed. If we bury them with him, it'll be damned tricky for you to appear as the legitimate heir."

"I saw him stick the envelope within the folds of the hooded robe."

"Then take it out."

"You can do it just as well as me, cousin."

"There you go again, Henri. You're spineless."

"Go ahead and mock. I won't back down from a fight in the light of day. But at night, in complete darkness, I'm not going anywhere near a corpse. I stand by my decision."

"I know. Cowards often choose to adhere to their principles when it suits them," Richemonte said. "I'm going out to collect the papers. In the meantime, have a look around and tidy up the place. I don't want to leave any remnants of blood, a sure sign of unnatural activity. Those who will surely come to visit the marabout tomorrow must not become suspicious. I want them to believe that the old man died alone while his son was absent on some errand."

Richemonte stole the documents and helped to eradicate the last remnants of blood. Having completed their task in silence, the two murderers extinguished the lamp and left the hut with their prize.

They walked to the cover of the trees. Despite their long and physically demanding journey, they were far too excited to feel tired. In order to pass the time, they returned to their quiet conversation, dwelling on the abundance of material they had gleaned from the marabout's confession to his son.

"Is your sister Margot still alive?" Henri asked his relative during a lull in the conversation.

"I don't know."

"What about her husband?"

"That damned Hugo von Löwenklau, the favored of the old field marshal? I can thank him for all my misery. I wish he was in the devil's clutches this very minute. I have no idea, since I haven't been home for many years."

"This Lieutenant von Löwenklau, the one we want to pay a cordial visit, could he be a relative?"

"Of course! Undoubtedly, he's Margot's son. That fellow hasn't the slightest idea that his loving uncle is planning a little get together, one that will cost him a few drops of blood and likely deprive him of his camel-laden property," Richemonte said, his eyes glowing darkly. "I sense my time has finally come. For years, I've yearned for an opportunity, even a glimmer of hope, and it has eluded me thus far. I've slaved and served others my whole life without seeing my hope come to fruition. But now, I see the glimmer of its fulfillment. I want revenge, revenge on Löwenklau and his lineage. And if it's possible, a little vengeance on the whole German nation. After all, it was their presence in Paris that led to all of my problems in the first place. Then came that damned Marshal Forward, who ensured that my contemporaries advanced in rank while I was forced out of the army. Perhaps Satan will see to it, once I'm living in France again, to blind a segment of the populace into starting another war with us. Then I'll do my utmost to see their blood flow in the streets!"

If it hadn't been dark, one could have observed the gnashing of his teeth, always indicative of his inward agitation. Despite his reminiscence, Richemonte was in a good frame of mind.

"Who could have predicted this?" reflected Henri. "That we would reach our goal so quickly."

"Yes, and what a goal! Two Sainte-Maries are dead, and one Richemonte will become a baron. This extraordinary turn is far beyond the boldest of hopes. We can be content with that."

"What news will you bring to Governor Cavaignac?"

"Bring?" asked Richemonte, surprised. "None. I'm going to send him word."

"Through who?"

"Through Poisson, the commander at Biskra. We'll be going there next. So much has occurred on our little adventure that we need to change our plans. This is the last servitude I plan to perform for the governor. I'm sick of all this subterfuge."

"Will he learn what happened to the marabout, and his true identity?" Henri asked.

"What's gotten into your head? He'll only find out that the pious Hajji Omanah no longer poses a threat to him, because he has died. That's all he needs to know."

"What about our wages?"

"I'm certain we'll receive some compensation. We'll certainly obtain it after we rob the German's caravan."

"Fine with me. I'm still not clear how you plan to involve the *Beni Hassan* in the ambush and saddle them with the blame."

Richemonte looked away from his younger cousin. "Leave that to me. I've more or less worked it out in my head. All that remains is the actual implementation... and its eventual success."

"Do I have to remind you that I insist on Saadi's death?"

"As far as I'm concerned, we should eliminate every last one of them, starting with your sweet Liama," Richemonte said, ignoring Henri's dirty glance in his direction. "You'll find out soon enough where your blind pursuit of love will take you. I've done my part by warning you of this unequal union. Now it's up to you to see if you can shoulder the blame, not to mention the consequences of your stubbornness... which will surely come."

"Let me worry about that, cousin," he replied quickly in an effort to divert another lecture. "You won't find the opportunity to revel in the consequences of my folly, as you put it." With that final, sharp retort, Henri put an end to their conversation.

The aroma of the desert air, borne by the wind, still whispered in the tree branches like the beating wings of a fleeing soul. The stars still glimmered in the south, oblivious to the earlier, dreadful disruption of the serene mountainside.

When Arthur had prayed according to his father's wish, *My life and my end is yours. Into your hands, Father, I commit my spirit*, his pain and the suppressed sobbing had been meant for his father alone, and yet it had also become his own dying prayer. He was meant to leave the desert, starting a pilgrimage to his father's home, but now he had embarked on an entirely different journey toward a distant place, higher and more wonderful than all the cities and lands of the earth.

The horizon had barely begun to lighten when both murderers plunged once more into their task of burying the clay pot with its gold pieces and jewels. They quickly found a suitable place, albeit only a temporary one, for their riches. They noted a few landmarks so as to be able to locate their ill-gained treasure in the future. They took one final visit to the forlorn hut, satisfying themselves in the breaking light of dawn that they had eliminated any sign of the gruesome deed.

Both men grabbed the stiff limbs of the corpse and dragged it deeply into the nearby forest. They armed themselves with two available spades and commenced to dig at a suitable spot. They tumbled the body of the marabout's son into the pit and quickly threw the fresh earth on top of him. This morbid task didn't take long.

They headed back down the mountain, shifting their concern to their horses. To their relief, the animals were still exactly where they had left them. The horses had recovered somewhat from their strenuous journey and eagerly carried their masters eastward toward their new goal, Biskra.

CHAPTER TEN
Inseparable Friends

Two full years had elapsed since the events on *Rue de Grenelle* in Paris, while in the south of Algiers three riders rode down into a valley. Instead of riding horses, they sat on mounts of a different sort, high-legged camels that were well-supplied for a long journey. Their camels stemmed from a particular breed of grey-haired specimens commonly known as *bischarin* camels.

Two of the riders were European and, judging from their demeanor, one was the servant to the other. Both foreigners had a military look about them. The third rider was a Bedouin and seemed to occupy the role of guide. He spoke in a mishmash of Arabic, French, and Italian, an amalgamation of language typical of the north coast of Africa.

Although it was still mid-morning, the sun's heat could be felt reflecting from the sand and nearby stones. It was no wonder the two travelers were looking to find a suitable place where they could escape the worst of the midday sun.

"Is there a shady place nearby where we could make a brief stop?" asked one of the sojourners.

"No, *Effendi*,"[10.1] said the guide. "Once we have crossed to the far side of the valley, we will find some solace in the shadows of the mimosa trees and jutting outcroppings."

"How far is that?"

"We should arrive by midday."

"Are you sure that the area is inhabited by lions?"

"Of course! There you will find the *lord of the tremors*, who has already victimized many of the tribe's livestock."

"Then let's get the camels moving a little faster," one of the Europeans suggested. "I want to arrive at a timely hour."

Their guide produced a plain wooden flute with three small holes. As he started to play a simple melody, the camels cocked their ears and immediately doubled their pace. They plodded eastward, without any sign of letting up. The burning sun rose higher and higher, and just as it reached its zenith, their guide's promise of reaching the encampment was fulfilled. The valley diminished ahead of them, giving way on both sides to an encroaching stone facade. The small forests of mimosa bush, which promised a reprieve from the scorching sun, presented a different kind of obstacle, in the form of thousands of sharp thorns.

"Allah be praised!" called out the guide. "Do you see the tents, *Effendi*?"

"Where?"

"On the left side of the valley. That's where we sons of the desert sometimes seek refuge from the prowling eyes of lions. Let's ride over there."

"Do you think we will receive a favorable welcome?"

"Yes," the guide assured him. "They might even give us some salt, bread, and hopefully dates. These Bedouins are not like the *Tuaregs*, whom you can't turn your back on."

On one side of the valley stood five lonely tents dwarfed by the stone walls. In front of them, a few camels and horses were tethered. A small number of sheep grazed nearby. Just then, as if on cue, the tent coverings were thrown back by the inhabitants as they emerged bearing a small sampling of salt and bread, the surest sign of hospitality in the region. They even shared a small quantity of dates with the newcomers.

The *Bey el urdi*, the sheik of the tribe, called the guide aside. "Who are these two strangers with you?" he asked.

"Two French nationals," was the guide's reply.

"I don't care for the French. How soon will they leave?"

"Once they have dealt with the *lord of the tremors*."

"The lion?" he asked in alarm. "*Allah il Allah!* Do they intend to kill it?"

"It would seem so. They heard he's been prowling around the valley."

"His lair is nearby, probably in the next valley, the one visible from here," the sheik said, casting his eyes warily at the newcomers. "But there are only two of them!"

"Still, they intend to take on the fearsome beast!"

"Allah has robbed them of all common sense," he said with conviction. "Sixty of my men have ridden out against the lion already. It killed four and wounded many others without us causing him any harm."

"Didn't you hear the story, how one Frenchman went out by himself to claim his own lion?"

The sheik scoffed. "These French are nothing more than fleeting ghosts. They shouldn't concern themselves about such things."

The Bedouin guide returned to his patron and related what he had learned from the sheik. The Frenchman glanced toward the next valley, mentally estimating the distance from the camp.

"We will stay here overnight," he allowed. "Then at daybreak, we will try our luck. Finally! Finally, we have an opportunity to hunt a lion with a chance of success."

160

"I too revel at the opportunity of seeing one up close," agreed his servant. "I find it most peculiar, Captain, how your betrothed came up with the idea of sending you into the desert with the hope of getting the lion's skin and eye teeth.[10.2] It's one thing getting here, but much more difficult to accomplish the task."

"Are you afraid, Gunter?" joked his master.

"No. After all, a lion is only a large cat," replied the servant.

"Hmm, a considerably larger one. Yet I feel exactly the same way. I've never seen one in the wild. Perhaps we could embark on a little scouting trip in the afternoon."

"A trek into the gorge at the end of the valley?"

"Yes, but on foot! It should only take half an hour."

"I'm with you, Captain."

They commenced their journey a short time later as if it were nothing more than a Sunday afternoon hunting excursion for rabbit or prairie chicken. The Bedouins watched them leave, shaking their heads. The whole notion of hunting a lion was incomprehensible to them.

The two men walked at a steady pace across the breadth of the valley, their paths culminating at the narrow valley entrance. There they encountered mimosa shrubs and terebinth trees interspersed by broken rock strewn over the uneven ground. They were cautious, recalling the sheik's warning that a full grown lion had established his lair in the recesses of the valley. Despite the danger, they hoped to discover his tracks, which might lead them to his hideout. They would then return with the breaking of dawn.

Familiar with its well-known habits, it was reasonable to conclude that a lion seldom appeared at midday. However, if the animal was disturbed during its habitual afternoon rest, he could venture forth, irritable and bad-tempered, posing an even greater danger than usual. While they worked their way over and around the many boulders, the servant suddenly halted, gripping his master's arm.

"For God's sake, what's that over there?" Gunter asked, pointing toward a particular outcropping.

The captain followed his outstretched arm, flinching momentarily. Whether it was out of surprise or fear, one couldn't tell. "*Sapperlot!* A lion!" he managed to whisper. "A live, genuine lion and not something you would expect to find in a zoo. Should we risk it?"

A large specimen of the breed approached slowly and majestically from the far side of the valley, seemingly aware of its superior strength. If it continued on its present course, the lion would notice the two hunters within minutes.

Gunter was no coward and wanted to show his support for his master. "Let's take him on!" he said. "He's even larger than I imagined. Who knows if we'll get another chance tomorrow? Which part of the body do you aim at to be assured of a good shot?"

"Aim for the left flank," instructed the captain. "In other words, go for the heart. Only in extreme cases would you consider aiming at the head, and only then through the eyes."

"Excellent. We'll conceal ourselves behind this shrub. He won't see us here. Each of us has two shots, that's four all together. That should be enough."

They followed their plan. Both men lowered themselves into a kneeling position, lifting their rifles up to their shoulders. The predator was barely thirty paces away from them now and about twenty paces higher in elevation.

"Take the first shot," ordered the captain. "I'll follow with mine in reserve."

Gunter took careful aim and pulled the trigger. Although the bullet had left the muzzle, the lion remained motionless. He followed up with a second shot, striking the lion in the side, but it didn't seem to cause it significant injury. The lion instantly determined the bush where the attack had originated and let out a deep, bone-piercing roar, bounding toward them. He would have needed at most four or five leaps to reach the hunters.

"Dear God! We're done for!" yelled Gunter, throwing himself to the ground. His earlier bravado came literally crashing down on him. The captain, however, remained motionless in his kneeling position. Just as the lion leaped into the air, he fired his first shot, quickly followed by his second. The massive animal seemed to constrict in midair and crashed to the ground. A short hollow growl escaped from the predator, followed by a spasmodic movement of its paws. And then it lay still.

"Thank God!" exclaimed the relieved servant. "Those were the shots of a marksman! I could see my life flashing before my eyes."

The captain remained silent, instead walking over to the animal. As he examined it, he wiped a bead of sweat from his brow.

"My first and last hunt!" he declared. "It only lasted three seconds, but I inwardly died five times before it elapsed." He stopped to ponder if the men in the camp had heard the noise. "Now for our reward. Let's skin him and pry out his eye teeth."

Not only was this time consuming, but extraordinarily laborious. It took them several hours. They had barely finished the task when the sound of approaching hoof beats stole their attention. Looking up, they waited patiently while two riders came into view, riding down into the valley. The two lion hunters were still concealed behind the bushes, occupied with the animal carcass.

The riders closed the distance quickly, coming to a stop in front of the bushes without noticing the captain or his servant. The older man sported a long grey beard. Although both men wore the traditional *burnus* of the Bedouins, the older one spoke to his companion fluently in French.

"Look! The valley is coming to an end," he said, pointing ahead. "We have to be careful. Ride ahead and scout out the area for any sign of activity."

The younger rider complied, galloping away. He returned a few minutes later.

"I spotted five tents in Wadi Guelb," he reported.

"How many people did you see?" asked the older one.

"I counted nine men."

"We can't allow them to see us. The success of our plan will create quite a commotion, and the governor will question each traveller in order to discover those responsible."

"Where did that German spend his last night?" the younger man asked.

"At the Saadi oasis. We'll reach it if we keep riding to the east. My spies told me as much. We'll have to leave the area, unnoticed by anyone. The *Beni Hassan* will be blamed and rounded up for their complicity."

"Where are we going now?"

"We'll quickly retrace our path, then ride circumspectly in a large arc toward the east. We have to hurry, or else Löwenklau will get away with his riches."

They turned the horses and headed back along their previous track as the two unsuspecting witnesses to the conversation looked at one another, dread showing on their faces.

"What was all that about, Captain?" asked the servant. "If I heard right, those two were planning to rob someone."

His master jumped up, grabbing his rifle. "Dear God!" he said in disbelief. "They mean to ambush my friend Löwenklau and plunder the caravan. Our chance meeting with the lion proved providential, Gunter. Now get up! We have to get back to camp and devise a plan to beat them to their target."

Gunter would have liked to get some clarification, but there was no time. They gathered up the cumbersome lion fur and ran as best as could be expected down the incline, back toward the tents. Once they arrived, they still had difficulty convincing the Arabs that they had shot and killed a full grown lion. But the men had no choice but to accept their word when they were presented with irrefutable proof in the form of the lion skin and massive eye teeth. Even as the men became jubilant, the captain turned aside, addressing the guide.

"Are you familiar with the Saadi oasis?" he asked.

"Yes, *Effendi*," the guide replied.

"How far is it to travel there by camel?"

"It's about one-fifth of a day's journey."

The captain looked off into the distance determinedly. "We must break camp right away and head there."

"*Effendi,*" said the surprised guide, "my animals are tired."

"I'll pay you what you feel is required to cover the hardship."

"But is it that urgent?"

"Yes. The lives of others could hang on our actions."

"Are you willing to pay me sixty of your French gold pieces?" When the captain nodded, the guide smiled. "Then I'll instruct my men to saddle up."

Fifteen minutes later, they were racing away on their trustworthy camels. Even though the camels hadn't fully rested, a horse would have had difficulty catching up with them. There was nothing but desert as far as the eye could see.

Shortly before the day gave way to evening, they spied a few palm trees on the horizon.

"What is that in front of us?" asked the captain.

"That's the Saadi oasis," reported the guide. "We have arrived in time, just as I promised."

The 'oasis' was nothing more than a waterhole, and one of the poorer ones at that. Perhaps two dozen palm trees covered the sparse landscape. The three riders approached, noticing that it was already occupied. They spotted about twenty passenger camels as well as the load variety. Despite the number, there were only five men. These rose from their sitting position, curious about the newcomers.

The captain jumped from his camel and immediately began to examine their faces, seeking to recognize one. Before he found the right one, a voice, rich and clear, called out to him.

"Kunz," the man began in German. "Goldberg! Is that really you?"

The captain turned at the sound of his name and scrutinized the one who had spoken. "Gebhard! Löwenklau! *Moor! Bedouin!*" he called in astonishment. "How can anyone recognize you? You're as black as the devil!"

"A surprise visit! What a wonder to see you here," Gebhard Löwenklau exclaimed. "How did you manage to get this far into the Sahara?"

"I'll tell you later," replied Kunz, his voice taking on a serious tone. "But first, I came to warn you."

"Warn me? About what?"

"About an ambush."

"Damn! Who's planning to attack me?"

"Two Frenchmen, disguised as Bedouins, aided by a tribe called the *Beni Hassan.*"

"Who are the two Frenchmen?" Gebhard asked.

"I wasn't able to find out."

"Where is the ambush to take place?"

"East of here, just before sunset."

"Really? What luck that I chose to remain behind."

"Yes, you've been spared," Kunz observed. "But what about your things, your property?"

"They're all laden on the pack animals. I knew that the story of my adventures and riches would be exaggerated, spreading like wildfire before me. I allowed the main troop to precede me, and I followed half a day's journey behind. This is the reason you were able to find me here."

"Then your main company is lost."

"Undoubtedly," Gebhard said. "I'll send a messenger after them. Hopefully he'll arrive in time to warn them."

"What if he gets there too late?"

"Then there's nothing I can do about it," Gebhard said regretfully. "Thirty warriors from the *Ibn Batta* accompany them. If they're decimated, it's probably a just reward for their previous deeds. All these fellows are robbers and murderers. Although these thirty men were paid to be my protectors, they never ceased in stealing from me. I can honestly say I'm glad to be rid of them. But now, for God's sake, tell me how you came to be in the Sahara."

Kunz smiled to his friend. "I came as a lion hunter. Don't you see the animal skin on my saddle?"

"Really? Did a lion jump out at you along the way?" he joked.

"Yes, indeed. Were you as fortunate?"

"Often, my friend. Actually, it just occurred to me why you've chosen to play the part of a lion hunter," Gebhard said, eyeing his friend.

"Well, how come then?"

"You're here on a holiday, right?"

"Yes."

"The way I see it, your Hedwig and dear stepmother have aspirations to turn you into a famous person. Therefore, you converted your leave into a pilgrimage to the Sahara, hoping to bag yourself a lion. Am I on the right track?"

"You've found me out," Kunz admitted, feigning embarrassment. "I'm to procure a lion's skin and the eye teeth, and even come home with news of your accomplishments."

"You can do even better than that," Gebhard said. "Take me home with you. What has Ida been doing?"

"Ida, the tame one?" teased Kunz. "She's been dying for your company, while my untamable one seems content to send me out in pursuit of lions. Aside from that, I've been promoted to captain."

"And I've become a *Moor*, just as I promised you. I congratulate you on both counts, my friend."

"Thank you, Gebhard."

The chief subject of their conversation naturally continued, centering around their providential meeting at the desert well, with one coming as the savior of the other. It was Captain von Goldberg's turn to fill Gebhard in on events from back home, after which Löwenklau began to expound on his adventurous trek through the desert and the magical road to Timbuktu.

In due course, it became night, the stars climbing higher and higher in the sky. Finally, shortly after midnight, the dispatched messenger returned.

"Were you able to overtake them?" asked Löwenklau.

"Yes," was his monotone answer.

"Were you able to warn them?"

"No."

"Why not?"

"They no longer needed my warning," the messenger explained. "They were all dead. Murdered!"

The news caused no small consternation, yet the remnant was grateful for having escaped certain death. Gebhard, along with the most valuable treasures, had escaped the looting Tuaregs. Unfortunately, thirty *Ibn Batta* warriors, and a considerable number of merchants who had joined the caravan out of fear for their safety, had also been killed and plundered. Though it hadn't been an unusual hold-up, it certainly demanded an exemplary and swift punishment.

"What are you going to do now?" inquired Goldberg of his friend.

"I'm changing my itinerary and heading north. I have little choice."

"Well then, I'm going with you. We'll be going through territory whose occupants aren't nearly so opposed to Europeans. When are we leaving?"

"Right away. I'm not waiting for morning."

"Why not?" Kunz asked. "My camels are still tired."

"I think it's possible," said Gebhard, "that the robbers may have discovered my absence, and that I wasn't among those attacked. They could have pressed one of the guides and learned my plan to remain behind, choosing now to pay me a belated visit. It's better to be prepared and avoid a confrontation with the Tuaregs. I've become too familiar with the dark side of these vagabonds."

Löwenklau gave the order to pack up and break camp. Before long, the small caravan started its procession to the north. Guided by the light of the stars, the two friends journeyed away from the safety of the oasis.

They hadn't left a moment too soon. Just a few minutes elapsed from their departure when a hoard of Tuaregs swarmed over the oasis. They were the same marauders who had attacked the main part of the caravan, now eagerly looking to complete their plunder by capturing the German explorer. To their chagrin, they had missed him and were forced to leave empty-handed.

❧✠❧

A few days later, a long line of French *Chasseurs d'Afrique* proceeded down a well-traveled mountain path from the north, heading toward the enemy territory of the *Beni Hassan*. Two notorious men, the traitor Richemonte and his cousin Henri, rode on either side of the commander at the head of the column. Their one and only piece of advice to him was to annihilate the *Beni Hassan*.

"Is it likely that we'll find resistance?" Poisson, the commander asked.

"Probably none at all," replied Richemonte. "This bunch has demonstrated their cowardly ways long enough. They only seem to find courage in conducting nightly forays of mayhem and robbery."

"Are you certain that they are responsible?"

"Absolutely! You'll likely find some of the effects from the caravan in their tents."

"How many people succumbed during the attack?"

"Thirty warriors from the *Ibn Batta*, one head guide, fifteen workers, the chief camel owner, and a German officer with his expeditionary entourage."

Richemonte certainly knew the truth, that Löwenklau hadn't been among the dead, but he added this lie for effect. It was he himself, accompanied by his relative, who had driven several of the plundered camels into the vicinity of the *Beni Hassan*'s encampment, leaving the animals to graze. He was convinced that the tribesmen would find them, and after a brief search to locate the rightful owner, would appropriate them for their own. In his mind, this would constitute sufficient proof of their guilt and complicity in the attack.

The commander planned on reaching the camp in the middle of the night. His troops surrounded the village so that when the guiltless inhabitants emerged from their tents in the morning, they faced an armed wall of determined soldiers.

Sheik Menalek wasted no time in sending a messenger to the commander. Acting on Richemonte's advice, Poisson allowed the *dschemma*, the gathering of the elders, to come to him and thus be assured they didn't pose a threat. Naturally, this didn't only include the eldest men, but also some of the younger men who had distinguished themselves.

So it came to be that Saadi, the son-in-law of the sheik, was found among them. The men were immediately bound and subjected to a stringent interrogation.

"You're responsible for the hold-up of a caravan formerly under the protection of the *Ibn Batta*," was the repeated accusation.

"No," came the unanimous answer. "We're innocent of this crime."

"We'll investigate and search your camp," the commander threatened. "The evidence will confirm your guilt."

"Of course you'll find evidence," replied Menalek, deciding it was in their best interest to be forthcoming. "Late yesterday, our shepherds came across four laden camels that had wandered near our camp. Our men conducted a search of the immediate area, finding the remnants of an attack not too far away. They found plundered bodies, apparently belonging to a caravan that had strayed onto our land. We chose to bury the bodies, according to the rules of our holy Qu'ran. Naturally, we retrieved those things from their bodies which we deemed useful to us. That's what you'll find."

His answer was dismissed as a pitiful excuse. More and more men were dragged out of the camp, until the entire complement of warriors lay bound on the ground. The verdict was swift and terrible: death by firing squad. News of the decision brought the women and children to an indescribable wailing, resulting in near panic. Some wanted to flee, while others sought to fall at the feet of their unmerciful judges.

The judgment was to be carried out the very same day, at noon, when the sun reached its pinnacle in the sky. At about this time, Richemonte's cousin Henri crossed through the soldier's line, oblivious to the wailing around him. He walked the length of the tents, stopping only at the sheik's tent. When he entered, he found the man's wife and Liama prostrated on the floor, lamenting for their husbands. They jumped to their feet when they spotted the intruder.

"*Sallam aaleikum* (peace be with you)!" he greeted coldly.

"How can you greet us with peace," called out the heartbroken wife, "when our men are faced with death?"

"They won't escape it. However, I bring peace to your tent. Has Liama already become Saadi's wife?"

"Yes," her mother answered.

Liama's recent marriage had heightened her outward beauty, but she had neglected to dress herself with the usual care because of her sorrow, leaving little of her body to the imagination. Henri was nearly mad out of lust for Liama, feasting his eyes on her beauty.

"The sheik must die," he said firmly. "Saadi as well!"

"Oh Allah! Is there no recourse to the decision?" pleaded Liama.

"None."

The young woman approached him with outstretched hands. "You're the soldiers' friend," she said. "Our men are innocent of this crime. You have a lot of influence. Perhaps you could intervene for them?"

"I have been allowed to save only two men."

"Which ones?" both women asked at the same time.

"I may choose them," he proclaimed.

"Oh, please, save my husband, the sheik!" called the mother.

"And save Saadi, who's innocent!" called her daughter.

"What thanks can I expect if I comply?"

"Ask for whatever you desire," replied the sheik's wife.

"Will I receive it?"

"Yes."

"In that case, let me remind you that I desired to make Liama my wife, yet she was withheld from me. If she agrees to become my wife, then I'm prepared to intercede on behalf of the sheik and Saadi."

Liama was stunned by the proclamation, turning pale at the news. Her mother, however, was less shocked.

"Will you keep your word?" asked the mother.

"Yes," replied Henri convincingly.

"Swear it!"

"I swear it by the Prophet's beard!"

Liama wrung her hands in dismay. "He can swear, but I'm not going with him."

"Do you want to shoulder the blame for your father's death?" lamented her mother.

"I cannot go with him. I don't love him. I belong to Saadi!"

"No," interrupted Henri. "He releases you to save him and your father."

"Prove it!"

"Here," he said, and produced a parchment, containing French and Arabic markings. "This is a document signed by the French commander, and witnessed by the sheik and Saadi. Are you familiar with the sheik's seal?"

"Yes," they both replied.

"Then look here and read it for yourself."

Her mother couldn't read, but Liama spelled out the edict endorsed by her father and her husband. In it, they implored her to accompany the bearer of the document, thereby rescuing the sheik and his son-in-law, which would be pleasing in Allah's sight.

"Are you familiar with their *hamaïls*?"[10.3] he continued.

"Yes," they replied in unison.

"Here they are!" he proclaimed, producing two *hamaïl* copies of the Qu'ran, which they immediately recognized as belonging to the men. It was more than enough proof to convince them.

"I believe you now," said the mother. There was no way for her to know that the unscrupulous Henri had forged the document and obtained the *hamaïls* by force.

In the meantime, Liama had sunk to her knees, sobbing with indecision. "Oh Allah, oh Allah!" she cried. "They're forcing me to comply, but I can't! Oh Allah, Allah, what should I do?"

"If you don't comply, they will surely die," he replied coldly.

"My daughter, consider your duty to your family!" her mother reminded her.

"Yes, consider it well," agreed the hooded Frenchman. "I'll wait outside your tent and give you a few minutes to think things over. But don't delay too long. Time is precious."

He stepped outside. A unified lament arose from the confines of the little village, and yet he discerned Liama's hopeless moaning from within.

Suddenly the two women heard a salvo of gunfire, a resounding shrill and terrifying call from the camp. Henri walked back into the tent, nearly running into the sheik's wife. Liama stood to the side, leaning against a pole, white as a ghost.

"What happened? What did they do?" her mother asked, trying to contain her fear.

"The soldiers just shot the first five men," he replied.

"Oh Allah! Was the sheik among them?"

"Not yet, but in two minutes another five men will be rounded up, including Saadi and the sheik."

"Liama is going with you!" she called out terrified.

"Is it really true?" he asked the beautiful *Moor*.

"Yes," she breathed.

"Then put on your traveling clothes. I'll see to it that the soldiers spare your men's lives."

A short time later, the perimeter of the *chasseurs* parted. Two horses and a camel were allowed to pass through the line. Richemonte and his cousin rode in front, while the camel carried an *atuscha*,[10.4] occupied by a heartbroken, beautiful young woman who felt she was living through the worst day of her life. It was Liama, who would eventually become the willing tenant of the dark tower near the Castle Ortry.

CHAPTER ELEVEN
Ill-Gained Favors

Several years passed after the events of that horrible day. Hugo von Löwenklau, the favored lieutenant of the former Marshal Forward, lived in relative seclusion on his estate, enjoying the fruits of his financial dealings. Because of his loving wife, Margot, he experienced an earthly joy that few men managed to duplicate. Only once did a deep sadness encroach on their joyous lives, and that was attributed to the passing of Margot's mother, Madame Richemonte.

Occasionally, Hugo had that pensive, faraway look about him that often pointed to the empty, dark place in his memory that served as a constant reminder of his brush with death. Hugo would sit for hours, debating this unsolvable point with his trusty friend Florian Rupprechtsberger, who had left his employ at Jeannette to become more than a servant to the Löwenklau family.

Hugo also sought to grasp that which had eluded him for so long, yet it was impossible for him to recall the location of the buried war chest. If Margot happened to come across the two men caught up in conversation, she could immediately guess the theme of their lively discussion. She would tenderly put her hand on Hugo's neck and probe good-naturedly, "I suspect you've enveloped yourselves in the story of the buried war chest. Isn't that the case, dear Hugo?"

"Unfortunately, yes!" he would respond, whether out of frustration or anger it was hard to tell.

"Can't you for once leave it alone? How often have I pleaded with you, and still you haven't let it be."

"I've often tried, dear Margot. Believe me when I tell you that when thoughts about the strong box work their way into my mind, I'm powerless to stop them!"

"But my love," she countered, "not only is it in vain, but it's also redundant. Even if you were able to recall the burial place, you still don't have the right to retrieve it."

"Why not, my dear?"

"Because it's French property. Your appropriation of it would be considered nothing less than theft. After all, it's not a German chest, or one belonging to our allies."

"I can't fault you there," he admitted. "However, if war was ever declared between the French and Germans, and we occupied that territory again, we'd have every right to acquire that which has eluded our side for so long."

"I only pray that such a bloody event does not happen again."

"I agree with you. Still, the way things stand right now, it would be beneficial to me if I could remember its location. I could benefit from the substantial finder's fee. After all, the French authorities have also been searching for it."

"I know, Hugo, but let it be! We're not suffering financially. We don't require such a reward."

Hugo chose not to respond at that point, leaving her to believe he had calmed himself, even though he continued brooding inwardly.

Margot was quite right when she said they weren't struggling financially. Their two estate holdings provided more than enough income to furnish their needs. Besides, they had inherited the large Jeannette estate from the late Baroness de Sainte-Marie and had been diligent in improving it over the years, turning it over to a capable steward who ensured their interests were looked after. Its value had risen considerably, even though they seldom visited.

Their son Gebhard had returned from Africa having accomplished what he set out to do, by leading a successful expedition to Timbuktu. He published his research and was rewarded with all sorts of accolades, resulting in high standing among the academic and scientific communities. His success encouraged him to continue in the field and he took leave from his military duties in order to participate in further expeditions. These resulted in still more honor.

Since there wasn't the slightest prospect of war on the horizon, he requested a lengthy leave of absence from his military responsibilities. Gebhard was granted the request, especially since his superiors recognized his worth to the expeditions for his country. Rather than confine him to mundane regimental duties, he was released with many well wishes and often remained absent from home for extended periods of time.

Gebhard fulfilled his other dream and married Ida de Rallion. She loved him with all her heart, finding the same fulfillment in her marriage as Gebhard's parents had found in theirs. Of course, she wasn't thrilled to see him absent for long periods. Yet she was honored to be married to a famous and well-respected explorer, feeling a double measure of blessing each time he returned home. While he occupied himself with various assignments in foreign lands, she found a measure of consolation with her supportive in-laws. Then, when she was rewarded with the birth of their son, and later with a daughter, the constant waiting for his return wasn't as painful as it had once been.

Ida baptized their son with the name Richard, and their little daughter as Amelia. Father and mother were both thrilled to have been blessed with them, but it almost seemed as though their love toward them was surpassed by that of the grandparents. Naturally, the young boy wanted to follow in his father's footsteps as an officer, and consequently his upbringing reflected this course. The encouragement from his parents, grandparents, and teachers provided a platform to show that he was capable of accomplishing the tasks set out before him and performing them scholastically with distinction.

While the Löwenklau family basked in a rich and nearly untroubled life, a dark and menacing cloud formed itself against them in the southwest. Napoleon III, initially president of France, was elevated to emperor. Though it gave the Löwenklaus no reason to celebrate, the appointment was a welcome sight for Captain Richemonte and his adopted son Henri, who up until now had waited in vain for an opportunity to carry out their plans.

As soon as the nephew of the famous Corsican became emperor, it stood to reason that all those who clung to the traditions of the former regime and had supported the former emperor in his exploits would take advantage of the current opportunity to serve him. They were not to be denied.

Napoleon III, who by no means possessed the immense mental faculties of his uncle, did what he could to emulate his predecessor. He was pleased to be able to step into his shoes, yet it was nothing more than an imitation of the great emperor's accomplishments.

What benefited Napoleon III was the current political situation in Europe. The crown shined with what many thought to be the genuine article. The glitter with which he adorned himself was mistaken for the brilliance of a diamond. What his uncle had accomplished through sheer genius by becoming emperor over half the world, the nephew sought to replicate through clever manipulation and sleight of hand maneuvers. He hoped that his escapades would sway the diplomats and endear himself to the world.

People marveled at his understanding of politics, which is exactly what he intended. After all, he was enjoying the recognition and admiration of the masses. If the first Napoleon had understood how to cultivate genius among the lower classes of the people, then his nephew imitated him here as well by never missing an opportunity to assemble for himself such vessels, suitable to cast a glimmer of artificial light on his precarious throne.

What actual worth these men possessed became apparent once his throne collapsed. Perhaps there were only two men who had actually understood his throne's worth, or rather the lack of it – Bismarck[11.1] and Moltke,[11.2] under whose wielding the entire house of cards of his reign came tumbling down.

One such elevated patriot, Count Jules Rallion, who considered himself belonging to the emperor's inner circle, had already demonstrated his honor by sidestepping Gebhard von Löwenklau's challenge. He had fled out of cowardice, only to return immediately after Gebhard's departure, seeking to ingratiate himself into Ida's former good graces. He was instead met by disdain and his advances were rejected. Not only was the reprimand painful to bear, he had to witness the departure and eventual marriage of his beautiful cousin to a German officer.

His hate for Löwenklau steadily grew and quickly included Kunz von Goldberg, who had managed to capture not only the heart of his other cousin, but also the approval of their austere aunt. How he would have enjoyed getting revenge on the Germans! But sadly, he found no suitable opportunity. He possessed neither the wherewithal nor courage to accomplish it.

Even though he lacked both of these qualities, though, he managed to weasel his way into Napoleon's court. A count's nobility and peerage were sufficient relief to mitigate the disappointment of not being able to bring the advantage of his own nobility to fruition. The outcome was that his underhanded and selfish aspirations were perceived in a positive light by a splendor-seeking king bent on furthering his influence and power base.

Rallion knew how to impress the empress and win her favor. It was thus widely known that the best way to gain the ear of the ruling couple was through the count's influence. This certainly appealed to the enterprising Captain Richemonte, who was polite when the situation required it and inconsiderate of others when it suited him. At last, Richemonte found an opportunity to make himself useful to the count. He was thus admitted into his circle, after which it wasn't difficult for his diabolical nature to gain a certain influence over the weak-minded Rallion.

Richemonte quickly found an occasion on which to recount the story of Baron de Sainte-Marie, who had died a well-respected marabout, leaving behind a son. The son was in possession of the necessary documents to legitimize himself as the rightful heir of Jeannette. Count Rallion listened with great interest at the unfolding saga as Richemonte explained how Napoleon himself had once spent a night there and in the process lost his heart to a beautiful mademoiselle.

"Who was this lady, Captain?" Rallion asked quickly.

"My sister!"

"What? You have a sister?"

"Yes, my worthy Count."

"A sister who was admired by Bonaparte?" Rallion asked, surprised. "How is it that you haven't introduced me to her? I should take exception to that, Captain. A lady who merited special consideration by our great emperor would have been received as *persona grata* at court. You've committed a great sin of omission, one which I'm reluctant to forgive."

"It was not my intention to commit this indiscretion, dear Count," Richemonte apologized. "Had it been possible for me to introduce you to my sister, I certainly would have done so. You see, she no longer resides in France, but has instead relocated to Germany."

Rallion looked at Richemonte in astonishment. "To Germany?" he asked. "How could she possibly think of settling down with the enemies of our beloved great emperor?"

"She would most certainly not have used quite the same descriptive words you have chosen," Richemonte allowed. "She wasn't worth the emperor's attention. She rebuffed him, choosing instead a mere German lieutenant, who she eventually married."

"Really? Was she married in Germany?"

Richemonte nodded sadly. "Unfortunately, that's precisely what happened."

"Ridiculous! What a travesty!" exclaimed the count fiercely. "How dare she turn her back on the country of her birth. And yet, I'm certainly acquainted with other wenches who have chosen those impertinent German barbarians over us. One should address these sorts of women with more than mere disrespect. I am telling you this, even though the one whom we spoke of is your sister. I am speaking as a patriot, and I trust you won't hold my comments against me."

"I take no offense. It couldn't be further from my thoughts! My sister's disloyalty has brought about such revulsion in me that I've broken off all contact with her."

"Really? You don't keep in touch?"

"No, though I am thinking of re-establishing a line of communication with my brother-in-law, via an advocate. It's this family, after all, who had the audacity to take up residence and possession of the Jeannette estate. The rightful owner is actually the Baron de Sainte-Marie, whom I have told you about."

"You don't say!" the count said, stepping back in surprise. "Is that what happened? Perhaps this set of circumstances is worthy of closer examination. What is the brother-in-law's name?"

"Löwenklau," said Richemonte.

The count did his best to mask his feelings, but couldn't avoid a show of dismay and amazement. "Löwenklau?" he called out. "How is that possible?"

"Are you familiar with the name?" asked the captain, just as surprised as the count.

"Oh, more than just in passing!" he replied. "What is his first name?"

"Hugo," said Richemonte.

The count contemplated the name for a brief moment. "While I visited my aunt, I became acquainted with a Lieutenant von Löwenklau who was proud of the fact that his father was well thought of by the old barbarian, Marshall Blücher."

"No doubt he was referring to Hugo, his own father."

"He went by the first name of Gebhard."

"That's right," Richemonte said. "I haven't been in Germany for some time, but I have made inquiries about the family. Hugo von Löwenklau has a son who goes by Gebhard."

"Ah, now I recall something else," said Rallion. "My aunt found out that this Hugo von Löwenklau married a Parisian woman, Margot Richemonte."

"That is my sister," confirmed the captain. "His son, this Gebhard we just spoke of, married a French lady by the name of Ida de Rallion."

The count's expression took on a darker shade, a pronounced sign of an irrepressible hate. "And this Ida de Rallion is my cousin," he said.

Richemonte searched the count's face. His shrewdness allowed him to come to the right conclusion. Such hate could only stem from a lost inheritance or spurned love, perhaps even both at the same time.

"I hope this cousin, who I may also refer to as disloyal, hasn't caused you much grief?" asked Richemonte.

The count showed his frustration by making a fist. "We were nearly betrothed to each other," he revealed. "But if your sister preferred a lieutenant to an emperor, then I suppose I shouldn't wonder that my own cousin decided to favor such a one over me. Damn, how I loathe those Germans! And I especially hate anyone by the name of Löwenklau, or anyone remotely connected to their breed!"

The captain slowly nodded his head in agreement. He gritted his teeth, a sure sign that he was angry about something. And yet, a miniscule smile played across his face, one that a more observant man than the count would have attributed to the fact the anger was strangely appealing to him.

"My hate for the family seems to coincide with yours," he said, secretly observing Rallion. "I would give much to be able to exterminate the whole lot of them!"

"That's exactly my desire!" Rallion exclaimed. By applauding his forthrightness, the count had unknowingly taken the bait. "Unfortunately, my influence doesn't reach that far. All I can do is grit my teeth and shake my fists at them. Nothing more, my dear Captain."

"And yet we have the means at our disposal to deal those Löwenklaus a decisive blow," Richemonte said thoughtfully.

"How so?" asked Rallion, beginning to pay more attention.

"By forcing them to forfeit Jeannette."

"Ah, really! That's true! All that remains then is for your protégé to be recognized as the Baron de Sainte-Marie."

"Exactly! Nothing stands in our way. We have all the necessary documents on hand."

"May I examine them?"

"With your permission, I will procure them and also introduce you to the one whom you refer to as my protégé."

Rallion smiled crookedly. "I would be delighted. It shouldn't take too much to invoke the emperor's curiosity. It is my hope that he will ask to speak to both of you. I imagine he will take up your cause once he hears that Bonaparte had an interest in your sister. But to be able to do so, I need to be better informed about the whole matter than I am at present. Would you please explain to me how your sister met the emperor?"

Richemonte was only too happy to comply. His report dealt with the hold-up in the Argonne Forest as well as Napoleon's overnight stay at Jeannette. This, however, was the only truthful part of the account. He then embellished, fabricating events and twisting the truth, all in an effort to portray himself in the best possible light.

"So that's how it happened!" the count commented when he finished. "Interesting. It's a most intriguing tale! I must confess to you, Captain, that I felt a warm sympathy for you the first time we met. Now that I have a clearer understanding of your circumstances, I think an opportunity will present itself to vent your frustrations against this German family. I am not a man to drive another to destruction, but I will never be able to forgive a Löwenklau. Let's shake on it, as a sign of our commitment to support each other when it counts. We need to show those who have offended us so openly that a Frenchman will not tolerate an endless barrage of insults."

Nothing could have pleased Richemonte more than this offer. He immediately accepted by reaching for the outstretched hand offered by his new ally.

"I'm committed to this cause with all my heart," Richemonte said. "It lies in each man's nature. Yes, it's even the noble duty of everyone who calls himself a man not to dismiss an offense without seeking revenge. We will fulfill this pledge by bringing it to reality."

"You're right," Rallion said. "I have been instructed to appear before the empress this very day, and I will not hesitate to bring this unusual matter concerning the Baron de Sainte-Marie to her attention. Roman de Sainte-Marie's complicity in his wife's murder should have no bearing on the son. Insofar as this man is the son of a common girl, it shouldn't present a problem either. The rights of a nobleman supersede those of a commoner. Present yourself with your charge tomorrow at my residence and I hope to enlighten you with the prospects that may lie ahead."

The proposed meeting took place as scheduled the following morning. It was evident that Richemonte's hopes of carrying out his plan were finally becoming a reality. The emperor insisted on a private meeting, which included the empress, who was a remnant of the highly proclaimed Spanish court. She prided herself in gleaning things not commonly meant for a fine lady. The empress was curious to learn about the last love of Napoleon, and prepared herself in advance to meet the man who would serve this delicacy for her.

Captain Richemonte knew exactly how to take advantage of the situation. He illustrated to the emperor his earlier adventures and assignments as vanguard, portraying himself most favorably. In fact, he made himself to appear as a martyr. According to his account, he had left the army with the assurance of returning one day, validated and exonerated.

Napoleon III asked to see all the relevant material that pertained to the long lost son of the dead Baron de Sainte-Marie. When he was finished examining them, he declared that he was satisfied with their legitimacy and was prepared to turn the matter over into the hands of the most competent professionals.

CHAPTER TWELVE

A Formidable Accomplice

While Richemonte was outlining Henri's legitimacy to the emperor, Gebhard was returning home from a trip. So it was that the entire family was on hand to witness the shocking news delivered by a government official. It seemed that the former Baron de Sainte-Marie, absent for so many years, had died and left an heir, his son, Arthur de Sainte-Marie. The aspiring baron had now returned to his home country, asking to be recognized and claiming his rightful inheritance.

The family immediately enlisted the services of a highly respected lawyer. After reviewing the documents, the lawyer simply shrugged his shoulders and promised to look into it. The advocate sought out the advice of his contemporaries, who replied in much the same manner – by shrugging their shoulders.

The Löwenklau family soon received further correspondence from Paris, explaining that the claimant had satisfied the authorities with his documents. The baron's son had even been legitimized by the emperor himself. The Löwenklaus had to decide whether or not to embark on a lengthy and expensive litigation, whose end was uncertain, to which the answer was a unanimous no. Hugo and Gebhard decided to do the honorable thing and quietly relinquish their claim to Jeannette. Truth be known, they knew that the new owner could have pressed them to pay compensation for the time they had been in possession of the estate.

It was no small loss and the family sought to console themselves. Although they had to surrender the considerable estate, however, they were by no means on the road to the poorhouse. After all, they were still in possession of two other holdings that no one could take from them. But as was often the case, that which seemed impossible could turn into a frightful reality. This emerging thunderstorm in the southwest had struck but the first of many lightning bolts. It remained to be seen if all its energy had been spent, or if some new devilry was in the works.

The illegitimate Baron de Sainte-Marie had arrived and taken up residence at Jeannette. He did not act of his own volition, but was under the constant prodding and supervision of the old captain. Richemonte's goal was twofold. Even though he wasn't the principal owner, his cousin, the newly appointed Baron de Sainte-Marie, was under his control and did what he desired. Secondly, he was able to finally avenge himself on his lifelong enemies.

The new baron played a wretched role, unaware of its repercussions. Only once did he attempt to challenge the captain's authority, but to his chagrin was quickly and masterfully rebuked. Richemonte made it clear that he was in charge of all his affairs.

"But who is the master here?" Henri interjected. "You or I?"

"I am," was the firm and convincing response.

"Really? Who is the baron here? You or I?"

"Of course you're the baron," Richemonte said, "but only as a result of your actions as a murderer. You shot and killed the rightful heir to take his place. I'm telling you once and for all that you're not going to control me! I'm warning you, Henri. If you continue to provoke me, it'll cost you everything you have, including your nobility."

"What? Are you implying that you'll go so far as to accuse me publicly?"

"If it comes to that."

"But it was you who helped me to remove the heir."

"Prove it!"

"Well," began the ill-prepared baron, "prove that I alone was responsible, without your complicity."

Richemonte looked down at him. "Don't speak like a child! I'm certainly not going to reveal how I plan to deal with you. You know full well that you're not on par with me. Be content with the knowledge that you, a former spy, are now a nobleman, have a worthy title and name, and lead a comfortable and carefree life. You should be grateful that you got your wish, namely that you now possess the most beautiful wife on the earth!"

"You mean Liama?"

"Who else?" asked Richemonte in surprise.

"She's not my wife!" Henri argued lamely.

"That's none of my concern. If you're so stupid, having failed to consummate your marriage, then it's your own fault."

"We haven't even been married. She has remained a follower of Islam."

"No one needs to know that!"

"And she hasn't allowed me to touch her," he whined.

"Your manner in dealing with her is deplorable," chided Richemonte. "Your infatuation with her goes past your ears[12.1] and clouds your intellect. You pussyfoot around her like a pigeon handler with his doves. She's completely under your control, and yet you don't dare touch her. Someone else could make sense out of this, but not I."

There was a simple explanation that eluded Richemonte. When faced with chaste and pure femininity, a villain is often powerless to act. The captain, well-acquainted with his cousin's idiosyncrasies, could have come to the same conclusion. Both men had conspired and tricked Liama into leaving her home. She had trusted them to keep their word and so she kept her side of the bargain in order to save the life of her father and husband.

She had plenty of opportunities to observe her captors, which had made her suspicious. Liama was filled with doubt, even questioning whether or not they had fulfilled their promises. She demanded proof that her father and husband were still alive, but was never the recipient of such news. If she despised the two Frenchmen before, her fears for her loved ones and being constantly ignored by Richemonte led her into a deeper hatred for both men.

Liama often contemplated escaping her tormentors, but didn't know how to accomplish it. She didn't understand French, much less speak it. She was treated almost like a prisoner and was keenly aware that she was rarely left without supervision.

Richemonte had initially been against the maddening love that had enveloped his cousin, but he had his reasons for consenting to this request. Prudence told him to keep a close eye on Liama, since she posed a formidable opposition to his plans.

The poor, betrayed woman would have eventually carried out her plans, by fleeing her confinement, if it hadn't been for a singular, life-changing event. She became the mother of a beautiful daughter, in whose innocent face she perceived Saadi's features. The earlier union to Saadi, blessed by the sheik, had been consummated, and now its reminder came through in the wonderful form of a child. Since she couldn't give her love to the father of the girl, she concentrated all her efforts on the baby. She nearly forgot her misery and decided to live her life for her daughter. It was her love that gave her strength and perseverance, enabling her to fend off the demands and advances of the baron.

Henri was relentless in his pursuit of her, visiting her daily in the rooms allotted to her, rooms which she wasn't allowed to leave. He tried to work his way into her favor by granting her more freedom of movement. Yet her woman's intuition revealed to her his weakness and she realized that the baron was completely powerless against the captain. Liama understood for the first time that it was actually Richemonte who dictated what transpired on the estate. It seemed to her the more she resisted the baron, the more his insatiable desire drove him to possess her.

Memories emerged from his past, robbing him of peace and tranquility. Dark, sinister shadows moved through his dreams, stirring up recollections of shots and the splattering of blood around him. When he would finally awake, it would seem as though he had actually fought with real adversaries. Henri moaned and whimpered to himself during those times.

There was only one man who was able to calm him – the old captain, who started with threats, but then had to resort to action, all in an effort to banish the ghosts that had taken hold of the baron's sanity.

Such attacks, once a seldom occurrence, were now taking place more frequently. On some occasions, Richemonte's threats and cajoling were insufficient to quiet him down. While in this state, besieged by fear, anxiety, and despair, Henri called for Liama, and Richemonte was clever enough to cave in to his pleas. Liama, the victim, had become the solace for the one who had deceived her. One comforting look from her was sufficient enough to bring Henri back to sanity. Perhaps it was this simple kindness that saved him from a life of utter madness.

Richemonte knew of her burning desire to be free from her invisible shackles. If she managed to escape from her confinement, it would lead to his undoing. It required constant vigilance to keep an eye on her and it stood to reason that his inconsiderate and unscrupulous nature would eventually lead him to carry out a final solution, thus ensuring the secrecy of his past. But just as dangerous was the baron's madness, whose outbursts could only be managed and subdued through Liama's intervention, therefore necessitating keeping her alive.

Liama had given birth to a girl, later baptizing her with the name Marion. Although Henri knew she wasn't his offspring, he accepted her because of his passion for Liama. Her young life was the unseen chain that confined the unhappy mother. Liama would never have abandoned her child. The astute captain comprehended this certainty and so shifted his attention to the child, thus ensuring the mother's cooperation. This was more than enough to derail any of her thoughts of escaping.

The surrounding townsfolk were given little news of the family situation. They knew that the baron was married to a foreigner, but they dared not ask for more information for fear of being reprimanded. Every once in a while, a tradesman would catch a glimpse of the beautiful, secretive woman, but why she chose to live in such seclusion was a mystery to all. Then again, perhaps the truth lay in the fact that upper class people, especially ones of nobility, were different, resorting to their own whims.

Even when Count Rallion came to visit Richemonte at Jeannette, Liama refrained from socializing. The captain knew the most innocent encounter could lead to the truth being revealed. It was highly unlikely for the count to insist on seeing her. Rallion inquired out of politeness as to her well-being, but was otherwise indifferent to her affairs, choosing not to pursue it. When his visit would come to an end, he sent his regards to the mistress of the house, and that was all. His mannerisms were perhaps somewhat unusual, but understandable under the circumstances.

Rallion and Richemonte had come to appreciate each other as time passed. Each man regarded the other as a suitable means to an end. If the count was cowardly and without scruples, then the captain showed the same cowardice, coupled with inconsideration. The former carefully wielded his plans out of cunning, while the latter forged ahead, sometimes with near reckless abandon. Both men complemented each other whenever they pursued the same goals, which occurred frequently.

Their private conversations often turned to the Löwenklau family. They enjoyed an immeasurable sense of satisfaction knowing that they had succeeded in displacing the family from Jeannette and their joy would have climbed to new heights if they could have devised a way to wipe them out entirely.

On a particular evening, the two men were occupied with this now familiar discussion while sitting in the captain's study. They employed a near diabolical shrewdness, seeking to find a plausible way to rid themselves of the Löwenklau problem. Yet for all their efforts, they couldn't come up with a satisfactory result. They parted company for the evening, each one intending to get some rest.

It was Richemonte's custom to bring his financial affairs in order before retiring for the night. He was in possession of a considerable sum of money, having just received it from a grain merchant. Since he purposed to count it and record the amount in his ledger, he pulled up a chair to his writing desk. He quickly completed the task and had just locked the money away when he thought he heard soft footsteps in the hallway. He listened carefully. Yes, there was the noise again, steps in the hall. Someone was out there, creeping closer.

The steps stopped near his door. *Who could it be?* he thought. *Perhaps a servant with an important message? Not very likely. I've just counted the money. A thief, perhaps?*

Richemonte quickly made up his mind to be prepared and extinguished the light. He took his loaded *terzerol*[12.2] from his night table and crawled into bed. He pulled the covers up to his neck, thereby hiding the fact that he was clad in street clothes. With the little pistol in his hand, he lay still, waiting for what he suspected would come next.

He didn't have to wait for long. Almost imperceptibly, a key was inserted into the door lock. He had had the foresight to remove his own key, and slid the bolt into place. According to his understanding of locks, it wasn't possible to enter the room without first bypassing the bolt via a proper key. To his surprise, though, he heard the bolt retract quietly. He distinctly felt a cool draft as the door slowly swung open.

The captain listened intently, holding his breath without realizing it. The room was perfectly still. He couldn't detect even the slightest sound. It was obvious that the intruder wanted to satisfy himself that the captain was sleeping. Richemonte intended to play the part, and breathed the slow, rhythmic breaths of feigned slumber. The act must have convinced the intruder, because Richemonte heard soft steps approach his bedside.

There was another pause, followed by a quick beam of light, which lit up the corner of the room. The captain kept his eyes closed for a moment, then dared to open one just a fraction. He made out the figure of a man, clad in dark clothing, standing only three feet from his bed. He was holding a small pocket lamp, illuminating the sleeper. There was no sign of a weapon and his face was shrouded with a mask as he observed the captain's sleeping form. Richemonte continued his deception with his calm, regular breathing, but was prepared to act at the slightest sign of danger by withdrawing his weapon from under the bed covers.

The masked man seemed satisfied. He left the bedside and noiselessly approached the writing desk. In doing so, the shine of the lamp fell on the door, and the captain noticed that the door was locked again. The thief was clearly experienced and knew what he was doing. As Richemonte watched, he reached into his pocket and retrieved a key, which fit perfectly into the slot of the box where he kept the money. The man opened it, removed the money bag, pocketing it with the familiarity of someone who had regularly handled it before. He quietly closed the box, locked it, and pocketed the key. All that remained was for him to turn around and leave in like manner.

This, however, Richemonte did not intend to allow. The captain was clever enough to realize that he had to gain control of the small lamp if he was going to have any success in overpowering the thief. He had to avoid a struggle in the dark at all cost. Just as the thief turned from the bureau, Richemonte jumped out of his bed and leaped past the startled man, grabbing his lamp in the process. He placed himself between the man and the door, allowing the light to shine on his quarry while he held his *terzerol*.

"*Halt!*" Richemonte commanded quietly but firmly.

The thief was caught completely off guard, failing to move a muscle. Then, having composed himself, he turned toward the window, abandoning the attempt to escape through the door.

"I said stop!" said the captain, this time more forcefully. "That window is not for you, you vagabond."

Richemonte couldn't believe his eyes. The man didn't seem perturbed at all. Instead, he was holding a long knife, prepared to use it to force his way out.

"Man, put that knife away this instant, or I'll fire!" said Richemonte decisively. The thief realized he meant business and lowered his hand.

"Drop the knife, or I'll shoot!" repeated the captain. "One... two—!"

But before he got to three, the thief put the knife away. He may well have been a bold man, but he was sensible enough to figure out that a knife was no match for a bullet.

"Put the money back on the bureau!"

The man hesitated, but as Richemonte took a step forward, still pointing the *terzerol*, he turned around and retrieved the bag, placing it on the desk.

"Now, remove your mask!" the captain ordered.

"I won't do that!"

The thief had remained silent up until now. The captain nearly winced at the unexpected sound of his voice.

"Hang it all! Did I hear you right?" he replied, astonished. "You don't intend to uncover your face?"

"No!"

"I believe I know the answer!"

The man remained silent.

"You're ashamed to reveal it," Richemonte continued. There was something about his voice that reminded him of one of his servants. "It's more disgraceful to steal from your master than from a stranger. Am I right, Jacques?"

Still no answer. If the thief was affected in any way by the captain's guess, he didn't show it.

"Well then," contemplated the captain, "if you choose to remain silent and refuse to show your face, it'll be worse for you. I'll be forced to summon the servants. If you were co-operative, I might be persuaded to deal with this nocturnal visit differently."

Richemonte wasn't the type to show kindness in this sort of situation, yet he was struck with an idea, one which in itself was more profitable than if he exposed and punished the thief.

"Is that really true?" asked the man. "Are you prepared to reconsider your position?"

"Yes."

"Then give me your word of honor!"

"Ridiculous! One doesn't give his word to a rogue. Remember that! I didn't say I was going to absolve you of any punishment. However," Richemonte hinted, "it's possible that it could occur, should you prove to be more compliant. For now, though, I'm not going to make any promises."

"It seems I'm in your hands," said the thief in resignation. "I hadn't counted on that damned pistol. I have no choice but to give myself over, whether into mercy or punishment."

"All right! Remove your mask."

The man obeyed. He removed the mask, revealing the face of a man approaching thirty years of age. This was certainly not a face one would characterize as belonging to a scoundrel. His features were smooth, nearly handsome. Richemonte was reminded that it was often the unassuming faces that were most apt to fool people.

"Jacques!" exclaimed the captain. "So I wasn't wrong after all when I thought I recognized your voice. My own servant breaks into my study!"

Jacques caught something comforting in the old man's tone, and his facial features took on a nearly flippant expression. "But he was caught in the act!"

"Yes, man! Getting caught breaking in is much worse than merely breaking in. At least, that's the way I see it. You made a dreadful mess of it!"

"Captain, I certainly won't do that again!"

"What do you mean? Breaking in or getting caught?"

"That," Jacques began coyly, "I'm not sure of."

Even though the old man tried, he was unable to maintain an angry face. Ordinarily he would have ground his teeth in his characteristic manner, but this incident was unique.

"Are you crazy?" he asked at last. "Are those the manners of a scoundrel who's been caught in the act?"

"No," laughed the man. "They are the words of a trustworthy man who's not afraid to say what he thinks."

"Perhaps, but you still don't know if you'll cease with your break-ins after you've been admonished."

Jacques' expression was inscrutable. "You're right. I don't know."

"*Zounds!* Scoundrel! What am I supposed to make of you? Haven't you learned that only genuine remorse leads to forgiveness?"

"I've heard it, yes, but I don't believe it."

"Jacques, you're hopeless."

"A fact that could prove profitable for me. I've often observed how it fares well for the worst of people, while the honest ones are mostly unlucky and miserable."

"But that's not the natural course," Richemonte pointed out, "and one certainly can't proclaim the exception to be the norm."

"Certainly! In fact, I've chosen to emulate the very embodiment of this exception."

"Really? Who would this 'exception' be?"

"You, yourself!"

"What! Me? Damn it, don't play that game with me. It could easily lead to your demise."

Jacques was not to be deterred. If he had momentarily faltered when he was caught, he was now in control of himself. A cynical smile played across his face, as he shrugged his shoulders. "Is it really your intent to lead me there, Captain?"

"Do you think I'm joking?"

"Yes, that's exactly what I think."

"That's too much! I'm telling you, now I'm even less inclined to be lenient."

In response, his servant bowed almost irreverently. "Captain," he responded, "I believe that you'll show restraint. I know of a way to persuade you."

"Really? I'm most curious to see what that could be!"

The thief contemplated his next words carefully and then, in a carefree gesture, tilted his head to the side. "There's no risk on my part to fill you in," he said. "Captain, may I suggest that we continue our discussion openly and calmly?"

Richemonte's eyes widened in amazement at Jacques' placid and audacious manner. "You've almost convinced me to allow you to negotiate your own terms," he said.

"That's how I see it," the servant replied with a smirk.

"Bastard!" Richemonte looked at him indignantly.

"Pah! It's because I'm a charlatan that you can best make use of my talents. If you recall, my first servitude was under Count Rallion."

"Why the reminder? It was the count's recommendation that persuaded me to consider your services."

The servant shrugged his shoulders, smiling wryly. "Don't hold too much stock in that," he continued. "Why do you think the count recommended me? It wasn't what you think, Captain. On the contrary, he was happy to be rid of me!"

Richemonte nearly dropped his *terzerol*, taken aback by Jacques' insolence. An indecisive expression appeared on his face. "Hang it all, man! I'm getting confused with your brand of logic."

"Not I, Captain! You see, the count put me in charge of certain matters that weren't suitable for just anyone. I therefore gained considerable insight into his affairs, ones which you wouldn't want strangers to look into. The count probably noticed that my respect for him started to wane the more I became familiar with his dealings. He probably reasoned that he could benefit from releasing me under good circumstances, and it just so happened that you were in a position to acquire a dependable and discreet servant. He naturally recommended me to you favorably, all the while happy to have me gone without having to face the repercussions of having me dismissed outright."

"If that's really true, then I'm not beholden to him."

"Believe me, it's true," Jacques said. "When I entered your employ, I made the same discovery that I made when I worked for the count."

"What discovery do you mean, you scoundrel?"

"Just as with Rallion before you, I am expected to perform in extraordinary circumstances without receiving extraordinary compensation for my services."

"Dammit! I could strangle you for your impertinence!" the old man yelled.

"Oh, and speaking of strangulation, I've heard that it's one of the more pleasant ways to die!" he remarked obstinately. "For example, I fulfill the role of guard over the baroness and her little daughter. This is no small feat, considering it requires constant vigilance, day and night. However, a bonus for all my hard work has failed to materialize."

"Your audacity is too much to handle!"

"Suit yourself!" Jacques said with a shrug. "Luck has always passed me by. My goal was to earn enough money so that I could live from my investments without worry. That goal seemed to elude me until I came to a decision to advance my plan. I noticed today that you received a nice little sum. I already had a key to your box at my disposal—"

"Ah! That's it!" interrupted Richemonte. "Who manufactured the duplicate key?"

"I did," he said slyly. "I might as well tell you that I was previously a locksmith. I knew it was your custom to slide the bolt at night after you turn in. One day, while you were absent, I examined your lock and adjusted the mechanism so that the bolt would slide back when a key was inserted from the outside."

"Then you also had a key for my door lock?" Richemonte asked.

"Naturally! Tonight I intended to procure my long sought after bonus. Everything was ready and the thought that something might go wrong hadn't occurred to me. Could you please explain how it was that you came to be on your guard?"

This was turning out to be a most unconventional conversation between a master and servant. The captain, who was a villain in his own right, couldn't understand how his servant had mustered the impertinence to speak to him in such manner. He simply couldn't believe his ears.

"Scoundrel!" he growled. "Did I hear you right? You're demanding that I supply you a clarification of how I came on to you?"

"No, I didn't demand it, Captain. I merely asked."

"The devil can divulge it, but not I! I thought I might go easy on you, but now I can see what a calculating patron you really are. I'm going to think twice before allowing a softer judgment to take place."

"Oh, I'm sure you won't venture into anything that might cause you harm," Jacques said. "You're much too clever for that."

"What harm could possibly come to me when you're safely fettered and tucked behind bars?"

"The ensuing fallout, if I should choose to unshackle my mouth."

The captain's eyes flared up in anger. Had he been able, he would have consumed the servant with fire.

"Heaven and hell!" he exclaimed. "Are you threatening me?"

"Yes," replied Jacques, as he drew himself up to his full height. "Do you really find that so surprising? I must admit, my break-in was carried out a bit too carelessly. I've always been cautious in such things. I considered that, if I should be caught, I shouldn't have to fear the outcome. If I looked a little shocked, it wasn't because of fright as much as merely being surprised in the act."

The captain fought to maintain his composure. He thought about lashing out against the upstart with his fists. He placed the *terzerol* on the table and clenched his fists, as though intending to strike. Jacques, on the other hand, didn't show the least bit of concern. Instead of being afraid, he stepped closer and spoke to his master cold-bloodedly.

"I certainly hope you're not intending to challenge me, Captain," he cautioned. "I'm not unfamiliar with hand-to-hand combat, having been trained as a soldier."

"What? You were a soldier?" Richemonte asked, gritting his teeth. "Since when do thieves merit the honor of a soldier?"

"But it's true. Thieves, robbers… even murderers have served. They're not only elevated to soldiers, they're promoted to officers! It's possible for the worst scoundrel to advance to the rank of captain, or legionnaire, or even higher."

Richemonte's upper lip lifted awkwardly. "What or whom do you mean by that remark?" he demanded.

"Whom? Hmm. That could be very revealing. All I'll tell you for now is that I gained my experience as a soldier in Algiers."

The old man's moustache dropped immediately, and the gritting stopped. "What?" he asked dumbfounded. "You served in Africa?"

"Yes."

"In what capacity?"

"With the *Chasseurs d'Afrique*," he laughed.

Richemonte's face paled. He started to wonder if Jacques had been referring to him earlier when he stated that the biggest scoundrel could elevate himself to the rank of captain.

"Damn it, why didn't you tell me any of this before?"

Jacques shrugged his shoulders. "I didn't think that you would be interested."

"How long were you there?"

"Long enough to have picked up some Arabic."

The old man involuntarily stepped back. An uncomfortable feeling shuddered through him. "Ah!" he said almost spitefully. "So you understand Arabic, then?"

"Tolerably."

"You were instructed to watch over the baroness. Did she speak in Arabic?"

"Yes, she did."

"With you?"

"No, not one word."

"With whom, then?"

"With the toddler, little Marion."

"Don't lie to me," Richemonte said, offended.

"Why should I lie? I see no reason to deceive you."

"How could she speak to the toddler, who only babbles to herself."

"Haven't you ever observed a mother and her child?" Jacques asked. "Haven't you listened to a young mother talking to her newborn, calling it all sorts of sweet names and sharing what's on her heart?"

"Ridiculous. Nothing but old wives' tales."

Jacques sighed softly at the captain's ignorance on such matters. "No, it's true. A mother's heart is full of love and she desires to share it with her infant, knowing full well that she doesn't understand a single word. But when the infant's eyes look into the mother's, she allows herself to believe that her beautiful child understood something."

"Nothing but foolishness!"

"I don't think so. What she speaks about is often relevant and fruitful. If a typical mother, who's not lacking in company, speaks often to her child, how much more will a mother who's afraid, lonely, and confined just like the current baroness? What do you think she would say? What secrets will she entrust to the child?" The former *Chasseur d'Afrique*'s eyes revealed a sharp, triumphant look, which was directed at Richemonte.

"Well, what for instance?" he asked haltingly.

"She will disclose why she's so poor, so miserable. She'll speak about her home in the desert, about the cruel deaths of the *Beni Hassan*, about Saadi, the real father of the child—"

"Heaven and hell!"

"She'll talk about the *fakihadschi*, Malek Omar," continued the servant undeterred. "And about his son, an accomplice, Ben Ali, who really can't be his son."

"You're making this up."

"I'm only repeating that which I've heard."

"You must have been dreaming."

"Oh, on the contrary, I was wide awake and very attentive. For now, all this is speculative. Its significance would only come into play in front of a judge. All I need to know right now is if you're still intending to expose me as a thief?"

Richemonte was completely taken aback by his revelation. He stuck his hands into his pockets, as if the attempt to hide them might settle his rising anxiety.

"Sit down!" he instructed.

While Jacques took a seat, Richemonte paced back and forth, finally locking the door. He then came back and addressed Jacques in a suppressed voice. "So, is it really true?" he inquired. "You overheard the baroness when she spoke to her child?"

"Yes, Captain."

"And she actually spoke of the things you mentioned earlier?"

"How else would I know about her circumstances?"

"What did she actually talk about?"

The servant's face took on a calculating and reserved expression. Had a painter been present and observed his face, he would have been able to portray the very personification of shrewdness onto his canvass. "About many things," he replied.

"I need to hear them all!" Richemonte demanded, slamming his fist on the table. "Do you understand? I have to know!"

"Hmm. I can't really say."

"Why not?" asked Richemonte.

"Because I can't recall every detail this instant."

"Then reflect. Try to remember."

"It's not as simple as you might think," Jacques insisted. "Demanding it won't help. It could take days, even weeks, before it becomes clear again."

"Ah, now I understand you, you rogue. Just don't think that your vague intimations, which you only heard in passing, could in any way place me in a predicament."

Jacques merely smiled knowingly. "Oh, they're more than just vague whispers. Besides, why isn't the baroness given the opportunity to learn French? Why is it that no one else is allowed to speak to her?"

"That's none of your damned business!" Richemonte replied testily. "Let's get something straight. It's not up to you to raise issues that don't concern you. It's incumbent upon you to answer me without reservation. Now, tell me truthfully, have you spoken with the baroness?"

"No, not a word!"

"You're lying! I don't believe you!" Richemonte countered.

"Well, then you take me for being dumber than I am. It was important for me to glean as much as I could. Therefore, I had to pretend that I didn't understand any of it. If the baroness had suspected in the slightest that I understood even a little of her ramblings, she would have stopped. I would have waited in vain to satisfy my curiosity."

"You weren't supposed to eavesdrop on her, Jacques!"

"What was I supposed to do, Captain? Cover my ears?"

Richemonte was too preoccupied with what may have been revealed about his past to recognize that his servant was taking advantage of his position, even playing with him.

"I'm going to inquire with my daughter-in-law," he said, asserting himself. "I'm perfectly capable of drawing the truth out of her. I'll get to the bottom of this and see if you've been telling the truth."

"By all means, go ahead. I have nothing to lose."

"I certainly hope so. Now, tell me, what were you planning to do with that money if you were successful?"

"What else could I do in the interim but to bury it?"

"Weren't you concerned that you would be suspected of the theft?"

"I don't see how," Jacques said.

"It would have been obvious to all that the thief had to come from within."

"Pah! I wouldn't have left a trace of my handiwork. None of the locks were tampered with. You were in possession of the only key. The theft would have remained a mystery and never been solved. As I said, I would have buried the money in a safe place."

"What about your skeleton keys?" Richemonte asked. "I naturally would have conducted a thorough search and they would have incriminated you."

Jacques shook his head. "You would have searched all over and found nothing. I would have buried them as well."

"Yet coincidence and treachery are the devil's tools. Something could have tripped you up." Richemonte searched Jacques' face. "The safest option for you would have been to flee."

Jacques didn't miss the clever way that the captain had laid the bait. "Do you think me a novice? I'm not that foolish. I would have drawn attention to myself if I had fled!"

"Hmm! I'm beginning to see that I've underestimated you. I naturally assumed that, since you got caught, you hadn't prepared yourself adequately, a reflection of your inexperience."

"I've already told you that I was convinced I could have extricated myself if I was caught. In other circumstances, I certainly would have escaped."

"Are you that sure of yourself?" Richemonte asked.

"Absolutely! A determined robber has to be prepared to remove anyone in his way rather than risk capture and imprisonment."

"I can see that you're someone to be reckoned with."

Jacques nodded self-assuredly. "Possibly!"

"You talk about a break-in as though you've already had previous experience."

"I won't deny it."

"Even that you're prepared to involve yourself again?"

"Certainly not here. You can rest assured that your cash box is safe from now on."

"But elsewhere?"

The thief examined his master for a moment while he considered his next words. "It all depends on how you plan to deal with me," he said at last. "If you dismiss me without a good referral, I wouldn't be able to find a suitable position and I would be forced to look after my own interests."

"What if I dispense with the termination?"

"Are you willing to keep the fox in the stall?" Jacques asked suggestively.

"No," Richemonte answered. "I would rather attract a different sort of animal. A leopard is well-suited for the hunt and mayhem, but a smart man knows how to reel him in, training him for his purposes."

The servant nodded silently, aware of the implication. "I had considered something similar," he said. "Long before I inserted my key in your lock, I had devised a backup plan."

The old man, who had been slowly pacing back and forth, stopped in front of him.

"If that's true, Jacques," he said encouragingly, "then you're a man I can make use of. I'm inclined to let you off the hook."

"So that you can employ me as a leopard?" laughed Jacques.

"Exactly."

"Well, give it a try, Captain."

"Are you in agreement?"

Jacques chuckled casually. "Why not? But you have to make it worth my while."

"I'll see to it that you won't be lacking. But what's most important here is boldness, cunning, and deception."

"I have no shortage of those qualities. Tell me, Captain, how can I be of service to you?"

"Patience! Patience!" Richemonte said. "First of all, I have to be sure I can trust you."

"Aren't you assured of that?"

"You don't believe I'm going to trust you all of a sudden without giving it a second thought?"

"Haven't I proved, through this break-in, that you can depend on me in similar circumstances?"

Richemonte gave that some thought. "Perhaps. Yet... Hmm, I don't know. Something's missing that may yet prove vital."

"What?"

"Hmm. If only you understood German..."

Jacques rose from his chair. "Who told you that I don't?" he asked, laughing.

"Heavens! Do you understand German?"

"Tolerably," he said. "Perhaps more than just tolerably."

"Where did you learn to speak it?"

"From my governess."

Richemonte initially thought he was joking, but changed his mind when he saw Jacques' serious expression. "You really had a governess?"

"Several, in fact. Not one could last long. After all, I was a wild boy. My parents let me get into all sorts of mischief. Rather than being thankful, I can attribute all my problems to their leniency. It's their fault that I've become what I am."

"Who was your father?"

The thief stared ahead into the lantern's flickering light for a long minute without replying. *What thoughts from the past might be racing through his mind?* Richemonte wondered. *Is it a shadow from the lamp, or a sign of an inner tenderness?*

Suddenly, Jacques motioned dismissively with his hand. "Pah! One shouldn't concern himself with regrets from the past, but rather leave them be!" Jacques replied hoarsely, the tinge of softness fading quickly. "I'm sitting on top of a mountain, the snow on the verge of sliding down it in the form of an avalanche. Perhaps I'll be buried under it, or I'll avoid it with a last minute extrication."

Richemonte narrowed his eyes. "So who was your father?"

"Allow me to dispense with the answer. It can't benefit you, and it wouldn't make sense for me to fabricate a lie. Suffice it to say that my current circumstances weren't prophesied while I was still in the crib. It's of no consequence who I was a long time ago. I want to forget about it. I want to leave it where it belongs – in the past. I want to remain that which I've become."

The captain extended his hand toward him. "My thoughts exactly!" he said. "I can tell that I can depend on you. If you were able to cast a small glimpse into hidden things through the baroness' ramblings, then you've recognized that my fate wasn't a welcoming one. I concur with your assessment. Forget about the past, grasp the present, and plan for the future. I was able to accomplish it and I'm convinced you'll succeed in becoming master of your destiny. A man can't wrestle one iota more from his fate than he's actually worth. Can I depend on you?"

Jacques grasped the offered hand and shook it. "I'd like to think that I'll prove myself."

"All right," Richemonte said. "Now let me speak plainly. Are you reluctant to get involved in a dubious errand, particularly if it involves a sizeable reward?"

"Not at all."

"Even if it were to involve a difficult break-in?"

"I welcome the challenge."

"What if you were surprised in the act and someone tried to grab a hold of you?"

"Pah! I would ensure I was suitably armed."

"That means you would make good use of your weapons and defend yourself?" Richemonte asked.

"Absolutely. If someone attacked me, he would soon regret it."

Richemonte paused, coming to an important detail. "What sort of compensation would you ask for?"

"It would depend upon the complexity of the undertaking and the value of the reward, Monsieur."

"Both requirements have yet to be determined. I just need you to clarify something for me. You mentioned that you were a locksmith, and you intimated that you've held a position that wasn't an ordinary one."

Jacques nodded. "Correct on both counts. I fell from the lofty position I was born into, choosing instead to try my luck in worldly pursuits. I eventually became interested in the mechanics of locks. As luck would have it, one of my colleagues was experienced in the trade and was willing to take me on as an apprentice."

"I'm satisfied with your explanation," the captain finished. "It seems that this has turned out to be a most fortunate day for you. It was fitting that you chose to try your skill on my box. I trust I've laid your fears to rest and that you can remain in my employ?"

"Yes, I'm not concerned anymore."

"Even if you had doubts, let me dispel them with this gesture. Here, take this."

Richemonte opened the bag on his desk and removed a handful of gold pieces, giving them to his new confidant.

"Thank you, Monsieur!" replied Jacques, pocketing the money. "If this unexpected present is any indication of the upcoming venture, I'm satisfied that I'll have an opportunity to add to my resources. You'll be satisfied with my performance."

"I hope so! I'm expecting that you'll show me your finest quality. As far as the rest goes, we'll continue from here as though nothing has happened. Good night, Jacques!"

"Good night, Captain!"

The servant left quietly, walking to the part of the castle where the servants were housed. He opened the little lamp in his room and slumped into a chair. He supported his head in his hands and pondered the events of the evening. The flickering light cast shadows that enveloped his face. He wasn't paying attention to what was going through his own head. Was he thinking about his parents, on whom he had shouldered the blame for becoming the person that he was, a daring and skilled thief? It was hard to tell! Did he know himself? His thoughts railed within the confines of his mind without demanding of himself any accounting for his past. The wick of the lamp flickered a few times and then went out, rousing him from his musings.

"Darkness," he grumbled. "That's the way it is with the light of one's youth, luck and life. But I'm going to make sure that when I light the wick anew, it'll represent my new beginning, without worry and fear!"

It's all coming together, he thought, *and I'm glad I didn't misread the captain. He considers himself to be superior to me. He erroneously believes that he'll find a forthcoming, thankful, and pliable tool in me. He's decided to use me for his purposes until he no longer requires my skills. But that's where he's wrong. I'm prepared to assist him in his ventures only so long as it's to my advantage. But if he tries to betray me, he'll find out what I'm really capable of.*

CHAPTER THIRTEEN
A Fiendish Plot

The captain joined the count the following morning at breakfast. Contrary to his normally serious disposition, Richemonte's face seemed almost cheerful, a detail that didn't escape Rallion.

"What good news have you received so early that allows you to be in such a good mood?" asked the count.

"It wasn't this morning, dear Count," replied Richemonte. "It occurred last night, right after you left my room. The news is significant. In fact, it even concerns you."

"You're making me curious."

Richemonte smiled. "Do you remember the matter we discussed just before parting last night?"

"Of course! We were talking about the Löwenklau family."

"As I recall," continued Richemonte, "we were unable to come up with a single suitable solution, one that would cause the family maximum discomfort. However, I'm pleased to be able to tell you that an extraordinary idea has come to me."

"If it's beneficial to my interests, and feasible, it's worth more than gold," Rallion commented. "I trust you'll fill me in."

"Of course I will," replied the captain. "But before I do that, let me relate another lucky incident, one which also occurred last night. You see, someone broke into the estate."

The count's jaw dropped in surprise. "A break-in?" he asked, looking expectantly at Richemonte. "Here at this castle?"

"Yes. In my own bedroom."

"Heavens! What daring! But you called it lucky. How is that possible?"

"Yes, that remains to be explained. A most fortunate and significant turn of events." It was evident by the count's facial expression that Richemonte's logic eluded him.

"Only the devil can make sense out of this!" Rallion observed. "I consider a break-in beneficial only to the perpetrator, while bringing all sorts of calamity to the owner."

"I can see you've never been a friend of daring exploits," said Richemonte.

The count's forehead creased, his answer coming across less cordially. "Are you questioning my courage?" he asked defensively.

"Not at all," laughed Richemonte. "There are various kinds of courage."

"That's new to me. Courage is courage, *n'est-ce pas?*"

"No, there are distinctions," Richemonte qualified. "There is the courage of thoughtfulness, the courage of love, the courage of hopelessness, and yes, even the courage of cowardice."

"Hmm, the last one seems to contradict itself."

"Not at all. It certainly was foreign to the one who broke in last night."

"What did he steal?"

"Nothing. Nothing at all. He was unsuccessful. Wasn't that fortunate for me, since I had over twenty thousand francs in my cash box?"

"That was lucky," replied the count, relieved.

"Not only that, but I managed to surprise the thief in the act, grabbing hold of him. Wasn't that lucky as well?"

"What! You actually confronted him? All on your own?"

"Yes," the captain confirmed proudly.

The count couldn't believe what he just heard. "Unbelievable!" he exclaimed. "How could you have been so careless? To think of grabbing hold of a robber without help. What if he had been armed? He could have injured you!"

"He didn't resort to violence."

"All right, but you said that he had the cash box open."

"Yes. He had already pocketed the money bag, but I forced him to give it back."

"Captain, I find that simply dreadful!" Rallion said. "This is clearly an example of your youthful bravado. I cling to my portion of courage and cunning, but to confront a thief in the act and demand that he relinquish his booty..." He paused for effect. "It could have very easily turned against you, judging from the countless stories we hear nearly every day." But the more he thought about it, the more puzzled he became. "It occurs to me that I didn't hear or notice anything indicating a robbery had transpired."

"What did you expect to hear?"

"Cries for help," he suggested. "Perhaps even the sound of fighting."

"It all went down very quietly."

Rallion frowned. "I don't understand. Was he alone?"

"Yes. Fortunately, it was just the one man."

"Have you arranged to put him in chains and turn him over to the local authorities?"

"No, it hadn't crossed my mind."

"No?" the count asked, more dumbfounded than ever. "Why not?"

"Because I let him go."

The count's expression changed from curiosity to shock. It was as though he had just received devastating news. He stared at the captain, speechless and uncomprehending.

"You let him go?" he finally managed to say. "You must be joking."

"I'm quite serious."

"What utter carelessness! Why allow a thief, a robber, to run free? He'll just find another victim and break into his house."

"That's precisely why I allowed him to go free!"

"So he could break in elsewhere?"

"Yes," Richemonte revealed. "For that very reason."

"I thought I'd heard of everything, but this is ridiculous. You've gone mad, Captain!"

"Not in the least. I settled the matter after careful consideration, something seriously lacking with most people."

"But where is he then, if you let him go?"

"Here in the castle."

The count suddenly tucked his feet under his chair and looked furtively around the room, as though the culprit might spring from a nearby hiding place at any moment.

"Here? In the castle proper?" he asked, bewildered. "Is that really true? Did I hear you right?"

"There's nothing wrong with your hearing," the captain replied amusedly. "The man is presently here in the castle. He is one of my servants."

"*Parbleu!* Does he serve me as well?"

"Of course."

"Was he armed when he broke in?"

"He was in possession of a long, sharp dagger."

The supposedly courageous count jumped from his seat. "That's quite enough," he said. "No, it's more than enough. Captain, may I solicit you for a favor?"

"Certainly, if it's within my power to carry out."

"I'm sure you can. Please, arrange this instant for my coachman, so that he can get the horses ready for my departure."

Richemonte merely looked at his guest wryly. "But whatever for, my dear Count?"

"I have to leave at once," Rallion announced. "Surely you don't expect me to remain here and place myself in danger, giving that robber ample opportunity to break into my chamber? I happen to have just enough courage and daring to overcome the usual obstacles. I have on occasion acted in a foolhardy manner, but it's been my experience that a prudent man is only courageous, bold, and cunning when the affair doesn't involve life and death. I have no desire to fall victim to an enterprising armed robber."

The old captain snickered quietly while playing with the ends of his moustache. "Yes, I've noticed you've been daring in your exploits. Of that I'm sure," mocked Richemonte. "However, in this instance, you won't have to exhibit any prowess. You see, I've completely disabled the thief, making him harmless."

"Is he really incapable of harming anyone?" asked the relieved count, taking a deep breath of air and sitting down again. "How could you possibly allow him to go free and yet ensure he won't come back a second time? How did you pull that off?"

"To begin with," started Richemonte, "I carried on a friendly conversation for some time, and in the end rewarded him for the break-in."

"Rewarded him?" Rallion asked. "Captain, I can tell you've been fibbing, having some fun at my expense. You've been saddling me with this fairy tale to determine if I really have courage, if I have what it takes." He paused, coming up with an idea of his own. "If I may impose on you, I would like you to give me an opportunity to occupy that same room you were in when the robbery took place. If he should try to break in a second time, I'll rattle his bones the same way a school boy assembles stones and glass in a kaleidoscope."

"Hmm, I don't doubt it," laughed Richemonte. "Unfortunately you won't get the chance to put your courage to the test. Everything I've told you is completely true. The man won't enter my room for the second time as a culprit, but as an accomplice."

"As your accomplice? Heavens! It sounds like you're in cahoots with this scoundrel."

"That's what I have in mind."

"*Sapperlot!* I simply don't understand you. You provide me with impossible riddles, ones I can't solve, even though I pride myself in having my fair share of intellect."

"I have no intention of putting your mental acuity to the test," Richemonte said. "I'm well acquainted with your skills. I'll try to clarify this by telling you that the attempted robbery has given me an idea whereby we can finally get our revenge on Löwenklau. A plan so clever, so devious, and so final that he won't ever overcome its impact."

No sooner had Richemonte uttered the name of their archenemy than the count moved his chair closer, wanting to catch every word.

"Ah, really?" he asked quickly. "Let's hear it."

"I intend to use this man as a tool to accomplish that which has eluded us thus far: a way to ruin the lives of our enemies once and for all. Even though it may sound improbable, let me assure you that it is a workable plan. Listen! Here's what I have in mind. But we need to be quiet. I don't want anyone to overhear my plan."

They conversed for some time in whispers. Richemonte's eyes glowed with malicious anticipation as he outlined the scheme. As he listened, Rallion's face conveyed tension that slowly won over to satisfaction.

"Well, what do you think of my plan?" the captain asked, gloating.

"Splendid, wonderful. It's very cleverly thought out."

"It will be carried out like clock work."

"And the best part is that we don't have to risk anything."

"Exactly. You won't have to enlist any of that daring courage you spoke of earlier!" quipped Richemonte with a touch of irony.

"Absolutely not!" the count agreed quickly. "But what about the money? How do we come to an agreement?"

"Just as old friends would in similar circumstances."

"So we divide the spoils."

"Exactly."

Rallion nodded. "That's fine with me. But who will procure the money?"

"Both of us, each one according to his resources. You're much richer than I. I'm convinced that I could come up with 100,000 francs myself."

"I can come up with the rest. How much do you think we'll need?"

"I don't know yet," Richemonte admitted. "We'll certainly have to offer a large sum, a figure beyond the actual worth so that it won't be rejected. Still, we won't risk much by it."

"Of course, we'll have to consider that we're both known to them. I'm afraid they won't deal with us directly."

"We're not going to be foolish enough to conduct the transaction using our own names. Certainly we wouldn't do it in person."

"Ah! Now I understand you. Are you planning on using a middleman?" Rallion asked.

"I wouldn't have it any other way," said the captain. "We'll enlist the service of an agent who can accommodate us for a few hundred francs."

"How will this industrious servant, your Jacques, accomplish the task?"

"He'll seek an introduction with the family."

"Are you suggesting that he do so in the capacity of a servant? How would we know they're in need of one?"

Richemonte shrugged, as though the detail was an unimportant one. "I don't think we should base our entire plan on something so trivial. I've contemplated various possibilities and come up with a workable solution, one that guarantees his admittance."

"He'll have to travel to Berlin."

"Even further," he said. "Events which befall my friends and enemies are always brought to my attention. Only circumstances pertaining to those who are indifferent to me do I ignore. I've ensured that the Löwenklau family is always kept under surveillance. I happen to know that they spend a lot of their time at their estate in Breitenheim, the one that was bequeathed to them through Blücher's intervention. Only one of their brood is currently absent. Gebhard is on an expedition to the Orient. This little fact is of considerable importance to us."

"How come?"

"It allows us to introduce Jacques without suspicion. Haven't I told you that Jacques served with the *Chasseurs d'Afrique* in Algiers?"

"Yes."

"Well, Gebhard von Löwenklau has also traveled to Algiers."

The count snapped his fingers, calling out in surprise. "Ah, now I see the connection!" he exclaimed. "It's genius, sheer genius. You're a damned clever man. If our current venture doesn't quite work out, you still have a future as a diplomat, Captain!"

"Do you think so?" asked Richemonte ironically.

"Of course. If I said it, then you have to believe me. After all, I'm a diplomat. Now then, Jacques was supposed to have met Gebhard in Algiers. Where is this estate of Breitenheim?"

"It lies in the Prussian district of Gumbinnen, a short distance from Nordenburg."

"Gumbinnen?" Rallion asked while making a face. "The devil can gather up all these hard to pronounce German names. My tongue gets twisted and sprained every time I run across one of them. Where is Gumbinnen?"

"Near the Russian border."

The count's eyes widened. "That far? Well, it doesn't really matter. Jacques' story will be that he met Gebhard in Algiers. While on a trip to Petersburg, he just happens to come through the area near the Löwenklau estate. It occurs to him that Gebhard lives nearby, so he takes a slight detour to visit him, only to discover that he's absent. Naturally, he'll be invited to stay and won't decline their generous offer of hospitality."

"Yes, that's the plan."

"A formidable one. But there are some further considerations."

"What possible problems could there be?"

"For one, Gebhard won't have mentioned this friend in any of his correspondence with the family."

"Why would that present a problem? No doubt Gebhard has made a large number of friends along the way. He couldn't be bothered to write about them all in much detail."

"All right," Rallion said, accepting the captain's point. "It stands to reason that they will also ask Jacques where he met their relative in Algiers. How can we be sure that his answers don't contradict what they know of Gebhard's travels?"

"That's simple. I've looked after it," Richemonte said. "Even though these Germans crisscross the globe on their endless expeditions, they're relatively ignorant in the areas of science and culture. To compensate for their shortcomings, they insist on documenting everything they see, hear, and think – you get the picture. They positively relish the joy of keeping meticulous records, and Gebhard is no exception. I've heard that he's written a book about his exploits and—"

"Heavens, what absolute nonsense!" interrupted the count. "Who in their right mind would contemplate purchasing such a book. It's nothing but trash."

"There are plenty of gullible people who would do so," the captain said sadly. "After his return from the Sahara, he apparently didn't waste any time in slapping together a mishmash of his adventures."

"What utter nonsense! What is in this book?"

"His experiences."

"What responsible German would even show interest in Africa? Not one single person. What does any German even know about Africa? It's well known that the Germans are the worst geographers anywhere. Most of them have never even heard of Algiers. It's no wonder, since they live so far north." Rallion rolled his eyes. "Algiers belongs to us, the French. It's only the French who have been entrusted with exploring the Sahara, and consequently we have the sole right to write commentaries about that part of the world. The Germans shouldn't venture anywhere near it."

"I concur wholeheartedly with your views," Richemonte assured him. "Even so, that audacious Löwenklau has written a journal that has already been translated into French. This is an example of our country's benevolence. An honorable publisher came forward, taking on the task of sorting through the deplorable manuscript and trying to make something out of it. Eventually, they paid out an honorarium to him, to be charitable. Since I've been following his exploits, I've made a point of purchasing the translation. It resembles a diary and clearly spells out what transpired from day to day. I'll supply our Jacques with the book so that he can become familiar with the details and respond with correct information if asked."

As the morning waned, they continued to discuss as many relevant details as they could think of that were crucial to the success of the plan.

By the time they were finished, the storm front building in the southwest was on the verge of dispatching yet another lightning bolt against the Löwenklaus, one with the potential to cause considerably more harm than the last.

CHAPTER FOURTEEN

A Deceptive Gentleman

A fashionable carriage pulled up a few weeks later in front of a sizeable business entrance on one of the busiest streets in Berlin. The carriage's lone occupant, a tall, slender, and well-dressed man, was identifiably French to those around him because of his attire. He lightly stepped off the coach and walked up to the front door. The name etched in the glass was the same as the one on the large overhead sign: Samuel COHN, broker and real estate agent.

The stranger opened the door and stepped inside.

"Is Monsieur Cohn available?" he inquired of the clerk in French.

"Yes, Monsieur," the clerk replied in limited French. "My boss has just arrived." He bowed respectfully.

"Here is my card. You may announce me right away," said the newcomer, handing the employee his business card.

The young man barely glanced at the offered card while making several further bows, nearly covering all thirty-two markers on a compass card. He hurried off on his new errand, breaking into a run as though having been bitten by a host of tarantulas and scorpions. He rushed through the door into the adjoining room, occupied by several clerks working at their stand-up desks, and threw open a door at the far end.

"Mr. Cohn, Mr. Samuel Cohn," he called out. "Please stand up, sir. There's a nobleman here to see you and he's just identified himself to me as a count. You shouldn't be sitting when you receive him. I believe he intends to conduct a business deal."

The owner, an enterprising Jew, nearly ripped the card out of the clerk's hand, scrutinized it for perhaps a fifth of a second, then bowed to the card he was now holding, an action evidently meant for the bearer himself.

"A count!" he exclaimed. "What an honor! Admit him this instant."

The clerk's intention was to hurry back the way he came, but the moment he turned around, he ran into the stranger, who had followed him in.

"Monsieur Cohn?" the count asked.

"The honor is mine, all mine!" Cohn said, making several formal bows while closing the office door behind his guest. "I'm Mr. Cohn, Samuel Cohn, broker and agent."

The count sat down, making himself comfortable on the divan. He pulled a cigar from his pocket and lit the end with a match. "I am Count Jules Rallion," he announced with an air of self-importance.

The broker's next round of pedantic pleasantry was cut short by a dismissive wave of Rallion's hand. "Please, let's dispense with all formality. I believe in conducting my business dealings succinctly. Now, I would like to discuss some business with you."

"I'm sure this will benefit us—"

"Yes, I'm sure profit will result," Rallion interrupted. "Now, let us get to the heart of the matter. Is the name Löwenklau familiar to you?"

"Löwenklau? Yes, yes indeed," replied the Jew. "A fine and honorable name. Good reputation, good people, punctual in repayment—"

"Fine, fine!" the count said, cutting him short. "Do you know where the family currently resides? A short response will suffice."

"As you wish, worthy count. The family occupies the estate at Breitenheim, in the vicinity of Nordenburg. They also happen to own a second estate, situated near—"

"Very good," Rallion interrupted. "I'm familiar with its location. Do you know per chance if either one is for sale?"

The Jewish broker made a long face before answering. "For sale?" he asked, registering surprise. "Why would they want to sell either property? I'm not even aware of any lien or mortgage against them."

"That doesn't matter to me!" Rallion replied reprovingly. "My interest is in buying the property. I have traveled through the region, and I like the layout and condition of the estate. I am looking for an agent to negotiate on my behalf. If you feel there is nothing to be gained, I will seek another."

Cohn paled, then sought to discourage him one final time. "But my dear Count, the proprietor has no intention of selling."

Rallion rose from the divan, getting ready to leave. "All right. If you have no skill in persuading the owner to sell, I will look for a more competent negotiator."

The broker jumped up, dismayed at the implication. "Please remain seated, worthy Count! Don't leave! What others merely contemplate, Samuel Cohn will bring to pass. Are you prepared to obtain the titles *partout*?"

"*Partout*?"

"Apologies. It means at any cost."

"Yes, at any cost," confirmed the count.

"Well, I'm afraid it could cost you a considerable sum."

"Why should that concern you?" Rallion asked. "Don't you realize the current value of the two properties?"

"I was unaware of it until now. How much are you prepared to offer?"

"It doesn't matter. Plead my case until they reconsider. I will gladly pay the required sum."

"How soon do you wish to proceed and what form of payment do you prefer?"

"I wish to proceed immediately, and I prefer to deal in cash."

"A bank draft would suffice just as well."

"I deal in cash," replied the count obstinately.

The experienced broker had never encountered an arrangement or client so peculiar. The Frenchman almost behaved like an Englishman, not bothering to count his guineas due to his extreme wealth.

"Very well!" agreed Cohn. "I will personally confer with Monsieur von Löwenklau. When should I depart?"

"Right away."

"And how shall I communicate news of my success?"

"I have other business and will therefore travel with you as far as Rastenburg," the count said. "I will await your personal report there. We can discuss your fee once we're under way." Rallion paused for a moment, then lowered his voice. "I have only one stipulation. I want to keep my name out of it. I don't want the proprietor to know that it's me who is purchasing the property. Is this possible?"

"It's not easy, but Samuel Cohn manages to accomplish what others cannot."

"Excellent! In that case, I will be leaving for the railway station shortly. Please make your arrangements and follow me quickly. I'm unaccustomed to waiting."

The count left the office, leaving behind an agent so excited he was nearly in a state of frenzy. Despite all that had to be accomplished in such a short time, Cohn managed to arrive at the station with just minutes to spare. He purchased the ticket and joined the count in his compartment just as the train began to pull away from the station.

❧✠☙

A few days later, an elegant-looking carriage traveled along the road to Nordenburg. The road traversed the forest belonging to the Breitenheim estate, intersecting with an access road that led onto the property. The wagon turned onto the access road and within five minutes, it reached an open courtyard. A young, well-groomed gentleman disembarked. Two farm hands, occupied with chores, hurried over to offer their services.

The gentleman approached them. "Does this estate belong to Monsieur von Löwenklau?" he asked in French.

One of the men looked at the other, who didn't speak a word of French, then stepped forward. "Yes, Monsieur."

"Is the gentleman at home, available for a visit?"

"Yes, Monsieur, he is at home. Hopefully he is unoccupied. Please, if you would care to follow me inside."

The gentleman kept pace with the worker, and walked across an immaculate courtyard, toward the main house. Once inside, he was led into a spacious foyer, where he left his business card with the farmhand. The worker disappeared into the house, only to return after a brief absence, beckoning the newcomer to follow him again.

They crossed two rooms, entering a third, which appeared to be the owner's library. Charts and maps were strewn about the tables and chairs, and bookcases jammed with books encroached upon three walls, stretching all the way from the floor to the ceiling. The study was sparsely furnished, with no trace of luxury, letting the gentleman know that the owner was unpretentious.

A comfortable chair was situated in front of the center bow window, and in it sat a manly figure who instantly left an impression on the guest. The man had short, snow white hair and a full beard of the same color that complemented a lightly tanned face, from which shone a pair of clear, blue eyes unexpectedly translucent for a man of his age. Contentment rested on the old man, though on closer inspection the tips of his magnificent moustache curved slightly at the corners of his mouth, which, though slightly down-turned, hinted at a trace of anxiety.

The man's stature was broad and tall. He held an open book in his hand, evidently reading without the aid of spectacles. In this way, he almost resembled Karl the Great,[14.1] whose shoulders had so easily borne the weight of armor too burdensome for the average man.

Across from his chair, a large mirror hung suspended from a pillar at the base of which stood a second piece of furniture, a settee. Seated here in the midst of several satin pillows was a woman, a matronly shape of exquisite beauty crowned with a head of snow white hair, who didn't elicit any less interest than her elderly husband. Her sickly face had a waxen appearance, yet the mild look that shone from her deep, dark mysterious eyes relayed a conciliatory tone. Her splendid forehead remained devoid of lines despite her advancing years. Her almost youthful round cheeks and firm chin, which gently blended into her white neck, together confirmed the truth that a woman doesn't show her age so long as she retains her vitality.

The lady's pale lips, which had at one time beckoned to be kissed, were beginning to show signs of thinning. The elegant woman sat in a withdrawn position, suggesting that at times she bit her lips, as though suppressing an inward pain in moments of deep contemplation when she felt she wasn't being observed. The lower portion of her body was covered by an ornate woolen blanket that extended all the way to her feet. Was it possible that this elderly lady, whose eyes still possessed the shimmer of joyous remembrance, carried within herself an inner pain?

Who were these two elderly people? They were Hugo von Löwenklau, the favored lieutenant of the famous Marshal Blücher, and his wife Margot, who had chosen to marry her Prussian lieutenant instead of bowing to an emperor's love.

Protruding from under the edge of Hugo's white hair, a purplish stripe, the length of a finger, ran from the scalp to his nose. This was the scar he had endured, a daily reminder of the ghastly saber strike that had nearly cost him his life. Instead, the blow had left behind a gap in his memory surrounding the events leading up to it.

Margot held her hands together, folded as though in prayer. Yet it was only a gesture, devoid of comforting words. The gesture was meant to convey an inner peace that showed itself around the eyes and was accompanied by a smile that permeated her entire being. Just as sweet, pure aroma permeates the blossoms of the Reseda flower, her eyes were fixed on the center of the room where a boy trotted back and forth on the floor, pretending to be a noble steed. A daring young girl occupied the 'saddle' on his back, laughingly trying to motivate the already sweating horse into a gallop by pummeling him on the hind quarters with her little hands. Such a sweet little girl had already figured out that she could go unpunished by good-naturedly wielding her authority over the stronger sex.

Taking in the scene with radiant eyes was a second woman with a Madonna-like appearance, clearly the mother of these two children. She was the breath of loveliness, as though love had yet to seal her heart, mouth, and mind. It was Ida de Rallion, Gebhard von Löwenklau's wife. It was unfortunate that her husband was absent to witness the splendid scene.

The serene moment was interrupted by the arrival of the farmhand, who presented a card and announced the arrival of the gentleman who had inquired after the master of the house. Hugo took the card and contemplated the inscription.

"Jacques de Lormelle," he said out loud so all could hear. "I'm not familiar with the name. Have you ever heard of it, my dear Margot?"

"No, Hugo," replied his wife.

"What about you, dear Ida?"

"Me neither, Papa."

"Well, we'll find out right away. Admit the gentleman," he said, turning to the farmhand. The worker left the room to fetch the stranger.

Within moments, Jacques entered the study and was greeted formally by its occupants. He showed his familiarity with courtesy by offering a requisite bow. In doing so, he avoided facing the often cold, curious, or even glaring glances that embarrassingly plague first-time visitors.

Löwenklau, laying his book aside, rose from his window seat and approached the newcomer. He extended his hand and greeted him in French, having made the assumption from the card that they were the recipients of a French visitor.

"Welcome, Monsieur de Lormelle! My name is Löwenklau, and these ladies are my wife and the wife of my son. My grandchildren are engaged in cavalry maneuvers, which I ask you to overlook. Likewise, would you make an allowance for my wife who is unable to greet you by getting up? The pain in her lower limbs prohibits her from rising."

Jacques hadn't expected such a warm greeting. From it, he couldn't help but feel like he was considered an old acquaintance of the family. He approached Margot and kissed her outstretched hand.

"I wouldn't want you to place yourself in any discomfort on my account, Madame," he said tactfully. "May God give you pleasure in the happiness of this moment." He motioned with his left hand at the two children, while at the same time taking Ida's hand with his right, kissing it as a sign of respect. His mannerism and courtesy were so subtle and unassuming that he made a favorable impression.

"Please, take a seat," invited Löwenklau. "Consider yourself in the presence of family."

"Thank you," he said in German, bowing again. "I would think that relatives would invoke the use of their native tongue. Please allow me to make use of it, and forgive me if my command of the language is somewhat lacking."

"We will do our best to be lenient," the matriarch replied, nodding with a friendly smile.

"I'm convinced of it," replied Lormelle. "It was clear to me from the outset that I have been included in a family circle ruled by a scepter of love, grace, and gentleness. This is all the more precious to me since I only expected to be admitted as a friend."

"As a friend?" asked Ida. "Oh, then you must surely mean my husband."

"Gebhard?" asked Margot. "Do you mean my son?"

"Yes, the gracious lady isn't mistaken," replied Jacques. "I'm currently on a business trip to Petersburg, but since I was in the vicinity of my friend's home, I decided to step out of my way for a visit. Gebhard and I met in Algiers."

"In Algiers?" asked Hugo. "Monsieur de Lormelle, this is a pleasant surprise. Unfortunately, my son is currently abroad on business. Nonetheless, you won't be disappointed with our hospitality. Again, I bid you a heartfelt welcome." Hugo extended his hand a second time, reaffirming the invitation. "I pray, Monsieur, that your commitment in Petersburg is not too pressing."

"Not at all. I am traveling mostly out of pleasure," Jacques said. "That said, I am probably already running late, as so often happens."

"Oh, don't concern yourself with expectations and schedules," Hugo said. "Those waiting for you in Petersburg should grant you a little grace for your travels. A short rest here at Breitenheim could be beneficial for you. What do you think, Richard?" Laughing, Hugo had directed the question at his grandson, who quickly bucked his little sister and walked over. The boy's expression was somewhat serious as he placed his hands behind his back.

"Have you seen my Papa, Monsieur?" he asked.

"Yes," Lormelle replied, matching the boy's serious disposition.

"Did he like you?"

"Of course, and the other way around as well."

"Well, that's the main thing," Richard said. "You may stay."

It was the solemn way Richard spoke and the forward way in which he had approached their guest that suggested his manner was more than that of a spoiled child. His explicit approval of their guest's stay was just the beginning of an animated conversation. The little granddaughter climbed into her mother's lap while Richard withdrew, finding a place for himself on the nearby steps. He seemed preoccupied with a picture book, but his eyes kept returning to the visitor's face. The only one who caught his furtive glances was Jacques himself.

Later, Hugo assigned him two rooms and gave him the opportunity to rest after his long trip. Alone in the room, Jacques approached the mirror and examined his outward appearance. A confident smile reflected back at him.

Hmm, I don't find anything unusual about my looks, he mused. *I'm convinced that I made a good impression on the family. If the saying is true, that the first impression is the decisive one, I can be more than content with my debut. Why is it then that the boy kept looking at me? Could it be true what they say, that a child can be the best judge of character and can be more accurate than the astute evaluations of a grown man? The boy seems intelligent and I get the feeling he doesn't like me. I'm sure it was his love for his father that persuaded him to grant his consent, because it's clear that he has an antipathy toward me. Since his parents value his opinion, and even lean in his favor, I need to be more mindful of him than the rest.*

As soon as Jacques concluded his inner contemplation, his time alone was cut short. He was summoned to supper, which they had rearranged to suit their guest. Since he had previously been in the employ of several refined families, he was accustomed with the role he now needed to play, to convince them of his elevated social standing. At dinner, he succeeded in winning the family's acceptance, with the exception of the boy, who continued to resist his attempts.

The rest of the day was spent inside with the family. They had decided that he would most likely be too tired from his travels to do anything too strenuous. By the next morning, however, the situation had evidently changed. Hugo asked Jacques if it suited him to take a small ride with him through the estate, since he desired to inspect the field work of his farmhands. The Frenchman naturally gave his consent, excitedly anticipating the opportunity to speak with Hugo alone. He hoped to steer their conversation toward an important subject they had yet to discuss.

The aged grandfather demonstrated that, despite his advancing years, he was still a confident and accomplished rider. The Frenchman, who hadn't had a lot of instruction in this area, had difficulty keeping pace with him for fear of embarrassing himself.

They stopped for a light meal at a nearby workhouse. During the course of their simple lunch, Jacques began turning the conversation toward his intended topic. "In their determination to cultivate larger tracts of farmland, I have found that the Germans are more diligent than the French. Would you agree with me, Monsieur von Löwenklau?"

"I don't see it quite as simplistic as that," replied Hugo slowly, contemplating his remarks, "because I don't have enough experience in such things to make an accurate assessment. If I were to follow your logic, I would have to conclude that the French are more committed to tilling smaller tracts of land."

"That's what I meant."

"Well, as I see it, it has less to do with individual accomplishment and the difference between the two nationalities as it does with the current state of the economy of our two nations. France leans toward cultivating land for the purpose of winemaking, and therefore it's more suitable to subdivide it into smaller plots."

"You may be right," Jacques said. "Still, when I look at the exemplary condition I find your estate in, I'm forced to return to my original view. It must be a real joy to be the proprietor of such an estate."

"But my dear Monsieur de Lormelle, it sounds as though you're not in possession of any holdings yourself."

"My family is not only well-off, but rather rich. Wealthy, in fact. Surely you must know that we Frenchmen live for enjoyment, and when we need to work, we occupy ourselves with literature and art, science and politics, rather than with the problem of parceling off land. We can't seem to convert it into prosaic crops like potatoes, beets, or even corn."

"Yet it's these crops that are the most essential," Hugo reminded him. "Likewise, art, knowledge, literature, and even, in a certain context, politics are affected by them."

"I agree wholeheartedly, and yet I would rather paint them on a canvas or write a book on the cultivation of potatoes than actually dig those dirty bulbs from the ground."

Hugo smiled at him. "The one who aspires to write a book on such a topic better not have only seen them in a picture. I agree that the life of a laborer is primarily a sober and difficult one, but it does have its benefits. It guards one against superficiality and dispersion, making a man conscientious and earnest. It gives him a love for his land and steers his thoughts to his creator and the giver of all things. When I allow the newly harvested kernels of rye or wheat to slip through my fingers, I suppose I feel the same satisfaction as an artist who brings his vision to life on a canvas."

"I must confess," pondered Lormelle, "that I hadn't considered the concept of farming in quite that way before. I was always content when my stewards and workmen paid me the rent. When I allow the gold pieces to slip through my fingers, they seem more valuable than the heads or kernels of harvested crops."

"But isn't it true that gold would be worthless without the other? The metal is merely a symbol, a form of exchange. The worth that we derive from farming stems from its inherent hardships and rewards."

"I can see your economic perspective lies on a more national scale," Jacques said. "I, however, am not prepared to debate such issues. Could it be true that one's love for his little parcel of land, in effect his love for his country, propels him to a higher form of patriotism?"

"That's the way I see it," agreed Löwenklau.

"Then your holdings must be close to your heart."

"Indeed. They represent much value and satisfaction."

"To the extent that you wouldn't part with them?"

Hugo paused, considering the unexpected remark. "It would take much to persuade me to sell."

"Even if you were offered handsome compensation?"

"It would depend on what sort of advantages there would be in it for me. Actually, I find myself in the midst of contemplating this very point."

Much to his delight, the Frenchman found himself at the threshold of the topic he really wished to discuss. "Really?" he inquired innocently. "How so, Monsieur von Löwenklau?"

"I have been approached by an agent to see if I would consider selling both my holdings."

"Then the buyer must be a wealthy man."

"He seems to be."

"No doubt a local owner who's familiar with your estate's worth."

"Surprisingly not," Hugo revealed. "He's a foreigner, a Russian."

"What would compel him to settle down here?"

"I don't know," replied Löwenklau truthfully. "Besides, I don't have the right to ask him. I've learned that this part of the country pleases him and that's why he made the inquiries."

"He must have been impressed with what he saw here," Jacques said. "Just as I am."

"I suspect that was the case. He then contacted a broker from Berlin to make the necessary inquiries."

"An agent from Berlin? Isn't that cause for caution?"

"Honest and dishonest people come from all sorts of places. I have heard that this broker has a favorable report among his peers."

"I would be most curious to find out if the Russian is indeed willing to pay what this estate is worth. It's been my experience that when it comes to financial matters, Russians aren't always forthright."

"It's interesting that you would say that," replied Hugo. "His offer has led me to an unusual predicament."

"What could that be?"

"Well, his offer exceeds the estimated worth by 100,000 thalers."

"Really!" exclaimed Jacques, astounded.

"Yes, above the value of both properties."

"What will you do?" asked Jacques, trying to get a sense of the man's intent.

"I've never thought of selling. I'm far too comfortable here to contemplate selling and leaving."

"Even at your age?" he blurted out without thinking. "Please, excuse my brashness."

"Don't worry about it. I have often asked myself that question. It's likely I may not have too many years left to live, and naturally I would have to leave one day, leaving all this behind. I intend to leave it to my son. That would please me much more than to leave it in the hands of a stranger."

"True. But on the other hand, your son would benefit from an extra 100,000 thalers."

Hugo nodded. "Obviously, that's something I can't dismiss. I've just learned of an opportunity to acquire another estate that I could purchase with cash, even though it's of more value than my own."

"In that case, I wouldn't hesitate."

"I have certainly considered it, but it's not my decision alone."

"Aren't you the sole owner?"

"A husband and father can never act alone, particularly when the matter at stake is a financial one. I can't sell my son's inheritance without conferring with him."

"Yes, you need to communicate with him right away."

214

"I have already done so," smiled Hugo. "Actually, I communicated with him as soon as I received the generous offer."

"Then I fear you'll probably decline the offer, as advantageous as it is."

"Why do you say that?"

"Because Gebhard is currently in the Orient."

"Are you implying that his opinion, his answer, will arrive too late?"

"Yes, that's what I'm thinking. The postal connection is far from reliable."

"As fate would have it, Gebhard is currently at a location that is equipped with a telegraph."

"And have you received a reply?"

"No, not yet," Hugo said. "It's likely that he went on a small excursion and will probably return soon. I am expecting the messenger to arrive at any time."

After a lengthy pause, Jacques continued. "You have drawn me into this affair! I find myself curious to find out how my friend will respond."

"I expect he'll agree with the proposed sale."

"Do you have a basis for your certainty?"

"Yes," replied Hugo thoughtfully. "You see, it was always inconvenient for him to live here, being so far removed from the capital city. His scientific position dictated he should be accessible and thus live in closer proximity to the scientific community. The estate I referred to earlier is situated near a major rail line just a few hours travel from Berlin."

"That's quite fortuitous. In any event, you're right. Chances are, Gebhard's answer will confirm the sale. Would you be moved to sell then?"

Hugo tilted his head before answering. "I would, however, I have one other item to consider. While you were in Algiers, did my son tell you how I came into possession of the Breitenheim estate?"

"I recall some of the details," replied the Frenchman. "Didn't you receive it as a gift from Field Marshal Blücher?"

"It was through his mediation. Breitenheim is a gift from the former king."

"Yes, now I remember. It was given to you as an appreciation of the many services you rendered for your country."

"That which one receives as a gift shouldn't be taken for granted," Hugo said solemnly. "I have a moral obligation to keep Breitenheim."

"Really? How unfortunate. So you're bound because of your attachment to Blücher! To squander such an opportunity?"

"There may still be a recourse. It would certainly be deemed prudent to inquire with the appropriate government agency and see if the sale of the estate would be perceived as being ungrateful."

"Have you corresponded with them?"

"Yes. I arranged for a letter to be sent even before I telegraphed my son."

"I suspect that someone of influence, tact, and ability would have to act on your behalf!"

"Naturally. I have a relative... In fact, you must be acquainted with him. Are you familiar with the name Goldberg?"

Jacques, for his part, had received excellent information from Richemonte. "Of course," he replied right away. "Gebhard has told me much about him. He advised me in one of his letters, which I still possess, that Monsieur von Goldberg married the sister of your daughter-in-law."

"Yes, he is one and the same. He lives in Berlin and is often welcomed at court. He is the most suitable person to intercede on my behalf."

"Then may I congratulate you in advance."

"Oh, don't be too hasty."

"Are you still thinking that one or both could prove to be an obstacle?"

"Not really," Hugo admitted, "although the possibility still exists that the Russian won't pay the price I've set out."

"Heavens!" Jacques exclaimed. "Are you perchance seeking to profit for more than the offered amount?"

It seemed inconceivable to Lormelle that someone could turn aside such a large sum. He was concerned the old man would decline the offer. If that happened, he wouldn't be able to carry out his plan, his whole reason for coming to Germany. Not only was he intending to betray Löwenklau, but he had formulated a plan to cheat his own two accomplices, Richemonte and Count Rallion.

"Would you think," asked Löwenklau, "that the extra 100,000 thalers are adequate compensation for giving up an estate that has meant so much to all of us?"

"You'll come to appreciate your new home just as much."

Löwenklau shook his head slowly, smiling with moist eyes. "No, never!" he said. "I'm too old to get all caught up with another land holding."

"Are you intending to elevate the price?"

"Yes," was the firm response.

"What if the Russian backs off?"

"That is his prerogative. I'm not forced to sell my holdings. If he adds another 50,000 to the offer, I'm prepared to accept it. Otherwise there's no deal."

"It seems too much to me."

"Don't worry. A man who is that interested in my property will gladly give me what I ask."

Jacques didn't want to risk further comment. It occurred to him that Rallion and Richemonte would probably come up with the extra funds, bending to Löwenklau's will. The real beneficiary of the arrangement would be himself, since he was planning to abscond with the money.

The two men continued their ride, inspecting the estate without discussing its sale again. This was short lived though, because as soon as they returned to the main house, Margot, the matriarch, nodded in a friendly and disclosing manner to her husband.

"I have a surprise for you, my dear Hugo," she announced.

"Is it a good one?"

"Yes," she teased. "Can you guess what it is?"

"A letter from Goldberg?"

"No. Guess again."

"Hmm, it must be a wire from Gebhard then."

"Correct!" She applauded his insight.

"Where is it? Have you read it already?"

"No," she said with a slight hint of reproach. "Since when have I taken the liberty of opening your correspondence? The telegram was addressed to you, my dear. Here, have a look."

She reached for the telegram, fishing it out from under her blanket. All members of the family were on hand to witness the news. Even Ida, his daughter-in-law, was curious, wondering how her husband had responded to the query.

Löwenklau opened the telegram and read to himself. When he finished, he looked up at the others. "Well, what do you think he said?" asked Hugo, teasing his audience.

"Read it out loud!" they pleaded.

"Very well," Hugo said. "It's quite short and to the point: *Sell it. I am doing well. A letter is on the way. Greetings and love to all. Gebhard.* So, he's in agreement. Is that to your liking, Margot?"

She slowly caressed a strand of hair, answering so quietly that it was barely audible. "You know that I'm happiest when I'm with my family," she said.

Hugo knew her only too well. He approached her and kissed her tenderly on the lips. "I know that, Margot," he replied. "You followed me from your home in Paris, settling on this estate. If we leave here, we won't be going separate ways. But I'm telling you all, I wouldn't sell the estate where we've experienced so much happiness for just any small sum."

Thus the matter was settled.

CHAPTER FIFTEEN
No Honor Among Thieves

Count Rallion stayed in the finest hotel in Rastenburg, albeit under an assumed name. Waiting for news was taxing his patience. Although he attempted to pass the time by absorbing himself with the contents of the local newspaper, he found he kept rereading the same article over and over, failing to concentrate on the story. Just as he was about to toss the paper aside, he was interrupted by a knock at the door.

"Come in," he called out.

Two men walked into the spacious room. The first man turned out to be Samuel Cohn, his broker, but the second man was unfamiliar to him. The proprietor of the real estate firm bowed politely, a gesture that was seconded by his associate.

"I came here," Cohn began, "to present to Count Rallion the gentleman who is prepared to purchase the two land holdings, only to turn them over to his Grace. The estate actually stemmed as a gift from the Prussian Field Marshal Blücher, the Prince of Wahlstadt, because he—"

"Enough!" interrupted the count angrily, ending the broker's needless introduction. "Let us keep the conversation to matters at hand. Who are you?" he asked, turning to face the stranger.

"I am Count Smirnoff," was his reply, as he bowed formally.

Rallion raised his eyebrows. Even though the newcomer wore a decent suit, he wondered how Cohn had managed to arrange for an actual count to handle the other part of the transaction.

"Are you a Russian?" he asked him.

"No, Polish."

"Are you living in exile?"

"Yes."

"Can you verify your identity?" Rallion asked.

"Of course," Smirnoff said. "Since this is a business deal, I came prepared with the necessary documents."

"Are you with means?"

"Unfortunately not."

"No doubt you have been informed by Mr. Cohn regarding the transaction I have in mind."

"Yes, he has already filled me in."

"For your part, what sort of compensation are you seeking?"

"I have been offered two thousand thalers."

"I will ensure that you receive the prescribed sum, but only when the deal is concluded," Rallion explained. "What assurance do I have that you will sell me the land holdings once they have been turned over to you?"

"My word of honor, Monsieur."

Rallion suppressed a sneer, choosing to respond with a deprecating smile. "I don't doubt your word, but you must agree with me that I will need to satisfy myself further, considering the large sum at stake here."

"I'm not aware of any other way. Remember, I'm not a rich man."

"I know of one. As soon as you have fostered the deal, you will receive the money for the purchase price accompanied with a promissory note, signed by you, also for the same amount. As soon as I have bought the land holdings from you, I will dispose of the note and provide you with two thousand thalers in cash. Are you satisfied with this arrangement?"

"Of course."

"Should you hesitate in fulfilling the agreement," the count went on, "I will present the promissory note to the authorities, and they will force you into compliance. In that case, you would forfeit the two thousand."

"Oh, Count Rallion," interrupted the Jewish broker, "you can rest easy knowing that I have chosen the right man, one who can be trusted implicitly. You don't have to entertain all the reasons why a man like Count Smirnoff would involve himself in a—"

"Stop this incessant blabbering!" interrupted Rallion. "You know I am not a fan of long-winded discourse. When did you arrange to meet with Löwenklau?"

"There was no mention of a firm date," Cohn said. "He was awaiting a reply from Berlin."

"Is it likely he has already received it?"

"Yes, it's possible."

"Then it would be better to get under way. Do you have any other business to conclude?"

Cohn shook his head. "Nothing. I only wanted to speak to your Grace and to assure you that Count Smirnoff is fully capable of carrying out—"

"Fine, fine!" interrupted Rallion again. "I am now acquainted with the count. If you are finished, I see no reason to delay your departure. I will wait for your message so that I can forward the funds."

"Regretfully," stated the broker, "the distance stands in the way of bringing this to a quick conclusion. Wouldn't it be easier for all concerned if your Grace would travel closer to Nordenburg?"

"I have no intention of meeting with Löwenklau."

"If you wish to travel as far as Drengfurth, you would still be far enough away to avoid a chance meeting. There is room in our carriage, Count."

Rallion's only answer was a dismissive hand gesture.

"Does the postal service send mail to Drengfurth on a daily basis?" he asked.

"Certainly."

"Then I will go with their coach," Rallion decided. "You can leave immediately."

Cohn left with Smirnoff after he received instructions from Rallion outlining where he was to meet him in the next city. The count then inquired about the mail schedule, learning that the next coach was scheduled to leave early the next morning. He decided to make use of the service rather than to procure his own carriage.

It was still dark when morning came and Rallion approached the mail carriage to tender his ticket. The coachman was already sitting on the buckboard, which meant that the coach was due to depart shortly. The count learned that only one other passenger had purchased a ticket on the mail run and he was about to climb aboard when he noticed that passenger already seated in the rear of the carriage.

"Move over!" the count commanded.

The coach's lantern lit up Rallion's face, making it easy for the stranger to assess the brash intruder.

"What for?" asked the other man, surprised.

"I am not used to traveling this way, facing backwards."

"Neither am I!"

"Well, I paid for my ticket and expect a good seat."

"Me, too!"

Rallion was growing frustrated. "Monsieur, I am a nobleman!"

"Sir, I am one as well."

"*Mille tonnerres!* I am going to speak to the coachman about this."

"As you wish."

The annoyed count stepped down from the carriage and approached the coachman, still seated on his lofty perch.

"Driver, ensure that I receive the seat I have paid for," he demanded.

"Let me see it," the man said phlegmatically, stretching out his hand.

"What?" Rallion asked.

"Your ticket."

"Oh, here it is." He handed his ticket up to the driver. The man held it close to the lantern, trying to decipher the numbers in the poor light.

"It says number two. That's the seat assignment for the left rear. The other gentleman has seat number one, which he purchased last night. If you're not satisfied with your seat selection, you can sit on the opposite side, facing backwards. Those seats are empty."

"Now, listen here. This is what you're going to do. I am Count—"

"What I am going to do?" interrupted the coachman. "You may be a count, but you're passenger number two. Therefore, you can take your place in your assigned seat. This coach leaves in one minute. He who hasn't boarded by then will be left behind, and that's just the way it is! *Basta!*"

The count was tempted to remain behind, but he didn't relish the prospect of staying another day on account of his wounded pride. Reluctantly, he climbed aboard with his suitcase, inside of which was cash to purchase the two properties.

But he didn't intend to remain quiet for long about his disappointment regarding his seat assignment.

"You said you're a nobleman?" he asked the other passenger, taking the seat opposite him.

"Yes," was his curt response.

"Well, in fact, I am a count."

"Likewise."

"Sir, I am going to demand satisfaction from you." Mocking laughter was the only response. "Didn't you hear me?" reiterated an angry Rallion.

"Of course I did."

"What is your answer?"

"Didn't you hear my response? I laugh at the mere suggestion."

"Monsieur!" Rallion said through clenched teeth. "Don't you realize what is implied when one seeks satisfaction from a gentleman?"

"Oh, very clearly."

"I demand that we settle this by way of a duel!"

The mystery man inclined his head agreeably. "Fine. I would welcome it, though I fear nothing will come of it."

"Then you're nothing but a miserable coward."

"Definitely not me," the man said. "Most likely you."

"Monsieur," Rallion countered angrily, "your manner is very irresponsible."

"Not at all. I know only too well just who I am dealing with."

"Well, with whom?"

"With a person who faints at the first sign of a saber and runs away when faced with the prospect of a pistol shot."

Although he was in a strange land and unknown to the general populace, the stranger's words left him feeling exposed. "I repeat," said the count, "your manner is deplorable."

"And I am telling you that I have no desire to continue this little discussion. I am tired and I am going to get some rest. At daybreak, I will address you and continue our chat. But if you have the intention of provoking me any further, I will slap your face so hard that its force will propel you through the door and out onto the road!"

The stranger spoke with such conviction that Rallion actually feared an attack. It seemed to him, despite the darkness, that his opponent's arm was already poised to strike him. For this reason, he decided to remain quiet, instead making himself comfortable for the journey ahead.

The time passed with taciturnity. The wheels spun endlessly on the roadway, their monotonous sound broken only by the occasional admonishment and whip by the coachman. The count was restless, but the coach's silence, coupled with its steady movement, had a nearly hypnotic effect, making him sleepy. He gripped his suitcase, pulled it closer to him, and closed his eyes.

When he opened them again, the night had given way to a new day. Naturally, his first thought was to scrutinize the man opposite him. It was difficult to make any kind of assessment of him. All he could see was a pair of boots, a hat, and a cloak that enveloped his upper body. Peering from beneath the hat were two dark probing eyes.

As soon as the stranger noticed that the count had awoken from his slumber, he loosed his cloak, revealing an aristocratic face augmented by a trimmed beard. It struck Rallion that he must have seen this face somewhere before, but he couldn't remember where and when.

The passenger removed a case from an inner pocket, withdrew a cigar and, without asking the other's permission, lit it. He rolled the little window down and looked outside, checking on the coach's progress. He pulled back his head after his evaluation of the countryside, examining Rallion with calculation and disdain.

"So, my fellow traveler," he started. "You claim to be a count like myself. I trust that this is a suitable time for you to continue our earlier conversation. I make it a point of looking into a man's eyes, particularly one who affronts me."

"So do I!"

"I doubt that. Your courage seems only to flourish in darkness. You are nothing but a rogue, a scoundrel, even a vagabond, whose looks remind me of an encounter with an ugly spider. I have no qualms about telling you what I think of you to your face, since I am convinced that you would choose to bow out rather than giving me satisfaction."

Rallion's face paled at the insult. He balled up his hands into fists. "If I didn't already find your manner deplorable, I would show you how I respond to such vile accusations." He spat the words out.

"Pah! Of course you cling to your position, knowing full well that you intend to evade the encounter. But I'm not going to let you get away so easily this time. Since you took it upon yourself to demand the best place in the carriage, you have demonstrated by your actions that you possess neither life experience nor courtesy. As you chose to make an issue out of it, even though I have every right to occupy my seat, you have shown that your actions are those of an escaped lunatic. I certainly could have given you a slap, which was more than an empty threat, believe me. I decided not to because of a single and unusual detail." These last words hung mysteriously in the air between the two men. Then, with Rallion waiting for him to finish, he added, "We are related."

The count made a dismissive gesture. "What! Me? Your relative?" he asked. "You must be dreaming!"

"I am most certainly awake. Aren't you the brilliant Count Jules Rallion?" he mocked.

"Dammit! How do you know me?"

"My dear cousin, how can you be so blind? Because I know you so well! I know exactly what your challenge, your demand for satisfaction, represents. As soon as I commit myself to your demands, your first response will be to jump out of the carriage and run clear across the open field for the safety of the next town."

"I will attempt to convince you otherwise," Rallion said. "But first, how is it that you consider yourself my relative?"

"Don't you recognize me?"

Rallion looked across the carriage vacantly. "I have no clue who you are."

"Well, let me refresh your memory. Our last meeting was on the occasion when Gebhard von Löwenklau demanded satisfaction, which you declined, leaving town in a hurry."

Suddenly, a knowing realization dawned on the count. "The devil!" he exclaimed. "You're not, you can't be—"

"Well, who then?" interrupted the stranger smiling.

"Count Kunz von Goldberg, the—"

"—the husband of your beautiful cousin Hedwig!" he finished in his stead.

"Yes, that's who I meant."

"Of course it's me, my dear Count," Kunz revealed. "I'm astonished to find you here. But before I ask you under what circumstances you happen to be here, we need to bring the little matter of satisfaction in order. My brother-in-law, Löwenklau, doesn't live far from here. This presents the best opportunity to settle that outstanding matter. However, I trust you would do me the honor of settling our current disagreement. Look outside, Count. Do you see that forest, just this side of town?"

"Yes," acknowledged the count warily.

"Well, there is a forester's house in the wood. I know the man personally, and he has some exquisite dueling pistols in his possession which I believe he would make available to us as a favor to an old friend. We can proceed into the woods and settle this as gentlemen. I'm convinced only one of us will leave alive, and that person will be me. Understood?"

Rallion found himself facing a determined, unsettling look in the other man's eyes. "Of course, I understand!" he replied. "However, I beg to differ as to who will leave the forest alive!"

"That remains to be seen."

The discussion ended just as the mail carriage rolled into the small town, stopping in front of the local tavern to collect mail and passengers.

"Fifteen minutes, gentlemen!" announced the coachman as he dismounted. Rallion emerged from the coach and disappeared from view through the tavern's door. Goldberg followed slowly, a peculiar smile playing across his face. He reached the bar area, finding it empty, except for the barman.

"Did anyone enter here?" he inquired.

"No, sir."

Kunz ventured out through a side door into the courtyard where he found a busy farmhand working in the garden with a spade.

"Has a stranger come this way?" he asked.

"Yes, sir," replied the man, stopping to look at the newcomer.

"Which way did he go?"

"Through the gate, into the lane!"

Goldberg continued on to the gate, just managing to catch a glimpse of someone ducking behind a bush. He laughed to himself and returned to the tavern.

More than half an hour passed before the worker once again heard the sound of approaching steps. He turned, surprised to see Rallion, the first stranger, walk back in from the lane. Rallion ignored the worker and walked right past him, striding into the inn.

The innkeeper was sitting down, enjoying his pipe when the count stepped inside.

"*Sapperlot!*" he cried, recognizing the former passenger. "Didn't you arrive with the mail coach?"

"Yes."

"The mail clerk was looking for you."

"What for?" asked Rallion unperturbed.

"Well, he couldn't wait any longer."

"What do you mean, couldn't wait any longer?" he asked shocked. "Don't tell me the carriage has left."

"Twenty minutes ago," replied the barman, amused.

"Dammit! The mail clerk said he was stopping for fifty minutes."

"Your ears must have been plugged, Monsieur," he said reprovingly. "The coach stops for fifteen minutes, and not a minute longer."

"I heard him say fifty. I am going to complain," the count said lamely.

"You can try, but it won't do you any good. Besides, the other passenger said we needn't bother looking for you."

"Ah! Why was that?"

"You know, I'm not sure. Where are you headed?"

"As far as Drengfurth."

The barman sighed, shaking his head. "There are no more coaches going there today."

"Is it possible to rent a carriage?"

"No. No one in our little village has a carriage for hire. As I recall, though, a delivery wagon is due through here in the afternoon. I'm sure there would be room for you."

"Then I will have to wait. Tell me, how far do you have to go to circumvent the forest?"

"How far?" he asked dumbfounded. "That's no forest, just a clump of trees. You could walk through it in two minutes."

"Isn't there a forester's house there?"

"No."

"Really? Not even a forester?"

"What for?" asked the barman, scratching his head.

It finally dawned on the count that he'd been made a fool off by Goldberg. He bit his lip in an attempt to suppress his frustration. He was about to reply to the innkeeper when he heard an approaching wagon. He rushed to the door and spotted a carriage coming to a stop out front.

"Has the mail already come through?" the coachman asked, addressing the emerging innkeeper.

"About half an hour ago," said the barkeep.

"Many thanks. Adieu!"

The driver was about to pick up the reins, when he heard a shout from inside the coach. "Wait a minute!" called out the lone passenger, swinging open the door and dropping down to the roadway. Captain Richemonte blinked in the bright sun when he turned to walk into the tavern. Before he could take another step, he was met by Rallion coming out.

"Captain! What a surprise to see you here!" exclaimed the count.

"Indeed," replied Richemonte. "It was by chance that I saw you standing at the window."

"What a reunion! Tell me, what prompted you to travel to these parts?"

"What do you have in the suitcase?" he asked, pointing to the case in the count's hands.

"The money."

"Ah, really! Put the case inside. We can discuss things in private while we go for a little walk. The horses can rest for a few minutes." He took the count's arm, leading him back toward the garden. "Did you really think, my dear Count," he asked, "that I wouldn't concern myself any further with our affairs? How far has it progressed?"

"My instinct tells me we could conclude it today, tomorrow at the latest."

"Really, that quickly?"

Rallion explained where things stood with the business deal. "The last thing I expected was to see you here, Captain."

"Isn't it?" laughed Richemonte. "I've come to avert an unpleasant end to our business. You see, I've discovered a flaw with our plan."

"What flaw?"

"Just consider what we've brought into motion thus far. Once Jacques disappears, it's only natural that Löwenklau will learn the identity of the true purchaser of his estate."

"So what? How can this knowledge harm us?"

"More than you might think. You are his enemy. That German will no doubt connect the sale with you because of his enmity toward you. He will turn to the police and they will conduct a search. Do you know what they will find?"

"Well, what?"

"That Count Rallion, the buyer, was in cahoots with the thief, Jacques de Lormelle."

"Hang it all! But I have to stay in touch with Jacques!"

"No. Not under any circumstances. That's why I've chosen to come after you."

"How did you find me?"

"I knew the agent's address. Even though you used an assumed name, I was able to learn that you went to Rastenburg and booked passage on a mail coach. I decided to obtain a rental carriage, hurried after you—and here I am!"

"That worked out well! So, you want to conclude this with Jacques?"

"Yes," Richemonte said. "You have to be in a position not to show any connection. At worst, all they can say is that you were in the vicinity, but they won't be able to prove that you spoke to or conspired with Lormelle."

"How do you propose to meet up with him without being spotted by others?"

Richemonte spoke while looking up and down the street, seeing no trace of the mail carrier. "Leave that to me! Tell me, though, how you happen to be here without transportation..."

"Yes, my dear Captain, that's a different story altogether. I climbed into the carriage this morning and who do you think came aboard? Take a guess."

"A member of the Löwenklau family?"

"Not a Löwenklau, but in truth just as serious. It was one of their relatives, the Count von Goldberg."

"Your cousin's husband?"

"Yes."

"I thought he was presently occupied in Berlin. What was he doing here?"

"I have no idea."

"Did he recognize you?"

"I'm not sure," Rallion lied, continuing reluctantly. "But as soon as I recognized him at daybreak, I decided to disembark."

"I applaud your foresight," Richemonte said. "Wait a minute. Didn't you tell me that Löwenklau was awaiting an answer from Berlin before making an informed decision?"

"Yes, that's what I was told."

Richemonte smiled to himself. "Well, it stands to reason that Goldberg represents that answer. He decided to come himself rather than simply send a letter. We can be certain the decision is imminent. Let's return and get ready to depart."

"How far are we traveling together?"

"As far as Drengfurth. You will disembark there without anyone seeing you in my company. I will get the coachman to drop me off at a place that won't lead to suspicion. If I need to speak to you, I will contact you there. We have to be extra vigilant to make sure we aren't seen together."

❧✠☙

Kunz von Goldberg had continued his ride on the mail carriage in relative peace without the count for company, yet he felt an inner restlessness over his unexpected meeting with Rallion. He had no idea of the significance of that fateful meeting.

His unexpected arrival at Breitenheim was well-received. As soon as he disembarked, he hurried to the familiar common room where the family liked to spend their time. Along the way, he came across Margot and her daughter-in-law Ida. He hugged both ladies and then inquired after the patriarch, Hugo.

"He's occupied with his guests," replied Margot. "Ah, dear Kunz, I haven't even told you who has arrived."

"I'm sure I will find out."

"One of them is the Polish Count von Smirnoff, the prospective buyer, and the other is a broker from Berlin who is assisting him. My husband anxiously awaits your answer."

"I chose to bring it in person and offer you my advice, since Gebhard is presently absent."

"We're greatly indebted to you. What news do you bring us?"

"Good news," Kunz announced. "There's not the slightest reason for you to alter your plans. The state's position is that the Löwenklau family is the proprietor of the estate and can therefore do with the land as they please."

"I'm afraid Hugo will elect to sell."

"Are you apprehensive?" asked Kunz concernedly.

"Don't you think I'm reluctant to leave this place after so many happy years?"

"I don't doubt it for a minute. Yet, consider all the advantages the sale represents."

"Does the pecuniary benefit take into account what we will miss once we have moved away?"

Kunz smiled at her reassuringly. "Yes, I'm convinced of it, dear aunt. I had a feeling you might have some reservations about the sale, and that's why I came here to put your mind at ease."

"Are you trying to persuade me to agree?"

"Yes, and I want to be up front with you both. I'm only asking you to consider this from the viewpoint of your grandchildren. Your little Richard is destined to become an officer. Increasing your wealth by the proposed 100,000 thalers will go a long way toward meeting his future needs."

"That may be. We women don't deal with the intricacies of numbers and check books. We rely on our feelings, which nearly always ring true."

"So, you're not in opposition?"

She smiled in resignation. "No."

"What was Gebhard's answer?"

"He sides with you. He urges my husband to sell."

"Now, do you see the advantage? I'm sure you'll soon get used to your new accommodations. Uncle Hugo will agree with me."

Kunz was right in his prediction. Löwenklau had asked for another 50,000 thalers, to which the Polish count requested a few hours to consider the proposal and left, promising to return soon. Smirnoff telegraphed Rallion for instructions at his earliest opportunity. Rallion was at first surprised, then consented to the new amount, convinced he would soon be in possession of both holdings plus the purchase money.

The transaction was concluded later under the watchful eye of witnesses and the local advocate. Smirnoff produced the required amount in gold thalers and bank notes, as witnessed by those present. The entire sum was transported in a suitcase, originally supplied by Rallion. When asked about its return, Smirnoff answered politely that since he was no longer in possession of the funds he wasn't concerned with the case and therefore presented it to Löwenklau as a gift.

Hugo took the case himself to his room and locked it in his cabinet. Coincidentally, Jacques, who was on his way to his own room, met him in the hallway. Once inside his own room, Jacques opened his large traveling suitcase and discarded some clothes, revealing two objects. One of them was an identical case, the same size and color as the one Smirnoff had presented to Löwenklau.

I'm going to fill it with stones, the Frenchman mused. *What a shock it will be when he opens it and finds rocks instead of gold thalers.* He picked up the second object. It was a satchel containing a set of skeleton keys. *A skeleton key is a wonderful invention,* he continued. *This one opens the old man's room and the other one the armoire, where he'll probably stash the suitcase. All that remains is for me to wait for my opportunity.*

Just as he pocketed the two keys, he heard a strange noise near the window. Startled, he stopped in his tracks and listened intently. Someone was throwing sand against the window. Perplexed, he quickly hid the small case within the big one, approached the window, and carefully opened it.

"Psst!" he heard from below.

"Who's down there?" he asked in a subdued voice.

"Are you Monsieur de Lormelle?"

"Yes, of course."

"Can you come downstairs?"

"What for?"

"I will tell you shortly. Please meet be by the chestnut tree."

"Who are you?"

"You'll find out. Hurry!"

"All right," Jacques said. "I'll be right down."

He left his room, being sure to lock up behind him, and made his way downstairs. The dining room was full of guests and family, whom Löwenklau had invited to help celebrate the sale. The servants were occupied with catering to their needs, making it relatively easy for Jacques to slip out into the garden undetected. He gingerly walked over to the prescribed tree, where he spotted a dark shape.

"Jacques?" whispered a man's voice.

"Yes," he replied. "Who are you?"

"Ah, you don't recognize me," said the man, in his normal undisguised voice. Jacques took a step back.

"Is it really you, Captain?"

"Of course."

"But what are you doing here? If you're discovered, all is lost."

"Not at all. To begin with, no one knows I'm here, and they won't get their hands on me. I surmise that Löwenklau has just received the funds?"

"Yes, about fifteen minutes ago."

"Then you don't have the money yet?"

"No."

"Well, what could they say if I was spotted? Anyway, after much deliberation, I decided to risk coming here myself. I'm glad I was able to meet you before you concluded your business, since there has been a change in plan."

Jacques hesitated. "May I inquire what this change of plan entails?"

"According to our scheme, you were to abscond the minute you stole the money."

"And I intend to do just that."

"No," said Richemonte convincingly. "It won't work."

"Why not?"

"Because they will immediately discover who the perpetrator is."

"I have no issue with that, so long as we get the money."

Richemonte shook his head. "No. We can't allow ourselves to be so careless. The authorities would immediately investigate and stumble onto your trail. You would be apprehended and us along with you. You have to stay for the time being."

"What! They would search my quarters and find the missing money."

"Don't be stupid! Instead of hiding the money in your room, you bring it to me. I will find a safe place for it."

"Ah, not a bad idea." If there had been sufficient light, the captain would have been surprised to see the determined expression on Jacques' face.

"Isn't it?" asked Richemonte. "I thought you might agree. They will discover the theft, conduct a thorough search, but find nothing. The theft will remain a mystery, and you can depart without giving it a second thought."

"Unfortunately," Lormelle said with a sigh, "that won't work, either."

"What do you mean?"

"Well, I'm a stranger here. Because of the timing of my visit, the police will still check my credentials and discover I'm not the upstanding gentleman I've been pretending to be. That would end it right then and there."

"How could they discover your real identity?" Richemonte wondered. "Count Rallion spent a considerable amount of money to provide you with excellent documentation."

"Perhaps. But what if they wire Gebhard and seek to confirm my relationship with him?"

Richemonte almost scoffed. "They won't do that."

"I fear they may nevertheless, just like when they wired him about the proposed sale."

"As his friend, you have the family's trust," Richemonte reassured him.

"True, but not the trust of the police. They will scrutinize each person on the estate, most certainly any stranger."

"In that case, I will advise you if they happen to use the telegraph to inquire about your credentials."

The truth was that each man was lying, desiring to betray the other. Jacques easily saw through the captain's scheme to saddle him with the theft. Rather than kindle Richemonte's mistrust, he decided to put him at ease.

"Will you really be able to find that out?" he asked.

"Of course," Richemonte replied reassuringly. "I will arrange it."

"Well then, if that's the case, I will trust your assessment. I won't bring suspicion to bear on me, and I can return to my country without incident."

"Exactly. I'm glad we're in agreement. As you can see, these are important considerations that we can't dismiss."

"Where will I meet up with you?" Jacques asked.

"It won't be necessary for you to leave."

"Why?"

"Count Rallion will buy the property from Smirnoff and show up as the new proprietor. By that time, you won't have to leave at all. Do you understand?"

"Now it all makes sense to me."

"Very good. Now, when will you bring the money down?"

Jacques paused, thinking it over. "I can't say for sure. I have to wait for the right opportunity."

"Where is the case?"

"In the old man's room."

"Have you ensured that you have the right keys?"

"Yes, they fit perfectly. Do you see the two lit windows in the corner room, Captain?"

Richemonte peered upward, spotting the lights on in the house. "Yes, what about them?"

"That's Löwenklau's room," he lied. "The children are currently in there with the governess. I have to wait until they leave."

"That's unfortunate," replied the captain. "I'll have to wait for a long time."

"Hopefully not too long. Besides, one should exercise a little patience when facing the prospect of such a windfall."

"Don't preach to me, you scoundrel," Richemonte said. "Go back and prepare yourself. I'm going to make myself comfortable in the grass and be content in knowing this whole affair rests in your very capable hands."

"Of course," Jacques said, and left.

Once he was gone, the captain leaned back against the base of the tree, and passed the time by thinking over their conversation.

He really isn't that bright, he thought. *Jacques has no idea that he won't receive a single thaler. He'll be lucky to get away unscathed. Once I have the case, he'll need to prepare himself to answer any incriminating questions. The best part is that this will ruin the Löwenklau family financially. Somewhere up in that house is my dear sister Margot,*

Napoleon's lost love. If she only knew that I was nearby, waiting to get my hands on that money.

Even though her family is ignorant of her declining health, I managed to find out that her doctor is concerned about a malady that inwardly pains her. Coupled with the shock of losing all that money, it stands to reason that it could affect her health profoundly, perhaps even to the point of death. Wouldn't that be something! I couldn't orchestrate my revenge more convincingly. Not only that, but I'll be handsomely compensated!

Jacques, occupied with his own thoughts, slipped back into the house. *That old schemer is looking to betray me*, he mused. *But he won't be able to. I can see him laughing already, thinking he won't have to give me any of that money. He knows I wouldn't be able to defend myself, since I'm the thief and wouldn't want to incriminate myself. The old captain is quite the calculating scoundrel, but he'll find out soon enough that he's the one who made a mistake.*

He made it back to his room undetected. Reaching into his satchel, he retrieved a small flask and went about oiling the two skeleton keys. He paced back and forth, deep in thought, when he was struck with an idea.

"*Zounds!*" he mumbled, his expression quizzical. "What a thought! Why not carry it out? Hell's bells! I'd like to see the old captain's face when he opens the case and finds my note."

Jacques sat down at the table, took some writing paper, and wrote a few lines on it, making sure the letters were large and prominent. He waited just long enough for the ink to dry, then pocketed the paper.

He left the room and made his way back down to the dining room, where he participated in the lively discussion. He stayed for a while, satisfying himself that no one would be leaving the celebration any time soon. Then, he slipped out again unnoticed, returning to his own room. He opened his large suitcase and removed a coil of rope, along with the smaller case. He took both items, leaving behind the larger suitcase. Jacques left the room again, locking the door.

All was quiet in the hallway, the celebration situated in the other side of the building. Deftly and noiselessly, the thief made his way to Löwenklau's room. He inserted the key, which was followed by an almost silent click as the door opened. He walked inside, quickly closing the door and locking it behind him. This would ensure him privacy and a warning if someone happened to come along. Even if that were to happen, he could still escape through the open window.

The Frenchman, familiar with his trade, decided not to risk lighting a lantern. Instead, he struck a match and surveyed the room in the dim light.

The suitcase was nowhere to be seen, leading him to the obvious conclusion that it was stored away. He produced the second key and inserted it into the lock of the armoire just as the match went out. He unlocked the large dresser, feeling in the darkness for the prize he knew had to be there. He felt an object in the corner. It was the suitcase. He removed it carefully, replacing it with the twin he'd brought. Jacques remembered to lock the armoire again.

Next, he unraveled the rope. He fastened one end to the case and lowered it out the window to the ground. The thief had oriented himself during the day, becoming familiar with the external layout of the building. He had discovered a cedar shrub below the window that would conceal the suitcase perfectly. It was so dark that even if someone were to walk past, they wouldn't notice anything.

Lormelle unlocked the door and opened it a crack. Convinced that no one was out in the hall, he came out of the room, relocked the door, and stole his way downstairs, quietly finding the outside door. The theft had gone off without a hitch.

When he found the case lying in the bush where he'd left it, the key was still in the lock. He carried the case to the far side of the garden, gingerly opening it. Jacques emptied the case of its valuable contents, replacing it with stones and twigs, not forgetting his penned note. He added some leaves for good measure and closed the case, locking it. He carried the newly packed case to the opposite side of the garden, where the captain was waiting for him.

Richemonte heard him coming, but quickly retreated behind the chestnut tree, not knowing who was approaching.

"Psst!" whispered Jacques.

The old man kept quiet.

"Psst! Captain!" he repeated.

"Who is it?" Richemonte asked.

"It's me, Jacques."

The captain breathed a sigh of relief. "Well, were you successful?"

"Yes, as you can see," he said, pointing to the small suitcase.

"Let me have it."

Jacques turned it over. The captain felt the case in the semi-darkness, yet had to control himself from shouting with joy.

"*Encroyable!*" he exclaimed. "So it worked out?"

"Completely."

"Did anyone see you?"

"No one. But, Captain, will I receive what you promised?"

"Certainly! Don't you trust me?"

"Why shouldn't I trust you?" Jacques asked. "It was only a fleeting thought. But I wish I could get a small advance for my work. You see, I've nearly come to the end of my resources. Who knows what I'll need in the next few days before I meet up with the count."

An unusual, compassionate feeling passed through the captain. He was in possession of a fortune and felt a sense of exuberance. He reached into his pocket, fished out a small purse, and handed it to Lormelle.

"Here, take this," he said. "There are a few gold pieces inside. I don't have any more with me. It should tide you over until I can pay you the rest." Richemonte peered suspiciously to his right, then to his left. "It's time I got going. I have a long way to carry the case. Good night, dear Jacques."

"Good night, Captain."

With that, Richemonte disappeared into the night. Once he had traversed the garden, he stopped momentarily to catch his breath.

That went better than I thought, he mused. *I only gave him about fifty thalers for his trouble. He even said good night! I wonder what he'll say later, when he finds out that's all he'll get! Ideally, I would rather have kept the whole fortune for myself, but then I'd have to contend with Rallion, who has considerable clout at court. No, I can profit more from his influential ways than if I kept back his share of the proceeds.* The old man took a moment to look behind him at the lights shining from the windows of the estate. *Good night, Löwenklau! Good night, dear Margot. I'm sure you'll remember this evening for a long time.*

Behind him, Jacques strolled back to the house engrossed in his own thoughts. *Idiot*, he thought. *He even gave me a handful of gold pieces. How he'll grind his teeth when he realizes that it was I who betrayed him! Serves him right. I have to look after my own interests.*

Jacques returned to the party and sought out a servant. He instructed him to advise anyone asking for him that he wasn't feeling well and had retired to his room for the night.

Once there, he opened his window and looked out. Satisfied that no one was standing below, he tossed his traveling cloak and leather case to the ground. He fastened the rope to the ledge and climbed down. He donned his cloak, picked up the leather case, and crept to the corner of the building where he had concealed the treasure, quickly filling the case and jacket pockets.

Jacques de Lormelle turned before vanishing into the night and bid a final adieu to the place that had received him so warmly.

CHAPTER SIXTEEN

Misery Upon Misery

Because the festivities had ended at such a late hour, the guests chose to spend the night instead of traveling through the night. The following morning, Samuel Cohn and Count Smirnoff were the first to leave. They had a pressing appointment and had to drive to Drengfurth to meet up with Rallion, who was eagerly awaiting their arrival. To their surprise, they not only found him awake, but packed and ready to travel.

"Did something happen?" asked the Polish count. "It appears like you're ready to leave."

"That is certainly my intention," Rallion admitted. "Unfortunately, I suffer from a recurring malady that often appears at the most inopportune times. Last night, I had a relapse and was forced to send for a nurse, who remained with me all night. Out of concern for me, even the proprietor stayed awake. I have to return to Berlin in order to find a better doctor than I found here."

Of course, it was nothing more than a ruse, a carefully staged alibi. This way, the nurse and hotel personnel could swear that the count hadn't left his room.

"What about us?" asked Smirnoff.

"Tell me, how did it go?" asked the count, ignoring the question.

"It all went according to plan. I stand here as the legal representative of your property."

"Show me the papers," instructed the business-minded Rallion.

"The title and necessary documents are all here," Smirnoff explained. "What would have taken a couple of weeks was accomplished in merely two days, allowing us to conclude the business quickly. Money certainly has the power to expedite a transaction! I wish I was in a position to exert this kind of influence."

"That will soon be the case, dear Count. The second part of our business can just as easily be accomplished in Berlin, so we'll conclude it there. We can even travel together. Once we're finished, you'll receive your payment."

Captain Richemonte was familiar with the count's scheme and had planned on a rendezvous with Rallion in Berlin. They had settled on meeting in an ordinary guesthouse on the outskirts of the city, rather than a conspicuous hotel where they would risk being recognized.

After his arrival in Berlin, Rallion went to the prescribed meeting place and inquired after Richemonte's room, which had been rented under an assumed name. Rallion obtained the number and, armed with anticipation, mounted the steps.

"Finally!" exclaimed the captain once the count was seated across from him. "The wait was becoming unbearable."

"Why? Didn't you have anything with which to occupy yourself?"

"Pah! What was I supposed to do?"

"Count the money!"

"I had no intention of doing so alone."

"Why not?"

"Caution," Richemonte answered simply.

"Really? I half-expected to hear that you had come here empty-handed."

"Did you think our little coup had failed?"

"It was always a remote possibility," Rallion said. "So, Jacques came through?"

"It worked out perfectly," confirmed the captain.

"Fine. But he won't get anything for his efforts. That should serve as a reminder of his previous hoodwinking. Did you keep the case hidden?"

"Yes," Richemonte said with a nod. "I concealed it in a special box, declaring that it contained mineral samples."

"That was clever of you. Where is it?"

"Right here." Richemonte pulled the large case out from under his bed. He cut the ropes and opened it. Inside, they found a collection of stones and the little suitcase, which both men admired, reminded of its costly contents.

"A sample case!" laughed the count. "What a fabulous idea! No doubt the police are searching for it right now. We will appropriate the money, then send the rock samples with the case back to the police. Thanks to you, Captain, this coup was brilliantly conceived. Think of it! To purchase two land holdings, paid for in cash, and steal the money back. What a grand idea! Now, let's have a look."

"Unfortunately, the key is missing," Richemonte said, pausing. "Evidently, Jacques didn't find it. Löwenklau must have kept it in his pocket."

"Then we'll have to resort to some tools."

Richemonte merely smiled, producing a hammer and chisel. The little suitcase was no match for the powerful blows of the chisel and the lock gave way after a few strong blows. When the lid popped open, both men peered at the contents with curiosity.

"What is that?" asked Rallion, shaking his head. "Leaves!"

"And a piece of paper," added the captain. "That Löwenklau is a curious fellow, to have covered the money with leaves. All these Germans are insane. I wonder what's in the note."

"He probably copied the serial numbers of the bank notes for future reference. What foolishness! Now he's left with nothing to deliver to the police. We don't have to worry about the issue of those numbers."

As the count prattled on, Richemonte glanced at the paper. His eyes widened as he read and he snorted through his nostrils like a wild animal.

"Heaven and hell!" he cursed. "We needn't concern ourselves with tendering the bank notes!"

"Great, isn't it?"

"Yes," he said sarcastically. "Too bad we won't be able to declare any of it."

"What are you talking about? What's wrong?"

"We can't tender the money," Richemonte said slowly, "because we don't have it."

"What do you mean we don't have it?" asked the count, looking dumbfounded. "Here is the very case that contains the money."

"Yes."

"What's on that paper?"

"Here," Richemonte said, passing the paper to his companion. "Read it for yourself."

The count took the paper, reading it out loud:

> "To my dear friend and colleague Richemonte, as a memento of the treasure your mouth watered after.
>
> - Jacques de Lormelle."

Rallion's eyes darted back to the captain, not comprehending what he just read.

"Isn't it clear enough?" Richemonte asked. "Don't you understand what this means?"

"What is there to understand? No, he couldn't have betrayed us!"

"What else could it be? Let's have a look."

They carefully went through the contents of the case, but found nothing else in it but stones, leaves, and twigs.

"He betrayed us!"

"Betrayal and theft!" Richemonte exclaimed, his face contorting into a hideous grimace. "I'm going to find him and crush him."

"Could it be that he plotted this with Löwenklau?" asked Rallion.

Looking aghast, Richemonte contemplated the possibility. "Dammit!" he murmured. "It's possible."

"Perhaps he guessed that he wasn't going to get anything in return for his trouble and decided to reveal everything to Löwenklau!"

"That's highly unlikely," Richemonte said, reconsidering. "He would have had to disclose the fact that he's a thief."

"Yes, that's true."

"It's more likely that he simply purposed to betray us all along. He kept the money and substituted the stones."

"Mineral samples!" the count spat the words like a curse.

"We should leave immediately... go back and try to capture him."

"Ridiculous! We underestimated him once, Captain. He will be long gone by now."

"Nevertheless, I'm going to find him," Richemonte raged, ranting to vent his anger. "I'll hold him for the police, identifying him as the thief!"

The count, although dismayed over the loss, was more composed. "No, it would only bring us harm. If we were able to find and capture him, he would probably confess everything and tie us in as his accomplices. We would face the same fate."

"We could deny the allegations and prove to the police that he acted alone."

"Perhaps," Rallion allowed, "but we would be taking an awful chance. I fear that in the long run they would still believe him. The smart thing would be to send out discreet inquiries. My business here is concluded, and I have the documentation to prove I'm the new owner. We should destroy the case, which could only implicate us. Better yet, let's burn it in the fireplace and leave."

When Richemonte remained still, his eyes staring at the case, Rallion continued. "My dear Captain, we have accomplished what we set out to do. We have avenged ourselves on Löwenklau. We have only lost the extra amount, the money we had to come up with to satisfy Löwenklau's sale price. If we play our cards right, we may still succeed in capturing Jacques and the full amount."

Both men had come to the realization they had been betrayed by a cunning and resourceful thief. Richemonte's anger slowly subsided, giving way to the reality of his victory in avenging himself.

They burned the case and a few hours later were sitting in a railway carriage, heading back to Breitenheim to complete their mission and search for clues of Lormelle's disappearance.

Löwenklau bid farewell to Samuel Cohn and Count Smirnoff the following morning, unaware of the heavy loss he was about to incur. It wasn't until after breakfast that the advocate who had conducted the sale proceedings suggested that it would be prudent to record the serial numbers of the bank notes. Hugo left the table and went to his room to fetch the traveling case. He unlocked the armoire and removed the case.

The first thing he noticed was that the key was missing. This little oddity stood out because he specifically remembered leaving the key in the lock. He had a cursory look inside the armoire, but couldn't find it. Hugo called for the official and outlined the inconsistency. It was decided to forego summoning a locksmith and to break the case open immediately.

Once the suitcase was forcibly opened, a shock spread through the household that was difficult to describe. The official issued an order prohibiting anyone, servants included, from leaving the estate without permission. A trusted servant was sent to bring the police, who upon their arrival immediately commenced a thorough search of the premises. The stolen sum was so staggering that any consideration for the feelings of individuals was of secondary importance.

Madame Margot was still in her room when the discovery of the theft was made. She had been unable to walk by herself for some time due to her ill health. She heard the commotion out in the hall: voices shouting, people hurrying, confusion not normal to the household. She rang the bell, calling for the servant girl to no avail.

As the noise outside grew louder, Margot was gripped by fear. Her fear rose in proportion to the growing noise out in the hall. She tried to rise from her chair, finally succeeding only with great pain and discomfort. Supporting herself on the furniture, she slowly worked her way toward the door, arriving weakly and in pain. Margot opened the door, finding a servant hurrying past her.

"Wilhelm! Wilhelm!" she called out to him. "What's happening?"

He stopped in his tracks, realizing he had been addressed. "Oh, dear lady," he said disheartened. "There was a break-in. You've been robbed. Victimized!"

"A break-in? A robbery? Dear God, what was stolen?"

"Everything!" he blurted out. "The whole fortune."

It seemed as though she had been struck on her head. "Our whole fortune?" she moaned.

"The purchase money... stolen from the suitcase... locked away."

"Oh—God... God... Sold!—Lost!—Fore—!"

She meant to say *foreboding*, but instead collapsed, unable to get the word out. The servant ran to find Löwenklau, who stood among the family members enveloped in his own shock.

"Gracious, sir," Wilhelm called out. "Hurry! Your wife has collapsed!"

All those who heard his proclamation hurried after the servant, leaving Hugo in his place, unmovable. Had a servant not supported him, he would have sunk to the floor. At last, aided by his servant, he managed to stagger his way to his wife's chamber.

241

He found her resting in bed. Her eyes were open, staring straight ahead as though she had died. A brownish frothy substance oozed from the corners of her mouth. Hugo collapsed next to her with a cry of dismay.

The prudent advocate immediately sent a servant to summon a doctor. The doctor, who arrived in a timely manner, was not able to offer much encouragement for Margot's condition. Having examined both man and wife, he concluded that she had suffered a debilitating stroke and had only a few days, perhaps a few hours, yet to live. Hugo himself was stricken with grief and had succumbed to high fever, which could prove very dangerous. Only a strict and carefully followed regimen would bring him through it.

In all the confusion, as the clouds of misfortune began to release their rain on the unsuspecting family, it became clear just what could be accomplished through a caring heart. Ida, the daughter-in-law, had failed to utter a single word when the unhappy news spread like wildfire. Her whole being seemed to be numbed by tears, yet she was the only one who grasped the severity of the situation. She declared that she would take over the care of her in-laws, forbidding anyone else to approach them.

During the confusion and fear, the lamenting and crying, no one had paid attention to the French guest, save one – a child. Richard had been lying in his bed when he heard all the yelling and running. He became curious, got up, and looked out his door, witnessing a confusion he had never seen before. He spotted a familiar face nearby, and though the man was crying and perturbed, Richard guessed that he would probably speak to him. It was Florian, the old coachman, wandering down the hallway, not like a drunk man but as one who was having trouble organizing his thoughts.

"Florian! Florian!" called out the boy. "Come here. What's happening? Why is everyone running back and forth?"

The old servant came over, took the boy's head into his hands, and bent down to kiss his soft hair.

"Richard, dear Richard," he managed to say, still crying. "A terrible calamity has befallen us. Your grandmother and grandfather—"

"What about them?" asked Richard, concerned.

"Oh, nothing. They're sleeping," Florian said, reconsidering his instinct to tell the boy the truth. "But someone has stolen all their money!"

The little boy looked at Florian through clever eyes. "Is that why you're crying?"

"Yes."

"They will have to return the money!"

"No, the thief is long gone."

"Who is the thief?"

"No one knows, but we're looking for him."

"Where was the money kept?" asked the inquisitive boy.

"In Grandpa's room."

"Oh, Florian," exclaimed Richard with youthful joy. "Then I know who the thief is!"

The old coachman was convinced this was nothing more than a child's whim. "Surely you don't know," he cautioned.

"Yes, I do. I know exactly."

"Well, who is it?"

"Monsieur de Lormelle."

"Dear God!" replied Florian. "Don't let anyone hear you say that."

"But why not?"

"Because Monsieur de Lormelle is a distinguished gentleman, and a good friend of your Papa. Certainly not a thief!"

"He may be a distinguished gentleman," Richard said, "but I don't like him. Last night, he was all alone in Grandpa's room."

"Did you see him go inside?" asked Florian, becoming more attentive.

"Yes."

"When was that?"

"It was last night, when all the visitors had gathered in the dining room."

"Was he with your Grandpa in his room?"

Richard shook his head, recalling the details of the encounter. "No, Grandpa was with his guests downstairs. I was restless. My little sister was asleep, and I wanted to join the others in the feast. I stood up and was going to call for you so you could dress me. But when I opened the door, I saw Monsieur de Lormelle in the hall. He was so quiet that I thought he wanted to surprise me. I closed my door, leaving it open just a crack."

The old servant was listening intently. "What did you see then?"

"He pulled a key out of his pocket and unlocked Grandpa's door. He went in, but came out after a long time."

"Was he carrying anything in his hands?"

"No, Florian. I didn't see anything."

"Curious, most curious. Will you repeat what you just told me to others?"

"To whom?"

"To Uncle Kunz." When Richard nodded to the question, Florian continued. "Even if he's accompanied by the police?"

"Even then."

"Wait a moment. I'll fetch them right away."

He returned shortly, followed by Goldberg, the advocate, and a policeman. The boy related his story once again with childlike pride.

The advocate followed the disclosure with considerable interest. "Have you already spoken to Monsieur de Lormelle?" he asked Goldberg.

"No. I hadn't thought of him until now."

"Likewise," said the policeman. "Isn't it curious that he hasn't come out of his room with all this racket going on? We should pay him a visit."

They went to his room, finding the door locked. This in itself was peculiar. When repeated knocking failed to garner a response from the occupant, the policeman instructed that the door be forced open. One of the servants procured a pry bar and performed the task.

Jacques was absent, his bed not showing any sign of having been slept in. The window was open, and it stood to reason he had left that way, since the door had been locked from the inside. Kunz looked outside, noticing the rope hugging the wall.

They searched the suspect's clothing, finding nothing unusual, but as the policeman moved the suitcase, he discovered something far more revealing – a ring with skeleton keys hanging from it. Jacques had neglected to remove this all-telling tool of his handiwork.

"This man is the thief," proclaimed the policeman. "These keys speak for themselves. With these instruments, he was able to gain access to Monsieur Löwenklau's room and also unlock the armoire. The owner had left the key in the suitcase, making it like child's play to steal the contents. The thief then climbed out the window so as not to be seen by the servants. I will instruct the authorities to conduct a search of the surrounding area."

The officer's suppositions weren't entirely correct, but he had drawn the right conclusion regarding the identity of the thief. The police alerted other jurisdictions, seeking to apprehend the thief, but to no avail. A man as clever and calculating as Jacques Lormelle had planned his escape with no less efficiency than the theft itself. He not only eluded the police, but remained at large for a long time to come.

CHAPTER SEVENTEEN
A Death in the Family

The doctor's dire prediction had come true. Hugo von Löwenklau succumbed to a dangerously high fever which lasted for several days. As he fought for his life, he hallucinated about land holdings, robbers, and stolen war chests. The doctor held out little hope for his recovery because of his advancing age. Madame Margot died on the fourth day without regaining consciousness. The house, once filled with so much joy, was now a repository of grief. Poverty, sickness, and death had precipitously found a way into the lives of the German family.

Kunz von Goldberg, in particular, reproached himself for supporting the decision to sell, feeling responsible for persuading the family to go ahead with the transaction. He wired Gebhard right away with the news. His friend replied quickly, stating he would return home with all possible speed, and confirmed what Kunz already suspected, that he knew no one by the name of Jacques Lormelle.

Goldberg decided to take holiday leave and be of assistance to the family, now in disarray. He even wired his wife, enlisting Hedwig's aid during this difficult time. But before her arrival and the granting of his leave, two unexpected visitors arrived. It had been five days since the tragedy. A servant approached Kunz von Goldberg, advising him that two strange gentlemen were seeking a meeting with Hugo von Löwenklau.

"Surely," inquired Kunz, "you informed them that your master is sick and unavailable for any meeting."

"Of course," agreed the servant. "That is why they requested to meet with you, Monsieur."

"What are their names?"

"They preferred to advise you themselves."

"Interesting! Bring them in."

Shortly thereafter, the two strangers were ushered in. No sooner had Kunz laid eyes on them than he jumped out of his chair. It wasn't Rallion who captured his attention so much as Richemonte, whose eyes he tried to penetrate with his stare. Anyone who had seen that face was incapable of forgetting it. And Kunz had seen it, in Algiers, shortly after the lion hunt, at the time unaware of his true identity.

The two men bowed, but it wasn't what one would attribute to a gesture of civility. Kunz suspected they intended quite the opposite.

"Are you Monsieur von Goldberg?" asked Rallion, mockingly.

"As you know full well!" replied Kunz. "No doubt you've come to explain your sudden disappearance from the mail carriage," he added sarcastically.

"Oh, I intend to clarify entirely different things."

"Perhaps you will finally grant me satisfaction," Kunz said condescendingly.

"Of course! That is my chief reason for coming here. I have come to inform you—"

"Please," interrupted Kunz, "aren't you going to introduce the other gentleman?"

"Actually, I intended to do so later, but as you wish. May I introduce to you my good friend and colleague, Albin Richemonte."

Goldberg failed to move a muscle or utter a single word as his mind digested the news. He was schooled as an officer, and had the fortitude to control his facial expression. *So*, he thought, *this is the devil who has tormented the Löwenklau family for so long.* Not a single muscle twitched in Goldberg's face. His eyes rested with a cold, calculating glare on Richemonte.

"Please continue," he said, turning back to Rallion.

"Right away. As I understand it, Monsieur Löwenklau has sold his current holdings to Count von Smirnoff."

"Correct."

"I believe one of the stipulations of the sale was that the new owner could take possession of the estate after thirty days."

"Yes. But how does this concern you?"

"Well, allow me to inform you, as you seem to represent Monsieur von Löwenklau, that I have purchased the holdings from the count, assuming all the inherent rights."

Goldberg's only response was a low whistle through his teeth. A thousand thoughts and suppositions bombarded his brain.

"I trust you understood what I just disclosed to you!"

Goldberg nodded slowly and thoughtfully, digesting the implication.

"I understand you very well," he replied evenly. "In fact, I perceive that you disclosed more than you intended. Would you please accompany me?"

He opened a nearby door and allowed the two men to step through ahead of him. They stopped in their tracks. The room was furnished with black drapes. It was strangely empty of table or chairs. For that matter, it was devoid of any furniture at all. Situated in its centre was an imposing *castrim doloris*,[17.1] with black crêpe material decorating its platform. Displayed on either side were large, ornate burning candles that, with all the windows covered, provided the only light in the room. The flickering light accentuated the coffin on the platform, drawing the gaze of the two men, helpless to avoid its magnetic lure.

The once lovely Margot, the object of affection of the emperor, was the occupant, clad in a bright white gown. Her lovely mouth was tightly sealed, the beautiful eyes were closed, and the once radiant cheeks had fallen. Skin that at one time had shone in ivory tones was now grey, and her majestic, dark colored hair had lost its luster.

No one else appeared to be in the room, and yet they heard the soft cries of a little boy sitting on the far side of the raised platform. His words, "Grandma, my dear Grandma," were cut short as he heard the door open. The boy receded from view, hiding behind the satin folds of the curtain.

Kunz von Goldberg climbed the steps and, with his right hand, pointed at the deceased. "Do you recognize this lady?" he asked, his voice trembling with emotion. "I told you earlier that you have revealed to me more than you probably intended. You admitted that you purchased the property of the deceased through a third party, allowing a fourth to steal the payment to facilitate your revenge. This dear lady has become a victim of the reprisal, and even now her husband is struggling to escape death. I place my hand on the stopped heart of this fair lady, and I swear by God Almighty that I won't rest until all your deeds come to light and you have found your true reward. Count Rallion, you share in the complicity of her death. Do you dare look into your victim's face? Captain Richemonte, do you feel the burning of hell fire in your heart when you glimpse your sister's body? Probably not, since you're a devil in your own right and have no fear of hell. Rest assured in the knowledge that a day of reckoning will come when you won't find a single soul to plead for your mercy. Leave now! There is no room for those who have murdered this angelic being."

Kunz pointed with his left hand toward the door. Rallion was deeply affected, reeling with a dread he couldn't seem to shake. He turned to leave, but Richemonte grabbed his arm. "Wait a minute!" he pressed him, sensing the count was losing control.

Richemonte climbed the steps and approached the coffin, assessing the corpse with a cold, distant look. There wasn't a trace of emotion in his impassive face. It almost seemed as though he was missing that place in his heart, the seat of emotions so vital to human existence. His aim in life had been to pursue his sister, not out of brotherly love, but for selfish gain. And now, as she lay dead in repose before him, he hadn't the slightest regret because he had no conscience.

After a moment, having viewed her as one would examine a wax statue, he calmly turned back to the others and shrugged his shoulders. "Why should I pity her?" he uttered, breaking the silence. "Despite all my efforts, she failed to see that which was best for her. I didn't want to believe it, but there really are people in this world who desire to have it all, yet fail to find true contentment."

Goldberg's spirit reeled. It was a travesty like no other. "Bastard!" he erupted in anger.

"Was that meant for me?" asked Richemonte blandly.

"Yes, you. No one else."

"You're out of your mind, Goldberg."

"I have a mind to throw you out of this house. Only my respect for this dear lady holds me back!"

"Monsieur von Goldberg," said Rallion, shaking off his previous inhibition. "Take care that it won't be you who gets tossed from this house."

"Coward!" was Goldberg's reply.

"Coward?" asked Rallion. "Each man wages his own battles. While some engage each other with firearms, the unassuming miner works steadily underground, being no less courageous than the first. Gebhard von Löwenklau was once foolish enough to confront me. I took on his challenge, but declined to fight with him in the traditional way with weapons of his choosing that were familiar to him, an accomplished officer. The exercise would have been pointless, with the outcome one-sided and unfair. Instead, I opted to go for other weapons, not desiring to fight him for his life, but rather for his financial existence. Who is the winner, I ask you now?"

Goldberg took a step closer. "Ah, now I understand you!" he called out. "You finally admit that the blow against the Löwenklau family was orchestrated by you."

"Pah! Think and guess all you like!" he countered. "Don't be so naive in thinking I came here for the express purpose of robbing them of their money, which is illegal. I'm satisfied to be the owner of an estate once owned by my adversary. If you're prepared to continue the fight, I'm up to the challenge. I'm letting you know that I don't intend to actually live here. Instead I will entrust the estate to a competent steward. If you want to contest the sale, you certainly have the judicial means at your disposal. However, in thirty days, make sure my representative doesn't find anyone on the estate who's opposed to my taking up residency. I would be forced to seek the help of the authorities to defend my own property. Adieu, Monsieur!"

He turned and abruptly left, with Richemonte following close behind.

❧�֍❧

The calamity had struck hard, affecting all members of the Löwenklau family. In a way, it was a blessing that Margot was spared the repercussions to come. She was buried in a private ceremony. All the servants mourned the passing of a lady who had cared for the welfare of all.

Hugo von Löwenklau clung to his strong nature, despite his advancing years. The fever hit him hard, bringing him to the brink of death. Nonetheless, he persevered, aided by his family's loving care. His convalescence took some time. Having lost everything he owned, he was no longer living at his beloved Breitenheim, but in rented accommodations arranged by Kunz von Goldberg. Although he was not alone, living with his daughter-in-law and her children, he still felt lonely, nearly abandoned. Hugo deeply missed his wife Margot, his soul mate. He wasn't immediately advised of her passing, under strict orders from his physician, but when he was told, the news hit him hard. It seemed that he was destined to experience another bout of sickness. It took all his family's love to side track his thoughts from the tremendous losses he faced and steer him away from depression.

At last, Gebhard arrived. Even while he was abroad, he had been aware that his mother had died and his father was very sick. He knew they had lost their holdings, victimized by a swindler, and, worst of all, that their enemy had taken possession of their estate. He had done everything he could to expedite his return, but it hadn't been possible to return any sooner.

He took matters into his own hands, taking up the investigation commenced by the police, and together with Goldberg labored at unraveling the disappearance of Monsieur de Lormelle. Unfortunately, there was very little to go on. It was clear to both that there was a definite connection between the theft of the purchase money and the almost immediate sale of the property to Rallion. Gebhard found that the solution was shrouded in an impenetrably bureaucratic mist, leaving all his inquiries fruitless. His only hope of success lay in capturing the thief, the so-called Jacques de Lormelle, but he wasn't able to find even the slightest trace of the scoundrel's whereabouts.

In the meantime, another misfortune announced itself in the form of a letter. The writing was conducted in black ink and the envelope bore an official-looking seal. It had originated from a notary in Paris, and was addressed to Gebhard.

> *Dear Sir:*
>
> *I regret to inform you that your close relative, the highly regarded Countess Juliette de Rallion, has passed away, having suffered a stroke. Unfortunately, she died without having left any instruction or testament regarding her possessions.*
>
> *For this reason, and the fact that your wife Ida and her sister, Hedwig von Goldberg, have both married foreigners and relocated to a foreign country, it behooves me to inform you that the prescribed time to contest the outcome, according to our current laws, has elapsed. The*

*estate therefore falls to the last remaining relative of the deceased,
namely Count Jules Rallion.*

Respectfully,

Erneste Vafot
Notary and Advocate

The good aunt had seemed destined to survive to an old age, and Gebhard had made it no secret that he hoped she would leave a little something for her nieces. This would have been an enormous help in their present situation. Now this last hope was dashed as well. Their enemy, Count Rallion, once again benefited from the outcome.

What mattered now was for him to roll up his shirtsleeves and go to work, holding off the advancing arm of poverty. Although Gebhard had a good friend in his brother-in-law, Kunz von Goldberg, who availed his resources to him, he chose to work rather than take advantage of his friend. Gebhard decided to utilize his experiences and observations from his many excursions. He wrote books, periodicals, and dissertations, and had the pleasure of seeing his work become recognized and rewarded financially. He was successful in making a modest living by employing his writing skills, something which proved very satisfying.

Time, however, didn't stand still for him, and with that reality came the demands that life and necessity dictated. His son Richard attained the age when he could enroll as a cadet in military college. Unfortunately, this required resources he didn't possess. Kunz von Goldberg helped him out as best as he could, but it was evident that the costs of such an education would mount from year to year. It wasn't Gebhard's style to solely rely on his brother-in-law's resources, and so he sought to find other ways to supplement their income.

On one particular day, grandfather, father, and mother sat together, coming up with and discarding plans that seemed impossible. There was one idea that at the outset came across as purely adventurous. It was usually Grandfather Hugo who steered the conversation toward it.

"The war chest, my boy," he said. "If we could only get our hands on it."

"It doesn't belong to us," Gebhard reminded him. "It's French property."

"True. But France would pay a handsome finder's fee to the one who found it."

"All right then! Where should we look for it?"

"I can't properly recall anymore," Hugo admitted. "I have a strong feeling we have to look in a southerly direction from where it had been buried. Even though Blücher kept my original drawing, I had the foresight to make a copy, which I still have in my possession."

The suggestion recurred among them so many times that Gebhard finally decided to give it serious consideration. Ida, though quiet, did her best to support her husband in the new venture.

On another afternoon, they were sitting in the small garden of their rented house, once again engrossed in talk about Hugo's favorite topic. The patriarch became more animated as the conversation progressed.

"That's fine, Gebhard!" he exclaimed. "If you're not going, I'll go in your place."

"You?" questioned his son. "I'm afraid not!"

"Why not?" asked the old man obstinately.

"Because even now the old injury is giving you a hard time. You need your rest and you have to avoid any sort of exertion."

"A trip is no exertion!"

"It could very easily turn into one!"

"I don't see how."

"Climbing a mountain and searching for an unfamiliar place is not what I would call convalescence," Gebhard admonished. "Furthermore, we need to do it without attracting attention to our activity. You can't wait for suitable weather. In fact, the worse the weather, the more you can be assured of keeping prying eyes at bay."

"Hmm, you could be right. I suppose I'll have to pass on it. But you, Gebhard, couldn't you give it a try?"

"If that's what you want, I'll do it. But how do we get started?"

A voice from behind them answered in Hugo's stead. "That's not too difficult!" said Florian, the former coachman. He had long ago come to Germany with Hugo and hadn't deserted them when they fell on hard financial times.

"Not difficult?" asked Gebhard. "How did you come to that conclusion?"

"Simple. I'm going with you."

"You? Let me think about it."

Like Hugo, Florian was older and showing his age. Gebhard looked the former coachman over, trying to evaluate if he was up to the rigors of such a journey.

"It seems to me," said the grandfather, "since I can't participate, that our Florian is the only one familiar with the lay of the land."

"Will he be able to remember some of the countryside?" Gebhard asked his father.

"Of course!" replied Florian. "I was in the ravine where the chest was first buried. It was on the same day when we were attacked that Captain Richemonte murdered Baron de Reillac."

Gebhard smiled, turning his eyes toward the old man. "I know, you've told us often. Will you be able to find the same ravine again?"

"Of course!"

"Describe the way you need to take!" prompted Hugo.

"The way leads to Bouillon, past the tavern where you once stayed and along the water until you come to the alder trees. Then you turn left, following the small path into the mountains, until you reach the old coal hut on the far side of the clearing. The way continues for a short while, until you come across the ravine on your right hand side."

Hugo nodded enthusiastically as Florian described the path. "Quite right," he agreed. "Many years have passed, though, and much has probably changed since then, making the terrain difficult to recognize."

"Perhaps, but the mountain is still there. And I doubt if anyone filled in the gorge," said Florian, making his point.

"True," laughed Hugo. "What happens when you've found the ravine?"

Florian shrugged. "We follow your little map, always holding to a southerly direction."

"Do you think you're up to such a strenuous journey?"

"Me?" asked the servant in his most convincing tone. "I would travel around the world if it would give you pleasure to send me!"

"Then I won't stand in your way," Hugo said. "You may go with Gebhard. Now that we've made our decision, we shouldn't put it off any longer."

The trusty Florian showed unexpected enthusiasm in being allowed to accompany Gebhard. "That's fantastic news!" he said, beaming. *I could even use the excursion to pay my relatives a visit*, he thought. *The old ones have long since died, but their kids are there and I still write to them. Perhaps I can notify my nephew and advise him of our proposed trip.*

Florian turned again to Hugo. "And then there's the money," he added. "Perhaps you'll become as wealthy as before."

The latest news brought Ida's curiosity to the forefront. "What portion of the treasure could we hope to keep?" she asked.

"Can't you guess?" Hugo asked with a short laugh. "To answer the question for myself, I sought the advice of a qualified advocate without giving away what I really had in mind. He did some checking with other colleagues and later told me that a war chest that had been buried for that long falls within the guidelines of buried treasure. Guess what the finder would get to keep under current French law?"

"Maybe a twentieth? Or a tenth?" suggested Ida.

"No, my dear, the finder can claim half for himself, while the landowner keeps the other half."

This latest revelation kindled a fervor in the men, propelling them to make preparations for a quick departure.

CHAPTER EIGHTEEN
The Shepherd's Daughter

Captain Richemonte, the true ruler over Jeannette's affairs, left the impression that his 'son', the young baron, and his reclusive wife were in charge. The baron's psychological state hadn't improved much. In fact, he had become more sullen. The memory surrounding the marabout's death in the Sahara plagued him constantly and the thoughts of his complicity in the death of so many Bedouins dragged him further into a shadowy world, leaving him brooding for long periods of time. At night, he envisioned the spirits of those he had murdered, imagining himself fighting against them. It was clear to the captain that he couldn't allow Henri to remain unsupervised. He also couldn't entrust anyone else with the task, for fear of their secret being exposed.

Eventually, Richemonte was forced to consult an experienced doctor. He supplied the physician with all the information he could without arousing the man's suspicions. The sympathetic doctor could have prescribed sedatives, but instead suggested that a change of scenery would do the patient a world of good. The rigorous demands of a journey would be sufficiently taxing on his body to release toxins that would translate into a healthier psyche.

The captain cursed to himself over the deplorable state of his adopted son's condition. He considered ridding himself of the burden, which in itself wouldn't have presented a problem to his conscience, since he didn't have one. But prudence persuaded him that such a risky ploy could lead to his undoing. If the Baron de Sainte-Marie were to suddenly die, there would be no immediate heir apart from a member of the Löwenklau family. In the end, the baron was spared an untimely end due to Richemonte's hate for his nemesis.

Richemonte wouldn't have undertaken the journey himself had he not received an unexpected message from a source in the Berlin telegraph office. The informant, having been on his payroll for some time, had intercepted a wire from the Löwenklau house, with the sender being Florian. This in itself was not particularly important, except that it mentioned a hasty trip to the Ardennes. Armed with this bit of news, he decided to undertake a short holiday, a hiking trip of his own into the mountains. The trip would be a departure from everyday life at the castle as well as a fulfillment of the doctor's suggestion to participate in more physically demanding activity. He proposed to go into the Ardennes and then into the Argonne Forest, hoping to uncover their plans. Planning for the trip was relatively easy. The captain ensured that a young, able-bodied servant was to accompany them, making himself available should the baron succumb to one of his episodes.

Upon setting out, they took a mail carriage to Chalons, disembarking at Bar le Duc. They hiked through the extensive Argonne Forest, ending up at Launoy. As predicted, the physical demands of the trek had a positive effect on the baron. If he dismissed a few mild outbursts at the outset, then Richemonte was pleasantly surprised to see that even the young man's melancholy, which hadn't left him in months, seemed to wane, replaced by a more even-tempered outlook. His disposition improved from day to day to the point that he was cheerful, talkative, and even interested in things going on around him. Richemonte had to be careful not to bring up negative reminders of his past, something that could easily throw him back into his melancholy state.

A pleasant little village was situated between Launoy and Siguy le Grande that was inhabited by good, hard-working people. Only one family, by the name of Verdy, was actually without means. The shepherd Verdy lived in a small hut that served as accommodations for both man and livestock. He was indeed poor and only owned that which he could carry with him. His income was meager and would have left a larger family hungry, but fortunately for him, his family consisted of just three people: himself, his wife, and one daughter, Adeline.

Adeline was the apple of his eye, yet caring for her occupied him more than looking after his flocks. Many villagers felt that such a pretty name wasn't suitable for a shepherd's daughter. She possessed little of value and was ostracized and avoided by the children of the more wealthy neighbors. Although she lived in seclusion, she would have rather dressed in nice clothes and learn to appreciate the finer things of life.

The shepherd's daughter was also vain, and as she became older her vanity grew along with her. She liked to admire herself in a mirror and compare herself to other girls, coming to the conclusion that she was the best-looking one among them. She wanted to groom herself and improve her appearance, but she lacked the means to do so. She looked for ways to earn money, but the prospect of working at the local market and serving the rich girls didn't appeal to her ego.

One day, Adeline was struck with a fabulous idea. Her father had some experience treating sick animals and he often sent her out into the nearby fields and forest to search for plants that had healing properties. Since she was aware that chemists needed herbs and plants, often purchasing them from local gatherers, she decided to venture out on her own, collecting plants and selling them to chemists. It was relatively easy work, and it brought her enough income for the things she needed.

Before long, Adeline acquired shoes, stockings, a colorful jacket, and several skirts. Attired in these new outfits, she soon noticed the admiring glances of local boys. Those who had previously ignored her, or made fun of her lower standing, were now changing their tune.

During Adeline's lonely outings into the forest, she occupied herself with all sorts of thoughts, some good and some less so. Having grown up being despised by the local girls, her heart grew embittered. She strayed from wholesome thoughts and moved toward inappropriate ones. It was no wonder that she contemplated ways of seeking retribution.

But how? she wondered. *There must be a way that I can get back at those pompous girls.* The longer she thought about it, the closer she came to a solution, until finally it came to her. *Ah, now I have it! I could have the best revenge by pursuing the most sought-after young man in the village – the mayor's son!*

From that moment on, Adeline began to cast her lures after him. The other girls quickly noticed her advances and scoffed at them, but what really mattered was that the boy himself viewed her as the prettiest of them all, allowing himself to be corralled. At first, they met haphazardly, often seeing each other in less public areas where they wouldn't be watched.

After a while, they made plans to meet publicly. Although Adeline was a shepherd's daughter, she was clever enough to persuade the young man to take her to a local dance. It became a real triumph for her to be seen by all, dancing with the mayor's son, who had no intention of dancing with any other young lady.

Even though the lad was upstanding and had honorable intentions, his parents opposed his choice. They confronted him with questions about the relationship and demanded that he no longer see Adeline. The boy listened to their disapproving advice, then promptly ignored it. The two friends still met in secret.

During one of these secret meetings, she faced her lover with an ultimatum, tears streaming down her face. She said that she felt unloved and unhappy having to keep their relationship secret. She feared the villagers would find out soon enough when the growing life inside her eventually became too great to keep private. The young man snapped out of his self-absorbed mindset and it dawned on him that such a union, between a poor shepherd girl and the son of a mayor, wouldn't be in his best interests. As the reality of the revelation sunk in, he began to pull back. When she noticed his reluctance, she demanded an explanation, her tears flowing freely down her cheeks. She was hoping her tears would fall like warm drops on the heart of her headstrong lover. But her cries had the opposite effect of what she had intended, washing away the last remnants of his love for her.

The boy decided to leave and never speak to her again, bringing out the abandoned Adeline's stubborn streak. She held out hope that he would recant and come back to her. She went looking for him at the local dances, but what had once been a source of joy for her was nothing but agony now when she found him dancing with other girls. At first she just cried, feeling worthless, unwanted, and sorry for herself. Gradually her feelings changed to anger, and finally to revenge.

How can I pay him back, she asked herself. *Me, the dirt poor girl, and him, the rich landowner's son. If only I could find a man who was richer, more refined than him. What a reprisal that would be!* She left the hall with this thought on her mind, pondering its merits. Once she was back home in the hut, she fell asleep, seeking to find a way to appease her agony.

One fine Sunday evening, she decided to return to the dance hall. Those around her were all having a good time, but she remained alone. Each young man passed her by, failing to ask her to dance. Then, all eyes turned to two strangers who had come in the back door to watch the dance. No one seemed to know who these well-dressed gentlemen were.

The older one sported a grey moustache, and his dour look suggested he wouldn't make good company. The second one was much younger. Perhaps he was the older man's son. Even he wasn't a young man anymore, but there was an appealing, endearing look about him that drew the admiring glances of the young women.

The two men watched the dancers for a while. Finally, the older man stood up, apparently bored with the proceedings, and left the hall. The younger man remained behind, his gaze continuing to follow the dancing couples. Adeline noticed that his eyes darted from one girl to another, as though evaluating their loveliness. Finally, it was her turn to be scrutinized. She lowered her eyes, feeling her cheeks turn red. When she opened her eyes after a while, he was still watching her, with a friendly smile on his lips.

He must like me! she thought. *But who is he?* Time and again, she noticed his glance returning to her face. At last, he nodded ever so slightly to her, but only enough for her to notice. She turned red again. *Did he notice I was looking at him, too?*

Adeline felt her heart beating under the bodice of her dress as the stranger left his place and walked along the perimeter of the hall toward her. Those who were seated during the pause in music respectfully allowed him to move through. When he approached her bench, near panic struck her. *What if he keeps walking? What if he stops? What will I say?*

The thoughts had barely made it through her head when he stopped next to her. "All alone, Mademoiselle?" he asked politely.

Should I reply? she pondered. *Of course. It would be impolite not to.* All eyes were on her and the stranger. Seeing his friendly manner, she decided to respond to his question.

"I am always alone, Monsieur."

"Why, my child?"

"The others are rich," she said. "I am poor!"

"What does that have to do with anything? Are they too proud to associate with you?"

"Yes, very proud."

"Ridiculous!" he exclaimed. "What could a farm boy or farm girl possibly boast about? Surely not about education and refinement!" His words had a profound effect on her. Too bad the others hadn't heard them. "Have any of them asked you to dance?"

"No," she whispered, her face blushing from the confession. If her admission bothered him, he didn't let on.

"Don't worry about the others. Do you like to dance?"

"I do enjoy it, although I have little opportunity."

"Are strangers permitted to participate in the festivities?"

"Who would dare to deny them, Monsieur?"

"Well then, would you do me the honor of the next dance, Mademoiselle?"

Adeline's heart seemed to be at the point of bursting. She held her hand over her bust, worried that her breathing might tear the bodice of her dress.

"You're joking!" she whispered.

"Oh no, this is no joke!" he reassured her. "I like to dance, too, but it's been a while since my last trip to France. I've come from a foreign land where dancing is viewed differently. Will you deny me this simple pleasure?"

"Oh no, Monsieur!"

"Then, please, join me. The music is just starting!"

The musicians began with a waltz. The newcomer put his arm around Adeline's shoulder, took her right hand into his left, and started the first turn.

Adeline was beyond thrilled, allowing him to lead at will. She closed her eyes as they floated across the dance floor, unaware that no one else was dancing, afraid to offend the stranger by getting in their way. It was only when the couple stopped dancing that a few fellows dared to step out with their partners.

The new couple danced several more songs before taking a break. During the pause between songs, another stranger approached the dance floor, addressing the couple.

"Baron," he said loud enough to be heard by all, "the captain is wondering if you will be joining him for supper?"

"No," he responded. "Tell him that he needn't wait for me. I will eat later."

The messenger, actually a servant from Jeannette, bowed and returned to the guesthouse.

"Well?" Richemonte asked him, already sitting at the supper table.

"The baron said not to wait for him," replied the servant.

"Really! I wonder why. Is he still enjoying the dance hall activities?"

"It would seem," replied the man haltingly, "that he is actually taking part."

"Really? What's he doing?"

"The waltz had just finished, but he still had his arm around the girl's waist."

The captain's face took on an amused look. "What sort of nymph was she?" he asked. "Pretty or plain, tall or short, heavy or thin?"

"On the contrary, she is quite good looking."

"Well, we're not known in these parts," he said. "All right, then. Let him have his fun. I'm going to retire after my supper. You can stay up and wait for him!"

Back at the dance hall, the messenger's announcement had created quite a stir. A captain, even a baron, had come to visit their village! Not only that, but he was dancing with a shepherd's daughter!

Adeline danced in a sea of bliss. She was so happy she could have hugged the whole world. She was dancing with a baron! Finally, here was her retribution to her unfaithful lover, who was standing in the corner trying to figure out if he should be angry or not.

The baron escorted her to a table, ignoring the bench where he had first met her. The table somehow seemed more appropriate.

"Will you allow me to join you, Mademoiselle?" he inquired, bowing before her.

Having to be asked permission was a consideration that had never occurred to her. She managed a smile, allowing herself to bask in the moment. "I'm not accustomed to such honor, Monsieur," she replied.

"But you're worthy nevertheless. Do you know how beautiful you are, my child?" Adeline blushed deeply, remaining quiet. "I wish," he continued, "that I was a farmer's son, like those I see here." When she didn't respond again, he went on. "Can you imagine why I would say such a thing?"

"No," she managed, although she guessed the answer.

The baron leaned in toward her, smiling. "Were I a farmer's son, I could come here and dance with you as often as I like."

"Oh, Monsieur, then you would surely become like all the others," she said dismissively, "preferring a rich girl over me."

"No," he insisted. "I would always choose the one who pleases me, and that is you. Do you still have parents?"

"Yes. They're both alive, living in the village."

"What does your father do?"

"He's only a shepherd."

"Only! Why do you use that word? Each man is complete in himself if he knows his place," Henri said. "Now, you might think I'm presumptuous by asking, but... do you have a lover? Will you answer me truthfully?"

"I don't have one," she replied, turning red.

"Are you telling me the truth, Adeline?"

"Of course, Monsieur."

"But you've had one before, am I right?"

She looked down at her feet, embarrassed to continue.

"This is the first time I've met you, Mademoiselle. I'm unfamiliar to you in every way, and I have no right to ask you such intimate questions."

She looked up quickly, examining his face. "And yet," she began, "I want to give you an answer, Monsieur. I had a lover, but he doesn't talk to me anymore. He shuns me because his parents have forbidden it."

"Really? Is he here tonight?"

Adeline nodded. "Yes."

"Will you point him out to me?"

"He's over there at the far table, getting a glass of wine," she said, pointing him out.

"That's him?" exclaimed the baron a little too loudly, glancing at the exposed man. "He has no taste. None whatsoever, Mademoiselle. You wouldn't be happy with a man like that, always wondering what his parents will coerce him to do." Henri paused, looking her in the eyes. "You've been more than obliging with me. May I presume to ask you a few more questions?"

"Yes, I'll be as forthright as I can."

"Would it be contrary to your customs if I were to invite you to dinner?"

"No," she said, "but it wouldn't be appropriate for us to dine alone."

"So it would have to be here?"

"Yes. Out in the open, for all to see."

He shrugged. "Fine. Would it appear forward or out of the ordinary if I were to escort you home?"

"Yes. People would talk, and I would be held in low esteem by the people in these parts."

"Still, I would like it very much if you would give me the opportunity of escorting you home."

Adeline found herself in a quandary. *I've dreamed of dating someone more distinguished than the mayor's son*, she thought. *My dream has come true! Should I spurn this baron's goodwill by declining his offer? Even if I accept, I'll face bitter recrimination.*

The baron could see her anguishing over her answer, but could also see that she was giving his offer serious consideration.

"Could we arrange it so that no one would know?" he suggested.

"What would you think of me, Monsieur?"

"I would conclude that you're a perceptive young woman."

"But what compels you to accompany me," she asked, "since we've only just met?"

Henri looked at her admiringly. "If you can't see it, I can't explain it to you. Men enjoy listening to good music," he said, indicating the others in the room. "Even more so, they enjoy being in the company of a beautiful woman. It would be easy for me to leave the hall before you and meet up later. It's a lovely evening and I would very much like to extend it with a walk."

"It would make more sense if I left earlier, and then waited for you."

"Why's that?"

"It's not customary for a girl to wait for a gentleman," she explained. "Those here wouldn't easily come to that conclusion, thinking instead that I've gone home."

"Ah, you're not only beautiful, but also clever. So, may I accompany you?"

She hesitated, still trying to make up her mind. "I'm not sure. To give you my answer, I would have to first ask you an important question."

"Go ahead and ask."

"I don't wish to embarrass you!"

"Your words won't offend me."

"Well, then," she began, treading carefully, "are you married?"

The baron had suspected she might ask him this question. He wasn't quite sure how to respond. "No," he replied after a brief pause. "I was, but my wife died."

"Then you're a widower?"

"Yes."

"In that case, I'm permitted to accept your invitation. At the conclusion of the dance, once you leave the hall after me, continue on the right side of the village until you reach the last house. I will wait for you there."

Henri nodded in agreement. He would have liked to shake her hand to seal the deal, or even give her a kiss, but such an act would have stood out and invited reproach. They stayed a while longer at the dance hall, spending quite a bit of time on the dance floor. They even shared a meal together. The other guests might have felt envious of them, but they never showed mistrust. When the two finally parted company and the baron politely bid her good night, all suspicious thoughts from those watching evaporated.

He waited for a few minutes after she had left before making his own departure, leaving the hall in the opposite direction. He found his servant at the guesthouse and instructed him that he was going for a walk, and wouldn't need him to wait up. The servant was to ensure that the door to the guesthouse remained unlocked.

Henri found the alluring Adeline at the preordained place. She didn't hesitate taking his arm as they strolled together down the tree-lined street. They talked about both everything and nothing, conversing unpretentiously about small topics significant in and of themselves. He placed his arm around her waist, something that surprised her, but she didn't object. He stole a kiss, meeting her lips with slight reluctance, which he easily overcame.

Adeline gave him the impression that she would have handled herself in like manner with other men. On the way back, they walked side by side, their arms wrapped closer around each other. They stopped often, feeling the need for lingering kisses.

When they reached the outskirts of the village, the baron let out a sigh.

"Oh, how quickly the time flies," he said regretfully. "I'd like to get to know you better."

"Is that so difficult?" she asked.

"Perhaps I could stay another day."

"Will you be able to convince your relative?"

"I'll get him to see it my way," Henri said. "Will we be able to meet again?"

"If that's what you'd like."

"Yes, I'd like that very much. Can you tell me where?"

She stopped walking and pointed to the right. "Do you see that clump of trees in the moonlight?"

"Yes."

"You'll notice a tall oak over there during the day. You'll find me under the oak at one o'clock. I'll be collecting plants."

"Ah! A good idea. I will help you, Adeline."

"Good," she said with a smile. "We will accomplish more that way. Good night, Monsieur."

"Good night."

What followed were a series of hugs and kisses more passionate than ever. It seemed as though they had known each other a long time already. Sadly, she walked toward her parents' hut while the baron headed for the guesthouse, like a man who had enjoyed a fine, if not unexpected, evening.

Chapter Nineteen
The Missing Strong Box

While Henri was out with the shepherd's daughter, an important development was playing out at the guesthouse. As Richemonte was sitting down to his evening meal, two new guests entered the inn. These two men, also an older and younger combination, took seats at a nearby table. A peculiar sensation passed through Richemonte as he watched them, feeling as though he had seen the older man somewhere before. He kept his eyes on them as they ordered supper and a bottle of wine, being served by the innkeeper.

"Is a gentleman by the name of Laroche staying here?" asked the older man.

The innkeeper nodded. "Yes, Monsieur."

"Do you have a room for us?"

"Are you the two gentlemen Monsieur Laroche told us to expect?"

"Yes. Did he say anything about our arrival?"

"Only that he's expecting you. He's still awake and booked in room number three."

"That's good. Please arrange for a room of our own!" He turned to his younger companion. "We don't need separate rooms, do we?" he asked.

"No, we can stay together, Uncle Florian."

On hearing those two words, Uncle Florian, it was as though a bright light illuminated Richemonte's deepest memory. *Yes, now it all comes back to me. Not only have I seen that face before, but I knew him quite well once upon a time. That's Florian Rupprechstberger, the former coachman at Jeannette. What business does he have here? Florian lives in Berlin, now a servant to the Löwenklau family. His arrival here must be connected to that telegram. And who is this so-called Monsieur Laroche who is supposedly waiting for them?*

Richemonte considered these and other questions and quickly realized that Laroche's room was directly next to his own. Reasonably confident that he hadn't been recognized by Florian, Richemonte acted quickly by going upstairs. He walked quietly up to his room, inserting the key into the lock with care. He quietly closed the door behind him and pulled up a chair, positioning it next to the locked connecting door to the adjoining room. He made himself comfortable, inwardly preparing himself for what might follow.

Finally, after a lengthy wait, he heard footsteps in the hall. Someone knocked next door.

"Who's there?" asked a voice from within.

"It's me. Florian."

The door opened, and the guest entered.

"What carelessness to use your real name in the corridor! It would be prudent to use assumed names!" the occupant chided, overheard by Richemonte. "You're very late. I would have thought the light to be inadequate at night to permit much of a search."

"I hope you will forgive me," Florian said. "It was good that we decided to split up! We covered a lot of ground that way."

"Really?" the other man asked quickly. "Were you successful in your search?"

Before answering, Florian tossed the question back at the other man. "What about you, sir?"

"No, I wasn't so fortunate."

"You had the detailed drawing with you. But, going from memory, I believe I came across the site. The trees have grown somewhat and new brush work has cropped up in places, but it all coincides with what I remember: the terrain, the hollow, the trees. It all fits. In fact, only the stump is missing."

"It could have rotted out with time. Did you examine the ground?"

"We weren't carrying any tools other than our walking sticks and my knife," Florian said. "The war chest would be buried deeper than I could reach with a knife. We'll have to obtain a spade tomorrow to conduct a more thorough search."

"Of course! For now, it's sufficient to determine whether or not we've discovered the right place—"

The dance music within the guesthouse started up, canceling Richemonte's hope of hearing more.

"Dammit!" he said in a subdued voice, just barely remembering to keep his voice down so the men in the next room wouldn't overhear him.

The war chest! he thought. *They're out looking for it, and it sounds like they've discovered where it was buried. This Laroche must be one of the Löwenklaus! Finally, one of my informants pays off. The chest will be mine!*

Although the loud music droned through the wall, the captain distinctly heard the door open and close next door. Florian must have left, meaning there wouldn't be much more to overhear. Richemonte decided to undress and lie down. But sleep evaded him as memories from the past filled his mind, evoking his previous anger and frustration. He tossed and turned in his bed all night, finally getting up at the break of dawn, giving up on catching any sleep.

In leaving his room, the captain had to be careful not to be seen. First, he attended to his servant's room, instructing him in how he should conduct himself in his absence. He then returned to his own room and got dressed quickly so as to be ready to follow the treasure hunters when they left.

When the guests started to wake up and move about the hotel, he snuck downstairs and left instructions with the proprietor that they were not to be disturbed. Since the innkeeper felt privileged to have such distinguished guests staying with him, Richemonte was certain he would comply with the request. Afterward, he returned to his room and remained on the lookout. His only regret was that he wasn't carrying a weapon. He was in possession of a hunting knife, but that was only suitable for defensive tactic. Only under extremely unusual circumstances would he even consider using it for an attack.

At last, Richemonte heard movement next door. The occupant, unlike himself, had probably had a good night's sleep, judging from the fact that he rose late. After a few minutes, the man left his room, heading for the restaurant. About half an hour later, Richemonte, looking from his window, saw three men leaving the guesthouse, walking slowly yet purposefully down the lane.

The first two were Florian and his relative, but the third man, although unfamiliar, had an unmistakable resemblance that Richemonte would have wagered money was a Löwenklau. He quickly left his room and rushed to see Henri, who was still in his bed.

"Already awake?" Henri asked. "Do we have to leave right away?"

"No," replied the captain. "You can get up at your leisure. We're not leaving today."

"We're not?" exclaimed the baron, just as excited as he was surprised. "Then what's on the agenda for today?"

"I don't have time to fill you in on all the details. I have to leave now and will probably return tonight. I hope you won't be too bored while I'm gone."

Richemonte had no idea how pleasing this news was to Henri. While the young man took his time getting dressed, the captain quickly left the guesthouse, not wanting to lose sight of Löwenklau and his companions. He followed the lane they had taken, spotting them at the end of the village.

They soon left the road, walking across an open field. The men then came across a plough, finding a shovel and pickaxe leaning against it. The two implements were a welcome sight. They picked them up and left in a hurry, not wanting to run into the owner. Richemonte used whatever cover he could find, following at a distance. The terrain was uneven, enabling him to keep them in sight while keeping himself hidden. When the trio finally reached the forest, he had to close the gap for fear of losing them.

Henri, on the other hand, was enjoying his breakfast, recalling with pleasure his nocturnal outing the night before. He instructed the servant to remain at the inn while he headed out for his prearranged rendezvous. He could easily make out the oak tree from afar, since it dwarfed the nearby trees.

Adeline was already waiting there for him.

"It was nearly impossible for me to keep our appointment," she told him, permitting him to greet her with a kiss.

"Why?" he asked, surprised.

"Because my father insisted on going out himself, looking for plants I wasn't familiar with. He was entrusted with a few new 'patients' from the herd, for which he needed special plants. I was supposed to remain behind with my mother, but I managed to get an old relative to help out at home."

"You handled that well, my child," he said as a compliment. "Why don't we stroll through the woods and enjoy a few hours together?"

As the morning wore on, he failed to consider his remaining susceptibility to the painful memories of Liama. He didn't think about the consequences of his actions, choosing to focus instead solely on the alluring Adeline. He blabbered on about all sorts of things, revealing his name and the location of his estate. But his greatest blunder was far worse. Eventually, he asked her to marry him.

Adeline didn't immediately say yes. She was concerned by her lack of passion for him. He was upstanding and fun to spend time with, an attractive quality to be sure, but the deciding factor was that he was nobility. When he broached the subject of marriage, she couldn't pass up the opportunity to become his wife. And so, she minimized her own doubts and agreed, holding him to his promise.

I could become Baroness de Sainte-Marie! she thought to herself. *But could I actually go through with it? I would do almost anything... maybe even something underhanded.*

The couple meandered through the forest, taking a rest from time to time to revel in their newfound love. They failed to keep track of the direction, dwelling only on their happiness. They were sitting comfortably in a mossy area, caressing each other and making plans for their future, which only a few hours ago had seemed impossible to the shepherd girl, when they were interrupted by a shrill outcry.

"Dear God," she exclaimed. "That was no ordinary holler. It sounded like—"

She stopped speaking and held her breath, feeling shocked to her very core. As they listened for more, they both heard a cry for help, loud and horrible, as one would call out when faced with a life and death situation.

"What's happening?" she managed. "My father's in this part of the forest!" She grabbed Henri's hand and pulled him along.

"Yes," he agreed. "Someone's facing a deathly fright. Come on, we've got to help."

The baron ran ahead while she did her best to keep up. The two calls for help were coming from the same direction. They quickly came to an area where the base of the forest sloped downward into a sort of ravine. At the bottom was the scene of a fierce battle. Two men were trying to wrestle a third man to the ground while he fought them with a knife. Not far removed, a fourth man lay on the ground, unmoving and presumably dead.

A short distance from the fighting was a wide, freshly dug pit, from which a shovel and pickaxe protruded. The first two men were Florian and his nephew, while the third man, who fought wildly with his knife, was Richemonte. The fourth man, wounded in the chest, was Gebhard von Löwenklau.

Henri took in the scene and correctly perceived that his relative was outmatched and in great danger. Although he had no idea what the conflict was about, he felt compelled to stand by Richemonte. He half-slid, half-ran down the steep embankment without being detected by the three men. He picked up the pickaxe and swung it at Florian with such force that it shattered the old man's skull with a single blow. While Florian collapsed in a heap, he concentrated on the other, younger man, striking a glancing blow. Richemonte seized the opportunity and grabbed Florian's nephew.

"Ah, it's you," he called out to the baron. "What luck! Come on, hit this one as well!"

The young man couldn't move. He saw the raised pickaxe and cried out in terror, falling victim to its wielder. He collapsed next to his murdered uncle. Richemonte tried to catch his breath, realizing he had fought against formidable adversaries.

"How did you happen to come here?" he asked, nearly out of breath.

Henri stood as still as a statue. Still holding the implement, he was staring at the bodies of the two men he had killed.

"Well?" pressed Richemonte.

The baron shifted his gaze to the captain. "What did you say?" he managed to ask.

"I want to know how you came to this place."

"I went for a leisurely walk. Dear God! The pickaxe is covered in blood, and so is your knife."

Richemonte looked at it and smiled with a grimace. "Of course it's bloody!" he replied matter-of-factly. "I just stabbed him." He pointed to Gebhard's body a short distance away.

"Who is he? Why did he attack you?"

"Attack me? Pah! It was I who ambushed him."

"You? How come?" Henri's eyes glimmered with insanity and the tone of his voice was that of a man who no longer had control of his mental faculties. The sight of blood had reawakened the old memories.

"You don't know this man," said Richemonte, pointing to Gebhard. "He was digging the hole with the other two. Can you imagine why they traveled from Germany to start digging on this lonely mountain?"

"No," he said.

"Then I'll tell you. It concerns the old war chest, that strong box we were after. It's buried here."

A measure of sanity returned to the baron as his eyes lit up. "The strong box?" he called out. "Dammit! We'll be even richer."

"Yes, we'll have millions. This man is Gebhard von Löwenklau, the one we were after in Algiers. He managed to elude us then, but now I've settled things between us. This other man is the coachman Florian, and the third one is his relative who I overheard last night."

Henri approached the edge of the pit. He looked down, still holding the axe in his hands. His expression once again assumed the strange look that was a precursor to a relapse.

"The money is down there!" he called out, jumping into the pit. "The strong box! I have to get it. I have to find it." Without giving the captain a second thought, he started hacking away at the earth.

The captain was about to clarify a few things, when he heard a noise behind him. He turned and stood mesmerized as two newcomers slowly climbed down the embankment.

Meanwhile, at the same time that Henri had rushed down to help the captain with his enemies, Adeline remained in the forest where he had left her frozen in her tracks. She wasn't easily rattled, and was even about to follow her betrothed when she heard fast steps approaching from behind her. She spun around and came face-to-face with her father. He recognized his daughter immediately and came to an abrupt stop. He held a long knife in his hand that he used for digging up roots.

"What are you doing here, girl?" he asked in astonishment. "I thought you'd be at home! Who was calling? Who's in danger?"

"Look down there!" she replied, pointing to the hollow. Her father looked down into the melee just as Henri felled Florian with the pickaxe.

"Look! A murderer!" he said out loud. "I have to get down there."

She grabbed him by the arm, holding him back. "Hold it, father!" she admonished him. "One of those men is my lover, a baron. If you want me to become a baroness, then be quiet and don't get involved until I tell you to."

He looked down at her, his face overwhelmed with confusion. "You, a baroness?" he asked.

"Yes. Now come down with me, but follow my lead."

Richemonte watched as they approached. The thought of discovery and losing the treasure made him immediately suspicious. His face was a mask of deception. He gripped the hilt of his knife tighter when he saw the shepherd was holding a long knife of his own in front of him.

Richemonte became instantly uncertain. *Two witnesses to murder*, he thought. *Will it come to another fight?*

"Captain, don't be afraid of us!" Adeline called out to him. "We're on your side. We're here as friends."

"What?" he asked. "You know me?"

"Yes. I've been keeping the baron company in the woods. Naturally, he told me all about you."

Richemonte narrowed his eyes. "Who are you?" he asked warily.

"My name is Adeline Verdy. My father is the local shepherd in the village where you've been staying overnight."

"Ah! So you're the girl from the dance last night?"

"Yes."

"Did you arrange to meet with the baron in the forest?" he asked sarcastically.

"Yes, that's right," she replied evenly.

"Then you're a *courtisane?*"[19.1]

"I don't know what that means," she admitted. "I'm sure you'll find out soon enough who I really am, Captain."

"Fine, fine, my venerable lady! Did you see what just happened here?"

"Naturally!"

"Did you hear what we talked about?"

"Of course. I heard every word."

"Go to hell!" he shouted. "How dare you seduce my companion and sneak around with him in the forest! What gives you the right to get mixed up in affairs that don't concern you?"

"On the contrary," she countered. "This concerns me as much as it does you. And I can prove it! In that pit over there, there is a buried strong box, a real treasure. Those three men over there wanted to dig it up, but you murdered them, with the help of the baron. I want to see if there is really a treasure down there. Father, don't let your guard down, but hold onto your knife. The captain is not to be trusted!"

Adeline walked over to the pit to evaluate the baron's efforts while her father bent down to examine the dead men. Richemonte was taken aback by the girl's attitude. She displayed a sort of bravado that dismayed him. He suspected she was therefore in possession of certain facts that gave her reason not to be afraid of him. He decided to be cautious and approached her father.

"Were you also with the baron in the woods?" he asked the shepherd.

"That's none of your concern!" barked the man, not knowing how to respond. "We saw how you murdered those men. We'll deal with the rest later."

"Really! Are you by chance considering sharing in the spoils?"

"What we want, shouldn't concern you right now. Why don't you see if the chest is really buried there?"

The captain's upper lip lifted, revealing his long yellow teeth. He would have liked nothing more than to stab the man and his meddling daughter, but was kept at bay by the man's knife. In reality, he wanted to find out what those two were really after, so he chose to ignore them for the time being and assist Henri in the digging. He climbed into the pit and picked up a shovel.

Like a madman, Henri worked without slowing down, which to a large extent reflected his current mental state. The hole became deeper and gradually wider, yet failed to yield any trace of the wooden box.

The shepherd, standing at the edge of the cavity with his daughter, felt as though he was in a dream. His daughter had aspirations of becoming a baroness! Nearby lay the bodies of three strangers, and in front of him two men worked feverishly to unearth a military strong box. It all seemed ludicrous to him.

One half hour followed the next without the slightest results. Finally, frustrated and tired, the captain climbed out of the hole.

"Nothing, absolutely nothing!" he exclaimed, disappointment dripping from him like sweat. "This fellow, this Löwenklau, must have been mistaken. He spoke of a drawing, a sketch, which he tried to interpret. Where could it be? Where did he leave it?"

He looked everywhere, but couldn't find any such sketch.

"Did he perhaps pocket the paper?" she asked confidently. "Father, why don't you search the dead man?"

It seemed unlikely that they would find the paper on the ground. It had been trampled during the wrestling match. Further, Richemonte had shoveled so much earth around the area that looking for it now would have been pointless. The old shepherd walked over to Gebhard's body, turning it over to be able to search the contents of his pockets. As he did so, blood started to flow again from the unseen wound, and the apparently dead man moved his arm.

"Dear God!" blurted the shepherd, startled. "He's still alive!"

"Really?" asked Richemonte. "Not possible!"

"I know it seems unlikely, but his hand moved."

The shepherd, who had prepared ointments and medicinal potions for livestock, was somewhat familiar with the treatment of human maladies. He conducted a thorough examination, coming to the conclusion that the German was indeed alive.

"He really is alive," the old man proudly confirmed. "He didn't die."

"Will he regain consciousness?" asked Richemonte with interest.

"Probably, but not for some time. The wound goes deep and still poses a danger. He could be saved if properly cared for, but before he regains consciousness, a strong fever will grip him."

"We have him under our control," Richemonte observed. "In time, we could force him to reveal his secret. If he dies, the secret dies with him. But if he lives, he could prove to be a hindrance!" He played with the ends of his moustache as he contemplated the reality of his words.

Suddenly he turned, facing the girl. "Mademoiselle," he said in a nearly friendly tone, "can you keep your mouth shut?"

"Yes," she replied.

"Can I depend on your father to do the same?"

"Of course."

"Can both of you keep this to yourselves if I promise to give you a portion of the treasure, assuming we will find it?" he asked, motioning to the pit and the bodies.

"Yes," she answered thoughtfully. "I only ask that this portion not be a meager one. What will you give us?"

"One-tenth."

"That's enough. We will remain quiet about today's events."

It was peculiar to watch both their expressions. The captain's face intimated his devious nature, as if he were a fox making a pact with a hen so that he could devour her even sooner. The girl, however, smiled slyly, suggesting much but revealing nothing.

"Then it's settled," continued Richemonte. "Chance has brought us together, and so it's fitting that we remain allies. What matters now is that we take the injured man to a secure location, where he can receive the proper care and eventually recover. Then we can interrogate him and extract his secret. Can you look after him in your house?"

"I think we can manage it, Monsieur."

"But no one can find out!"

"Of course," she assured him. "Prudence and discretion are paramount to our success."

Richemonte nodded. "Well then, that should suffice for now. We need to bandage the wound so he won't bleed to death." The instruction was meant for the girl's father, who accepted the task without comment. "Are you convinced that I'm responsible for their deaths?" continued Richemonte, pointing to the two dead men.

"Yes," she said, seemingly unperturbed.

"You're wrong. I'm not a murderer," he said in his own defense. "I will explain the circumstances, and then you can judge for yourself. Hopefully, you will realize how you've misjudged me."

Adeline smiled, nodding in agreement. "And you should become familiar with my plans," she said. "That way you will be convinced we mean you no harm."

"Ah, how come?"

"I will fill you in later. For now, there is much to be done."

"You're right. We can't move the injured man until it's dark. Until then, we need to make use of our time. We need to fill the hole."

"What about the corpses?"

"We'll put them in the pit." He turned to Henri, who was still in the hole. "Come out of there!" he shouted. Henri simply ignored the captain and continued digging until Richemonte had no choice but to climb in and grab him by the arm. Startled, the baron finally stopped working and followed him out of the cavity.

Henri was in the grip of a recurring mental sickness. He happened to glance briefly at the grotesque-looking corpses. Unable to help himself from staring at them, he tugged at his hair.

"God, I killed them," he lamented. "I'm the murderer! Where is the strong box? Where is it?"

"Be quiet," admonished the captain. "Do you want someone to hear and arrest you?"

"Catch me? Arrest me? No, no, I'll be quiet, but I'm still the murderer!"

"There are times when he suffers from delusions," explained Richemonte. "Things from the past."

"I will comfort him," Adeline offered and walked over to Henri, pulling him close to her. "Calm down! Be quiet. You're not a murderer!"

As he looked expectantly into her face, his eyes brightened a little. "I'm not a murderer?" he asked. "But who are you? Ah, now I remember. You're my dance partner, Adeline, the beautiful shepherd's daughter. No, I'm not a killer. You are my bride, my lover. Come here, I want to kiss you."

He pulled her closer and kissed her on the lips. She tolerated his impromptu manner as though she were accustomed to it.

"Adeline!" her father barked.

"Heavens!" commented the captain. "You two seem to be well-acquainted with each other."

"Perhaps that's why I want to help him in his state," she replied.

She then led the compliant baron toward a small clearing, where they sat down together as though they were on a stroll. Her father continued to stare, amazed at his daughter's intervention. She seemed to have turned into a different person.

"Hang it all!" the captain said to himself, irritated at the turn of events. *What am I supposed to do with her?* he wondered. *She could prove very useful, but she could also become a stumbling block. Which of the two will come to pass, I'll have to wait and see, and handle it the best way I can.*

He roped the shepherd into helping him to fill the pit. The man had been an honest soul all his life, and yet now found himself an unwitting witness to murder. He helped place the two corpses into the hole, working in a daze, and then helped to cover them with earth. He trampled the ground and scattered leaves and brushwood needles over the area. He did so without compulsion or thought, almost absentmindedly.

In the meantime, Henri and Adeline sat together, whispering to each other as lovers do. He revealed all sorts of important details about his past to her, the relevance of which struck home as evidenced by the stolen, triumphant glances she cast at the captain.

Evening finally arrived, signaling the time to transport the injured man. The shepherd fashioned a sort of litter from nearby branches. Richemonte and the old man used this simple stretcher to carry Löwenklau to the shepherd's small house. Henri and Adeline sauntered behind them, arm in arm, as if they belonged to each other.

Having arrived at the hut, there was still much to discuss and negotiate between the two factions, with issues finally settled and covered by the curtain of secrecy.

Back at the guesthouse that night, the servant was quite surprised to see Henri and the captain return so late. He was dismayed over the baron's mental condition, which only the previous evening had seemed to be more stable.

Henri struggled to maintain his composure and succumbed later to another episode of madness, alternating between calling for help and repelling unseen ghosts. The captain had no choice but to bind the ranting baron, with the servant's help, even stuffing a cloth into his mouth to stop the outbursts.

Under the circumstances, there was no way they could remain at the guesthouse. Richemonte arranged for a carriage and they loaded the delusional Henri onto it, leaving the little village in the middle of the night. The end of the excursion, which at the outset had looked so promising, had turned out nothing like they'd expected.

The two men could hardly contain the half-mad Henri. He envisioned the ghosts of the dead men as deep pits tried to swallow him. Lastly, he fantasized about the stolen war chest. He insisted that he had personally fought at major battles, including Austelitz, Magenta, Solferino, and others, coming away with stolen strong boxes. He cried out to Liama, then to Adeline, hoping to secure peace through their intervention as he was hounded by unseen spirits.

Upon their arrival back at Jeannette, Richemonte once again turned to qualified doctors, who convinced him that a change of location would still benefit the baron. The captain, who was no longer content at Jeannette, jumped at the chance of leaving once he learned of another estate that was for sale. He was able to work out a mutual arrangement whereby he more or less exchanged one property for the other.

He was happy to leave the old memories of Jeannette behind him. Even though he had been careful in his dealings, he realized that the local inhabitants were aware of certain details about his past that he wanted to keep to himself. He therefore chose to head for the new estate and home, the mysterious Castle Ortry.

CHAPTER TWENTY
Richemonte Upstaged

Richemonte embraced his new dwelling and hoped to start his affairs there anew. He was just getting acquainted with his new surroundings when one of the servants interrupted his solitude with news that a visitor, a young lady, was seeking an appointment. He was astonished to find Adeline, the former shepherd's daughter, in the hall, now attired as a lady of social standing. His first thought was that she had spent the money he had entrusted to them for Gebhard's care on herself.

"Have you brought me good news?" he asked, leading her into the parlor.

"Yes," she replied, taking a seat. "The injured man has recovered sufficiently. We don't have to be concerned about him dying."

"Did you discuss the war chest with him?"

"Of course. So far, he has refused to divulge any details."

"He won't keep it from me. I know how to persuade him to talk. We'll leave today. I will instruct my servant to make preparations for the return trip."

"Are you implying that I need to travel back with you?"

"Of course!"

"Then may I pay a visit to Henri before we go?"

"What for?"

"Well, naturally, I want to check on his well-being."

"Why should that concern you?" he asked warily. "You seem to have forgotten that he showed interest in you only when plagued by one of his episodes. It should be obvious to you that there exists a huge gulf between a baron and a shepherd's daughter. Therefore, there is no need for you to be concerned with him."

Adeline rose from her chair, her eyes flaming with anger. "You are mistaken, Captain!" she replied sharply. "The distinction between an honest shepherd's daughter and murderers, thieves, and spies isn't nearly as large as you claim."

"What do you mean by that?" he asked in surprise.

"I just wanted to make you aware that Henri has told me everything. While you were occupied with filling the pit, he revealed your shady past in great detail. And I mean everything! I'm acutely aware of my simple upbringing, but I want to show you what a grave mistake it would be on your part to disgrace me just because I am the daughter of a lowly shepherd."

"Really!" he said, a malicious look forming in his eyes. "It's just further proof of his insanity. Come with me, and he will recant it instantly."

"No, thank you," she replied, smiling calculatingly. "I've heard there are many little out of the way places in this old castle suitable for making unwelcome guests disappear without a trace." She straightened herself proudly to her full height. "It's time that I returned home. Then, by the German's side, we can discuss our opposing views and come to a mutual arrangement. If you fail to take me seriously, my father will go to the authorities and expose your evil deeds. After all, the man we're nursing back to health is the rightful owner of your estate and the real Baron de Sainte-Marie, the rightful heir after the marabout's death, was murdered by both of you. I'm warning you, Captain. If you fail to agree to my terms, you will perish, entangled in your inescapable past!"

Before the captain could formulate the words for a scathing response, she left the room, quickly escaping the estate in her rented carriage.

❧✠☙

The famous Marshal Turenne had once told the French Minister Louvois that "a disgruntled neighbor is the worst kind of enemy. One is forced to always be on his guard, on the *qui vivre*, and this mistrust is the basis for derailing any future attempts for peace. Victory then belongs to the one who manages to become the most cunning and ruthless combatant."

Although the celebrated marshal of France had spoken in the moment, his evaluation of the relationship between the nations of France and Germany had been inordinately perceptive, in that they probably would never change. The neighbor unwilling to pursue peace was France, against which Germany always had to guard itself. As evidenced by years of deceit and open aggression, Germany experienced the truth of Turenne's words countless times.

Frederick the Great's political astuteness and perception was more than enough to overcome France's cunning ploys. He was a less prominent sovereign who knew how to single out the enemy's intentions and use them to his own advantage by wielding his political and military watchfulness to outmaneuver the enemy's plans.

Napoleon Bonaparte had been land-hungry and cast his ravenous eyes on Germany. He had thrown the country into shambles, harnessing his princes to his victory carriage. Only the combined prowess of the English, assisted by the uniting of Russia, Austria, and Prussia, finally succeeded in taming the mighty eagle. Like a second Prometheus,[20.1] they banished him to the remote island prison that was his final resting place.

Since those days, a firm belief propagated in France that only a unification of all those forces would be enough to tame the mighty French again. Napoleon III followed his uncle's example, and his successes in Italy and the Crimea nourished his own arrogance. He managed to subdue the hapless Chinese in Palikao, near Beijing, and even ventured as far as Mexico. This caused him to become overconfident, eventually leading him to believe he was assured of victory much like his famous predecessor. He thought that no country would dare wage war against France without resorting to support from allies. Napoleon III overestimated his strength and underestimated that of his neighbors, especially Germany.

Germany is considered to be the phlegmatic personality of the European family. Underneath its quiet, unpretentious, and seemingly indifferent manner rests a powerful and resilient constitution. The Germans' patience, often taken for granted, gives others the false impression that one could pull on their proverbial beard without facing retribution. But beneath their outwardly calm demeanor lies an active sense of honor that, when rudely affronted, suddenly looms powerfully into action, curtailing any mistaken notion that they are a dormant or disinterested race. A German will pursue his enemy with such fervor that, as the old Blücher used to say, his 'ears will ring'. In such instances, the usually passive German develops such a mobility that the so-called simian agility of the French can't seem to overcome.

While Napoleon was busy conferring titles on his marshals and generals who had distinguished themselves in Africa, Russia, China, Italy, and Mexico, all Prussia had was the old workhorse Bismarck, supposedly past his prime, to lead the nation into war. Since the First Schleswig-Holstein War, other leaders had come to the forefront, but their influence was superficial and nobody took them seriously. Even though Prussian princes like Karl Friedrich had conducted strategic campaigns, they were considered mere foreplay, paving the way for larger campaigns. If there was any mention of a newly-formed military establishment, its news resounded in an entanglement of voices about its relevance, as though the entire matter was overblown and of minor importance.

The German Michael, as Bismarck was known, evidently possessed a portion of his mother's wit and had learned in European circles not to reveal all his cards, so as to be able to play his trumps at times of his choosing. The French considered him to be too unrefined to offer him the proverbial check, instead allowing him to partake in a game of checkers. If they baited him with a trump card, he held on to his own, discarding small counters. But Napoleon didn't realize that the clever German beast kept the matadors at bay, waiting for an opportunity to lash out at them convincingly.

If there was talk in Paris of Bismarck or General Moltke, his most trusted military strategist, the French regime shrugged its shoulders. Bismarck was perceived as an average statesman with unskilled tactics, while Moltke was merely touted as an officer and nothing more. The French felt they didn't need to pay much attention to such men, just as they would have ignored lesser playing cards.

After getting himself into an unpleasant setback in Mexico, Napoleon decided to mitigate the impact by engaging Bismarck in negotiations. He presented Prussia with an offer to enlarge its territory by eight million people. In exchange, he asked for Prussian-ruled Bayern and Hessen land holdings, situated between the Rhine and Mosel rivers. It was perceived as amateurish, even foolish, that Bismarck didn't jump at the offer. From this point on, it was obvious to Napoleon that he couldn't hope to deal with the pragmatic helmsman of the German state.

Napoleon was not to be deterred, however, and orchestrated a similar deal in Vienna. Austria agreed to the trade, giving up Venice and in turn promising Prussian-held Schleswig. At about the same time, the emperor declared to the French nation that he was in favor of granting more autonomy to the lesser German cities. By doing this, Napoleon had thrown his proverbial glove in Bismarck's face. The unyielding German retrieved it even-temperedly and picked it up again, a signal that he was up to the challenge.

In the meantime, over in Mexico, a poor Austrian duke named Maximillian was coerced by Napoleon and driven to his untimely death. He propelled Austria into a less than desirable position. Prussia declared war on Austria, relying on almost entirely unknown generals while Austria was prepared to counter with well-established, renowned marshals. Those in the know in Paris speculated that Prussia would soon be on the verge of a crushing defeat, preferably after a long and drawn out campaign by both sides. Such a long war would give France ample opportunity to conduct its own political chess game.

But that was not meant to be. Prussia proved victorious, vanquishing its rival just as one defeats his own brother. The war was over with such uncharacteristic swiftness that it had a ripple effect on each of the other German states.

And yet Napoleon had deeply underestimated the victor's strength. Through his ambassador Benedetti, he demanded that Prussia recognize the former border from 1814. Had Bismarck agreed, Germany would have had to cede the territory of Rhein Bayern, Rhein Essen, and even Mainz. In addition, Prussia was asked to relinquish its occupation of Luxembourg. If Prussia refused to comply, the reigning Napoleon threatened to declare war on Germany.

Without asking France's permission, Bismarck negotiated a lasting peace with Austria, sending Napoleon a message as if to say, "Fine, if you desire war, we won't stand in your way. But you won't get anything out of it!"

Acting on the advice of his ministers, Napoleon withdrew his threat. Instead, while dangling the prospect of Luxembourg, he turned to the king of Holland for support. Holland's king wasn't disinclined to accommodate Napoleon. When Bismarck learned of this, he stated openly that he wouldn't give his approval of their pact. He advised Holland of his newfound peace with the southern German states, leaving Napoleon admonished and repelled once again.

These repeated disappointments on account of Bismarck made a lasting impression on France's inner circles. The emperor's throne continued to lose luster as the various factions grew restless and clamored for attention. The consensus of many was to press for war against Germany. Even Napoleon's wife, Empress Eugenie, tried persuading her husband to go to war. In response, Napoleon stepped up his efforts to tangle with Germany and Belgium, but soon realized that even the best of his feeble attempts bounced off Bismarck's stern head.

France's emperor decided to pursue a military option and secretly instructed his forces to prepare for war. He recognized that, should he fail to bring Germany to its knees, his already shaky throne would collapse outright. In order to mask his true intentions, he announced that more than anything he desired peace in Europe.

Bismarck, however, wasn't fooled by the man's deceptive platitudes. He was convinced France was still looking for a reason to declare war and would eventually be the first to cross the border, breaking their fragile ceasefire.

Napoleon's weakness was to overestimate his own advantages, particularly in terms of military readiness. He inquired about its preparedness with the minister of war, General Leboeuf, and was given the news he was expecting – *Nous sommes archiprêt* (we are more than ready). But unbeknownst to Napoleon, Bismarck had managed to uncover even this latest news and already set into motion his own contingency plans.

CHAPTER TWENTY-ONE

Baroness Marion

In the spring of 1870, a steamship labored upstream on the Mosel River having left the city of Coblenz punctually at seven thirty in the morning. Its goal was to reach the city of Trier after an overnight stay in Traben-Trarbach.

Aside from the usual passengers, most of whom had paid for second class passage, a small company of young gentlemen climbed on board before its departure. They meandered nonchalantly through the throng, leaving little doubt to their fellow travelers that they considered themselves belonging to a higher class. They scrutinized the other passengers with cold, judgmental glances, taking their places under the deck cover without asking others if their actions had inconvenienced them or stolen their view of the beautiful countryside. They conducted their conversations in French, but spoke so loudly and inconsiderately that those in their immediate vicinity had to listen to their boastful discussion whether they wanted to or not. Ordinarily, this unrefined behavior would have been challenged, but here the other passengers chose instead to criticize them in silence.

One of the 'distinguished' passengers, Major Provost, sporting a monocle in his left eye, pointed with his walking cane toward the river bank.

"Dear Colonel, isn't it a pity that such a fine river and splendid countryside have been withheld from us?" he hollered for all to hear. "When will we march to reclaim this territory?"

"It has always belonged to us," replied the colonel. "How I detest these Germans!"

"You dare to voice your view while we travel through their lands, my good Rallion?" replied his friend, the scorn evident in his voice.

"Pah!" the colonel spat. "We know why we traverse their land. Don't you have to explore a territory before you can possess it?" His tone suggested a secret yet to be revealed.

Colonel Rallion, or Jean-Paul to his friends, was a handsome man, and since he had attained this high rank at such a young age, it stood to reason that he stemmed from higher circles and possessed influential connections.

"Dammit, Jean-Paul! Not so loud!" admonished Provost. "You could be perceived by these plain folk as some kind of spy."

"If it suits them! These ordinary people are quite harmless. A battle with their army should be amusing. Should a war break out, we'll all have an entertaining stroll through Berlin."

"No doubt we'll have a stroll," Lebeau, another officer, pointed out, "but it remains to be seen if it will be entertaining! These Germans are a typically boring people, rough, crude, and unpleasant. Turn around and tell me if you can find a single face among the many ladies on this ship worthy of being kissed!" he scowled.

"I'm going below to see if I can find something more appealing," added the colonel. He rose and climbed down the steep iron staircase leading to the cabins.

If anyone had spotted the two ladies sitting on plush ottomans nearby, they would have to acknowledge that at least here were two young women that would fit the bill. One was blonde and the other was brunette. The first one was of medium height, but had a fine figure that showcased her young form. Under her long, soft eyelashes shone the light of two sparkling sapphire eyes, inviting causal observers to look further into her tender soul. She was far from an imposing, ravishing beauty, but her charm and loveliness set her apart from the rest.

The brunette presented a much different picture. She was tall, like the Roman goddess Juno.[21.1] Her features were reminiscent of a painting of a Persian beauty, envisioned by an artist whose intention was to dim the appeal of all the other harem concubines around her in the scene. Her wonderfully shaped head carried a measure of full-bodied chestnut colored hair that would have presented much work for a servant girl. Her alabaster white face projected nobility, conveying a character without reproach. Her captivating brown eyes, flashed from underneath exquisite eyebrows, revealing an almond shape such as could only be glimpsed in the Orient. Yet their shape was not as pronounced as one would ascribe to Middle Eastern eyes. Her small, delicately formed nose was flanked by two rose colored nostrils, which tended to dilate energetically. The fine-sculptured mouth was of equally exquisite proportions, enticing one to partake of a sensual kiss. The woman's lips, beckoning of their own accord, were not overstated in their fullness, as would be the case with a sensual being. When the lady's lips parted in a smile, two rows of pearly white teeth came to the forefront, a picture of perfection. The most experienced dentist would have had difficulty finding even the slightest imperfection. Her teeth seemed to detract from her lips, yet it was this contrast that lent it magical overtones. Her lips moved gracefully, conveying spite and meekness, pride and humility, self-confidence and composure, boldness and womanly reserve. Only the future would dictate which of these traits would gain the upper hand in her life.

The young woman's figure was full and opulent, but not voluptuous, even though a pedantic critic might have posed the question if her bust, which threatened to escape the thin summer material of her bodice, drew the inevitable stares of passing men. Her ornate, formfitting dress was unable to conceal her figure. Her small but strong hands seemed destined to be held to a lover's heart with fervor. Protruding from under the hem of her dress were two elegant shoes whose delicate feet could easily have evoked the envy of thousands.

These two young women were caught up in an animated conversation. Even though they were alone, they conducted it in suppressed tones. An astute observer may have come to the conclusion that the subject entailed secrets of a feminine nature.

"But my dear Marion," said the blonde, "I had no idea of this news! I thought we always shared everything, but now I see, to my astonishment, that you've chosen to keep a closely guarded secret that which is most important to a girl!"

The brunette's brows came together in a slight frown. "On the contrary, dear Nanon," she corrected. "I haven't kept anything from you. I only received word of it in the letter I had just obtained in the mail. Here, look for yourself."

Marion's voice was strong and clear, resonating like a finely tuned bell. One could tell she was capable of modulating the perfect pitch, whether as an order to a servant, or in the form of a lover's whisper. It was a voice of rare quality, and yet soft and pliable. She possessed a voice of authority and the channel of gentle persuasion. Her voice was sonorous, yet warm. Her tone didn't come from her throat, but emanated from low within her chest as though stemming from someplace deep within her heart, the innermost part of the soul. The fortunate one to hear her voice was spellbound, captured like one who kneels in the shadow of a basilica, suddenly exposed to the reverberation of the magical *vox humana*.[21.2]

Marion reached into a decorative Moroccan purse which hung on her belt. The handle was covered with genuine Ceylon pearls. She retrieved a letter from her handbag, passing it to her friend. Nanon took the letter eagerly and started to read. While she read the contents, her beautiful face clearly conveyed amazement. When she finished, she handed it back with a grateful smile.

"That is quite extraordinary," she said, nodding her head thoughtfully. "You're supposed to pack and quickly return home to become acquainted with your appointed groom! Have you ever laid eyes on the colonel, this Count Rallion?"

"Never! I only know that the Rallions come from a well-established, yet impoverished lineage," Marion explained. The current head of the family holds the favor of the emperor couple, which is probably why his son has already attained the rank of colonel, despite his youth."

"How then did your Papa come to arrange this proposed marriage?"

"I'm not clear on that, but I'm sure I'll find out soon enough." Marion spoke in a deliberate tone so her friend could witness the lively movement of her delicate nostrils.

"Perhaps the colonel knows you already, Marion," Nanon suggested. "As your friend, I can openly tell you how beautiful you really are. If he's already seen you, it's possible that he strives to possess you."

A contemptuous smile played across Marion's lips. "That wouldn't be much reason to concede my freedom and independence," she said. "The man who wants to pursue me must understand that he not only has to gain my love, but also my respect. I will never just capitulate." She tilted her head back proudly. It was obvious to Nanon that Marion had a great deal of self-worth.

"Really? Do you hold to a standard, an ideal you fantasize about?" asked Nanon with a smile.

"Like most young women, I have one," she answered coyly. "But I realize this ideal is nothing more than a fantasy. Yet, it's peculiar, strange even..." She stopped talking. Her self-assurance, so evident in her radiant eyes, changed to contemplation as she stared out the open window at the waves.

The giant wheels of the steamboat churned the river water, spewing the far reaching dark waves whose foam-crowned walls reflected the sunshine in diamond sparkles.

"What?" urged her friend, breaking her reflective moment. "What's so peculiar?"

"It's strange, even wonderful," Marion replied, brushing a strand of her hair aside, "I once saw a man whose outward appearance embodied my ideal. I can't speak for the soul, but I was shocked to see the picture of my dreams suddenly appear in reality right in front of me."

"That is amazing," Nanon admired. "Almost miraculous. You're very fortunate, dear Marion. If only I could some day see the incarnation of my ideal! But tell me, where did you see this man? And who is he?" she added quickly.

"It was in the city of Dresden, and he was attired as an officer. I took a carriage to the famous city of Blasewitz. On the way, I happened to encounter a small contingent of officers on horseback. They rode past me like phantoms on steeds. Still, I caught a glimpse of his face, identical to the one from my dreams!"

"How interesting, Marion, how romantic. Did you see him again?"

"Not in person," she said with a smile, "but I found his picture!"

"Really! Please tell me! Did you make any inquiries?"

"How could I?" Marion asked. "Besides, you were awaiting my arrival in Berlin and I had to hurry. Do you remember me telling you that I visited a photographic studio while in Berlin? While I was waiting for the clerk, I found myself alone in the studio. I examined the portraits and landscapes hanging on various walls, some even lay scattered on tables. That's when I spotted his picture. The photographer had captured the same profile as the man who stormed past me on the road to Dresden." Her eyes became wistful again. "Dressed in his Ulanen uniform, he looked handsome and proud, the way I remembered. It was taken in quarter profile, and I saw a dozen or so proofs in a pile on the table."

"What luck!" exclaimed Nanon. "Do you know what I would have done in your stead?"

"Probably exactly what I ended up doing," smiled Marion. "I was all alone. No one saw me. I became a thief, just for a moment, and pocketed one of the picture cards in my purse."

Nanon clasped her hands together, caught up in the excitement of the story as though she had been there to witness the indiscretion firsthand.

"Then I might yet see your depiction of the ideal man!" her friend exclaimed jubilantly. "What a cunning, roguish lady, my proud Marion has turned into. Did you carefully preserve the photograph?"

"Of course."

"Oh, if only you had brought it with you!" Nanon said. "I'm beside myself with curiosity, wanting to see that dream-like face come to life in a photograph!" Her eyes, full of yearning, remained fixed on Marion's hands, which had returned to the ornate purse. She opened it a second time, fishing for the desired object. "You have it? It's in there?" Nanon asked, overjoyed. "Too bad you don't know his name. It would be impossible to contact the photographer without revealing you had pilfered the photograph."

"His name is on the back," commented Marion. "Here it is."

Nanon plucked it out of her hands almost too hastily. She turned it sideways, allowing the light to fall on the picture. She examined it from several angles to be able to provide an accurate evaluation.

"Such a distinguished, handsome head he has!"

"Isn't it?" commented Marion, her eyes shining.

"And the name?" she wondered, turning the card over. On the back was fine-scripted writing: *Cavalry master Richard von Löwenklau.* "A nice sounding name, isn't it, dear Marion?"

"Yes," she agreed, nodding her head. "And it's peculiar when you consider that Richard is my favorite name. *Richard the Lionheart* is one of my favorite stories."

"I always imagined Richard the Lionheart in a different light than this cavalry master," Nanon considered. "I would compare him to the hero Hüon, in Wieland's classic *Oberon*. That forehead, the eyes, the mouth, in fact the whole face stands out, something that appeals to me from the onset. I don't understand anything about physiognomy. I'd rather let my heart, my feelings, my intuition be my judge."

"Well, what does your intuition tell you, dear Nanon?"

"This man is self-confident without wearing his nobility. His strong upper body conveys a firm disposition. He's cunning and bold, and looks as though he could be a tough opponent in battle. He has the forehead of a thinker and his mouth suggests a comfort with eloquent speech, preferring the finer things in life. His disposition, to borrow from the scientific community, is a choleric- phlegmatic, which means he's passionate but slow to anger, he's tender and compassionate, but doesn't get caught up in the heat of the moment. Then—"

"Stop already!" interrupted Marion, laughing and snatching the picture out of her friend's hand. "You're conjuring up a psychological profile of the perfect man! If he really is as you make him out to be, he coincides with my image. My only regret is that I couldn't find out more about the Löwenklau family. Truth be known, I tried my best."

"You only had to purchase the Gothar nobility calendar!"

"It wasn't readily available, so I ordered one. Then came Father's letter, and I had to leave a forwarding address so they could send it after me. I'll have to be patient until I receive one. How unfortunate!"

Marion suppressed these last few words, hearing the approach of a stranger who turned out to be the obnoxious colonel, come to the cabin in search of lovely faces. When he noticed the two ladies, his face contorted into a look of pleasant surprise. He bowed deeply and immediately left the way he came.

That was the Baroness de Sainte-Marie! he thought to himself once he was back on deck. *Fortunately I caught myself in time. That could have been an unpleasant situation. She at least knows how to remain detached.*

"Well, did you find something of interest?" asked Lebeau.

"It would appear so," he replied. "But I'm still right. These Germans have no allure. I finally found a beauty down below, but as I foretold, she is French."

"And you didn't stay and keep her company? You left in a hurry!"

"Incidentally, because I know her. She doesn't tolerate being toyed with."

"Then she's worth having a look at," his friend laughed.

He shrugged his shoulders. "She's not only the most beautiful woman in Paris," Jean-Paul replied pensively, "but probably in all of France..." His words left his companions in disbelief. "...and will likely inherit several million," he finished.

"What's her name? Quick!"

"Her name is Marion, the Baroness de Sainte-Marie."

"De Sainte-Marie! Ah, she's certainly famous. I should go below and introduce myself. One should pay homage to such a beauty," advised Lebeau, actually rising from his seat.

The woman's name caught everyone's attention. "Hold it!" the colonel called out, grabbing his friend by the arm and pulling him back down. "Stay here! No one is going to embarrass this lady!"

"Why not?" he asked, wincing and holding his arm where Rallion had grabbed it.

"Because the right is mine alone. She's my betrothed."

They all looked dismayed at the revelation. No one had had any inkling that he was interested in a lady, much less engaged to one. And especially with the most famous beauty in Paris! They converged on him with all sorts of questions, often repeating themselves. He cut them off, and addressed them all at once.

"The story goes as follows," Jean-Paul began. "My father wrote to me, outlining that he had discussed the matter of my marriage with a good friend, and they had come to an agreement over his daughter. I haven't been introduced to the lady yet, but I couldn't find a reason to go against my father's wishes. The lady in question is the Baroness de Sainte-Marie. She has been away on a trip, much like myself. Undoubtedly, she has also been summoned home by her father. We find ourselves returning on the same boat without having seen each other, or being personally acquainted. It goes without saying that I'm going to exercise my right about my position. I'm now going to introduce myself and I forbid any one of you to upstage my visit!"

His facial expression instantly changed. He was no longer the joking, even-tempered man he had been. Whereas he was once handsome and neutral, the complete opposite was now evident. He became visibly pale, his lips closed in the middle, the corners of his mouth opened slightly when he spoke, his words discharging from the side. His forehead was creased and taut so the peak of his hairline nearly touched his eyebrows. Two deep furrows formed at the corners of his nose, progressing to his chin. All blood seemed to have drained from his face, receding down his smooth neck, whose malicious strength by no means waned from his large frame.

The biggest transformation, however, was evident in his eyes. They had been a pleasant grey color, but now turned darker, influenced by his sudden anger, to a nearly black color. They quickly changed again to a spiteful yellowish green that seemed to glow from deep within. It was as though the small veins of the eye suddenly swelled, giving the white matter a bloody appearance. As he turned around and climbed down the metal rungs to the cabin, they all stared without saying a word.

After a moment of reflection, only the friend wearing the monocle had something to say. "There he goes again," he exclaimed, "flying his devil's flag for all to see!"[21.3]

And he was right in his assessment. The colonel's facial expression had been clearly diabolical. Only the devil himself could have made such a face when he laid the foundation of hell. Such a face appeared each time the devil threw a condemned soul into the slough whose fires never went out. Such a face appeared when he delighted in the torture of those who suffered for their deeds and lost all hope for eternity. Anyone who saw such a face would have to conclude that Rallion could transform himself into a devil, a deceptively, cruel, unmerciful devil who didn't shun atrocity, had no regard for others, and didn't hold back from anything if it meant attaining his goal.

CHAPTER TWENTY-TWO
The Blundering Idiot

While the Mosel steamer was getting ready to depart for Trarbach, two gentlemen sat in a coffeehouse in Simmern, one of the capital cities of Bavaria. Although they were drinking a superior brand of coffee, the aroma seemed to be lost on them.

Judging by their demeanor, both men were preoccupied with a matter of considerable importance. They were dressed as officers, the older one carrying the insignia of a general and the younger one, about twenty-eight years old, that of an Ulanen cavalry master.

The younger officer, Richard von Löwenklau, was a handsome man. Even though he had sunk into the soft cushion of the sofa, it was clear that he had an imposing, broad-shouldered physique. His face sported a full beard, its blond color contrasting sharply against his clear blue eyes. Those eyes hinted at his peaceful disposition. Among friends, he was known to be a gentle giant. A solemn determination rested on his forehead, coupled with abundant energy. He didn't easily tire. A soft, impudent smirk concealed itself under the tips of his moustache, suggesting that he was quite capable of springing into action despite his good-natured temperament.

"Now then, my good Löwenklau," said the general. "Do you understand the nature of the assignment?"

"It seems simple enough, Excellency," he replied.

"Fine. You will have to develop the actual details on your own, but I'm confident your prior demonstration of tactics will serve you in good stead. The only thing that remains is to advise you of the personalities involved. It might be beneficial if you took notes."

Richard produced a wallet from his coat, extracting paper and pencil.

"The count of whom I spoke is Count Jules Rallion, a highly favored servant of Napoleon and a confidant of the war minister Leboeuf," the general began. "The other man to whom I alluded is the Baron de Sainte-Marie. The count has a son and the baron a daughter. Apparently they don't know each other, but the arrangement has already been made for them to be married. They will return to France and meet in a place called Ortry, not far from the Luxembourg border, in the area of Thionville. Sainte-Marie is the owner of the estate. He also has a young son from his second marriage, his first wife having died. This boy has been neglected in his upbringing, and the baron has gone through several governors without success. He finally decided to engage a German tutor for the young man. That's where you come in."

"What name will I be using, Excellency?"

"Andreas Müller. Here are your documents and letters of reference. Your success will depend on how you conduct yourself. Besides, I have arranged for photographs of those in question, so that you can become acquainted with them ahead of time."

He produced a number of photos out of the same dossier and presented them to Löwenklau one at a time.

"This one here," he continued, "is a portrait of Count Rallion, and this is his son Jean-Paul, the colonel. I also have a picture of the Baron de Sainte-Marie and his son Alexandre. The boy doesn't make a good impression and seems capable of all sorts of mischief. An impact of a different sort comes from his stepsister, Baroness Marion. Here's her portrait. I have to warn you of just how beautiful she is, because I don't know if even I could withstand those beautiful eyes, were I in your place." He handed the photograph to Löwenklau. No sooner had the young officer laid eyes on that face than he rose from his seat.

"What is it?" asked the general. "Do you know her?"

Löwenklau couldn't hide his embarrassment even though, as an officer, he prided himself on being able to conceal his emotions.

"No, Excellency," he replied, taking his seat again.

His superior eyed him with amusement. "It seemed like you do. Why were you so surprised then?"

The cavalry master hesitated before replying. "I can see that I'm obligated to answer you, so as not to arouse suspicion, Excellency," he said slowly. "On an afternoon ride near Dresden, I saw a beautiful young lady who made quite an impression on me as I galloped past her—"

"Ah, captivated by love!" the general said, laughing.

"Until now, I have done only my duty," said Löwenklau, defending himself. "I'm poor, and as you well know, I hope to improve my financial situation by way of advancement in rank. I've had little opportunity to contemplate amorous pursuits."

"Well, it's because you're without means that you have to look for a way to enrich your future."

"Pardon me, Excellency," Richard said, "but I don't agree with you on that point. I would like to enrich my life through marriage, but I don't want to depend on my wife for my welfare. I want to be in a position to choose with my heart rather than my pocketbook. That short moment during my ride toward Blasewitz could have become significant had it lasted longer. A few days later, I went to pick up some proofs I had ordered from a photographer in Berlin. While in his studio, I happened to notice the photograph of the same lady I saw on the road. I asked for a copy, but he didn't feel comfortable handing it over. I couldn't even find out her name since she didn't supply it, and promised to return for the photographs in person. His Excellency can imagine my astonishment upon seeing her photograph today, and finally learning her identity."

The general smiled. "Yes, I understand now. It shouldn't come as a surprise that a woman can leave such a lasting impression. But my dear Löwenklau, the task of accomplishing your mission will only grow more difficult now, more so than you imagine. It's not much fun having to present yourself as a teacher, a tutor in fact, to the lady who has captured your heart, while holding higher aspirations. Go with God's blessing, cavalry... I mean, schoolmaster!"

The general stood up and extended his hand. Richard shook it, half out of respect and half in friendship. He assembled the papers and photographs and left.

Once he arrived in his room, he pulled Marion's picture from the rest and examined it more closely. Then, contrary to his usual serious nature, he surprised himself by pressing it to his lips.

"Yes, it's you!" he whispered to himself as though she were standing right in front of him. *The one I have longed to find will be residing with me in the same castle! Not only will I see her, but I'll be able to talk to her, and be near her. But this Rallion, the colonel! Will he really marry her? They don't know each other, and so it can't be anything more than a marriage of convenience. Pah! I suppose I'll find out soon enough. My mission is now twofold. First, I have my duty to consider. And yet I also yearn to satisfy the longing of my heart! We'll soon see who gets the prize – the Frenchman or the German!*

Before long, it was time to get ready. He rang the bell, summoning his servant.

"Have you procured everything, Franz?" he asked him when the man appeared.

"Everything, including that damned hump," was his reply. "Are you really planning on strapping it on, Cavalry Master?"

Richard contemplated the question for a few moments before answering. "Yes," he finally answered. "I'll stick with my previous decision. It's listed in my papers, so I suppose I'll have to wear it."

"When will we depart, sir?"

"As soon as you're ready. It shouldn't take long. After all, you're a competent barber."

"But your splendid beard?"

"It'll grow back, Franz. The main thing is for me to leave this guesthouse without anyone knowing it's me. I'll await the wagon outside the city, then drive through Kirchberg toward Trarbach where I'll catch the steamboat in the morning." He paused, putting a finger to his lips in thought. "But we'll have to leave the carriage in the last village we cross before Trarbach. I don't want people seeing a poor schoolmaster arriving via coach. The general can make arrangements to collect it after I'm gone. In the meantime, we'll continue our excursion without anyone being the wiser. I'll arrive in Ortry as the new schoolmaster while you find other employment nearby from which you can be of assistance without drawing attention to yourself or fostering suspicion. Now, get to work!"

An hour later, Richard left the city of Simmern on the Kirchberger road with a new appearance, one belonging to the class of people that occupies itself with the understanding of education and philosophy. His stature, at one time seemingly tall and proud, was now crooked and bent over, probably as a result of many hours hunched over books and other scholastic pursuits, though he bore the look of a man who didn't allow such physical limitation to hamper the execution of his profession. He wore a tight, well-worn, but clean traveling suit. His long, black hair was already thinning and reached the collar of a coat that hadn't been in style in some twenty years. His faded top hat and faded blue umbrella were no better, and he tucked them under his arm as though they were much-beloved companions of his coat. To passersby, the brass-colored frames of his large spectacles stood as a reminder to his many years of service.

He meandered down the street for a while, until he was overtaken by a carriage. It was unoccupied and the coachman courteously permitted him to ride as a non-paying passenger.

The coach soon reached Kirchberg, but continued on through. Just before nightfall, they reached another small village, where Richard disembarked. He sauntered through the little hamlet until he reached a small forest, where he rested for a half hour. There, he was joined by the coachman, this time on foot.

"Is everything in order?" Richard asked.

"Yes, Cavalry Master."

"Don't call me that from now on. You don't know me, and when we later meet, you're to address me as Andreas Müller, doctor of philosophy. Understood?"

"Very well, Doctor!" said Franz.

"All right. Let's go."

They wandered together, reaching Trarbach with the onset of night, just before nine o'clock. They parted company, each one looking for his own guesthouse. Since Richard wasn't familiar with the village, he politely asked a townsperson for directions to the nearest tavern.

"Come on, follow me," the villager said. "I'm going for a glass of beer myself. Just keep in mind you won't have much selection. The ship from

Koblenz overnights here and the disembarking passengers usually choose all the best rooms for themselves."

Richard found that the prediction rang true. He was able to rent a small corner room in the attic, but its size was of little consequence to him. The common room where supper was served was fairly spacious.

A billiard table was set up in the corner and a number of participants were already playing. Richard could see that the players were French. More importantly, he realized that one of these loud and boisterous individuals was the very man he had been sent to spy on.

Colonel Jean-Paul de Rallion was among them and was the most jovial of all. He had come earlier from the room of Baroness Marion, to whom he had introduced himself as the man she was intended to marry. He didn't leave her side until he had obtained the best accommodations for her. She had captivated him, and he now found himself in a euphoric state, overjoyed to have obtained such a prize. He would have made a fool of himself just to impress her, hoping to win her hand.

Marion had been quite surprised when he disclosed his name to her. Her first reaction had been to dismiss him entirely, thus sending him a clear message of her independence. However, he acted so blamelessly, so tactfully, that she found it impossible to refuse his courtesy. He hadn't broached the subject of the arrangement made by their parents. In fact, his bearing and demeanor had been entirely polite. Therefore, she hadn't declined his offer to bid her good night at ten o'clock.

Jean-Paul had shown himself to be handsome and gallant. She hadn't felt any antipathy toward him and had decided to let her decision rest, for or against him, based solely on his character. Marion had been curious to learn about this Rallion family, which had exercised such influence on her father that he had bypassed the usual period of engagement, wishing to conclude the betrothal as quickly as possible, without tolerating any objections.

So it was that the gentlemen were in the middle of a billiards game when the chimes of a nearby clock sounded the tenth hour. Jean-Paul pulled his pocket watch out, comparing the time.

"Hmm," he mused. "It's that time already! You'll have to excuse me. I have to go upstairs and pay my respects to the baroness."

"Go on, then!" encouraged one of his friends. "I'll play for you."

"Would you please, Francois. Or maybe..." He looked around the room, reconsidering. His gaze finally found Richard, who was seated nearby and clearly following their game. "I don't want to impose, but perhaps I can find a temporary stand-in." He swaggered toward Löwenklau, stopping in front of him. "I'm Colonel Rallion," he said abruptly. "And you are?"

Richard calmly appraised the brash count. "My name is Müller, and I am an educator," he answered, ignoring Rallion's boastful arrogance.

"An intellectual?" Jean-Paul murmured. "Fine with me! Are you acquainted with billiards?"

"A little."

"Then play in my stead for a while. It should be an honor for you, no?"

Enjoying the opportunity to play along, Richard agreed to the count's rude entreaty. "Yes, it is. I will do my best."

"Of course you will! Now, I'm warning you, if I return and find you've ruined my game, you can forget about receiving a tip."

He left the room, but not before tossing a knowing look to his friends, intimating that they should have a little fun at his expense. They complied, but Richard allowed their jokes to wash over him, as if he weren't aware of their jabs. In turn, he played so poorly that the players erupted into laughter with each shot of the cue.

Jean-Paul returned in due course, dismayed that he had dropped so quickly in the standings.

"Monsieur Müller," he complained, taking Richard by the arm. "How could you have spoiled my game so quickly? You're nothing but a clumsy German oaf!"

"Undoubtedly, sir," Richard replied, bowing respectfully.

The response from the spectators was unanimous laughter. Jean-Paul joined in.

"I should punish you," he said reprovingly, "but then you're half a cripple, anyway. Perhaps you deserve a bit of tolerance. And yet I won't absolve you completely. I will allow you to attempt one more shot. If you shoot well, you may leave, but if you shoot poorly, you will have to get up on that chair and apologize to all."

"All right, Monsieur!" Richard agreed, picking up the cue stick. "Just one more thrust on your behalf?"

"Yes," replied Rallion.

"In your stead?" the German questioned. "Under your authority?"

"Of course! It's my number!"

Richard nodded determinedly, waiting for his turn. When it was finally time, he stepped up to the table.

"Now give it your best shot!" the colonel urged him on. "Go ahead!"

"Don't worry," Richard assured him, smiling confidently. "I'm convinced I'll hit the mark this time."

He pulled back and released a mighty shot, tearing a large hole in the billiard cloth. The outcome was predictable. The players all roared with laughter, with the exception of Rallion. He grabbed Löwenklau by the arm and shook it angrily.

"Idiot! Clumsy fool!" he yelled. "Don't you realize I'll have to pay for your incompetence?"

"Unfortunately, yes," Richard said politely, allowing the colonel to continue shaking his arm.

Realizing he wasn't going to accomplish anything by venting his frustration on the passive German, Rallion let go of his arm and called for the innkeeper. The proprietor assessed the damage, confirming that the tear was impossible to repair. He determined that the normal compensation needed to cover small patches would be inadequate, necessitating a larger sum to replace the entire cloth. The colonel reluctantly agreed. Not realizing that Richard had intended the accident as a punishment for his rude behavior, Jean-Paul ordered him to mount the chair to make his proclamation. Richard stepped on the stool, willing to continue acting the part.

"I respectfully ask for your forgiveness," he started in a loud voice, "that through me Colonel Rallion managed to rip holes through the cloth. I trust that the next time we meet it won't be me who has to ask for forgiveness. Good night!"

He stepped down and disappeared out the door before anyone could ask him what he had meant by those last words. Little did the gentlemen realize that the full significance of his words would become clear the following morning.

Richard had purposely left the room to avoid any more unpleasantness, deciding to retire to his room for some rest. Familiar with the layout of the guesthouse, he climbed to the first floor, having to traverse the entire corridor to access the steps to the upper level. The floor was covered by carpet, minimizing the sound of his footsteps.

He had barely covered half the distance when a door opened in front of him and a lady emerged. She was still speaking to the occupant of the room as she backed out.

"Again, I bid you a good night, my dear Nanon," she said. "Don't dwell too much on your ideal man, or else he may come to pass, like he did for me."

Just then, Marion turned around and noticed him. Both stood motionless for a moment, she out of fear and he in joyous surprise. Here was the living proof of his ideal! Her beautiful appearance in her nightgown spoke volumes that her covering was unable to hide. He had seen her outline and revealing bust as he had hurried past, but now she stood in front of him in all her beauty, providing a view appropriate only for a lady friend or husband. His blood rushed to his heart, causing his pulse to quicken. In an instant, he knew he had to have her at any price so long as it didn't infringe on his honor.

Marion felt trepidation, exposed in the hall to a stranger. "What do you want?" she asked, trying to curb her fear.

"Excuse me," he replied. "The carpet muffled my steps. I intended on going past when you came out."

Richard's tone had been disarming, quelling her anxiety. She lifted her lantern to illuminate his face without thinking that by lifting her arm she revealed more of her beautiful shape. He had to employ every ounce of control not to allow his eyes to stray to her bosom. As the light exposed him fully, her eyes widened in surprise, so that she stepped back a pace.

"Who are you?" she asked hastily.

"My name is Müller and I am an educator," he replied evenly.

He would have rather given his real name and rank. He even thought of saying, *I love you madly, you crown among women!* Instead, he restrained himself.

"Ah, what a resemblance!" she whispered to her friend.

"Yes, short of the beard!" exclaimed a melodious voice from the open doorway.

Richard had been captivated by the baroness, only now paying attention to the other woman standing in the doorway examining him. He bowed politely and rushed off down the hall.

"Dear God!" he heard behind him as he walked out of earshot. "The poor man has a hump, dear Marion. How unfortunate. But what do you think about his face?"

Startled by the encounter, Marion walked back into Nanon's room, closing the door behind her.

"He scared me at first!" she admitted. "So you noticed the resemblance as well?"

"You mean to the photograph of the cavalry master?" Nanon asked. "Of course, but I'm sure it's just a coincidence."

"No doubt! But you know, in that first moment, it was as if he was standing right in front of me, exactly the way I pictured him." She paused, then added, "Without the beard, of course! Good night."

"Good night, dear Marion!"

The baroness closed the door and walked a short way down the hall to her assigned room. She had only left it for a short while to spend a little time with her friend. As she stepped inside, she pondered the stranger, the educator, who bore such a resemblance to her ideal.

CHAPTER TWENTY-THREE
A Shipwreck

While the ladies turned in for the night, Richard sat at the open window in his small gabled room, his eyes gazing at the incoming clouds. Yet his mind was attuned to something other than the atmospheric conditions. He thought about the wonderful girl who had magically appeared as though from the heavenlies. He also pondered the strange words he had heard between the two ladies, the meaning of which escaped him. What had the baroness meant when she made reference to a resemblance? And what had the other one meant by "short of the beard"?

What troubled him, however, was that Colonel Rallion had been drawn in as well. Hadn't the general indicated that he and Marion hadn't met yet? Could this have been a mistake? Could this very same colonel be the basis of her ideal? He suddenly felt heavy, as though a sword had penetrated his innards. His life loomed in front of him like a dark ominous wall, threatening to crumble in and bury him in the rubble. He tossed and turned in bed, finally falling asleep with the first sounds of birds chirping, announcing the arrival of a new dawn.

He woke sometime later to the sound of a servant knocking on his door and announcing the imminent departure of the steamboat. He rose and dressed in a hurry. When he entered the restaurant, he found that most of the guests had already consumed their breakfast and busied themselves with preparations for departure. He quickly drank his coffee and rushed after them.

As he walked toward the ship, he thought about the baroness and realized he could have told her about his position as the new educator for her younger brother. Still, the fact that he hadn't mentioned it hadn't been a mistake on his part. After all, no introductions had been made and he wasn't obligated to address her.

The beautiful sunny day that had graced his earlier journey was replaced today by a cloudy, inferior one. A thick fog lay on the river and there was little indication it would break anytime soon. The air lay heavy and still on the countryside and, rather than the usual morning freshness, an oppressive and unpleasant weightiness carried it over the ship as it emptied into the fog laden river.

The captain was about to order the removal of the loading platform when Richard stepped on board. He bought a second class ticket from the purser.

Purchasing a first class ticket would have put a strain on a schoolmaster's salary. Having climbed on board at the ship's stern, he made his way through the first class section. In the midst of it, he spotted the already familiar French gentlemen.

"Look out!" Rallion called out loudly. "Here comes the German fool! Give him lots of room so he doesn't trip over anything!"

They allowed him to pass, laughing hysterically as he walked by. He nodded respectfully, even tipping his hat, purposefully misinterpreting their sarcastic faces as merely patronizing. Near the bow, and in second class, he spotted his servant Franz, who paid him no mind according to his instructions. Richard noted that he had also changed his appearance. In place of traveling clothes, he was wearing a large blue shirt, a matching pair of pants, and a red handkerchief around his neck. Over his shaved head, he wore an unusual *chapeau*, such as would be worn by the local inhabitants of Moseille or Meurthe. All in all, he looked like a traveler from the area of Metz or Nancy.

Richard had no idea how Franz had managed this remarkable transformation, but he was pleased by the man's resourcefulness. Franz had a good head on his shoulders and frequently demonstrated his trust and cunning. Richard passed him by, content to await until later for an explanation.

The ship was freed from its temporary berth and left the confines of the riverbank. Richard stood on the parapet, watching as the large wheels whipped the dark water below. When he looked up, he noticed a finely dressed man sauntering in his direction from the rear of the ship, making his way toward the front. His nearly military disposition, his immaculate beard and his gold *lorgnette*[23.1], gave him a distinguished appearance. His penetrating glance drifted over the passengers. As soon as Richard recognized his face, he quickly averted his eyes. He didn't want to be spotted by the newcomer. But it was too late. A slow, knowing smile spread over his face when he spotted Richard's humped form. He strolled toward him in a manner emphasizing his boredom. The man longed to break the tedium of the voyage at any price, even if it meant intruding on another man's privacy.

Richard noticed his approach and turned away, hoping he wasn't being too obvious. Regardless, the stranger continued toward him to start up a conversation. He stopped beside Richard, throwing a cursory glance at the thick fog.

"An unpleasant morning!" he announced. "The fog is so thick one could almost cut it with a knife. I'm afraid we'll encounter unsettled weather ahead."

Richard was painfully aware that the stranger knew his true identity, and even that of his disguised servant. The entire mission was in jeopardy, yet he had to respond.

"A thunderstorm is sure to follow," he said, disguising his voice. "We will have to seek shelter below deck."

Richard turned aside, intending to follow his own advice. The stranger however, placed his hand on his shoulder.

"You can stay for a while," the man said. "It'll be some time before the weather develops into a storm. Allow me to introduce myself. My name is Bertrand, a doctor in Thionville."

Richard had no choice but to face the speaker. "My name is Andreas Müller," he replied, bowing, "and I've been hired as an educator at Castle Ortry."

"Andreas Müller, doctor of philosophy, yes, I'm familiar with that name."

"Really!" said Richard, his anxiety rising.

"It's true. You see, I'm the family doctor for the Baron de Sainte-Marie. I know he's expecting you."

"But sir, how could you possibly know I'm the one he's expecting?"

"You yourself gave me the name, the same one mentioned by the baron. Besides," he broke off, lowering his voice conspiratorially, "I heard the same name from my herb collector, who I just hired last night in Trarbach." Richard, still unsure how to respond, motioned with his arm, which the doctor took as a sign for him to continue. "I ran into this man quite unexpectedly, and it turns out I owe him my life.

"I have to confess," he continued, "I served as a military doctor in the Austrian regime during the last German-Austrian entanglement. At one point, I was en route to a makeshift first aid facility near the town of Gitschin, not knowing that a Prussian Ulanen regiment was poised to attack the Austrian position there. I realized too late that there was no way to avoid being overrun. Fortuitously, I was thrown to the ground by shrapnel from a grenade. I lifted my arm in protest, but the Ulanen regiment flew toward me, their lances pointing menacingly ahead. The advancing line formed an impenetrable mass. It was a horrifying moment for me, despite the spectacular military impression they had made. The horses were bound to trample anything in their path, and I couldn't make out any gap in the line. I was trapped and resigned myself to being trampled by their unmerciful hooves.

"Suddenly, an officer must have noticed my feeble attempts to get away. He spurred his horse to double its pace and lunged ahead, coming straight for me. Just as he was about to shoot past, he bent down, grabbed me by my arm, and picked me up, throwing me over his knees like a sack of potatoes. Then, he led his regiment into battle. His timing was so exact, his execution so elegant, as if he had practiced the maneuver a hundred times before. My leg hurt and my head was spinning. I looked right and left, seeing the lances projecting forward. I heard the thunder of the horses' hooves. I saw the salvo of Austrian batteries flash in the distance. I witnessed the roar of the cannon fire exacting its toll on the advancing line. But any holes in the German line were immediately closed as they advanced on the infantry. I barely remember the small arms fire, and then I must have lost consciousness in the tumult of battle."

Richard listened intently, his eyes shining and his cheeks glowing during the recital. He seemed to have forgotten his precarious position. Enjoying the story, his fear of being exposed evaporated.

"When I came to," Bertrand continued, "I was lying next to a cannon in a conquered position. A Prussian doctor was tending to my injuries, and next to him was the First Lieutenant who had saved my life. Once I was bandaged, he put me into his servant's care, who had been shot in his right arm. The officer ensured that I got the best of care in the military hospital. I owe my life to that man, Lieutenant von Löwenklau, now promoted to cavalry master, and to his brave Franz. I haven't forgotten either one, and would recognize them in a crowd of thousands." He added a smile. "Even if they wore peculiar, outdated clothing."

Seeing the beginnings of panic in Richard's eyes, the doctor went on to explain himself. "I'm a German-Austrian, a German with all my soul. I had a relative in Thionville who had a significant medical practice. When he died, he left it to me along with all of his wealth. I had no reason to spurn such a generous offer. Last night, I was staying at an inn in Trarbach when I ran into Franz. You can imagine my joy in seeing him. He mentioned that he was looking for a simple job in the area, one that would give him time to look after his own interests. I hired him right away, and he's now my gatherer of plants and herbs. It's not necessary for me to go into things which I may suspect or deduce, Dr. Müller. I'm looking forward to seeing you in Ortry, and I want to reassure you on my honor that my one wish is to be of service to you and cause you no discomfort." He shook Richard's hand, then returned to his former seat.

Thank God for that, Richard thought, relief washing over as he watched Bertrand walk off. *The danger of being discovered is gone! Franz risked much when he took the doctor into his confidence, but the risk was well worth it. Of course, he has no knowledge of my mission beyond that I'm going to Ortry in disguise. Franz couldn't have told him what he didn't know.*

This Bertrand fellow is evidently cultured and genial. Perhaps it's even advantageous for me to have met him. His familiarity with the circumstances and persons at Ortry could prove to be of great benefit to me, and my problem of finding Franz a position is taken care of now. This way, he won't stand out or look suspicious. The position will be an asset, allowing Franz to be of service to me. It was providential of Bertrand to have attired Franz in the local garb as well, and considerate of him to seek me out and explain the circumstances, thereby laying my fears to rest. He even had the tact to return to his seat without drawing any suspicion.

Richard glanced over at Franz, who looked at his master apprehensively, wondering whether or not Richard was pleased with him. Richard responded with a good-natured smile, but tempered it by raising his eyebrows, hopefully communicating the importance of him not acting so liberally in the future on his own accord.

❧✠☙

The steamer made good progress as it passed Bernkastel. The fog showed no sign of letting up. They labored past Mühlheim, Wingerath, and Emmel, with the fog stretching over the waves in layers. Here, the river made a wide turn to the north, exposing the ship's vulnerable side to unseen obstacles. The current hugged the left bank, creating deep whirlpools that discharged all sorts of debris on the opposite side. The captain and helmsman needed to be extra vigilant.

The fog started to recede, but instead of it becoming lighter, an unwelcoming darkness settled over the land. The sky darkened and the clouds hung suspended low in the sky. Suddenly, a display of sheet lightning lit up the distant horizon. Heavy drops began to fall. Then, a blinding lightning bolt struck nearby, so intense and powerful that it felt like a massive bolt of fire had descended from heaven. A dreadful thunderclap was heard, followed by more rain that encompassed the entire river as the passengers on the foredeck instantly emptied into the refuge of the ship, Richard included.

Only the ship's crew remained at their stations. Against the oncoming storm, they were facing a difficult stand. Lightning bolt followed lightning bolt and thunderclap after thunderclap. The rain came down in buckets, so that the sailor entrusted with the job of lookout could barely see three meters in front of him. He clung to the mast for fear of being swept away by the deluge.

With the steamship already halfway past the treacherous bend in the river, the captain was hopeful of reaching Thron or Neumagen shortly, where the ship could lay over and ride out the storm. The ship's engine labored with all its power against the wind-tossed waves and the lookout's eyes tried to penetrate the wall of water in front of him, which seemed to be thrown at him with gale force. He heard something ahead slightly different than the incessant bellowing and roar of the rain and wind, a sharp cracking followed by a low moaning. He quickly turned to face the wheelhouse and cupped his hands, intending to warn the captain, but it was too late. He was jostled by a sudden crash and thrown forward onto a dark wooden mass that had collided with the steamboat.

The lookout's cry for help coincided with the warning cry from the captain and helmsman. The captain lost his footing and was thrown to the deck, knocking him unconscious, while the helmsman was unmercifully tossed into the tempestuous river. It was later discovered that the ship had collided with a large manmade barge that had broken its moorings upstream at the start of the storm and had been propelled downstream, striking the slow moving steamship with such force that the impact tossed many of its passengers from the shelter of the cabins. Anything that wasn't nailed down was thrown to the floor.

After the initial strike of lightning, Marion and Nanon sought shelter in the upper cabin. Faced with the prospect of sharing the small compartment with so many others, they decided to go back outside. Marion spotted Colonel Rallion across the deck and called out to him through the howling wind.

"Colonel, for God's sake! Help us!" she shouted.

He turned to face her, intending to answer, when a loud fear-laden voice drowned him out.

"Everyone for himself! We're sinking!"

On hearing the crewman's warning, Rallion wasted no time in abandoning Marion, quickly climbing the steps to the upper deck, a sea of passengers right on his heels. The two women were brushed aside and pressed into a corner. No one paid them any heed, squeezing them against the narrow opening leading further upstairs. People cried and yelled, ranted and swore. They pushed and shoved, all in an effort to get through the doorway. The thunder cracked and the lightning illuminated the desperate passengers, all clamoring to safety.

"God help us!" cried Nanon, cowering in the corner and holding herself back so as not to get crushed by the panicking crowd.

In this dangerous moment, Marion's decisiveness shot through. The proud, beautiful woman wrapped her arms around her friend. "Have courage," she said, comforting her. "The colonel left us momentarily to check on the state of things above. Just be patient. Surely, he will return and assist us in our plight!"

The disarray and confusion were even worse in the second cabin where all sorts of furniture had toppled, along with the items on them, and lay strewn about. The scraping and cracking of the bow against the barge, and the continual moaning and crackling of the logs as they jammed over top of each other droned on. The boiler tender and the machinist had abandoned their posts, leaving the engine to fight a losing battle against the logs. Since there was no one to operate the controls, the engine forced the steamship forward, resulting in the bow rising against the logs, while sinking in the stern. There was a huge crack in the front, like an explosion, sending a rush of water through the breach in the hull.

Frightened passengers wailed and fought their way to the door. In the middle of the confusion, Richard had the presence of mind to think about the baroness. *No doubt she's still on board,* he thought. Avoiding the panicking passengers, he worked his way over to Franz.

"Franz," he yelled over the calls of other passengers, roar of the deluge, and howl of the storm. "Have you seen two distinguished ladies go inside?"

"Yes, a blonde and a brunette," he replied. "They must be in the first cabin."

"Come on, hurry, we have to be sure!"

Richard leaped through the narrow door that led into the small kitchen and machine room. They found a small access door with steps that led to the upper deck. As they arrived on top, they first spotted the unconscious captain on the deck. At the back, Richard saw the French officers working at freeing a rowboat for themselves.

Richard ran up to them. "Hold on! Ladies first!"

"What! We need it for ourselves," Jean-Paul argued. "Get out of my way, idiot!" He jumped into the boat.

In the meantime, the ship sunk even lower at the stern, with the water rising up to the windows of the cabin. Richard saw that he had no time to lose. He gave up trying to convince the Frenchmen to give up the boat, especially since other passengers were already rushing over, yelling and screaming at them. He ran to the nearest steps, Franz at his heels, and headed down.

The two lovely girls were still cowering in the corner, holding onto each other. Although Nanon's eyes were closed, Marion saw the approach of the two men.

"Is it dangerous?" she asked.

Richard pointed to the window as the waves pounded the cabin wall.

"Come on, quickly!" he commanded, grabbing Marion's hand.

"Please, find Colonel Rallion!" she pleaded.

"He took off, saving himself," Richard said, not waiting to gauge their shocked reactions to the news. "For God's sake, we must hurry!"

The flooding river had nearly engulfed the entire ship. Water was pouring into the cabin from broken windows, and the ship was sinking fast. Without asking a second time, Richard reached for the baroness and in one motion swooped her into his arms, as though he had playfully picked up a child, and rushed with her toward the foredeck. Franz needed no prompting, and followed his master's example by picking up Nanon and hastening after him.

The danger had reached its pinnacle for those on the foredeck. The rain was no longer coming down in large drops, but falling in sheets, interspersed by lightning flashes. The bow had worked its way further up the barge, while the stern sank ever lower. Large logs and debris that had been ripped from the barge were being carried downstream, just as the small boat, occupied by Rallion and his friends, departed the foredeck accompanied by a hundredfold clamoring and cursing.

"Coward!" mumbled Marion. Then louder, as if embracing her fear, she said to Richard. "Now there's no hope for rescue. We're doomed!"

Richard lowered her feet to touch the deck and pointed to the churning waves.

"Will you place your trust in me, Mademoiselle?" he asked.

"It would be futile to swim against this torrent," she replied, her face turning pale.

"Nevertheless, we have to try," he said. Then, looking ahead, he reached out his finger to point. "Look!"

Richard spotted Dr. Bertrand, who in that very moment jumped overboard. Without prompting her, he took hold of Marion and pulled her after him toward the wheelhouse. The water had risen to the deck, forcing Richard to wade through it to get to the edge. Terrified, Marion looked for her friend. Nanon, nearly unconscious, hung on Franz's neck, who rushed past his master, slipping with his precious cargo into the wild river. Summoning her last ounce of courage, Marion put her arms around Richard as they plunged over the side.

The waves whipped against the men to such heights that Richard felt like he was lost at sea. The current propelled floating logs and debris around them, posing the greatest danger to the lucky few who had survived by swimming for their lives. As long as Richard could avoid the floating danger and stay above the waves, he would make it.

As a result of the bend in the river, the current pulled him to the far bank. Even though Marion was held above the water, the raging waves were too much for her. She cried out and fainted. Richard swam on his back, holding her up with his own body, ensuring the water didn't enter her mouth. She lay still on his chest, her eyes closed. As he swam he couldn't help but notice the gentle movement of her chest. Despite the danger around him, his eyes wandered back often, hardly believing his good fortune to have rescued the one he loved. Having just left the ship, he was a witness to its final sinking. The thunder and raging of the storm swallowed up the desperate cries of those still bound to the doomed vessel.

Franz was nowhere to be seen. In the steady, dense rain, Richard couldn't distinguish more than a few meters in front of him. Even so, he wasn't worried about Franz, who was also an accomplished swimmer. Although he couldn't see the riverbank, he reasoned that he would find land if he held to the left side of the river.

Five minutes went by, and another five elapsed before he spotted the eerie shapes of trees in the mist ahead, emanations out of the rain along the riverbank. He took a few strong strokes and ended up close to the bank. It wasn't easy to cling to the low-hanging branches without losing his precious cargo. After considerable exertion, he managed to pull himself closer, until his shoes found firm ground beneath him. He carried Marion up the bank and laid her in the grass, catching his breath.

Marion lay motionless, her face pale as a ghost. Her wet dress hugged her shapely form, revealing her lovely figure as though she had no clothes on at all. Richard ignored the rain, forgetting about the whipping wind and the roar of the river. His only thought was for the lovely woman who had so willingly trusted him. He sat down beside her, picked up her head, and kissed her on the mouth, over and over. Finally, warmth returned to her lips. She slowly opened her eyes as though coming out of a dream, her faint gaze on him.

"Richard!" was the only word to escape her lips during a short pause in the storm.

He sat upright. He had heard the name distinctly, witnessing the grateful smile as she closed her eyes again, drifting back into temporary unconsciousness.

She spoke my name, he pondered, shaking his head. *She couldn't have meant me. Was that Colonel Rallion's name? No, I'm sure he goes by another.* In her semi-conscious state, she had revealed the secret that she was in love with a man named Richard.

Richard felt a surge of momentary relief, even though the realization that her heart was spoken for caused uneasiness to creep into his own heart. But this was not the place to contemplate such things. It was imperative that he bring the baroness to shelter.

He noticed that there were well-tended fields along the river's edge, a sure sign that homesteads were nearby. With the baroness nestled in his arms, he hurried along the riverbank and came across a small path. He followed the path until it merged with a roadway.

He felt the baroness stir in his arms. Still only half-conscious, she wrapped her arms around his neck and rested her head on his shoulder. He felt her soft body and held her tighter, aware that he was prepared to fight her other Richard or any other to secure this wonderful woman's love. After walking for perhaps ten minutes, hardly noticing the burden of his beloved, he spotted a farmyard.

The roadway headed straight for a large gate, through which he entered. The owner, who happened to be on site, noticed that he was carrying a woman in his arms and rushed out to help. Richard briefly related the story of the disaster, creating quite a stir in the man. He dispatched all available farmhands to search for survivors, offering what assistance was needed.

Richard turned the baroness over to the women in the house, who in turn removed her wet clothes and put her to bed. Satisfied that she was in good hands, Richard went after the men and returned to the river, hoping to find Franz and the other lady in his care.

The downpour had abated, turning into a milder rain that allowed them a greater overview of the riverbank. The farmer spotted the funnel of the sunken steamship protruding awkwardly from the raging river. No one was visible on the river's edge. The barge had broken up and disappeared without a trace. There was little for them to do. Richard talked them into accompanying him by walking upstream. As they searched, Richard found a track through the grass, perhaps evidence of where Franz had made it to safety.

"It could belong to the man you're looking for," suggested the farmer. "Maybe he found our cabin."

"Where is it?" asked Richard.

"Over there, behind the alder trees."

They all walked toward it, finding a primitive looking structure built out of rough field stones. There was no door, just the rough hewn opening, and the only window was covered with straw. As they approached, a man came out. He was a little worse for wear, but Richard was relieved to see that it was Franz.

"Franz, is the lady with you?" asked Richard, happy to see his confidant.

"Resting on the straw," he said grinning. "She's still unconscious."

"Did she swallow a lot of water?"

"Not half as much as I did! Don't worry, Dr. Müller. There's someone with her far more proficient in distinguishing the living from the dead."

"Really?" laughed Richard. "Do you mean Dr. Bertrand?"

"Of course. He was already on the riverbank when I arrived with my lovely burden. Together, we carried her to this palace, managing to escape the storm."

"Ah, Dr. Müller," Bertrand said, getting up. "I must apologize for my sudden departure, but I knew that the ladies were in excellent hands and felt it was best if I could make it to shore in one piece, thereby rendering service to the afflicted. This lady is only unconscious. She should recover quickly if we can get her out of those wet clothes and give her a warm bath."

"There's a dairy farm nearby," replied Richard. "I will show you the way and we can carry the Mademoiselle. The baroness is already there." He took Nanon into his arms and followed the farmer back to the farmyard.

Once there, he led the doctor to a bedroom to care for the baroness while the women occupied themselves with Nanon.

As Marion regained consciousness, she was surprised to find a man alone with her in the small bedroom.

"Gracious lady," Bertrand said, excusing his presence, "I am a doctor and consider it my duty to look after your well-being since there are no nursing facilities nearby."

"Oh, thank you," she replied relieved. "Where am I?"

"On a dairy farm, not far from where the steamboat sank."

"Who brought me here? Is my savior alive?"

"He is doing well. He not only rescued you from the raging river, but also carried you here."

"Who is he, Doctor?"

"His name is Müller, an educator and doctor of philosophy."

"So he's German?" she asked.

"Yes. Do you feel his nationality somehow diminishes his noble feat?"

"Oh, not in the least. I am French, but by no means do I hate the German people."

"That won't sit well with the Baron de Sainte-Marie," smiled Bertrand.

"What? You know of my father?"

"Indeed," he answered. "I know him quite well. I've set up my practice in Thionville during your absence and have been selected to be your family's doctor."

"Then how is it that you know me?"

"I was also a passenger on the doomed ship, having barely escaped. I heard your name in passing, Mademoiselle. As you can see by my appearance, I have also survived the ordeal. How do you feel now?"

She paused, looking herself over. "I feel much better. I trust I escaped that horrible incident without succumbing to anything serious. How is my rescuer?"

"He possesses a strong and resilient nature. He has probably changed out of his wet clothes by now. But as for you and the other lady—"

"Ah, Nanon!" she interrupted. "I almost forgot about her. Was she rescued as well?"

"My herb collector, Franz, managed to save her, reaching the riverbank. She is currently occupying another room of this farmhouse. I'm certain she'll recover as quickly as you. I'll send for a few medicinal items from a nearby apothecary. There should be no reason for both of you not to resume your journey tomorrow."

"Dear God! Not by steamboat," she said with a shudder. "I will procure a carriage which should get us through Hetzerath to Trier. We should be able to access a train from there."

Meanwhile, Richard and Franz had removed their wet clothes and changed into temporary ones supplied by the farmer. The rain had stopped and most of the clouds had receded, revealing a clear sky. The sun's rays began to warm the cold earth.

Richard happened to glance outside, just in time to catch the approach of a few men. He recognized Colonel Rallion and his friends from afar. He withdrew from the window, not wishing to become another target for their tasteless jokes. The men ran into the doctor, who had just stepped outside to enjoy the warmth of the sunshine.

"You there, friend!" Jean-Paul called out, supposing him to be one of the farm workers since he too was clad in borrowed clothes. "Are you aware of the unfortunate incident with the steamboat?"

"Quite well, actually," replied Bertrand, smiling.

"The devil! Weren't you one of those on board?" he asked, studying his face. "You were in first class. Have any of the others survived?"

"I am only aware of four others."

"Who are they?"

"Two ladies and two gentlemen."

"Who are the ladies? Quickly!"

"Baroness Marion de Sainte-Marie and her friend, Mademoiselle Nanon."

"Thank God!" Rallion exclaimed. "I've been looking for her. Who brought her to shore?"

"Dr. Müller."

"Ah, the German fool!"

"Monsieur," said Bertrand reproachfully, "it doesn't seem particularly foolish to rescue a lady from certain death while others leave like cowards. If you hadn't appropriated the lifeboat, which seems to have disappeared, more lives could have been saved. You could have returned at least once to rescue more people. You'll be lucky indeed if your lack of action isn't judged too harshly." He turned around and left the chastised colonel standing there out in the open.

"No doubt another German," the colonel noted with disdain. "If we subdue this crude nation tomorrow, it won't be soon enough for me." He looked to the others. "Don't worry about him. Just look for the baroness so we can pay our respects."

He crossed the yard and entered the house, proceeding to the reception hall with the others following him. Richard, leaning against a wall, was in conversation with the proprietor. As soon as Rallion spotted him, he erupted into laughter.

"*Parbleu!* Now here's something funny!" he called out. "Look, our billiard player has transformed into a farmer! The jacket seems to sit well on his hump. I would have loved to see him swim!"

"I had to swim," said Richard, bowing politely. "I had the privilege of filling in for you once again, Colonel. Saving the baroness should have been your affair. No doubt it'll be you who asks for an apology today. I will, however, dispense with the formality of you having to proclaim it from a chair."

"Shut up!" Jean-Paul shouted, embarrassed. "Who gave you permission to concern yourself with the lady? Yet, I suppose your little swimming exercise has earned you a small tip. Here's forty francs," he said, reaching into his pocket and withdrawing two gold pieces. "That should be more than enough compensation for a crippled schoolmaster. If you approach her again, I'll smack you so that your crippled back snaps into a more manly form. Here, billiard fool!" He offered the money to Richard.

"I am a poor soul," replied Richard politely. "I will gladly accept your reward, with the condition that you explain to me if you really believe that the baroness' life is worth only forty francs." When Rallion, feeling slighted by his words, failed to respond to the comment, Richard continued. "I surmise that the amount is still too much for you to part with. Think about the transaction until we see each other again."

He left the room and retrieved his traveling suit, which had dried by this time. As he left the farm, he realized pleasantly that all he'd lost was his hat and old umbrella. Franz, now employed by Dr. Bertrand, remained behind, making himself useful to the doctor.

In the late afternoon, a lady appeared at the farmyard seeking an audience with the baroness. She explained that she was employed as a seamstress in Hetzerath. She then unveiled a number of clothing items, offering them for sale to the ladies as replacement for the ruined ones worn by Marion and Nanon. Marion was curious to learn how she had come to know of their presence on the dairy farm. The seamstress explained that a hunched over gentleman had come into her shop earlier in the afternoon, outlining the baroness' plight. He had asked her to accommodate his request the same afternoon and was prepared to reward her with two gold coins.

That must have been my rescuer, thought Marion. *The man is as resourceful as he is brave. His thoughtfulness has made the rest of my trip more bearable. How I wish I could see him again!*

The seamstress was rewarded for her prompt appearance, and sold each lady a suitable traveling dress.

CHAPTER TWENTY-FOUR
The Factory Director

If one traveled on the road that heads southeast from Thionville toward Stuckingen, one would come across a tributary of the Mosel and arrive at a fruitful region nestled with small villages and dairy farms. The Ortry estate was situated among these farms, complete with a castle. Although its outward appearance didn't present a formidable facade, the inner decor spoke volumes of the proprietor's affluence.

The proprietor was the Baron de Sainte-Marie. Having settled there just a short number of years ago, he was unfamiliar, even foreign, to the residents of the region. Even now, all that anyone knew was that his title had been only recently placed in the nobility registry. He liked to spend the winter in Paris, moving to Ortry with the advent of spring, often staying until late fall. The baron lived in seclusion and failed to socialize, but exerted considerable influence on the area through his business dealings.

Near the estate, down by the tributary where livestock once grazed peacefully, emanated the sounds of machinery in action. Huge chimneys eclipsed the trees and black iron wheels churned the water. Workers covered in soot labored with all sorts of hand tools and implements, and a soot-laden atmosphere lay over the entire factory, an unfortunate byproduct of the industrial revolution.

Baron de Sainte-Marie seldom visited the blackened buildings. Metroy, the factory director, had been appointed to oversee the entire operation. Quite often, though, a tall, gaunt, and withdrawn figure walked the distance to the factory, coming to inspect the goings on without saying a word. As he wandered through the facility, the workers admonished each other with a warning: "Be careful, the captain is making his rounds!"

The captain, of course, was the baron's father. Rumor had it that he was approaching ninety years, yet his stature was straight, his dark brooding eyes still had life in them, and his mouth bore the evidence of his original teeth. It was these teeth that one noticed, particularly if he was in a foul mood. In a characteristic move, his mustached lip curled up, exposing yellow teeth that he ground, reminiscent of a dog snarling at his adversary.

The captain never spoke to anyone; he neither praised nor criticized. But all who worked in the factory knew that he was the actual backbone overseer. If he stopped at a work bench, an anvil station, or in front of a blast furnace, then the workers exhibited twice the usual effort. If he spotted a worker's incompetence or lack of effort, he gritted his teeth, rolled his eyes, and walked away without uttering a word. The foreman would then approach the lazy worker a few minutes later with an irrefutable message: "Here is your severance pay and dismissal!" Once the old man was on his way back, the workers breathed a sigh of relief and they shook off the unseen influence he had exerted during his brief stay.

Other than his unscheduled visits to the factory, he didn't set foot outside the castle grounds, even though the forester assured those who asked that he had seen the old codger at night near the old abandoned tower. It was rumored that the tower was haunted by ghosts, which was why most people avoided the area altogether. Some men quietly laughed at this superstition, while openly clinging to the belief there were unusual things that occurred there.

Some time ago, the factory had been enlarged and more workers hired. It was rumored that Richemonte had arranged for the implementation of a firearms division. Wagon loads containing stocks and barrels from old rifles appeared from unknown locations and were outfitted with new mechanisms, an indication that technology was moving forward, even in Thionville. Once the rifles had been refitted, they were immediately shipped out, without the workers being the wiser about the intended destination. Large quantities of bayonets and sabers were also cast, with the captain paying specific attention to the quality of the final product.

Rumors continued to abound about the baron's mental health. Workers speculated that he was confined to his room most of the time, whining and lamenting. The old captain would be summoned to speak to him behind closed doors. When the baron finally appeared after several hours, he looked pale and worn out, as though he had survived a week-long malady. Although the baron was a handsome man, he bore a pale, waxen complexion that suggested an unusually sickly disposition of the psyche. His eyes were often glossed in a haze, he shuffled in his walk, and there was a worrisome shyness in his appearance, the basis for which defied any explanation.

His second wife, Baroness Adeline, exuded a totally different image. The opulent blonde carried herself proudly and was the one who ruled the castle, in some situations even daring to contradict Captain Richemonte, who was feared by all the staff. Her outlook was pretentious, and at times inconsiderate, even though anyone familiar with her traits would say that she had moments wherein she was easily influenced.

When present, the baron's daughter Marion managed to draw most of the servants' appreciation to herself. Unfortunately, she had been away in England for the last two years. Word leaked out she was expected to return soon by way of Germany. The complete opposite was true of her stepbrother, now well underway toward becoming a nuisance to all the servants, or anyone who crossed his path. Spoiled by his mother and mollycoddled by his tutors, Alexandre was the only one who meant anything to the cold-hearted captain.

Richemonte reminded him continually that he was the son of a Sainte-Marie, whose family looked to him to further the lineage. The boy, now thirteen years old, became proud, arrogant, imperious, and considered himself to be better than others. He derived his greatest pleasure from reminding the servants and workers that they had to obey his every whim and command. If one subordinate dared to contradict him, he or she immediately became the recipient of disfavor.

It was midmorning and a soft splashing came from Baroness Adeline's private bathroom. Anyone who had ever laid eyes on the decadent interior would have chuckled, knowing the baroness was pampering herself inside. The spacious room had no windows. The structure was eight-sided, with one of the walls forming the entry way for the door. The other seven sides were completely covered with murals of naked men and women in compromising positions. A large exposé of vineyards adorned the ceiling, and a rose-colored lamp hung from its center, giving an amusing appearance to the obscene figures depicted on the wall.

Situated under the lamp was a large marble bathtub that wasn't filled with water, but milk. In this soft, white bath, the body of the narcissistic baroness frolicked to the pleasures of her bath. The gracious lady insisted that milk was the only remedy for maintaining a clear and soft complexion, even into the later years. It was therefore no wonder that a considerable portion of the daily milk quota ended being used up by the baroness' health regimen, with the baron not seeming to mind the extravagance.

Whether Adeline's opinion proved correct was debatable, but one thing was consistent; she was always in a finer mood after her bath. And this day was no exception. She stood up out of the white milky substance and allowed the drops to fall on their own. As she dabbed with the towel, she considered the colorful images around her, comparing her attractive figure with that of the nymphs on the wall. She seemed to be pleased with herself. A self-confident smile played across her lips.

Indeed, she mused, nodding her head proudly, *if I were a man and beheld this sight, I would certainly fall in love with me. I know of no other who's so entitled to enjoy the finer things in life. The milk truly has wonderful properties. It protects and preserves the female body. The milk! Ha! What priceless irony. Not that long ago, I was forced to milk this white substance as a servant girl, and then sell it to others. Now, as the baroness, others gather it for me, and I can bathe in the same!*

She stepped out of the bathtub, slipped into her silken bathrobe, and rang a nearby hand bell. A maid came in, ready to attend to her needs. The maid toweled off her mistress, helped her change from the bathrobe into a fine cotton dress, and accompanied her to her boudoir to start her daily toilette.

"Is Alexandre already awake?" she asked her maid.

"For two hours already."

"Ah. What time is it?"

"Eleven o'clock, Madame."

"That means he rose at nine o'clock. I won't tolerate that. My boy doesn't have the same constitution as a blacksmith. What is he doing now?"

"I believe he is still with the captain, being schooled in fencing."

"Fencing lessons? For a thirteen year old?" Adeline asked. "I can see that I'll have to talk to my father-in-law about this. Alexandre has to develop more physically before he can be entrusted with a foil. Colette, have you seen the director?"

She shook her head. "Not yet. He usually comes at about eleven fifteen."

"Then pay attention! I need to speak to him before he sees the captain."

"I will wait for him on the landing, Madame," said the maid as she turned to leave, an amusing and all-knowing look escaping her eyes that slipped right past the self-absorbed baroness.

Situated above the baroness' boudoir was the captain's favorite room. It was furnished with simple and comfortable furniture, allowing him to look out unobstructed through any one of the three large windows. Two older style mirrors hung from pillars. Steel engravings of Napoleon I adorned the walls. They were interspersed with weapons of varying description and captured trophies of the various campaigns the captain had participated in while fighting for the famous Corsican. Once he had been a captain in the elite *garde*. He had fought and bled in France's wars and was now living in remembrance of those monumental years. Despite his advanced age, he still pined for a restoration of his country's former glory and was prepared to offer the few remaining years of his life to further the new successor's ambitions.

The old fighter, whose declining years had been unsuccessful in bending his physical body, resembled in a way a century-old dormant volcano, complete with the cliffs, schisms, and crevices that elicited warnings of an imminent eruption, whose smoldering reprisals were apt to erupt into furious and devastating discharges. Just like his body, his intellectual prowess hadn't waned. His eyes, still clear and unaffected by myopia, enabling him to gaze into the distance, were just as capable of penetrating objects up close. His guile and observation were feared by all he came into contact with. The result was that not a single person could boast of getting the upper hand over the old man. Simply put, he was a hard, regimented, stubborn man. His reputation as an unscrupulous businessman preceded him, and it was clear to all that once he had determined to do something, he would most certainly accomplish it.

Richemonte's only weakness, if it could be labeled as such, was his indulgence of his grandchild Alexandre, whom he shamelessly spoiled. Just as the maid had pointed out to her mistress, the young baron was receiving some basic instruction in the art of fencing from a master who still possessed sufficient physical strength and sharp eye to not only compete, but vanquish those who underestimated him because of his age.

They finished their exercises and sat on a divan in Richemonte's study, discussing the appointment of a German tutor who was to arrive at Ortry any day.

"But why did you select a German one, Grandpa?" asked Alexandre, already standing tall for his thirteen years.

"For a number of reasons, my son," replied the old man. "To begin with, your previous French teachers have been too independent. They've been limiting your instruction in certain areas. These Germans are used to paying attention and have traditionally proven to be the most reliable servants because they are willing to be led." The unspoken truth was that none of the previous tutors had been willing to idolize the young man in the way that he wished.

"Do you mean," began his protégé, "that such a man can become a thing of amusement? A servant? One who submits to the French?"

"Completely," Richemonte confirmed. "The second reason is that they claim to be well-educated and knowledgeable in such fields as geography and mathematics. Under this new teacher's tutelage, you'll learn more in a week than you learned in a month before."

"In effect, you're saying that the Germans are superior to the French!"

"Not at all! We are masters at practical living, yet they like to dream. They hunch over books, but know little of life. This Dr. Andreas Müller probably knows nothing about fencing, riding, swimming, dancing, hunting, shooting, conversing, or many other practical things. However, he'll be able to tell you much about Greece, Egypt, or China, without knowing much about Parisian social life and how the French nation defeated Austria at Magenta. The main thing is you'll learn the German language, not just in passing, but become proficient in it."

"What! I'm supposed to learn German?" asked Alexandre, turning up his nose in displeasure. "Why? I've no desire to become familiar with the language of barbarians and bookworms."

"You don't understand, my son," the old man patiently explained. "The time will come, perhaps sooner than I thought, when our eagles will rise, as it was with the great emperor. They'll fly over the Rhine and grip Germany with their sharp, victorious talons. Then we'll rule over the land that once belonged to us, the land that was stripped from us in the last war. An era will come when the brave will once again be rewarded with titles of nobility, just like with Murat and Beauharnais, like Davoust and Ney, and many others. The one who understands the language of his conquered people will be in a position to exert twice the might and influence over the subjugated. You *are* a Sainte-Marie, and you are my grandson. You deserve to count among these honorable ones." He rose from his seat, speaking animatedly and with passion. "You will fly with the other eagles to capture the reward that has eluded me because of the English picaroons that banished my emperor to an inaccessible island, just like the prophet of old, because they were afraid to bind the Corsican in chains."

The memory of the captain's missed opportunities and the emperor's defeat stirred him inwardly. His dark eyes flashed as he thought about Napoleon's exile, his mustached lip curled upwards, exposing his yellow teeth. By chance, his gaze drifted to the window overlooking the path that connected the castle with the ironworks. His face instantly grew calm again as his eyebrows furrowed in contemplation.

"But we'll talk about that later," he finished softly, his voice returning to its normal tone. "For now, go downstairs and see if the groom has harnessed the pony for your excursion."

Alexandre didn't have to be told twice, and left in a hurry. The captain's serious gaze returned to the path, scrutinizing a man who was now slowly making his way toward the castle. The visiting factory director, Metroy, had a stately, well-built shape, and his countenance was pleasing to the eye. He approached the castle, his head slightly lowered as if he were deep in thought. But on closer inspection, his eyes were searching the castle wall for a particular window, the one belonging to and occupied by the baroness.

"It's high time I brought this little charade to a quick end," Richemonte grumbled as he left his window, not wishing to be seen by the man below. *He's been quite enterprising, arranging everything to my satisfaction*, he thought. *The best part is that he was discreet about my affairs. But since then his demands have continued to climb. His infatuation with my daughter-in-law has become useful to me. I can use their relationship as an excuse to drive a wedge between us, ridding myself of him. I'll wait to confront him later in his own room. How fortunate for me that no one has discovered the secret passages of the old castle.*

Richemonte walked up to his armoire and opened it. He reached deep inside, his hand slipping between his clothes. The action resulted in a creaking sound as the rear wall of the closet slid back. He stepped into the wardrobe, bolting the outer door behind him, and strode through the narrow opening. The armoire concealed a false wall, perhaps one of many in the old castle. Someone familiar with the layout could easily maneuver between the walls, going from one level to another, or from one room to another. The purpose of these secret passages was clear, allowing the watcher to gain access to certain rooms, secretly observing and listening to the private conversations of the occupants.

A set of narrow stairs led down between the two walls. Richemonte was quite familiar with the way, descending the stairs in total darkness with complete confidence. He stopped at a familiar place, probing carefully with his hand. He located a loose brick, gingerly removing it without making a sound. A glass plaque with a matt finish became visible inside the cavity. It was situated in the baroness' boudoir just under the ceiling and had the same dimensions as the wooden edging, so that it blended with the rest of the décor, making it virtually undetectable to the casual observer. The design allowed for a limited overview of the spacious room and made it possible for him to eavesdrop on conversations so long as they weren't conducted in whispers.

Richemonte positioned his head so that he was able to look below into the room. The baroness was seated on an ottoman opposite him. She was wearing a thin, white morning dress, its folds held together with rose-colored lace. However, this sash was so loose that the top of her dress revealed the ornate blouse beneath it. The blouse had a low cut front, not supported by a typical corset, but by a flexible Oriental brazier. Her bust was partially exposed, suggesting that she had dressed in a hurry, when in actuality it was part of a cleverly executed plan. The man whose approach had been monitored by the captain now stood in front of her. It was the factory director who had been intercepted on the steps by Colette and ushered into her mistress' boudoir. He was holding a large book under his arm, one often used for financial record keeping.

"Please, Monsieur," said the temptress, reaching for the cumbersome journal, "put that away for a minute and sit down beside me."

"Forgive me, my dear Adeline," Metroy replied, "I can't dawdle. I must report to the captain. Quite likely, he has observed my approach through his window and will become suspicious if I tarry too long."

"That despicable old man!" lamented the baroness, casting a covetous look at the director.

"I know. He's become even more difficult lately. Not only does he keep checking up on me, he has no concept of rewarding me for hard work. If it wasn't for you, I would have tendered my resignation long ago."

Well, well, thought the passive meddler from his vantage point above. *It remains to be seen how much I can actually trust him.*

"Don't do that," she pleaded. "It would be unbearable here without you. But it's true. He doesn't like to be kept waiting. I'll try to contain my longing for you. Are you free this evening?"

"Yes, but not until later."

"How late?"

"Not until after ten o'clock, my dear Adeline."

"I'll leave the castle at that time and go for a walk through the park. Can you meet me there?"

He offered her a broad smile. "Nothing would make me happier."

"Then please, go for now, my love!"

Metroy picked up her hand intending to kiss it, but she moved it, offering her lips instead. His kiss found its mark and the satisfied director left her boudoir.

A short time later, the director arrived in the captain's study, finding Richemonte seated and occupied with paperwork.

"Have you come to advise me of the daily report?" asked Richemonte without getting up.

"Of course, Captain," he replied.

"I don't have much time right now. Is there something that can't wait?"

"Monsard & Co. sent payment."

"Finally," exclaimed a satisfied Richemonte. "How much?"

"Twelve thousand francs," advised Metroy. "Likewise, there is also one from Léon Siboult for eight thousand five hundred."

The captain tipped his head forward agreeably. "That is good news. Did you bring the monies?"

"Yes. I wanted to count both sums in your presence."

"We can do that tomorrow," Richemonte said. Then, looking up, he met the man's gaze. "Actually, I've decided to give you a bonus, as a sign of my appreciation for your thoughtfulness. Just don't make my generosity public knowledge. We'll discuss it tomorrow. *Adieu!*"

Metroy would have liked to acknowledge the rare compliment, but he knew his governor. Once he had pronounced his adieu, any further conversation risked stoking his ire. The director made the requisite bow and left the room. *Had I known he was occupied with other matters*, he mused to himself as he walked down the steps, *I would have remained with Adeline for another fifteen minutes. Who knows if she'll be in such a pleasant mood tonight!*

Meanwhile, Alexandre followed his grandfather's suggestion and attended to the stable. The groom was busy harnessing the pony to the smaller wagon that was suitable for taking the young baron on leisurely rides. He had barely finished the task, and was about to climb up on the buckboard, when Alexandre interrupted him.

"Hold on," he ordered the servant. "Climb into the carriage. I'm going to drive myself!"

"But, gracious sir, you haven't been taught that yet," pleaded the servant.

"Then I'll learn it today!"

The groom, already familiar with Alexandre's stubborn manners, recognized that a further contradiction would be useless. He obeyed his young master and took his seat while Alexandre picked up the reins and the whip, taking his place on the buckboard. The horse, heeding the signal, began to inch forward.

❧✠☙

At about the same time, the hunchbacked schoolmaster sat in a tavern in Oudron, dressed in a long coat and wearing large brass spectacles. For the time being, he was the only guest in the inn.

The innkeeper's wife came up to him, looking for some conversation and a break from her kitchen work. She obviously liked to talk, and in the space of ten minutes related her entire life story to the German spy, acquainting him with much village gossip.

"It seems to me," she said examining him more closely, "that you're a stranger in these parts, Monsieur?"

"Quite right," replied Richard.

"Where are you headed?"

"To Castle Ortry."

"Ah, I was born near there! Do you have relatives residing there?"

"No. I've traveled from far away. I'm German."

"That can't be!" she said loudly, taken aback. "You speak French so clearly and fluently, one might assume you were born near here."

He suppressed a smile. The woman clearly held the opinion that the inhabitants of her town spoke the purest French. In reality, her speech was laborious and sprinkled with foreign words.

"I had a good French tutor," he replied.

"He must have been from another region, then!" she concluded. "Are you staying long?"

"Probably, Madame. I'm going to meet Baron de Sainte-Marie, who has engaged me as the teacher for his son."

"Dear God! You poor man!" she exclaimed. "You'll have your work cut out for you there."

"How come?" he asked innocently.

"Because the baron's son Alexandre can be quite a handful. It seems he has a different educator every month. I've heard they can't wait to leave."

"That's most curious," Richard pretended. "Who's to blame for their early departure?"

The woman rolled her eyes. "Everyone else but the illustrious tutors. Oh Monsieur, the former owner was completely different. I worked there as a parlor maid before I met my first husband."

"Really? You've had more than one, Madame?" quipped Richard.

"Two, actually. And I've divorced the third," she said conspiratorially. "If you're wondering why, it's because I'm not Catholic. Well, Monsieur, as I've said, I was a maid and it's a real shame that the estate came into possession of the Sainte Marie family. I shouldn't have told you, since you'll be living there, but I couldn't help it. I can't stand that baron."

"Why not, Madame?" asked Richard, prodding her on. It was to his advantage to learn as much as he could about the family.

"Why? Dear God, there are so many reasons! Let me start at the top. First, there's the captain—"

"A captain," he interrupted her. "Who's that?"

"Who is he?" she asked incredulously. "Of course, you're unfamiliar with the circumstances over there. The captain is the baron's father, a relic from the old Napoleonic war, and probably close to ninety years old. He's a devil, Satan himself, a real Beelzebub. His hair is white, but deep inside beats a black heart. He rarely speaks to outsiders, yet holds such authority as if he were the baron himself. He's the one that founded the ironworks factory, and woe to the man who dares contradict him. Then there's the baroness—"

She paused to catch her breath. "The story goes," she added quickly, "that the baroness comes from the region of the Argonne Forest." She looked sideways, continuing with a smirk. "They say she was a shepherd's daughter. She prances about and makes herself out to be some sort of spectacle, claiming she has a following of countless admirers in Paris. She spends the whole day on her appearance, carries on like a little girl and tyrannizes the servants. She treads carefully around the old captain, but is otherwise the mistress of the manor."

"What about the baron?" Richard asked.

"Oh, he doesn't count for much. He's actually a decent man who goes along with what those two dictate, but he's not quite right in his head. He suffers from attacks, and that's when they lock him up. Sometimes he receives a beating so severe that he whines and laments. These episodes only occur in the summer. Strange, isn't it? During the winter, he lives with the baroness in Paris, completely normal. Then there's the young baron, Alexandre."

"The one I'm supposed to educate?"

"Yes. There's no other son. He's about thirteen years old and carries on like he's already grown up, like a real gentleman. He has no desire to learn from strangers. You can spend all your energy trying to motivate him, but it's a waste of time. I already know that come a month's time I'll be expecting you to pass by here again on your return trip back home. It's a mystery to me why they decided to hire you, since most of the residents of the castle despise the German race. Your mere presence there could prove dangerous for you, Monsieur. Germans aren't tolerated in these parts. I've even heard talk of war with them and—" She stopped in mid-sentence, as though she had said too much.

"Well, and?" he probed.

"It's only my way of talking," she evaded. "I tend to repeat what I've heard from guests who come through the tavern. If I were you, I wouldn't stay in these parts too long."

"Is there anyone else you wish to mention, Madame?"

"I could speak about the gracious mademoiselle," the woman prattled on. "But Marion's been absent a long time. She's living abroad, in England. I've heard that she's revered by her father, and hated by her stepmother. She's a classy lady, the young baroness, not at all conceited. She visits the poor and cares for the sick. Her mother was supposed to have been an angel, blessed with beauty, goodness, and kindness, but she died of a broken heart. Why, no one knows for sure. She was buried outside the castle wall because she was a heathen rather than a Christian."

Richard frowned. "A heathen? What do you mean by that?"

"Well, the baron brought her to France from a distant country where lions and tigers roam. She refused to convert to Christianity, and that's why they couldn't bury her on consecrated ground. Now she rests in a simple grave and haunts the old tower at night!"

"Really! Has anyone seen her?" asked Richard.

"Seen her? Incredible!" exclaimed the woman, astonished by the question. "Many have seen and heard her! She walks through the forest in her white robe, just like she used to before, with a hundred lights dancing around her. Then she suddenly disappears into the tower, appearing briefly at its pinnacle. When she leaves, you can hear the sound of chains rattling and clinking, as though a thousand ghosts were chained together. No one dares to go there at night."

"If no one dares to go, who then has witnessed this nocturnal hocus pocus?"

"The old forester," she answered. "At first, he was a young and courageous man who didn't believe in ghosts. He was determined to uncover the mystery. One night, he was confronted with the dead baroness' apparition and shot at the lights, but didn't hit anything. He was dismissed immediately because he had desecrated the blessed woman's peace."

Richard shook his head in contemplation. As bizarre as the story was, there was something there, even if most of it was probably exaggerated. It seemed to him that he would be getting involved with a most curious family that would affect his future profoundly.

At that point, the innkeeper's wife felt she had said enough and returned to the kitchen, giving Richard the opportunity to embark on the final leg of his journey to Ortry. The sun was shining pleasantly on this spring day, and he decided to enjoy the walk. His instructions hadn't specified an exact time, so it didn't matter to him if he arrived an hour early or an hour late. He knew the general direction and roughly where the estate was located. He wandered at his leisure, not keeping to the road. There was something freeing about being able to wander at length, and he took pleasure in arbitrarily following his own course.

His route took him through a small forest. Without worrying about not following a marked road, he continued through, crossing a meadow and arriving at an old stone quarry surrounded by steep, impenetrable cliffs. He decided to scale the cliff face from the side. When he climbed to the top, he reflected that the edge of the abyss hadn't been marked or sealed off. He saw the farmer's fields that encroached to the edge of the rock face. What if a farmer's horse or livestock spooked and approached the unfenced ravine. No sooner had he formed the thought than he was alerted by an outcry from a nearby field.

Richard saw a light wagon, pulled by a pony, careening toward the ravine at breakneck speed. As it neared, he realized that it was out of control, the buckboard occupied by a frightened boy who had dropped the reins and was hanging onto the sides of the cart for dear life. The hapless horse was galloping toward the quarry.

Rather than watch the scene unfold before him, Richard sprang into action. He ran diagonally toward the edge of the rock face, trying to intercept the out of control wagon. It was going to be close, he determined, since he couldn't match the speed of the horse. Richard's cool-headed nature came through. He couldn't stop the animal, but perhaps he could save the terrified boy. He braced himself, and as the wagon sped by, he reached his arm toward the frozen lad, grabbing the wide-eyed youth by the arm and pulling him from the seat.

In an instant, horse and wagon flew past him, careening in an arc over the rim of the ravine and falling into the abyss. It was only then that Richard realized a second person had been on board, cowering in fear on the floor of the carriage. He heard a loud crash from down below, and then it was deathly still.

The boy had lost consciousness and lay unmoving on the ground. By looking at his well-tailored clothing, Richard correctly assumed that he came from a wealthy family. While he examined him, he heard distant shouts from approaching farm workers.

"What luck that you managed to grab him!" exclaimed one man, running toward him. "It's the young sir!"

"Whom do you mean?" asked Richard.

"He's the young baron," said the man, bending with concern over the youth.

"He *is* alive," the German said, anticipating the next question. "He must have passed out from fright. Which baron were you referring to?"

"Alexandre, the young Baron de Sainte-Marie," a farmhand explained. "Hmm, this could mean a little reward. Come on, give me a hand. We'll carry him to the castle."

Two more workers stepped forward, collectively carrying Alexandre to the castle proper. Richard allowed them to proceed. He smiled to himself, recognizing they were more concerned about receiving a reward than acknowledging his deed.

Richard turned around and climbed back down into the quarry. When he finally reached the bottom, he was faced with a horrible sight. The carriage, smashed into countless pieces, lay atop the dead horse, which was nothing more than a grotesque mass of flesh. A short distance away, the disfigured body of a man lay sprawled on the ground. Richard supposed this was the groom. He surveyed the gruesome scene and instinctively knew there was nothing he could do.

He found a tarp and covered the poor man's body. He knew that the workers would advise the baron, who would make the necessary notification to the local authority. He scaled the face of the quarry for the second time that afternoon and hurried on toward Ortry.

❧✠☙

At the castle, the setting for a second breakfast was underway, with the family members assembled around the dining room table. It was obvious to anyone watching that the participants had no particular fondness for each other. They came one at a time, mumbled a sort of a greeting, and sat down. Baroness Adeline presided over the group. Richemonte barely acknowledged her presence, while Henri ate absentmindedly, making a face as though he hadn't the slightest idea what or where he was eating. After a few minutes of uncomfortable silence, the captain, aware of the boy's absence at the table, finally broke the silence.

"Where's Alexandre?" he asked.

"The young man left on a carriage ride, Captain," replied one of the servants.

Another period of stillness followed, this one lasting to the conclusion of their breakfast. They were interrupted by shouts of wonder, accompanied by frightened calls from the courtyard. Richemonte stood up and walked over to the window, where he managed to catch a glimpse of several strangers carrying something, only to disappear from his view into the foyer.

"What's happening?" asked Adeline, getting up from the table.

323

"Wait here while I have a look," the old man advised, the realization forming in his head that they had probably been carrying a person.

He left the dining room and met the workers coming up the stairs. When they spotted the master of the estate, they stopped respectfully. No one dared to verbally engage the old man unless he spoke to them first. Richemonte approached them, recognizing the lifeless form as Alexandre. The sight of seeing his favorite boy unconscious, perhaps even dead, would have affected many a man, but not a single expression crossed his hardened face.

"What's wrong with him?" he asked neutrally.

"He's not dead, gracious sir," replied one of the men, "only unconscious. The stranger who examined him assured us he was all right."

"What stranger?"

"The one who grabbed him from the carriage, just as the stampeding horse plunged into the ravine."

The captain's brows furrowed. This was the only outward sign of his concern. "Saddle a horse and ride to Thionville with all speed," he said, turning to one of his servants. "Find Dr. Bertrand and bring him here."

Then he instructed the farmhands to recount the story from the beginning. He asked about the stranger, but couldn't get any more information from them. The workers, intent on bringing the young baron back to the castle, hadn't paid any attention to the rescuer.

"He'll probably show up soon," Richemonte grumbled. "No one will pass up a reward. Well, come on, follow me!" he instructed.

They complied and carried Alexandre into the parlor. Richemonte returned to the dining room to inform the others.

"Alexandre is not feeling well," he announced frankly.

"He's unwell?" asked the baroness quickly. "What ails him?"

"He experienced a slight *malheur*. His horse got away from him."

"Oh my God!" the lady cried, jumping out of her chair.

"It fell into the ravine," Richemonte continued. "I'm sure the horse is dead and the wagon shattered on impact."

Adeline steadied herself against the table, feeling her knees starting to tremble. "And Alexandre, my child, my son?" she asked, turning white from worry.

"He was rescued at the last moment. Some workers found him and brought him to Ortry. He's resting in the parlor."

The baroness collected herself and staggered toward the door. Richemonte followed her. Even Henri rose from the chair and rubbed his forehead, as though he had to recall who this Alexandre actually was. Then, after a few moments, he slowly followed them.

The boy lay stretched out on a sofa. His eyes were open, staring into space, his self-awareness slowly coming back. The field workers stood at the entrance more interested in examining the plush decorations than in the injured child. The captain gave them a gratuity and sent them on their way.

Adeline kneeled by the sofa and hugged her son's head, tears streaming down her cheeks. Richemonte picked up the boy's closest hand and checked the pulse. Henri stood nearby, his attention riveted on a painting, oblivious to the scene unfolding before him. He was suffering from another spell.

"Mama, my dear Mama!" whispered the young man, slowly slipping back into consciousness.

"My son, my dear Alexandre!" she said. "How do you feel?"

"I feel very weak. It was so horrible!"

"I'll arrange to have you brought to your room."

"No," Alexandre pleaded. "I don't want to leave. I'm tired. I just want to rest here!" With that, he closed his eyes again.

The baroness lifted her teary eyes and looked questioningly at the captain. He nodded, agreeing to her unspoken request that he remain where he was. Henri approached his son, allowing his heavy eyes to scan the seemingly lifeless form.

"Alexandre!" he said, attempting to smile. He then turned abruptly around and inexplicably left the room.

The other two sat down on the sofa, intending to wait for the arrival of the doctor. Their love for the boy allowed for a temporary cessation of hostilities between them. Adeline hated the captain, and Richemonte despised the baroness, who in his mind was still nothing more than a shepherd's daughter. The feeling was mutual and they didn't bother to hide their revulsion. The apathetic Henri, the captain's supposed son and her husband, wasn't able to quell their distaste for each other, a fact that was known by the servants. It therefore remained a mystery to all why the captain had consented to Adeline becoming his son's wife.

Hurried steps approached, proclaiming the long awaited arrival of the physician. But it wasn't Dr. Bertrand who entered the room, but another practitioner who was somewhat familiar to Richemonte.

"Why did you come?" asked the captain inconsiderately. "I didn't summon you. I asked for Bertrand, my house physician."

"Forgive me, Captain, gracious lady," the doctor apologized. "You see, Dr. Bertrand is currently away on a short holiday. He asked me to fill in as required during his absence."

"When will he return?"

"The question remains if he will ever return," the doctor clarified, shrugging his shoulders. "He could be dead for all I know."

"Dead? What brings you to that conclusion?"

"He quite likely drowned, Monsieur," replied the doctor evenly. "Haven't you heard about the tragedy regarding the Trier-bound steamboat? It has been in all the papers. It apparently sank yesterday in the Mosel in a storm with all hands. A fierce thunderstorm hit the area to the south of the town, its ferocity rising to the level of a hurricane, something that has never been witnessed there. The ship collided with a large barge, which became dislodged from its moorings. I happen to know that the good doctor intended to return on that very same ship."

Richemonte stood up stiffly and approached the physician. "Is this news factual?" he asked, his voice trembling. "Has the story of the disaster been corroborated?"

"Yes. The investigating authority has already made inquiries, trying to compile a list of passengers so they can later inform the respective families."

"Then you have become the bearer of unspeakable news for us," the old man rasped. "My granddaughter, Baroness Marion, also intended to return on that ship. I just received her letter from Coblenz advising me that she was arriving today."

Since the residents of Castle Ortry rarely communicated with each other, the captain hadn't bothered to advise the others of the letter. If Marion was planning to come, she would simply show up on the estate. Adeline winced slightly at this latest bit of news.

"What?" she managed in a convincing, caring tone. "Our dear Marion was also traveling on that doomed ship? My savior! Two calamities in one day! Who can bear it?"

"Don't lose heart, my daughter!" Richemonte said, turning to face her. "There is still the possibility that some managed to survive the ordeal, or that some fateful incident caused her to delay her trip." He turned his attention back to Alexandre. "Please, Doctor, examine the boy!"

Because of the doctor's presence, Richemonte felt the need to speak some words of comfort and compassion, but his glance to her revealed his understanding that she wasn't in the least concerned for Marion's safety. In fact, he suspected she was inwardly rejoicing over her stepdaughter's untimely death.

The doctor approached the couch to examine Alexandre. After a cursory exam, he looked at the couple. "You can take some comfort," the doctor continued, "that the young baron is uninjured. He will recover quickly. If you don't mind, I'll send a servant to Thionville with instructions to procure some medication. I only hope that Baroness Marion has also conquered her ordeal, like the young Alexandre!"

CHAPTER TWENTY-FIVE
Doctor Müller

The physician had barely left the grounds when a servant approached the preoccupied captain.

"What is it now?" asked Richemonte.

"The new tutor, Monsieur Müller, has just arrived and requested to be introduced."

"Ah! What do you make of him?" asked Richemonte with growing interest. "What sort of an impression did he make?" The servant smiled surreptitiously, shrugging his shoulders while remaining quiet. "I see!" replied the old man. "If he leaves the same impression with me, I will simply dismiss him on the spot. You may admit him, even though we're not receiving visitors. Still," he mused, "we don't have to show much regard for a German schoolmaster. Tell him we have a young patient with us and that he should approach quietly."

Richard, having been briefed by the retreating servant, entered quietly. He bowed respectfully and waited to be addressed by the master. The baroness sized him up coldly, exhibiting shock.

"Well, I never!" she whispered. "It's almost insulting!"

Richemonte addressed the new educator with pitying scorn. "Monsieur, you're hunched over!" he uttered tactlessly.

"Unfortunately, I am," replied Richard evenly. "But I trust I will find favor with the household. After all, it's not a man's physical appearance that nurtures a child."

The old man made an inconsiderate, dismissive hand gesture before replying coldly. "But it's the stature that makes the first and lasting impression. How could my grandson possibly come to honor and respect you? Do you suppose we have the intention of disgracing ourselves by hiring a deformed tutor? I'm not prepared to accept you in this state. You are dismissed. Proceed to the servants' foyer and you will receive some compensation for your travel expenses. You can't expect more than that from me. We have been misled, yes, even betrayed."

"Good sir," replied Richard, "I plead with you to consider that—"

"Enough! Leave immediately!"

The shout woke Alexandre. The boy's glance fell on the newcomer. "Mama," he whispered, turning to his mother. "This is the man who saved me from falling into the ravine!"

Despite having been overwhelmed and fixated on the stampeding horse as it approached the abyss, Alexandre still recognized his deliverer. The baroness expressed her surprise with a quick movement of her hand.

"Is this true?" asked Richemonte, taking a step closer to the German. "Are you the man who rescued my grandson from certain death?"

"I was fortunate enough to be able to pluck him from the buckboard just as the panicked horse plunged over the precipice. I later climbed down into the ravine where I found a man's body in the wreckage. His face was unrecognizable, but I suspect it was the groom who allowed the horse to get away from him."

"Ah! I hadn't even thought about the stable hand. So, he died in the mishap?" The old man waved it off. "Then it's his own fault. It's not much of a loss. He should have been more careful. If he had survived, I would have punished him severely! Now, concerning you, Monsieur Müller, hmm!" He cast a questioning glance at Adeline. She understood him right away.

"It stands to reason," she said carefully, "that we're beholden to Monsieur Müller for his thoughtfulness, Captain. Still..." She shrugged her shoulders. On one hand, she felt compelled to acknowledge their gratitude, but on the other, she still had her reservations. Before she could express herself, Alexandre's voice interrupted her thoughts.

"Who is this man, Mama?" he asked.

"Monsieur Müller. He has applied to become your new educator," she replied.

"That's good," said the young man, showing signs of recovery. "I'm looking forward to it."

His two relatives looked at each other in amazement. Alexandre had never before expressed a desire to meet, much less anticipate, a new tutor.

"But look at him, my son," reflected his mother. "He's so... unseemly." She chose to avoid the words *hunched over*.

Alexandre responded in an impatient tone. He was used to getting his own way. "I find nothing wrong with his appearance. I don't want anyone else."

"Well then, perhaps we could give it a try?" she asked, addressing the captain with her remark.

Richemonte nodded thoughtfully. "Do you have your documents with you?"

"Here, Monsieur," replied Richard and removed a dossier from his coat, handing it to Richemonte. It was the same packet the general had given him in Simmern. The old man carefully read over each document to the end.

328

"You have excellent credentials. However, I only see accomplishments in literature, history, geography, mathematics, and a reference to several languages. It seems your countrymen place little worth on developing the outward skills of a person. Have you learned to dance, Monsieur?"

"I have never been rebuffed by a lady, Monsieur," replied Richard modestly.

"I wasn't referring to a schoolmaster's daughter or a seamstress," Richemonte said with a touch of sarcasm. "I was thinking of a real lady. Anyway, we'll see about that later. How would you fare in wrestling or horsemanship?"

"I am confident I would meet your approval."

"What about fencing or marksmanship?"

"I have received the proper instruction from qualified tutors in both."

"Hmm. What if I were to put your skills to the test?" Richemonte asked. "You see, I like to pick up a foil now and then."

"I remain at your disposal, sir," said Richard unpretentiously.

The old man appraised him with dark, penetrating eyes. It was clear that he didn't believe him.

"Well, in that case, I'm going to hold you to your word," he decided. "If you prove yourself by demonstrating your proficiency, you can consider yourself to be in my employ. But for now, find *l'intendant*, Monsieur Lussier, the governor. He will show you to the room, normally reserved for the tutor. I hope you will remain at my disposal as soon as I call for you, Monsieur!"

The formality of the introduction was over. Richard approached the still unwell boy and picked up his hand. "Many thanks for your friendly recommendation, my young sir! Your kindness has elicited my respect for you and I hope to prove myself worthy of educating you, so that you will attain the high recognition worthy of a Sainte-Marie!" He bowed to the other two and left the parlor.

The captain watched him leave. "That was well said," he remarked, partly astonished. "No one has proclaimed this before. He seems to know what a good name represents."

"His bow was most elegant," agreed the baroness. "Perhaps a little self-confident, but still respectful, completely without fault. We will have to evaluate him to see if he will be suitable for the task, despite his ungainly appearance."

Leaving the parlor, Richard sought out the head servant. When he spotted him, he immediately saw that Lussier was a staunch Frenchman. He wore a formal black coat, pressed pants, a white silk vest, and a pallid neck scarf. His large feet were pressed into shiny patent leather shoes, the cramped quarters making his posture and gait a little unsteady.

"Ah, it's you! You're the new tutor?" he inquired in a superior tone, appraising him. "My name is Marcel Lussier. Is this posture customary in Germany?" he said, mocking the newcomer's physique.

"Not likely," replied Richard neutrally. "Fortunately, I am an exception and trust you are capable of overlooking my outward deficiency in favor of my accomplishments. I have come to you so you can assign me a room."

"I will see to it. By the way, I need to point out that I am not here to serve you. As head servant, I am your superior."

"I have no objection to that, Monsieur. I only ask that you treat me with the respect I deserve. In my country, it's customary to pay homage to those who have demonstrated their understanding of how to attain the respect of one's peers. May I entreat you to show me to my room, Monsieur le Concierge?"

"You seem to speak a poor version of French, Monsieur," Lussier said as Richard turned to leave. "The word concierge signifies more of a doorman than head servant. You are to address me as *l'intendant.*"

"Very well, Monsieur. *L'intendant* it is," he said, taking the correction amicably. "Please, my room."

They walked past several servants who, when spying the tutor's ungainly appearance, showed their disapproval by turning up their noses at him, something which Richard ignored. After climbing several flights of stairs, Lussier stopped in front of a door high up in one of the turrets, flanked on either side by the castle facade. The room was outfitted with the simplest of furniture.

"Well, these are your accommodations," Lussier said, failing to hide his malicious enjoyment of putting Richard in his place. "A table, two chairs, bed, commode, armoire. I trust you have your own pocket watch, and that this," pointing to the sparse furniture, "will suit your comforts."

"Where does the young baron reside?" asked Richard.

"On the main level, next to the gracious lady's rooms."

"Isn't it customary to house the educator in closer proximity to his charge, *Monsieur L'intendant*?"

"Perhaps elsewhere," Lussier allowed, "but not here. In terms of peerage, the educator rates below the cook, so your lodgings should come as no surprise to you. The cook resides directly below you, not any closer to the master."

"Thanks for the information, Monsieur!" said Richard, dismissing the imperious housemaster who seemed determined to place the German on the lowest possible rung of the domestic ladder.

Richard paid no attention to the meager decorations. He walked up to one of the three windows in his quaint abode. A small smile creased his face. Surprisingly, he wasn't displeased with the poor accommodations. Luck had stayed with him, and he hoped it wouldn't desert him now. Lussier's arrogance couldn't provoke him to retaliation, and being Alexandre's deliverer had assured him of the baron's gratitude. *This recognition will probably increase on Marion's arrival. But then what?* he mused. *I'm not about to let uncertainty ruin my outlook.*

Richard gazed contentedly at the spectacular scenery in front of him. Far out to the west, the high Meuse hills were dwarfed by the towering tree-lined mountains of the Argonne Forest. Church steeples and structures from the nearby towns looked welcoming. To the right lay Thionville. Just below the castle rose the dirty structures of the ironworks, eclipsed by a smokestack, spewing black, pungent smoke into the atmosphere. Another window faced south, revealing a little park that stretched toward a nearby forest. The third window faced north, overlooking the flat roof of the main building of the castle. Richard didn't yet realize just how providential this would later prove. The fourth side, the east wall, had no window. It was wallpapered and bore an old dirty mirror. While his eyes took in the room's simple furnishings, he heard a soft, creaking sound. He walked up to the wall and listened intently.

Yes, I wasn't mistaken, he thought. *It's as if something, more likely someone, is moving on the other side of this wall, in an upward direction, probing with his hands.* He detected a slight rustling, as when a stone scrapes another surface. *What is this? Is there a false wall in this room? Could someone have come to spy on me? I'll have to look into this further, but I can't risk it now. I have to pretend I don't hear anything. What an odd castle! It may have secrets yet to be explored.*

Richard returned to one of the windows and pretended to be merely captivated by the view. At the same time, he concentrated, hoping to hear any unusual sounds. Since he didn't detect anything new, he left the window and lay down on his bed, still alert to anything unusual. He heard the same quiet rustling again. This time, it seemed to be coming from the ceiling. The sound seemed to move back down the wall and stop. He tried to hear more, but the room was completely still.

After a while, Richard rose and went to the north window, overlooking the flat roof. He lacked an instrument to make an accurate measurement, but as he compared the distance between the window and the outer edge of the turret with the inner edge of his room with his naked eye, he came to the conclusion that the wall was nearly one meter thick. When he gently tapped the wall, he deduced from the hollow sound that there was indeed a cavity between the inner and outer walls.

But what is its purpose? Richard thought to himself. *What other reason could there be but to eavesdrop on an unsuspecting occupant? And where is the opening whereby one can see into the room?*

He surveyed the entire wall and even looked behind the mirror, but couldn't find anything out of the ordinary. The suspected opening could only be near the oven pipe or in the wooden trim joining the wall and ceiling. He moved a chair against the wall, climbed up, and knocked gingerly. *I was right,* he thought. *Tapping the trim here makes a different noise. It even feels smoother. Unless I'm mistaken, this section isn't wood, but glass.*

Having made this new discovery, the only logical conclusion was that he was being observed. But by who? Were there other places in the old castle with double walls? It seemed lucky for him to have found out about the eavesdropping so early in his stay.

His eyes widened as another thought occurred to him. *What if I had changed my clothes during the presence of the eavesdropper? He would have seen my artificial hump and my secret would be out! I had better be on my guard and find a way to turn these secret passages to my advantage. I have to find out who is spying on me.*

His thoughts were interrupted by the arrival of a messenger, advising him that the captain was expecting him in the courtyard. He followed the summons and found Richemonte already waiting for him. He wasn't alone. Alexandre was with him, as well as Lussier, the haughty *l'intendant*. He was instructing two servants carrying weapons. Alexandre, still looking a little pale, appeared to have mostly recovered from his ordeal.

"Monsieur Müller," he said, approaching his new educator. "I've tried to sleep, but I'm restless. Grandpa said that you were about to go through several trials. I didn't want to miss that!"

The captain pointed to a corner of the yard. "Monsieur Müller, over there are several devices used for strengthening the upper body. Please, show us what you can do."

"Right away, sir!"

Richard walked over to the first object, a wooden horse. He braced himself, then without a running start or even using his hand for support, he jumped it lengthwise. Next, he walked to the horizontal bars and, without removing his upper clothing, gripped the bar with one hand and swung himself to the other side.

"Is that sufficient, Captain?" he asked, turning back to Richemonte.

"Did you see that, Grandpa?" praised Alexandre. "Until now, no one has been able to accomplish such a feat."

"True!" admitted the old man. Out of the corner of his eye, he saw a brown horse being led into the courtyard. "Monsieur," he called to Richard, "saddle that horse. I want to see how well you can ride."

A stable hand brought the horse closer while another carried the saddle and bridle.

"A saddle won't be necessary!" Richard told the stable hand.

"But Monsieur!" warned Richemonte. "This one's unpredictable and only used to one rider, namely me. He routinely bucks anyone else from the saddle."

The animal seemed to have been confined to the stall for several days. It was restless and pranced about, kicking its feet in the air and pulling on its halter. Without heeding the old man's warning, Richard approached the spirited horse, appraising it with an expert's eye. He nodded in recognition and smiled to himself.

"He's the son of an Arabian and an English mare. Am I right, Captain?" asked Richard.

"Indeed," replied Richemonte. "But tell me, Monsieur Müller, how did you come to that conclusion so quickly, something that... *Morbleu!*"

Richemonte jumped aside, startled. In a blink, Richard was on the horse's back. He grabbed the halter and began riding around the courtyard, defying explanation of how he had mounted the steed in the first place. The horse made every attempt to shake off the rider, but the young Löwenklau sat securely, as though he had been born to ride it.

The old man narrowed his eyes suspiciously. Did this Müller fellow know some secret that enables him to ride with such control? It certainly seemed like it. Richard had managed to calm the horse within the first minute, riding now with such confidence and elegance that he may as well have been performing in a parade. Suddenly, he brought the steed to a full gallop, leaned forward, and raced across the courtyard. In a spectacular leap, he hurtled over the brick wall surrounding the courtyard.

"*Mille tonnerres!*" yelled the captain. "He's going to break his neck. The horse is finished!" They all ran to the gate. They hadn't quite reached it when they hastily stopped in their tracks.

"Look out! Make some room!" bellowed Richard's deep voice. In the same instant, he came flying back over the wall again. He rode in a circle a few times to calm the horse, then dismounted with a leap.

"The devil! Where did you learn to ride like that?" Richemonte inquired.

"My teacher was an Ulan," replied Richard.

"Do all Ulanen ride like that, Monsieur?"

"Most of them even better!"

"I see," the old man noted, stroking his chin. "I've heard they're a wild people, the *Hulanes*. They live in the desert, marry at will, constantly add to their harems, and ride their horses to the ground." He quickly turned his mind to other subjects, refocusing his attention on Lussier, who was approaching with a loaded rifle. "Now, let's see how you fare with firearms!"

Richard didn't reply, trying to suppress a smile over the old man's words. He knew that Richemonte, like many Frenchmen, were ignorant in matters of geography beyond their own borders. The old captain mistakenly held the Ulanen for a race of wild nomads living on the eastern border of Prussia. They were often mistaken for the *Baschkiren* and other Asian peoples. As far as most Frenchmen were aware, they were hardly more than cannibals. It wasn't until after 1870 that they became better understood in general circles, quelling the unpleasant perceptions about them.

The captain took the rifle with a rear loading mechanism out of Lussier's hands. "Alexandre allowed a balloon to get away from him yesterday," he began, pointing to where a balloon tugged hopelessly against a nearby wind vane, its string entangled in its rotating blades. "The string got caught in the mechanism. I'm going to hit the balloon."

He lifted the rifle to his shoulder, aimed briefly, and let loose a bullet. The shot struck the balloon squarely. "There," he said proudly as the beheaded string dropped limply against the side of the vane. He handed the rifle, along with some ammo, to the teacher. "Now, it's your turn."

"Ah, a Mauser!" Richard observed, examining the firearm carefully. "I'm not familiar with this type, but I hope to hit the cord on my first try. Certainly, it won't take me more than two."

The spectators looked at one another in amusement. Richard loaded the rifle and aimed at the object. The shot rang out. A moment later, Alexandre let out a gasp as the pieces of balloon sank toward the roof, the cord having been severed.

"Remarkable! You're as proficient with firearms as you are in horsemanship and athletics," complimented the old man. "Finally, I want to examine your fencing skill. I sincerely doubt a German could measure up to a Frenchman." He waved for Lussier to step forward. "Our *l'intendant* is quite proficient with a foil. He was a premier sergeant with the *Chasseurs d'Afrique*. I make it a habit of employing retired military men. Are you up to a little fencing match?"

"If you require it, Captain, I will comply."

"Then let's arrange it!" said Richemonte, barely concealing a smirk. His white moustache curled upward, signifying some sort of looming calamity. He knew that Lussier was an above average fencer, and his arrogant nature would have liked nothing more than to spill a little of the German's blood out of sheer amusement.

Lussier had two identical epées in his hands and handed one to the unsuspecting schoolmaster.

"Monsieur Müller," he said, smiling, "would you be so kind as to indicate where I should strike your body?"

"These foils are very sharp, with the tips unprotected," Richard pointed out as he examined the foil. "We're not going into battle. Shouldn't we arrange for less offensive weapons and wear some protective gear?"

"Ah, you're afraid!" scorned Lussier.

"Of course I'm afraid," replied Richard steadily.

"And you have the nerve to admit it openly?" Lussier scoffed.

"Why hide the obvious? But you seem to misunderstand me, Monsieur. I'm afraid it's you who might be injured. Certainly I have no qualms for my own safety. Since you've informed me that you're my superior, am I permitted to strike you?"

"Of course, if you feel you're able to accomplish it! Now then, point out the place I should aim for!"

"I will dispense with naming it, reserving that right for myself so I can exercise my own judgment."

"I will grant you that much. So where shall we aim, Monsieur?"

Richard shrugged his shoulders. "I'm a stranger to these parts, not wishing to be ridiculed for my choice. You can take your preference."

"Very well," replied Lussier, trying to conceal a devilish grin. "These foils are designed for thrusting, but we can satisfy ourselves with a cut to the face."

"Just as you please, Monsieur," agreed Richard, "though I would point out the risk of you perhaps losing a nose or damaging the eye, not to mention the danger of ruining your silk neck scarf."

"Ah, you're mocking me! You think you'll gain the upper hand and cut my nose? I suspect the match will go the other way." Lussier turned to eye Richemonte. "Captain, would you confirm the details?"

Richemonte's face twitched with excitement. "I will allow the match, with the stipulation that no reproach falls on me," he said, turning serious. "You are both in my employ. If one should succumb to the other and become incapable of performing his duties, he won't receive any compensation from me. Is that clear?"

"Perfectly!" replied Richard.

"Excellent!" exclaimed Lussier a little hastily. "We can begin."

Over on the side of the courtyard, the baroness stood at an open window, watching the proceedings. She observed the trials which Richard had been obligated to demonstrate, catching every word conducted between her father-in-law and the German tutor. Another lady may have raised an objection over the latest development, but she relished the drama of a good fight, and leaned further out the window, not wanting to miss a single moment. She was a woman devoid of compassion.

Lussier, full of self-confidence, assumed the appropriate stance. Suddenly, the rapiers flashed – and a split second later, he cried out in pain, staggering back. He dropped his foil and felt his face, unable to stop the blood flow.

"The devil!" called out the captain. "That was a devastating blow!"

"It's what he wanted," said Richard solemnly, without boasting in his victory. "I regretted having to show up my superior, but now he sees how much he has yet to learn about the art of fencing."

Richard's lightning-like thrust had glanced off his opponent's forehead, catching the left eye, and splitting the nose in two. The eye was almost certainly lost, but he was still alive. The injured man howled mostly from the pain, but also out of anger.

"Take him to his room and send for a doctor!" ordered Richemonte, addressing a nearby servant. "Who would have thought that he would meet his match at the hands of a German tutor? Monsieur Müller, you're an accomplished fencer. I can see one must treat you with the utmost respect, despite your infirmity. You have passed your tests to my satisfaction, and you may assume the role of my grandson's tutelage."

"Thank you, sir," Richard replied. "This last trial was somewhat unusual, but since I value my face more than Lussier's, I had to defend myself."

That said he left the courtyard, returning to his room to clean up while *l'intendant* was escorted to his own to await the doctor's arrival.

Alexandre had watched the trials with interest, including the last match, short as it had been.

"Grandpa," he said to Richemonte after Richard had left, "this Monsieur Müller is totally different from my previous tutors. He's confident in his abilities and has no fear of you or me. I like him and I don't want to see him leave."

Back inside the castle proper, Baroness Adeline examined herself in front of the mirror in her boudoir, admiring what she saw there.

What a man! she thought. *All his efforts seemed like child's play. Even his leap was accomplished with perfect grace, not detracting from his manhood. And that jump over the wall with the horse! A simple miscalculation and he would have ended up injured on the ground, disgraced and seen by all. This German has a powerful physique, like an Adonis. Too bad he carries that ghastly hump. He makes the factory director look meek and compliant. No, this Müller is far more appealing...*

CHAPTER TWENTY-SIX

The Baron's Madness

Once Richard had returned to his room, he examined himself, but unlike the baroness, he did so for an entirely different reason. Fortunately, his wig was still in place. If it had come off during the trials, everyone would have clearly been able to see the underlying blond hair. It was a miracle the hairpiece had remained in place while he fought to save Marion in the Mosel. His entire mission hinged on these smallest details.

A servant appeared later with instructions that the young baron wished to go out with him. He looked forward to the opportunity. Richard needed to assess Alexandre's knowledge and abilities so he could design a suitable curriculum.

He descended the steps and arrived in the main corridor. A door opened, revealing an occupant unknown to him, who emerged with slow steps and lowered eyes. It was the baron, Arthur de Saint-Marie, presumably going to his wife's chamber. Although Richard didn't know him, he resembled the photograph supplied by the general. The tutor's suspicion was confirmed by the absent-minded expression on the man's face. Richard stopped out of respect, allowing the baron to pass by.

Henri approached slowly, coming to the realization that someone was standing in the hall. He lifted his lethargic gaze and stared at Richard. A remarkable transformation occurred in the deathly face. The eyes widened, displaying signs of recognition. The eyebrows pulled together and his mouth opened in unpleasant surprise. He stood transfixed for a few moments, disbelief etched into his forehead and arms outstretched as though trying to repel a foe. Suddenly, he turned around and ran back to the door from which he had emerged, accompanied by a loud raspy voice that warned of looming disaster.

"It's him, it's him!" he called out. "He's still searching for the strong box. Flee for God's sake. He's looking for the war chest!"

The baron disappeared, slamming the door behind him. Richard stood motionless, the lunatic's words having had a profound effect on him. A few doors opened, with Baroness Adeline appearing, as well as the old captain, who approached him none too pleased.

"What's going on? Who was shouting?" Richemonte demanded.

Richard mustered every ounce of his self-control to gain control of his emotions. Instantly, his face revealed a perplexed expression. He looked as if he wasn't able to comprehend something, shaking his head.

"I just came down the stairs," he said, "when a gentleman, unfamiliar to me, came out of a room, rambling about war and having to flee. What a singular prank!"

"What words did he use?" inquired the old man, pressing for an answer. "Tell me exactly what he said to you!"

"The words *war* and *escape*."

"Nothing else?"

"No, or at least I didn't catch others." Richard was wary of revealing the truth. He found himself standing quite unexpectedly on the brink of solving some of his life's most troubling questions, the ones revolving around his family and immediate relatives. Finally, the curtain of secrecy had lifted slightly, revealing solutions he gladly would have ransomed his life for.

How often had he, his dear mother, old wizened grandfather, and lovely younger sister prayed on their knees for a glimpse into the mystery of their father's disappearance? All their prayers had seemed to be in vain. But now, after many years, after giving up all hope, came a glimmer, so out of the blue... not overpowering and blinding like lightning, nor bright and illuminating like the light of day, but like a slow precursor, the awakening of a dormant hope, such as with the breaking of dawn after a stormy night.

Watching the old captain, he knew he had to tread carefully.

"He's my son, the Baron de Sainte-Marie," Richemonte said stiffly. "He suffers from peculiar episodes. I'm not sure if I should label them hysterical or just unusual. He dreams of strange things, and then erupts, becoming vocal. Don't pay any attention to his ramblings. I've issued strict orders that all the servants are to withdraw themselves when he experiences a relapse. The presence of strangers can often heighten the severity of the episode. If you lend credence to any of his ramblings, I would be forced to dismiss you from my employ."

Richemonte was clearly agitated, his eyes glowing like coals, and he lifted his teeth into a snarl. In this brief moment, he had the appearance of a man who didn't give a damn about the world. "What were you doing down here anyway?" he asked gruffly.

"I was on my way to the courtyard," replied Richard steadily.

"What for?"

"The young baron is waiting for me. He requested that I accompany him on a walk."

"Then go find him! But I'm warning you not to reveal anything to outsiders about my son's condition."

The captain spun on his heels with a youthful quickness and headed through the same door the baron had disappeared into while Richard proceeded to the courtyard where Alexandre awaited him.

From her vantage point, the baroness had listened to the men's unusual conversation. With slow steps, she followed Richemonte into her husband's room, only to find it empty. From the adjacent closet, however, came a wailing sound, interspersed with the captain's threatening voice. As she entered, she saw that the captain had coaxed the hapless baron out of the closet. Henri was cowering on the bed, his head hidden under some pillows.

"He's here! He's here! I saw him!" lamented the baron.

"Silence!" thundered Richemonte. "It wasn't him!"

"But it was him!" Henri insisted. "He's searching for the war chest."

"I'm ordering you to keep quiet!"

"No, no—I'm not going to keep quiet. I simply can't," Henri cried out in his delusion, burying his face deeper into the pillow. "I don't want the strong box. I've already unearthed one. I've stolen the money box from Magenta. What use do I have for the one from Waterloo?"

The captain removed the pillow and showed him his fist. "Dammit!" he threatened. "One more word about the chest and I'll show you the real master."

"Not you! It's not you!" exclaimed the desperate baron, rising from the bed and looking at Richemonte with disdain. "You're the devil, Satan himself. But you're not my master. I still have control." He struck his head and chest for effect. "My master resides in here and he has crushed my heart and battered my mind. I don't want the chest. I'll return one and leave the buried one. Oh, my aching head, my poor heart. How it burns, how it pains me! Only the loving look of Liama can stop the pain. Where is she? I want to see her!"

"Silence!" Richemonte roared. "I'm telling you for the last time!"

"I'm not going to keep quiet! Oh Liama, my sweet Liama. Give it back, the chest, give it back!"

The captain's fist struck him not once, but many times, yet the sickly man continued to wail. Henri, subjected to the cruel chastising at the hands of his adopted father, didn't do much to defend himself. All the while, he persisted in calling for Liama. The captain's arms grew weary and he turned after some time to face the baroness. She had witnessed the brutal assault, and though she hadn't been a party to it, she also hadn't done anything to stop it.

"This relapse is more serious than the previous ones," Richemonte said resignedly. "I can't seem to intimidate him into stopping. We'll have to resort to the other method."

Henri continued to whimper.

"I'm uncomfortable with it," Adeline protested. "Do you derive pleasure by forcing me to—?"

"You will comply!" he interrupted her, barely concealing the underlying threat. Do you want the servants to find out what's really going on and what he continually wails about?"

"And if I don't, then what?" she asked, shrugging her shoulders.

"Then you will cease to be the Baroness de Sainte-Marie!"

Although Adeline took note of the implication, she dared to provoke him. "I'd like to know how you plan to pull that off, my dear father-in-law."

"It's the baroness that I want, the Baroness de Sainte-Marie!" called the deranged man, remembering her at last in his fractured state of mind.

"Silence! How careless of you to mention her!" said the captain angrily, striking the man again. He then looked back to the baroness and continued. "I know exactly how to bring you down. By God, I'm just the man to accomplish it! How do you intend to prove that you're his wife?"

"I have witnesses!"

"They're all dead!"

"You're their murderer," she argued. "But the mayor's journal and the church records will confirm my identity and position."

He faced her derisively. "I've arranged for the records to disappear," he said.

"Then you're a thief! I don't require documents or witnesses. All I have to do is to reveal what I know."

"Right! And spend the rest of your miserable life in prison," he mocked with a devilish grin. "Who will punish my son here? No one. He's unhinged. Who will accuse me? I wasn't there. Are you going to comply, or are you willing to forfeit your son's future as the rightful baron?"

Henri was squirming under Richemonte's embrace, who was trying his best to cover his mouth.

"You really are a devil!" Adeline uttered through clenched teeth, rising out of her chair.

"And you're nothing more than a milkmaid, a miserable peasant girl. Now, go and get changed!" he ordered, his eyes flashing with anger.

Filled with humiliation, her cheeks reddened. The baroness returned to her husband's living room and entered the adjoining bedroom. It wasn't particularly spacious and only contained a washbasin, mirror, and closet. She opened the cabinet, removing the only item of clothing inside. It was a farm girl's dress in the style customarily worn by girls in the Argonne Forest region. It seemed to have been kept there for a purpose, for a time such as this.

While the baron's moaning and whimpering continued resonating through the wall, Adeline removed her garment and put on the simple dress. She took some time to rearrange her hair. Even though she only needed a few moments, she took great care in presenting herself in the best possible light. She stood in front of the mirror as an opulent shepherd's daughter, pretty and alluring, ready to crumble moral walls of resistance. She contemplated her appearance for a minute, pleased at the transformation.

"I must be insane!" she muttered to herself. "All this for a madman! Oh, if only that German wasn't a cripple!" She blushed at the suggestion and reluctantly returned to the bedroom where Richemonte was still tormenting her husband.

"Finally!" exclaimed Richemonte, relieved. "See if your persuasive method works better than mine. I'll wait next door."

As soon as he had left, she approached the baron. "Henri!" she whispered softly.

Although he had once again buried his head under a pillow, he perked up at the sound of his true Christian name. "Who is it?" he asked. "Is it you, my sweet Liama?"

Adeline bent down to him. "Come on, my dear Henri," she said in a charming voice. "Look at me!"

He lifted his head and stared at her. A look of recognition crossed his pale face. "Ah, it's the pretty girl from the village well," he said weakly, trying to smile. "I rode through the town while you stood at the fountain. Did you see me?"

"Yes, I saw you ride past," she acknowledged, sitting down beside him.

"I inquired after you," he said, sitting up. "Your mother is dead and your father is a shepherd. Right?"

"Yes," she whispered.

"Do you have a lover, you pretty, virtuous girl?"

"No. I've never had one."

"Really?" he asked. "No one has kissed your lips?" He put his arm around her waist. His gaze became more confident as he appraised her, searching for an illusive memory.

"No one," she answered.

"Then your lips will kiss a baron's for the first time. Come, lean over. I want to taste love from your lips. Not just any love. Real love, the nectar of the gods."

She complied and moved her lips to touch his. He embraced her until her breast touched his chest. A strange change came over him as he passionately kissed her. He broke the embrace, pulling back with a confused gaze in his eyes. He examined her face, her hair, her figure, as if searching for something. He grabbed her hair, pulling her toward him for a closer inspection. The resultant assessment elicited even more uncertainty.

"Girl, you're lying!" he concluded. "That wasn't a kiss from virgin lips. The kiss of a young, virtuous girl is quite different. One who kisses like you has already experienced love. What is your name?"

"Adeline," she replied, showing signs of concern.

"Adeline?" he asked, struggling with a thought he couldn't make sense of. "Adeline? Ah, now I remember. Adeline, the shepherd's daughter, the secret lover of the mayor's son. The boy wasn't going to marry her, even though both had been intimate. She was clever, clever enough to marry the Baron de Sainte-Marie, convincing him that her lover's son was actually his own. That's who you are! Isn't that the truth?"

"You're mistaken!" she replied, horrified, putting her arm around his shoulder and trying to playfully pull him closer.

Filled with indignation, he shoved her back. "I'm not mistaken!" he shouted. "Do you take me for a fool? I've finally figured it out. You betrayed me once, but never again! You were spying on me when I was digging for the strong box—oh dear God, the war chest! And then, in order to ensure your silence, I had to put away my wonderful Liama—oh Liama, my sweet Liama!"

Henri pushed the baroness away with all his strength and buried his head in the bed again.

Usually when he was in the grips of one of his episodes, the captain's scolding pulled him back, and if that didn't help, Adeline's loveliness always did the trick. In the form of the shepherd's daughter, he could be calmed down and brought back to a semblance of sanity. But today, for the first time both strategies had failed to subjugate him. He began to whimper anew, forcing the captain to reappear.

"Well?" he asked his perplexed daughter-in-law.

"It's not helping," she exclaimed in frustration.

"Then you didn't give it your best effort," he chided.

"Liama, my dear Liama, it's you that I want to see!" called out the troubled baron. "Where have you hidden her?" he asked, clenching his fists and licking his lips.

Richemonte realized Henri was close to reaching the peak of his paroxysm. What would likely follow would be foaming at the mouth, grinding of the teeth, and renewed strength, making him difficult to control.

"What should we do?" he asked.

"Where is she?" Henri demanded. "Show her to me this instant or everything will be exposed!" His look was daunting, nearly out of control.

"Show her to him!" Adeline pleaded, backing away from her agitated husband.

"I see we have no other choice," Richemonte voiced, more to himself than to her. Turning to Henri, he asked. "Whom do you wish to see?"

"Liama, my lover, my wife!"

"But she's dead!"

"Dead?" laughed the baron with derision. "Don't suppose for an instant that you can fool me!"

"You were there when we buried her," the captain insisted.

"Buried? Of course we buried her, but then she rose from the grave. I want to see her. I must see her. I have to tell her that I have no desire to keep the war chest. I have to ask for forgiveness, even though I'm a murderer. We must go. I'm not waiting any longer!"

"All right, you can see her," the old man conceded at last. "Come then."

He took his arm and motioned the baroness to quietly leave the room. To his surprise, she didn't, instead stepping closer to him.

"I'm coming with you!" she announced.

Richemonte looked at her more out of surprise than anger. "What for?" he asked.

"I want to meet this picture of his past, the wax mannequin that captivates him and—"

"Pah!" he interrupted roughly. "This doesn't concern you!"

"And why not?" she refuted courageously. "I want to once and for all determine if you've been honest with me. I want to see the entrance to her chamber. I'm tired of being the brunt of your intrigue. I'm not going anywhere until you reveal the truth!"

"Ah Madame!" he mocked. "Are you familiar with the story of the veiled *Isis*?"[26.1]

"I am."

"Then you must know that the one who dares lift her veil must surely die."

"I've heard as much."

"Well then," Richemonte continued, "I suggest you stay far away from uncovering this veil of secrecy, since I deduce by your young age you're not quite ready to forfeit your life!"

"But, Captain," she stammered. "Are you implying that—"

"That you will die!" interrupted the old man menacingly. "If you attempt to meddle in my affairs, you will certainly die! That's exactly what I mean!"

"You wouldn't dare become my murderer!" she persisted.

"I certainly would, Madame," he responded coldly, stepping toward her. "I suggest you withdraw from this room... quickly. It doesn't matter to me whether the daughter of a pig farmer breathes her last on my account. Do you understand me?"

Henri stood nearby looking deranged, oblivious to the conversation. The old man had promised that he could visit Liama and that was all that mattered to him.

"And if I insist you respect my request?" she asked proudly.

"Then I'll demonstrate how much your request matters to me!" Suddenly and deliberately, Richemonte punched her in the face so that she collapsed unconscious on the bedroom carpet. He calmly walked over to a bell ringer, summoning a servant, who appeared shortly in the outer room. The captain met him there, as if nothing out of the ordinary had occurred and he was about to issue a mundane request.

"Her ladyship has just fainted," he explained. "Go and fetch her maid and help carry the mistress to her chambers."

As soon as the servant left on his errand, he took Henri by the arm and pulled him along. Two girls appeared shortly, accompanied by the servant, finding both men had left without a trace, even though they hadn't seen them in the corridor.

⋙✠⋘

This secretive coming and going was, of course, nothing new to the servants, but they still could offer no explanation. Richard had been fortunate, having been alerted to the presence of secret passages on his first day at Ortry. He was to discover far more revealing secrets during his stay.

The tutor left the courtyard with Alexandre and proceeded to the garden, taking the opportunity to view the outlying buildings. They sauntered into the small park and played a number of boyhood games, expending their energy by roughhousing. During this time, Richard allowed Alexandre the freedom to do what he wished. He recognized a personality trait within the boy. He would be led easiest if he gave the impression that it was Alexandre himself who was leading. In doing so, the boy came to respect and enjoy the company of his new teacher, who had no desire to enroll his pupil in a pedagogic regimen.[26.2] Instead, he allowed Alexandre to have some fun, even indulging him by hunting for pinecones.

Just as the young baron began to tire, a suggestion was made to walk to the little park hut for a rest. Richard had no objection and so they strolled over. Nestled in the wood, they found the little shack that had been outfitted with a simple table and a few chairs. Recalling that his room in the tower had a double wall, Richard noticed one wall of the little structure that was considerably thicker than the others. As he contemplated a reason for such an oddity, he heard a sound coming from inside that wall. It sounded as though a portion of the wooden wall had slightly shifted. He took the spectacles from his nose, removed a handkerchief from his pocket, and commenced polishing the lenses. He then rubbed his eyes, using the opportunity to look in the direction of the wall without being obvious about it.

I was right, he concluded. *A small opening is visible! I swear something is behind that wall. I'm sure that's the shimmer of an eye I see. Someone has positioned himself behind the wall to spy on us. Who could the eavesdropper be? Maybe the captain himself?*

It seemed obvious to him now. Quite likely, the system had been fashioned quite some time ago. Perhaps it operated on casters or some sort of track system.

344

Unfortunately, Richard didn't have the luxury to pursue the thought further. Foremost, he had to be on guard not to reveal to the watcher that he had discovered the gap in the wall. He wisely turned around and engaged Alexandre in a lively discussion. He looked unobtrusively around the room a few minutes later, and realized that the crevice had been closed.

His young charge rose and went outside to observe a hawk catching the thermals. For a brief moment, it became utterly quiet in the hut. A sound drifted up through the floor boards similar to one of keys jingling, followed by another that sounded like a heavy door straining against rusted hinges. Blessed with excellent hearing, Richard didn't miss the connection between the hidden listener and the passage below him, promising himself to look into it at the earliest opportunity. The sooner he could do so, the sooner he could unravel some of the castle's secrets.

After they had rested, Richard expressed a desire to visit the ironworks. Alexandre joined in enthusiastically, but their unexpected appearance was not welcome news to the factory director.

"Did the captain send you, Master Alexandre?" Metroy asked.

"No," was the young man's reply.

"Do you perchance have a permission slip?" the director asked, turning his attention to Richard.

"Likewise, the answer is no," the tutor answered. "Is one required?"

"Of course."

"That strikes me as unusual. I've visited similar factories and I've always been well-received by a proprietor who wished to showcase his production. I would think the owner would be pleased to hear that the reputation of his factory had garnered the interest of laymen."

"I might possibly concede the point," replied Metroy dismissively, "though you must realize that there are reasons for keeping some things from public scrutiny. For instance, we cannot allow our competitors to learn of our techniques and the latest developments in manufacturing."

"Do you consider me as an outsider, a competitor?" Richard asked, a smile on his lips.

"I take you for who you are, namely a man who's unfamiliar with our production line. You're not going to reveal what you don't understand, but I have my instructions not to let anyone in without authorization. I trust you will respect this request."

"Of course," replied Richard. "I have no intention of creating a problem for you, Monsieur. Adieu!" He turned to leave, having already found out what he wanted to know.

Alexandre was not so easily dismissed and stood his ground. "Does this also apply to me?" he asked.

"Yes, it does," responded the director mildly. "At least, it does when you show up without a slip."

"Don't you realize you can't dictate what I do or don't do?" the boy muttered indignantly. "You have no right to boss me around. If I were alone, I would look around at my heart's content, but I don't wish to leave Monsieur Müller by himself. However, I would remind you to address him with more fitting explanations about your responsibility here. He's a man who's more capable than you. You were simply rude."

Alexandre felt he had said his piece and left, hurrying to catch up with Richard, who had caught every word.

"Monsieur Müller," he said, "I have to tell you something."

"What is it?"

"I have never defended one of my tutors until now!" he said proudly.

"Ah!"

"This should be proof that I like you. I want you to stay for a long time. You're quite different from the idiots who came before you, and I don't want to cause a problem that forces you to leave. Tomorrow, I'm going to learn German!"

Richard was quite pleased with the progress he had already managed to make with the boy. Alexandre possessed many natural gifts that, until now, had been largely ignored.

Dusk settled in as they approached the castle again. When they arrived, they found town officials on site, having come to investigate the unfortunate accident leading up to the groom's death. They took their time with the necessary bureaucracy, necessitating that they spend the night. However, this in no way changed the routine of the castle's residents. Punctually at ten o'clock, they retired for the night.

CHAPTER TWENTY-SEVEN
The Schoolmaster Investigates

During the course of the afternoon, Richard's personal effects arrived at the estate. Among his possessions was a small pocket lamp he'd had the foresight to bring along. It had occurred to him that his stay at the old castle might eventually require the use of such a device.

When he perceived that it was quiet in the castle, he changed his clothes, this time in total darkness, not taking any chance of being secretly observed. He removed his cumbersome hump and donned a dark shirt and pair of matching pants so that he would blend in with the locals. He traded his boots for a pair of comfortable house shoes, because they made less noise. He decided against using the stairs, having already made up his mind to take a different route. He bolted the door, pocketed a loaded revolver, and opened the window facing north, swinging himself out onto the roof. The flat roof allowed him to walk erect, but prudence told him to exercise caution. After all, walking upright would make him susceptible to prying eyes below.

He reached the lightning rod conduit. He had noticed it during the day and evaluated the support structure with his sharp eye. It was constructed to old standards and consisted of four-sided iron rods supported by sturdy iron brackets at key intervals. This allowed him to climb up or down the structure without concern. Over time, the wall had lost its luster and some of the facade had flaked off. A careful climber could scale it undetected unless someone was looking for the unusual.

Richard clamped the iron bar between his legs and carefully started to slide down the framework. He slowly worked his way down, making it to the second story. He came to rest between two windows that were still lit. He dared a cursory glance into one and spotted the captain inside.

What's he up to? he asked himself. He watched as Richemonte carefully loaded a pistol, placing it in his jacket pocket. Then, the captain walked over to an armoire. Richard supposed he was going to select a coat, but instead the old man stepped into it, closing the door behind him. The watcher patiently waited for Richemonte to emerge, but after some time passed he realized he wasn't coming out.

What's going on? Is there a secret door leading from the armoire to another room?

That didn't seem to make sense, however. There was already a door between the two connecting rooms in that part of the castle. He smiled as another thought came to him.

Perhaps there's an access point in there to the secret passages in the walls. I'll have to be careful. The captain could be on his way to the park hut himself.

Richard climbed the rest of the way down and crept through the darkness to the park. The stars' light was sufficient in illuminating the way. As a precaution, he kept to the cover of the trees at the perimeter of the park. He was about to cross a clearing when he was startled by a voice beside him.

"Psst!" whispered a voice. "I heard you coming."

Who's that? It sounds like a female voice. He didn't have to wait long, as a soft hand reached out and touched his, embracing him.

"I thought you would have been here already," whispered the voice in the darkness. "I couldn't get away any sooner because the captain was just leaving with my husband. Then I had to put Alexandre to bed, but he further delayed me with tales of his new teacher. We don't have to go any further. Let's go to the bench under the ash tree."

She pulled him toward the spot without removing her hand. *What am I supposed to do?* he wondered. *She's clearly mistaken me for someone else. It sounds like the baroness, judging by her words.*

He had come out to investigate the shack, but he realized that this unexpected rendezvous would perhaps represent an even better opportunity. He calmly sat on the bench when they reached it, ready to continue playing the part of this woman's secret lover. Strangely, he had no pangs of conscience over deceiving her.

The lady unexpectedly took a seat on his lap. This in itself was proof that the man she had mistaken him for was on more than friendly terms with her, and probably had been for some time. As she snuggled up to him, he detected her full, lovely figure and knew instantly that he had been right. This was certainly Baroness Adeline.

But who does she think I am? I'll have to find out quickly.

The baroness seemed to have read his mind. "Alexandre told me," she began, "that he and Monsieur Müller paid you a visit this afternoon. Yet for some reason you denied them entry to the ironworks."

So the director is her lover, he concluded, sighing in relief. *I have roughly the same build as the director. My false beard nearly matches his, and I can imitate his voice.*

"It went against my orders," he replied quietly.

"I know! That crusty captain rules with an iron fist. Still, I wish you would show Alexandre more courtesy. He'll be your overseer one day. It wouldn't hurt to show the same courtesy to Monsieur Müller."

Since she had whispered to him, he followed suit, better able to disguise his voice that way. "Those Germans? Pah!"

"I know you despise them, just like I do, and that you would just as soon destroy them all, but I want to draw an exception for the tutor. Alexandre cares about him."

"That's unheard off!"

"Yes, but it's true. Alexandre hasn't ever cared for any of his previous educators, but Monsieur Müller saved his life. The German man seems to have won his heart. Actually, it wouldn't be entirely fair to compare him to other schoolmasters."

"Why is that, my dear?"

"Finally! Do you realize that's the kindest thing you've said to me so far tonight? *My dear.* You've been holding back!" Adeline cuddled up to him and kissed him with the passion of an ardent, disloyal wife. He dared not respond in kind. "Your kisses are cold, without feeling," she pouted. "I know how I could teach you a lesson..."

"What do you mean by that?"

"Well, this German, for example, could vie for my attention."

"*Fie donc!* That hunchback?"

"If you had seen him ride, fence, and shoot, you wouldn't think that. Anyway, his deformity really isn't his fault. I'd like to find out if his kisses are as fiery as his fencing skills."

It was obvious to Richard that the scheming baroness was only trying to make her lover jealous, and so once again he played the part. Wrapping his arms around her, he kissed her with feeling this time. Having committed himself, he was thoroughly unprepared for her passionate response. Not only did she grab his face, but she allowed her tongue to probe for his. Then suddenly, she pulled out of the embrace.

"What is that?" she questioned. "What happened to your tooth?"

"Nothing, why?" he replied.

"Well, just this morning I felt the gap between your front teeth."

"Oh, right! Truth is, I had the dentist replace my tooth this morning," he said, hoping to maintain his cover a little longer.

"Liar!" she accused. "There was no missing tooth, just a small space between them. Show me your right hand!"

Oh no, the fun's over, he thought, remembering the details of the director's appearance from his visit earlier in the day. Indeed, he had been missing a digit on his right hand, probably a result of a workplace mishap.

Before he could prevent it, she grabbed his right hand, feeling for the small finger. When she realized it was whole and intact, she jumped from his lap, ready to flee. She took two steps, but then spun around, having reconsidered.

"Do you know who I am?" she asked guardedly.

"Yes," he replied, deciding not to spare her the discomfort of the truth.

"Well, who am I?"

"The Baroness de Sainte-Marie."

"Fine. Now it's your turn to return the favor. Who are you?"

He stood up, approaching her. "I can't reveal that at the moment, Madame."

"If not now, might you later?"

"Perhaps."

"In that case, at least tell me what you do."

"I'm an officer," Richard revealed carefully.

"From where? Which regiment?"

"Unfortunately, I can't divulge that."

"You're lying! Officers are also gentlemen, and wouldn't think of embarrassing a lady by taking advantage of her."

"True. But under unusual circumstances, he may have to resort to keeping his identity secret, Baroness."

"Under what circumstances? What business do you have here this late at night? I'm unaware of any officer having permission to be here at this late hour."

What response can I give her? he wondered. Then, an idea came to him. "Have you forgotten, Madame?" he asked. "Think of Paris!"

"Really? You know me from Paris?"

"Is that so unlikely? How could I possibly forget you, having admired you since last summer..."

"And you really want to keep your identity from me?"

"At least for today, my lady."

"Then give me your word of honor that you won't reveal the contents of our conversation to anyone."

"I will gladly give you my word, and think fondly of our meeting. Is that enough?"

She walked up to him seductively. "Yes, but I still want to see your face." Wrapping her arms around his neck, she tried to pull him closer, without success. "Then at least give me one more kiss," she pleaded.

"With pleasure," he smiled. He leaned over and kissed her, yet at the same time covered her eyes with both his hands so she couldn't see his true face. Before long, he released her from his embrace, turned around, and disappeared into the darkness.

Adeline remained standing there, more surprised than fearful. *He's an officer and he gave me his word,* she assured herself. *My reputation remains intact. But who is he? Did he really come from Paris only to sneak around the grounds and be close to me? Is he perhaps stationed in Thionville? If so, he might come again. After all, he knows that*

I make nocturnal visits with at least one other man. He's handsome, well-built, and strong! That much I could tell from the embrace. I could smell a fine aroma coming from his clothes, or perhaps from his hair. I should have paid more attention.

But what now? Should I leave the director waiting? No. I gave him my word and I have to keep it. Reluctantly, and a little disappointed, she continued on toward the scheduled rendezvous.

❧✠☙

Richard left quickly, this time making sure his steps were soundless. Although he had been careful earlier, the baroness had heard him approach.

He reached the little hut, but just as he was about to enter, he heard a familiar sound inside. Someone was moving the boards. He immediately stepped back to conceal himself behind a bush. As he watched, a momentary burst of light escaped between the cracks in the wall. Then it was dark again. The door opened slowly and a man emerged. From where Richard lay prostrate on the ground, he could make out the man's features against the starlight. He immediately recognized the old captain.

What could he want here at this time of night? he asked himself. *Was there a connection, a secret passage, between the old man's room and the forest hut?*

Unfortunately, the educator had no time to further ponder these questions. Richemonte quickly and purposefully crossed the clearing. Richard rushed along the edge of the clearing, trying to keep pace while maintaining his cover behind the trees. He managed to hurry ahead of the old man, getting to the far side of the clearing and finding concealment behind a large oak tree. He made it just in time as Richemonte walked past, quickly vanishing into the night.

Even though he couldn't see the old man anymore, he was determined to follow him, keeping to the direction he had taken. Richard crouched down, electing to crawl the rest of the way. On his hands and knees, he detected a soft rustling just ahead of him, realizing that the captain was also advancing slowly. It wasn't long before he heard whispering voices nearby. He doubled his alertness. By now, his eyes had become accustomed to the darkness, and he could just make out the captain's shape. Richemonte crouched down behind a large tree near a bench at the edge of the clearing. Richard approached the area from the side, finding a comfortable spot at the base of the tree. He was situated closer to the bench than the captain, and found himself in a better position to listen.

Richard found himself a witness to the dialogue of lovers. The director, having found the baroness, was not nearly as reluctant as Richard had been earlier. He was certain the captain was also following the conversation and

351

probably on the verge of boiling over. Then, quite suddenly, the captain stood up and stepped out in front of the two lovers.

"Good evening, my dear daughter-in-law. And to you, Metroy," he greeted, his voice dripping with irony.

The director jumped from his seat, momentarily staring at his overseer, then bolted from the clearing as fast as his legs could carry him. He knew the captain only too well and feared a reprisal. Adeline, however, was unable to move her limbs, much less run. She tried to get up, but dropped despondently back onto the bench.

"Just as I surmised," Richemonte mocked. "Another farm girl outing."

"What are you doing here?" she asked, composing herself. "Where did you come from and why are you mocking me?"

"Don't tell me you were just enjoying the spring evening," he said with a laugh.

"Of course! What else would we be doing?"

"And I see you were enjoying it whilst in the arms of my factory director."

"Don't presume to judge me!"

"Oh, I saw it plainly enough. My eyes may be old, but they're still capable of seeing the obvious."

She squirmed uncomfortably as she anxiously began to concoct a series of plausible lies. "Don't you want to know how we came to be here?"

"I'm quite anxious to hear your explanation."

"When I tell it to you, you'll realize just how much you've offended me! I came here earlier, intending to enjoy the solitude of the park, when suddenly a dark shape appeared in front of me. I was frightened and must have fainted. It was Metroy who caught me when I collapsed. When I awoke, you were standing in front of me. That's all that happened."

The baroness tried to speak with righteous indignation, but her words had little effect on the captain's deaf ears.

"Why didn't you faint when you were confronted the second time, by me?" he mocked, crossing his arms. "Either you're only capable of one fainting spell at a time or the event merely exists in your dishonest mind. How can you possibly speak of fainting when I know from experience that you, a simple farm girl, possess nerves of steel?"

"Monsieur, please don't insult me further!"

"Pah! Don't play games with me! I laid here in the bushes, concealed for a full fifteen minutes. I heard every word, counted every gasp that spoke of your undying love, and numbered each and every kiss you stole. It might surprise you to learn that I also enjoyed kissing in my youth. Of course, I made sure to avoid all those unpleasant and unnecessary sounds..." He made a disgusted face. "Why do you insist on smacking your lips like a delivery man urging his horse, Madame?"

Despite her strong nature, having been confronted so boldly had indeed brought her close to collapse. "You are impertinent!" she wailed.

"Do you really deserve something better?" he scoffed. "Before you continue your lies, let me say that I know of the director's visit to your boudoir this morning—"

"Indeed!" she interrupted. "How does that concern you?"

"—and that you planned on meeting here—"

"Liar!"

"—and that you offered him your sensual lips in place of the customary hand," he finally finished, pausing to give her a chance to respond.

"Oh, who will save me from this devil!" she lamented.

"If you dare call me that a second time, I'll strike you down without hesitation, just as I did earlier!"

Richemonte lifted his arm threateningly, as though intending to make good on his threat. Richard was about to jump out to her, saving her from the captain's brutality, when he was unexpectedly spared from having to reveal his presence. Adeline snapped out of her passivity, rose from the bench, and rushed off in the direction of the castle.

"She can run all she wants," muttered the old man to himself, "but she can't escape me!"

CHAPTER TWENTY-EIGHT
The Ruthless Captain

Richemonte turned around and headed for the little hut. Richard followed noiselessly, hoping that this might present the best opportunity to find out how to access the secret entrance. Unfortunately, by the time Richard arrived, the old man had already disappeared through the hidden access point.

He crept closer and cautiously looked through the small window. A match flickered. The old man was about to light his lantern, clearly so certain he was alone that he didn't even bother closing the shutters. As Richard watched, he reached for a metal peg, which seemed to have originally been put on the wall for the purpose of hanging a jacket, and slid it to the left. A few boards moved in unison, retreating like a door on rollers. The captain stepped into the opening and closed the door behind him. It closed smoothly, not leaving a gap.

If Richard hadn't seen it for himself, he would never have guessed its hidden location. The schoolmaster snuck inside the unoccupied hut and lay down, pressing his ear to the floor boards. He caught the sound of retreating foot steps.

Should I follow him? he debated. *I may not get another opportunity to actually follow the captain.*

Deciding to go for it, Richard produced his own pocket lamp and lit the wick with a match. He reproduced the captain's actions from memory, locating and pulling the peg and sliding it over. He was rewarded for his efforts when the hidden door opened invitingly to him. He cautiously looked inside, seeing narrow wooden steps that led into the deep. He examined the interior of the door which had a large nail protruding from it, no doubt to facilitate the closure.

Once inside, his feet on the wooden steps, he tugged the nail and pulled the door down over his head. Carefully descending the steps with the lamp in his left hand and the revolver in his right, he began counting the steps. By the time he reached the bottom, he numbered over twenty steps that ended in a large, square cavernous room. It was devoid of furniture, yet contained an assortment of spades, pickaxes, and other digging implements, the purpose for which eluded him.

This room had two exits, one that led toward the castle but had no actual door and the other toward the forest, which was sealed by a solid, metal reinforced wooden door. The underground pathway toward the castle was a large tunnel, measuring two meters high by a meter and a half wide. It was fashioned from bricks and appeared to be dry.

Richard decided to follow it. Since the captain couldn't be too far ahead, he pocketed his little lamp and walked ahead in the dark. From time to time, he took the lamp out, being careful to only allow a momentary flicker of light to illuminate the path, enabling him to avoid any approaching danger.

Richard made good progress, feeling his way ahead by touching the walls. At last, he spotted a glimmer of light ahead. It had to be the captain. Richard heard the old man's footfalls quite clearly as he closed the gap between them, taking great care not to be seen. He had covered a considerable distance when he noticed that the walls here consisted of large stones. Undoubtedly, he was under the castle.

Ahead of him, the old captain stopped, presumably to rest. As Richard slowed, the light began to fade in a vertical direction where Richemonte was climbing upward. Richard found a flight of stairs where the old man disappeared from sight, and decided to use the lantern to navigate his way up into the castle. When he lit the lantern, he found himself in a sort of central passageway, from which a number of staircases led upward. He concluded that this was where all the passageways in the castle ended up.

Richard could still hear the old man's footsteps. He slowly scaled the steps, going up several floors, until he saw a narrow beam of light just ahead. The teacher caught the distant sound of two voices. As he cautiously crept closer, he could distinguish them apart, realizing that it was the captain conversing with Metroy, the factor director.

A bright, rectangular beam of light came from an opening in the wall. Richard daringly crept up to the opening from which he could witness the unfolding scene. He crouched down just short of it so he could see in. The room was paneled in oak, with one section of the wainscoting comprising the secret door, now standing wide open. Metroy, visibly shaken, stood in front of Richemonte, who had appeared out of nowhere like a ghost.

"Get a hold of yourself!" admonished the old man. "You can see perfectly well I'm no ghost."

"But sir," Metroy stammered, "the manner of your entrance…"

"It's a secret entrance. That should be obvious enough!" replied the old man. "I've chosen to appear this way so that no one will witness my late arrival. Can you guess the reason for my late visit?"

"I would rather you tell me yourself, Captain."

"Fine! But please, my dear Metroy, have a seat," Richemonte invited conciliatorily. "Your entire body is shaking. What's wrong?"

"Oh, it's just the initial shock from seeing you coming in from out of the wall. I wasn't prepared for it."

"I can see you experienced a fright. Tell me, which caused a bigger shock, this one or the one in the garden?"

"My good Captain..." The director let his sentence hang awkwardly, unable to finish it.

"Well, weren't you in the garden?"

"Of course," admitted the man.

"With my daughter-in-law?"

"Yes."

"This has been an extraordinary day," continued Richemonte in a friendly tone. "I've had to do more than my fair share of intervention, something I'm not entirely comfortable with. But there are issues that can't be ignored. Why did you suddenly depart from the garden, Monsieur?"

"Because I thought that—" He stopped himself again, clearly embarrassed.

"Because you thought I might misinterpret your actions? Well, don't worry. The baroness has given me an explanation. She told me about her plan to enjoy the pleasant evening alone in the garden. Obviously, you had the same thought and surprised her. She must have fainted upon seeing such a dark shape creep out in front of her! You took it upon yourself to revive her."

The director breathed a visible sigh of relief.

"I must admit," continued Richemonte, "that I thought the worst of you for a moment. Perhaps because of your sudden departure. Why did you flee? Didn't you realize it would look suspicious? I absolve you of any perceived wrongdoing. In fact, I'll prove you can trust me. Do you have any paper handy?"

"More than enough," Metroy replied, relieved.

"Then take a sheet and prepare a draft of the transaction you detailed earlier. I haven't forgotten about your promised bonus. Where are the monies you had with you?"

"Here in my bureau."

"Please, count it now."

Richard saw the director remove bank notes from a drawer and, in a loud voice, counted the amount for Richemonte's benefit. It was the exact amount he had presented earlier.

"Both of these firms are cautious," commented Metroy. "They noted the serial numbers and initialed them. You can see the corresponding signatures, Captain."

"Yes, that should suffice for now," replied the old man. "And now for the receipt, Monsieur!"

"Why a blank draft, Captain? Don't you wish to finish it tonight?"

357

"No. I haven't made up my mind what sum I'm going to set aside for you. Tomorrow, I'll examine the extent of your work during the past week. Just enter today's date in the lower left, and place your signature in the lower right."

"As you please, Captain!" Metroy said, entering both as instructed and handing the document to the old man.

The captain took it from him and examined it carefully. "Now then, this should be sufficient punishment. Trust me, it's no reward!"

"Punishment?" asked the director, caught of guard. "Did I hear you right, sir?"

"You heard me. I intend to punish you! First, for daring to become romantically involved with the baroness."

"But you just explained how she clarified the situation—"

"Hmm, she certainly tried. But I'm not a man to be easily deceived by a woman. I know the whole story. Everything!" he said, letting out a sarcastic laugh.

Although Metroy paled at the revelation, he still sought to vindicate himself. "There must be some sort of misunderstanding, Captain."

"Not as far as I'm concerned. I laid myself down behind the park bench, listening to your entire conversation from my hiding place. Besides, as you can see from my knowledge of the secret passages, I also overheard your chat earlier in Baroness Adeline's boudoir."

The director slumped into his chair, closing his eyes in dismay.

"It was only this morning," continued the old man sternly, "that I learned of your arranged meeting. I also heard what you said about me. For example, you said that you extended your stay only to spend more time with the baroness. Tell me, does this deserve reward or reprimand?"

"Gracious, sir," exclaimed the shocked man. "I have served you faithfully. It's because of me that the ironworks have prospered."

"Served me faithfully? Ha! And now for the second reason for your punishment..."

"What is it?" asked the frightened Metroy. He knew the old man's mannerisms and knew better than to expect restraint.

"I deemed it necessary to protect my interests by searching through your personal effects."

Metroy gasped, working up a little courage. "What! You have no right!" Standing his ground now against the old man, he drew himself up to his full height. Here in his room he was master and chose to defend himself accordingly.

"Be quiet!" the old man barked, silencing his objection. "I have the ability to enter your room without detection. Let me remind you that everything contained in this room is my property. I'm in possession of skeleton keys that enable me to gain access to various doors, even your bureau. While you rushed to the park for your romantic meeting, I came here and searched the drawers of the writing desk. Can you guess what I discovered?"

Metroy realized that denial at this juncture wouldn't help his cause. Thinking that boldness would perhaps intimidate the old man, he approached Richemonte. "You actually dared to go through my belongings?" he asked indignantly.

"Of course!" laughed Richemonte. "What do you intend to do about it?"

"You'll find out shortly! Well, what did you discover, Captain?"

"Oh, many things. But I'm only concerned with one item." The captain reached into his document folder and produced a letter. He paused for a moment, as though intending to heighten the tension, then began to read it out loud.

> *To Monsieur Metroy, Director at Ortry:*
>
> *Having conferred with my superiors, I need to inform you that my government is not inclined to accept your offer. If there really are secret places where weapons are being stored, in order to equip franctireurs* [28.1] *and other insurgents, then that in itself is not sufficient grounds for action by the emperor.*
>
> *We don't feel it's necessary to advise your government of your actions, but we will keep your letter for future reference.*

"You intended to betray our noble undertaking for filthy lucre!" Richemonte declared, spitting out the words in disgust. "And you dared to write to the German government?"

"Only because of your stinginess," replied the director.

"Then you're admitting to this act of betrayal?"

"Why hide it?" said Metroy resignedly, shrugging his shoulders.

"Don't you realize that I planned and arranged for the construction of the ironworks? Each worker swore his allegiance to the baron. Any deviation results in punishment."

"Pah! You can't chastise me!" Metroy managed a laugh.

"And why can't I?" asked Richemonte, surprised by Metroy's bravado.

"Because the entire factory is under my control. You managed to intimidate me earlier because of my affection for Adeline, but I've overcome it. Do you think you're master of everything? Well, not exactly! I've prepared myself for a situation such as this. What do you understand about chemistry, galvanometers, or electrical current? This room is electrically connected to the factory and the corresponding storage rooms. All it takes is a little movement, a slight pressure drop, and all of it will explode. Then you can go about finding other means by which to equip your *franctireurs* against Germany!"

"Hang it all!" yelled the captain, shocked at the man's insolence.

"Now you see how things stand," proclaimed the director proudly. He was convinced that it was he who held all the trumps in his hand. "I have no desire to continue working for you, but since I've labored to bring the factory to where it is today, I would rather not destroy it. My only reason in offering my knowledge to the other side was to be compensated for my efforts. If you reward me with the same amount I requested from them, I would be satisfied in giving you my word that I would cease any hostility. I have advanced your cause through my knowledge and expertise. I've worked day and night for little remuneration. It's high time I receive my reward now."

The captain's brows furrowed and his moustache lifted awkwardly, revealing his yellow teeth. At the last moment, he managed to compose himself and remain calm.

"What sum did you expect to receive from the Germans?" he asked neutrally.

"Pah! A trifle sum, considering all my work! Only a hundred thousand francs. You'll pay for your close-fistedness with many lives if you choose not to come to terms with me."

"I truly hope so!" Richemonte crowed. "The time is coming when we'll take back what Blücher, Gleisenau, and York stole from us. So, my ironworks are really electrically connected with this room?"

"Yes. One firm signal from me and the electrical spark will ignite the powder and dynamite provisions."

"Will you give me your word of honor that you're speaking the truth?"

"Of course. As soon as I have the sum in my hands, I'll show you the conduit so you can neutralize it."

"I don't know," pondered the old man. "You're an unpredictable man. What if I pay you the amount and you still destroy all the stores?"

"My word of honor should convince you of my sincerity."

"Hmm, if only I could trust you!" Richemonte looked at Metroy pensively, but his eyes shone with a sinister light. "You demand a lot. But to save our enterprise—hmm!" He pretended to mull it over, but in the meantime, his furtive glances were surveying the room.

If he really concealed such a device in this room, he thought, *it could only be in his armoire or near the back wall. He wouldn't have laid the conduit in the front of the castle because it would have been discovered. It's important that I keep him close to the window.*

Richemonte sat down at the desk, taking the draft out of his pocket. "Well, a laborer is worth his wages," he conceded, pulling at the ends of his moustache. "I suppose I'm forced to accommodate your wishes in this matter."

"Are you prepared to give me the hundred thousand?" asked Metroy, nearly overjoyed.

The old man nodded solemnly. "I'll pay you what you demand," he replied. "You can read it later. Your signature is already on the document." He reached for the quill and commenced writing. "Have you offered our secret to anyone else?" he asked when he finished.

"No."

"When you made your inquiries with the German representative, did you perchance leave any information that might suggest the location of our provisions?"

"Do you consider me a fool? From what I told them, they may as well be out near Strasbourg."

Richard heard every word and knew the director was lying through his teeth. Indeed, the German government knew precisely where the stores were hidden, but the captain seemed satisfied. Richemonte rose from the writing desk, leaving the completed draft facing up.

"Then we're in agreement," he said, pointing to the document. "Go and have a look."

The captain slowly walked to the rear of the room, guarding it just in case it contained the location of the electrical conduit. Likewise, Metroy was as much surprised as he was happy to have dealt with the old man so quickly. He would be walking away with a considerable sum. Somewhat relieved, he sat down at his desk and reached for the document, which supposedly outlined the transfer of a hundred thousand francs. But to his horror, his eyes beheld a totally different edict.

I hereby confess, being full of repentance and mindful of the truth, that I have appropriated two large sums belonging to my employer for my own purposes so that I could settle my debts. As I leave this world, may God forgive me, being painfully aware of my unresolved mistakes.

Ignorant of Richemonte's plan, it was written on the same paper which he had earlier signed his name to. He was completely taken aback by this latest display of the old man's trickery.

"What is the meaning of this, Captain?"

"That I remain your master, not the other way around," laughed the old man derisively. "Even though you earlier purported the opposite. You won't obtain one *sou*. You're going to pay both for your treachery and for misleading the baroness, just as I planned all along!"

"Do you think I'm just going to drown, or take some poison, as a sign of my repentance?"

"Wait and see!"

Metroy shook his head furiously. "That's where you're mistaken. You're nothing but a liar and a crook! I'm going to prove to you that I haven't fabricated the story about the electrical connection. I'm asking you for the last time: are you going to hand over the money or not?"

"Not one single franc!"

"Then pay attention, and see how the fireworks explode!" He jumped out of the chair and moved toward Richemonte.

"Yes, pay attention!" exclaimed the old man. "But it won't be my ironworks that explode, but rather your thick skull!"

Faster than Richard would have thought the old man capable, Richemonte produced his pistol, pointed it at Metroy and squeezed off a round. The director stopped in his tracks, mortally wounded in the head, and collapsed to the floor.

Richard followed the proceedings between the two men with mounting interest, having no idea their discussion would end with the captain taking such drastic measures. The dramatic conclusion had developed with such rapidity that Richard had been powerless to stop it. For a moment, he considered revealing himself. He immediately thought better of it. Nothing he could do would change the terrible outcome. His first duty had to be to the mission. With this in mind, he lit his pocket lamp and used it to light his way down the steps, hurrying to get away before being discovered. Surely the shot would have awoken the sleeping household and they would soon he calling on Metroy for an explanation. Richemonte would be escaping quickly right behind him.

Back in the director's room, the murderer bent down to examine his victim, satisfying himself that he was dead. He then walked over to the bureau and realigned the confession note so that it would stand out. He had already pocketed the money. The captain hurried out the secret entrance and closed it carefully behind him.

Luckily Richard arrived at the juncture of the steps without a mishap and rushed through the underground passage toward the hut. He managed to open and close the secret entrance, leaving it the way he found it. He was grateful to have had the pocket lamp with him, without which such a quick flight wouldn't have been possible. He took a cursory look outside and then left the hut behind, rushing toward the castle.

Once he arrived, Richard noticed that many of the windows were lit, but to his relief no one was yet in the courtyard. He scaled the iron rods, grateful for the cover of darkness. When he reached the second level, he quickly glanced into the captain's bedroom. The old man, with an unkempt beard and hair, was already attired in housecoat and slippers. He was carrying a lantern in his hand and was about to leave his room. Anyone seeing his appearance would be immediately convinced that he had just woken up with the rest of them. He shuddered at the captain's diabolical nature.

Richard succeeded in reaching his lofty room without detection. He quickly removed his clothes, replaced his hump, and haphazardly threw on new clothes, leaving the impression that he had dressed while still half-asleep.

He hurried out of the room to join the excited, confused throng of assembled people congregating in front of the director's door. As it turned out, Richemonte had already authorized a forced entry, thereby being a witness with the rest to the sober, gruesome scene within. He sent for the justice officials who were staying overnight on the estate.

They soon arrived and took charge of the scene, instructing everyone, except the captain himself, to remain outside. They quickly discovered the confession document, and what followed was the natural course as suggested by the fabricated writ. The captain was questioned about the referred to sums, stating he had no idea that the money had been received. He suggested to them that they verify the facts by checking the ledger. The gentlemen indicated they would follow up on his recommendation. Next, they arranged for the body's removal. When the excitement finally died down, the castle's occupants resumed their interrupted rest.

The baroness had also awoken from her sleep at the sound of the pistol shot and rushed to the place of misadventure, but once there, she didn't want to look at the corpse. The man's death affected her, but only for a few moments. Without much prodding on her part, she was already contemplating her unexplained meeting with the secretive officer on whose chest she had lain. Occupied with more pleasant thoughts, she made her way back to her room, running into Richemonte on the stairs. Since no one else was nearby, he couldn't resist a taunt.

"He was a good-looking lover, wasn't he, Madame?" he mocked.

The unexpected jeer repelled her, and she held up her hands in an attempt to ward off their effect. "Murderer!" she shuddered. "Your day will come!"

A subdued sneer was the base response of the old man. He had extinguished a man's life with no thought other than ruthless calculation.

Richard was deeply affected and returned to his chamber unable to sleep. This first day at Ortry had been one of the most eventful of his life. First, there had been the discussion with the innkeeper's wife, then Alexandre's rescue, his actual arrival, the trials, the discovery of the secret entrances, the romantic adventure with the baroness... all of it finally culminating with murder. It was more than enough for one day, but for the most part, his mind returned to the most recent event.

Should I expose the murderer? he asked himself. *Morally speaking, I'm bound to. But shouldn't I exercise discretion, allowing my orders to supersede my moral considerations? Should I squander everything I've learned and negate sending an important report to my government on account of a stranger whose life can't be brought back? Could I successfully accuse Marion's grandfather of murder and see him put into stocks? What if the examining magistrate sides with the accused, an officer of the Emperor's Guard and knight in the Legion of Honor? I'm nothing better than a foreigner, a despised German teacher. I could show them the secret passages, but then what? The only solid proof rests in the bank notes, assuming I could find them, and Richemonte probably concealed them well, knowing their value. Besides, wasn't the dead man an enemy of Germany, even disloyal to his own country? What sort of family are these Sainte-Maries? I sincerely hope Marion, that wonderful woman, is nobler than the rest.*

These thoughts plagued and distressed him as he prepared to turn in for the night. He lay in bed tired, his mind racing, any hope of rest eluding him as he prepared for the next day.

CHAPTER TWENTY-NINE
Alexandre

Early the next morning, Richemonte was already awake, arranging for his most qualified people to come from the factory to help him search for the conduit. Despite their cleverness, they were unable to locate the circuit. The old, unwavering soldier couldn't shake the disconcerting feeling that they had missed something. If some worker were to accidentally come into contact with the hidden conduit, the resulting explosion would prove disastrous.

Monsieur Müller is gifted in many disciplines, he pondered. *What if he could discover the one thing the others could not?* The German's knowledge would be advantageous in their search, so he sent for him. Richard attended to the captain's study and was greeted with unusual friendliness.

"Monsieur," Richemonte asked, "are you familiar with the concept of electricity?"

"Somewhat, sir," he replied, guessing the reason for the question.

"Are you aware that it's possible to ignite powder kegs through the use of electrical current?"

"Certainly, Captain!"

"Could such a device be easily neutralized? If the conduit was located, could it be disrupted?"

"It all depends on how it was set up. I have some experience in the detection of these devices," said Richard truthfully, recalling his military service in the artillery corps.

"Ah," responded Richemonte. "In that case, I need to advise you of something. Did you know Director Metroy, the one who shot himself?"

"Only in passing."

"Well, this man concocted a diabolical plan before he killed himself, intending to blow up my ironworks. I have reason to believe that the trigger is concealed in his room. I've searched for it, but haven't been able to find any trace of such a device. Could I impose on you to give it a try?"

"I'm completely at your disposal, Captain."

"Then let's have a look."

They headed to the deceased man's room. Richard shuddered as he walked in, expecting the blood stains to have been removed. To his morbid surprise, however, they were still there, a solemn reminder of the captain's swift retribution. He surveyed the room now in the full light of day, looking at the bureau which had served as a table for Metroy's last testament.

"If there is an electrical connection in here," suggested Richard, "I would look for it near the back wall, not the front."

"Exactly what I was thinking," Richemonte said agreeably, nodding in satisfaction. "Please Monsieur, have a look around."

Richard's searching eyes glanced around the room, coming to rest on the old fashioned Lyon-style wall clock that spanned from floor to ceiling. It looked worn and neglected.

"Do you see something?" asked the old man.

"I would need to have a closer look, but I believe I have found something." Richard pushed the table up to the clock and placed a chair on it. He climbed up onto the chair so he could look between the top of the housing and the ceiling. Pointing toward the ceiling, he asked. "Who lives above this room?"

"*L'intendant*."

"Really? My superior!" smiled Richard. "Is he still in your employ?"

"Yes. He was a good non-commissioned officer, and a loyal *l'intendant*," Richemonte paused in memory of Lussier's recent injury. "Unfortunately, his face will never be the same. I intend to make an allowance for him, even though I had said otherwise."

"If I had known yesterday what I have just discovered, I wouldn't have spared his face." Richard smiled, looking down at the old man. "Rather, I would have removed his head completely! He is the director's accomplice."

"*Sacre bleu!* Is that possible?" asked the old man, clearly shocked.

Richard opened the clock's case and inspected the workings. "Monsieur," he said, "your ironworks and the lives of your workers literally hung on a single thread. Come see for yourself." As the captain stepped closer, the schoolmaster pointed to the side of the framework. "Do you see this single strand of horse hair? It's difficult to distinguish from the black background."

The old man was about to grab the strand when Richard shoved his hand aside. "For God's sake, don't touch it! If you were to pull on it even slightly, your whole factory would go up!"

"Really? One solitary hair?" asked the captain. "And it leads into the cabinet?"

"Yes. It's connected to an extremely thin copper thread, which leads through the top of the housing and into the ceiling. Lussier must have known about the connection. Chances are he was involved with the director. We should pay him a visit."

The captain nodded in agreement and proceeded out of the room without giving it a second thought. He mounted the steps and barged into Lussier's room without knocking. Richard followed close behind him.

They found Lussier alone and resting on his bed.

"What's the meaning of this?" Lussier asked, astonished. Recognizing Richard, he added, "What business do you have with me?"

"You'll find out right away, you rogue!" replied the captain. "Have a good look around, Monsieur Müller!"

The schoolmaster bent down in the far corner of the room, the section that was situated directly over the old clock. He examined the floor, then opened the window and looked outside.

"Have you found it? What do you see?" asked the captain, burning with impatience.

"Indeed," replied the schoolmaster. "Have a look for yourself, so you can be assured of my assessment. A thin copper wire follows the underside of the trim to that wall. A tiny hole permits the conduit through and it continues along the ledge until it reaches the front of the structure. It must have taken considerable effort and expense, particularly when you consider the work that had to be carried out in secrecy."

Richemonte couldn't contain his frustration any longer. He practically threw himself at Metroy's accomplice, grabbing the startled man by his shirt. "You swine!" he thundered. "Who talked you into this?"

The man, completely unprepared, was intimidated into a quick admission.

"It was the director, sir!"

"What did he offer you for your complicity?"

"Five thousand francs."

"He tried to get a hundred thousand out of me! And you," he said grating his teeth, "you tried to ruin me and kill my workers for a mere five thousand! Get out of that bed! You belong behind bars, you vagabond, you – you l'intendant!"

Although the old man hadn't been entirely convinced by Richard's earlier implication that Lussier was an accomplice, there was no longer any doubt in his mind. It was enough for him to vent his frustration on Lussier. The exposed man pleaded for mercy, but it didn't help. The incensed captain pulled a nearby cord, summoning a servant. Richemonte instructed him to fetch several men, who had the unpleasant task of seeing one of their own taken into custody and led away to the jailhouse.

Once Lussier was removed, the captain faced Richard. "Monsieur," he said with relief, "you've proven yourself more capable than all those in my employ. It seems you were meant to come to Ortry for our benefit. But now what?"

"We should go outside, sir," he responded, "so we can determine where the conduit enters the ground."

They walked outside and found the cable concealed behind a downspout.

"We can sever the connection here, right now, and eliminate the main danger," Richard explained. "The portion of the wire that's in the ground must be wrapped in some sort of insulation. It will be thicker and thus easier to detect. We should be able to trace it to the factory wall and see how it was dispersed from there."

"I have already taken up too much of your time, Monsieur," said Richemonte hastily. "Now that we have located the conduit, the rest should be easy. I have plenty of laborers for that. I don't wish to interfere with your plans with Alexandre."

Richard could understand the old man's reluctance. Richemonte had no intention of allowing Richard to catch a glimpse of his plans, least of all see the build-up of his munitions. The schoolmaster nodded as though he hadn't caught on and returned to his room, satisfied to have merited the approval of the overseer.

He hadn't been there for long when Alexandre came calling, looking for a companion for another outing. Richard gladly accepted, realizing that the boy seemed drawn to him.

"Did you know, Monsieur," started Alexandre as they walked down the stairs, "that one is better off being in your good graces?"

"Why's that?" asked Richard in surprise.

"Because calamity befalls those who despise you. The two men who insulted you have been punished. One has shot himself and the other is now confined to a holding cell, brandishing a nasty wound as a permanent reminder. I'm going to warn anyone who thinks about getting on your bad side, and that includes Marion."

"Marion? Who's that, Master Alexandre?" asked Richard, doing his best to feign ignorance.

"Marion is my sister," the boy stated. "My half-sister actually. But she's so fine, she may as well be my real sister. I've caused her much grief. I suspect that's why she had left, since I complained about her to Mama and Grandpa. But when I started to fall asleep last night, I thought about her quite a bit and a thought came to me – that I have treated her unfairly. I promise you that I'm not going to embarrass her again, Monsieur!"

"How is it that prior to yesterday those thoughts hadn't occurred to you?"

"Because I thought about our walk. You don't preach and you don't lecture, but I sense what it is you're trying to teach me."

Richard didn't reply. Instead, he bent down and kissed the boy on his forehead. He felt overjoyed in having profoundly influenced this young soul, who had already been led astray by those before him. They moved deeper and deeper into the forest, until they reached a stone ruin with the remnants of an old tower protruding from its midst.

"What sort of ruins are these?" asked the schoolmaster.

"This was the former site of Castle Ortry," explained Alexandre. "But all that's left is this old tower."

"Don't you want to climb it?"

"No, I'd rather not."

"Why not?"

The boy looked at him, guileless and innocent. "I've also disobeyed your predecessors in this matter," replied Alexandre. "Grandpa has forbidden me to come here and climb it, but I used to do so often. Now, I want to leave old habits behind me. Even though we're not going in, we can still see the grave."

He maneuvered between the broken stones, with Richard following close behind. When they came to a stop, they were standing in front of a small, ordinary mound, unkempt but adorned with wild flowers. Beside it was a massive stone block bearing a simple yet barely legible inscription: *Here rests Liama.*

"This Liama was Marion's mother," commented Alexandre. "Did I mention that Marion is coming back today?"

"Not yet, no."

"Well, she is. We thought she drowned when the steamboat capsized, but Grandpa received a wire this morning proclaiming that she will arrive at midday. She's coming with a lady friend."

Richard would have thought he'd have been overjoyed by the news that Marion was still alive, but his tone had been entirely matter-of-fact. The family ties among the Saint-Marie clan were loose, indeed.

"How will the family receive the young baroness?" asked Richard.

"Receive?" asked Alexandre, perplexed. "I suppose the servants will help her out of the carriage and she'll go to her room."

"Without showing her any sign of affection that they are glad to see her?"

Alexandre looked at his tutor with large eyes. "Will she be happy to see us?"

"I'm sure of it," Richard replied. "One just has to show her she's loved, and that she was missed during her absence."

"I'd like to do that, but how do I show her that I care?"

Richard was saddened to find that the young man's heart had been largely uncultivated in matters of love, even of the familial sort.

"I have an idea," he said, putting his hand on his shoulder. "Was the young baroness fond of her mother?"

"Very much so. She often visited her mother's grave."

"Then why don't we gather some of these wild flowers from her mother's grave and place them in a prominent place in her room? That way, when she comes in, she'll see them and feel as though they are a greeting from her own mother."

Alexandre's eyes shone with delight. "Yes, that's what we'll do. But we're not going to tell anyone, or else the others will squabble."

They sat down on the heathen woman's grave, gathering flowers for the one who captured their hearts. With the young baron it was out of brotherly love, while for Richard it was out of a passionate, deliberate longing for the fulfillment of his earthly bliss.

It was nearly midday by the time they returned to the castle. Richard spotted a considerable number of workers in the field between the ironworks and the castle engaged in removing the conduit cable.

He turned his attention back to his charge as they entered the castle. They first went to Richard's room and arranged the flowers into two bouquets. Alexandre took a piece of paper and wrote on it, *To my dear Marion, from her mother's grave. Alexandre.*

He then personally delivered the two arrangements. He placed the smaller one in the room that had been assigned to his sister's friend. He positioned the larger one, with the note, in Marion's room so that it would be the first thing she saw when she arrived.

CHAPTER THIRTY
An Irreverent Colonel

Richard chose to take his breakfast back in his room, where he could be alone for a while. He was still eating when he heard the sound of an approaching carriage. He rose quickly and walked over to the window, peering out.

An elegant coach had just pulled into the courtyard. A servant opened the door and a beautiful young woman alighted. It was her, the magnificent lady he had rescued from the raging Mosel. His heart pounded in his chest, surprising him. *But under what circumstances has she come? Will she stay, ready to face the challenges of her family, or will she quickly leave, fleeing toward a less repressive atmosphere?*

Just as Nanon was emerging from the coach, Captain Richemonte came out of the main building and approached the two women. He simply shook his granddaughter's hand and bowed to her friend.

"Second breakfast is being served," he said evenly. "Are the two ladies inclined to join us?"

"In about a quarter hour, Grandpa," replied Marion. "First we have to brush the dust from our clothes."

"All right, we'll wait," he said and left, walking back into the house.

After an absence of nearly two years, this was the extent of his welcome. Bitterness crept into Marion's heart, but she bravely suppressed it. Nanon had also anticipated a warmer welcome, but she cared too much for her friend to let her disappointment show.

A maid escorted both ladies into the castle. They elected first to visit Marion's room. As she stepped in, she saw that it was exactly the way she had left it. Except for one item. On the dresser, there was a large arrangement of wild flowers, accompanied by a note.

"To my dear Marion, from her mother's grave. Alexandre," she read aloud, her eyes filling with tears. "From my dear, dear Mama!" she called out, turning to her friend with a wide smile. "And Alexandre picked them! The unpleasant Alexandre, on whose account I left Ortry. Oh, how much I appreciate what he did today." She remained standing, allowing her tears to caress the wild flowers.

Nanon graciously stepped out, leaving Marion alone with her feelings, and opened the door to her own room. What both women failed to notice was that when she had walked out, Nanon had left the door open slightly. In the doorway stood Alexandre, listening to his stepsister's tender words. How beautiful she was! He almost didn't recognize her. He felt a momentary pang of sibling jealousy, then dismissed it. Creeping closer, he placed his arms around her waist.

"Marion!" was all he said.

She turned around and recognized him. "Alexandre!" she replied. She welcomed him with open arms and they embraced as brother and sister for the first time she could remember. For years to come, he cherished that moment. Richard's suggestion had paid off more than if he had lectured him with a thousand stories.

"How happy you've made me, my Alexandre!" she said, kissing her brother.

"A greeting from your mother, as suggested by Monsieur Müller," he elaborated.

"Monsieur Müller! Who's that?" she inquired.

"He's my new tutor, a German."

"A German tutor? Well, I suppose that makes sense. I suppose the German people know a thing or two about love. It's the most precious gift, you know."

"I wouldn't have thought of the flowers without him," he smiled. "We owe him this little happiness, dear Marion. It's on his account that I've decided to respect you from now on. But come to the breakfast table. Mama will be upset if we take too long."

A shadow crossed Marion's beautiful face. "I could also be upset over the fact that she didn't come out to welcome me, but since she's our mother I won't hold it against her."

The two ladies didn't bother waiting for their suitcases, deciding instead to attend breakfast in their traveling clothes rather than keep the others waiting.

Baroness Adeline and the captain were the only ones present. They rose out of respect for Marion's friend. The baroness' eyes immediately scrutinized her stepdaughter's appearance, her face paling. Two years ago, Marion had still been a tender bud, but now she had developed into a mature rose. She recognized she couldn't compare herself to the young beauty in front of her. Her previous dislike, which had been dormant during Marion's absence, now deepened, laying hold of her inner fears and developing into a deep-seated hatred. Still, she stepped toward Marion, giving her the expected embrace. But this action was nothing more than a formality performed out of obligation, happy to be absolved of it upon completion. Even Nanon was the recipient of a welcome by the mistress of the castle.

They began the customary silent consumption of the meal. No one said a word. Richemonte, feeling the silence almost too painful to bear, finally took the initiative and addressed his granddaughter.

"Marion," he began, "have you heard that a steamship capsized in the Mosel?"

"Yes," she remarked, looking at him with large, expressive eyes. "I'm sure I had wrote to you that we had intended to travel on the same ship. Nonetheless, you fail to ask the obvious question."

"What question? It's obvious to all that you traveled on another ship."

"Why would you draw that conclusion, Grandpa?"

"The fact that you arrived unharmed speaks for itself. Had you traveled as scheduled, you would have perished with the others."

Marion paused, lifting an eyebrow. "And yet, we were on that doomed ship. Fortunately, we were rescued by two brave men."

This last disclosure finally aroused some interest in the captain and the baroness. "Really?" asked her grandfather quickly. "Please explain, Marion!"

"Yes, tell us all about it!" Adeline joined in, doing her best to pretend to be concerned. "Dear God! What if you had drowned? What a calamity that would have been!"

Alexandre jumped out of his chair, showing his genuine concern by wrapping his arms around Marion's neck. "If I had known," he exclaimed with childish bravado, "I would have come to save you myself!"

She affectionately held his hand while recounting her ordeal in a short, yet meaningful account.

"Those two men must have been as brave as my Monsieur Müller," Alexandre commented when she finished the harrowing tale. "He saved me from falling into an abyss, you know. I wish I could have met these two saviors of yours. Did you know them?"

"The one who saved Nanon is Dr. Bertrand's herb collector. He resides in Thionville. Unfortunately, the man who rescued me left before I could find out his name."

During breakfast, the recent events surrounding Ortry were discussed, with Müller's name being mentioned prominently. Ironically, however, Marion remained unaware that Monsieur Müller and her rescuer were one and the same person.

They were still at the table when they heard the sound of hoof beats in the courtyard. Habitually, the captain rose from his seat and walked to the window. No sooner had he glanced outside than he smiled with satisfaction. "We have a visitor. He's finally here!"

"Who? Who's finally here?" Adeline asked.

"Colonel Rallion!"

"Ah, now there's someone worth greeting!" she replied, rising a little too hastily. She smoothed her dress so as to appear as regally as would befit the mistress of the castle and left the dining room with the captain.

The other two ladies felt compelled to follow out of courtesy, yet felt no compulsion to rush like the others had. Even Alexandre wasn't overjoyed.

"He could have stayed where he was," he said under his breath. "I don't care for that Rallion!"

Marion looked at her stepbrother in surprise, her expression nearly changing to one of agreement. *It's as if he spoke from my heart!*

By the time they reached the courtyard, they witnessed the captain and the baroness paying their highest respects to Jean-Paul Rallion, who had just disembarked the carriage. Smiling, he turned from them and greeted each of the ladies, bowing to each one and kissing their finger tips.

"Pardon the intrusion," Rallion said diplomatically, "but I chose to barge over here, knowing you had just arrived. I felt compelled to inquire after your well-being. These are dutiful pleasantries between us that simply cannot be postponed any longer."

Marion bowed formally without expression, choosing not to respond. Rallion turned back to the others, engaging them in polite conversation as they mounted the steps. It was during this moment that Richard came down the stairs. He stopped out of respect, allowing the entourage to pass him. Marion looked at the German man in surprise as a friendly smile crept across her face. Rallion recognized Richard, too, but his surprise at seeing him was of an entirely different variety.

"*Morbleu!*" he cursed. "If it isn't the billiard fool! What is *he* doing here?"

All those present looked in embarrassment at the offended schoolmaster to see how he would react. Richard, however, failed to acknowledge the colonel's presence. He bowed politely to the two young ladies and walked past.

Marion's face reddened. Whether it was because she was ashamed at Rallion's lack of tact or over Richard's apparent cowardice, nobody could tell.

Richemonte shrugged his shoulders in amazement. He couldn't understand why an accomplished fencer and marksman like Richard would allow himself to ignore such an obvious insult.

"My dear Captain," said the colonel as they reached the foyer, "what is that German fool doing here?"

"He's Alexandre's tutor," replied Richemonte evenly.

"*Fi donc!* What will our Alexandre possibly learn from him? The man only knows how to rip holes in billiard covers!"

Alexandre bit his lip, not wanting to respond out of anger. Something within him demanded a retort.

"Your comments are completely uncalled for, Monsieur," the young man said defiantly, turning his eyes to the colonel. "If Monsieur Müller wanted to, he could respond quite differently. He is my teacher and my friend, and I'm telling you now that I'm not going to tolerate your insults."

Rallion was taken aback by the young man's rebuff, but his surprised look quickly gave way to a sarcastic smile. "Ah, then I envy him. Such a fierce protector you are, Alexandre!"

"He doesn't need my protection," replied the youth. "He's man enough to take you on, and as a member of this household he deserves to be respected as such. Even so, I'm not inclined to allow someone like you to speak of him in such unfriendly terms. After all, he saved my life, I'm indebted to him!"

Marion cast a glance at her brother, a glance that conveyed both surprise and approval. His mother's face displayed pride at the boy's defense of his friend. Even the captain played with the ends of his moustache, a sure sign that he approved as well.

Irritated, Rallion responded with a haughty smile. "Saved your life?" he asked patronizingly. "Well, that's an entirely different story. This man seems to be predestined, going about the countryside saving people at will. He should be complimented for his actions."

"This is not a case of mere coincidence," Marion finally broke in. "This man is full of bravery and deliberation, two qualities which are often lacking in many. It's therefore little wonder that such people fail to act when it matters most."

A slight redness, perhaps born out of shame, spread across Rallion's face. Turning to face her grandfather, Marion continued. "You see, it's this monsieur who saved my life by swimming through the deluge with me."

"Really?" Richemonte asked, astounded. But that was all he managed to get out. His granddaughter had been facing death and was rescued. Her savior, as it turned out, was none other than the new German tutor. That was plain enough. What was the point of getting all worked up? The captain had been so consumed with his own intrigues that it hadn't even occurred to him to question Marion's incident, which had turned out all right in the end.

As the lady of the house, however, the baroness felt a compulsion to comment on the event. "Dr. Müller was also there?" she asked, registering surprise. "What a coincidence! Then we *are* truly indebted to him."

Alexandre reached for his sister's hand. "My dear Marion, you too owe him your life? Then he's twice as precious to me. I'm going to go after him and tell him myself." He jumped out of his chair and left the parlor without giving any thought to the feelings of Colonel Rallion.

Although he searched for his tutor, he wasn't able to find him. That's because Richard had left the vicinity of the castle for the solitude of the forest. He felt an overwhelming urge to be alone. Since it was still before the scheduled time for Alexandre's lessons, the time was his to spend as he pleased.

The arrival of the colonel had preoccupied the captain and baroness, insuring that his absence would barely be noticed. He had seen Marion for only a fleeting moment, but this had been enough to stir up his deepest emotions. He needed some time by himself to sort out his feelings for the beautiful girl. He had hardly paid any attention to Rallion's insult, allowing his own frustration to dissipate with the wind. He knew the time would come when he would have to contend with the arrogant man, but he felt assured he would prevail in the end.

The schoolmaster slowly strolled through the woods, occupied more with his thoughts than the direction of his promenade. Marion's image accompanied him, so that as he walked on he dreamed with his eyes open. He saw her enticing figure. He looked into her mesmerizing eyes. He heard the soothing tone of her voice, and it seemed as if he felt her heaving breast on his heart, just like when she had lain across his chest as he carried her from the Mosel to the dairy farm.

A quarter of an hour followed another. He wasn't paying attention to time, the loyal sacrificial love he felt for Marion superseding all concerns over the passing hours and minutes of the day and giving way to the whisper of eternity.

Suddenly, Richard was drawn away from his musings by the sound of a familiar voice.

"Ah, it's the doctor! God bless you!"

He looked up, and in front of him, on the small path, stood his faithful servant. Franz was examining him with an amused look.

"Franz, it's you," Richard forced himself to say after a moment. "How is it that you've come so far? Aren't you supposed to be in Thionville?"

"Of course, but you must remember that I'm employed as a collector of plants and herbs!" replied the servant. "We just arrived in Thionville today, and Dr. Bertrand immediately sent me out to go about my job."

"Then you came across me by chance?"

"Yes, just like you did," laughed Franz. "I saw you meander down that path, your eyes fixed on the ground, just like someone looking for plants. And I came here, eyes to the ground, like a man whose mind is fixed on a certain mademoiselle. It's therefore no wonder that two people could meet by chance."

The loyal, quick-witted servant knew he was allowed to make the odd comment to his master. For his part, Richard didn't take offense. The comment was light-hearted enough. In fact, he surveyed Franz's attire with amusement.

"So, you're already engaged in your duties as the 'plant man'?" he asked. "Do you have any skill for the job?"

"Of course, Doctor!" he said, taking the sack from his shoulder and letting it sink to the ground. He opened it for Richard to see into. "Look here," he said with mock importance. "My bag is already half full. There's moss, pine cones, ferns, oak leaves, wild grass, and cabbage leaves. But what the chemist does with this stuff, I have no idea. It's not important. Dr. Bertrand told me I was free to do as I please, but if it suited me, I could collect peppermint or mint, known here as *véronique* and *menthe pouirée*. Since I'm not familiar with either one, I thought I would just gather some pine cones and cabbage leaves. No one's going to drink the stuff and certainly no one's likely to die from it." He closed the sack and threw it back over his shoulder.

"You've ended up with a very lenient employer," Richard observed. "It was fortunate that we ran into Dr. Bertrand, although I would have preferred to keep my plans to myself."

"Oh, Bertrand is trustworthy. We can count on him," maintained Franz. "I've only known him a short time, but I can tell that he doesn't care much for the Frenchmen. There must be a reason why he's not enamored of them. Naturally, he guessed why we came here, but I'm convinced that he'll continue to support our efforts, not hinder them. Besides, it's good that we found each other. I'm eager to receive instructions from you, sir."

Richard walked into the nearby bushes to make sure the two of them were alone. "I can only give you an overview for now, not the specifics," he said, returning from his reconnoiter satisfied. "France's ruler is secretly plotting a war with Germany. He's orchestrating his efforts in secret, hoping to catch us unprepared so they can march to Berlin relatively unmolested. The emperor believes that the southern states' dissatisfaction with Prussia will prevent them from supporting us, and he's contemplating moving his supplies to the border. This would enable France to attack us en masse.

"Our objective is to glean news of these plans and to formulate a strategy to thwart their preparations. One of the key places of activity, if not the most dangerous, is right here at Ortry. I've been ordered here to observe and report on any unusual activity, and you are to support me in this risky endeavor. That's all you need to know for now, Franz."

"That's enough," Franz said with a nod, a grin flashing across his intelligent face. "I'm a foundling, a simple barber's helper, but I want to be known as the one who stole a glimpse at the braggart's cards. I've got lots of time and it's fortunate that they won't mistake me for a German."

"What makes you say that?"

"Well, Dr. Bertrand registered me as a Swiss worker from Geneva. As you may recall, I spent two years there learning enough French to pass as one from that region." He paused, scratching his head. "How am I supposed to communicate with you when I learn something of value? Where should we meet?"

"You can inform me of the lesser things through the mail, as long as you address your letters to Dr. Andreas Müller. The more important issues, however, we'll need to discuss face to face. My room is situated at the top of the turret facing southwest. From there, I can easily see the large linden tree, the one that stands next to the Thionville road. If you have important news, just clump down with your sack at the base of that tree. People will think you're having a rest, and I'll be able to see you clearly with the aid of my little telescope. You can monitor my window with a telescope of your own. As soon as you see my white handkerchief, proceed to this place so we can meet in private. Naturally, this can only work during the day."

"What about at night?" asked Franz, anticipating his next answer.

"You can pay me a visit, to my room."

"People will undoubtedly see me."

Richard considered that possibility for a moment. "Not if you're careful. You'll have to wait until after dark, when everyone's asleep, making sure no one is wandering about the courtyard. Then climb up the lightning conduit structure on the far side of the castle, creep across the flat roof, and knock softly on my window. The conduit supports are solid. I've already tried it out."

"That's good to know. I'll look at it tomorrow."

"There's one more thing. I need to make you aware of the old tower, the one that's in this forest—"

"I'm not familiar with it."

"Then I'll show it to you now. Rumor has it that it's haunted, but I have a feeling these ghosts are made of flesh and blood. It's not easy for me to leave the castle at night, but that's the best time for me to observe the tower—"

"That's fine, Doctor," Franz said. "I'll go in your place."

"But the ghosts!" laughed Richard.

"Oh, I happen to own a revolver. That should keep them at bay! Besides, a good club can work wonders."

"Of course. Still, I don't want you to place yourself in any danger. Our observations must be conducted in secret. I would prefer that you avoid any entanglements with strangers."

"Just as you please, Monsieur. What should I do if we run into each other in public, while others are around? How should I handle myself?"

"Simple. We don't know each other, and we have to speak French. At best, we can say that we traveled on the same steamship. Now, let's find that tower."

They walked through the dense wood and arrived at a broken heap of rocks flanked by the ruins of an old stone tower. The diameter of the base wasn't particularly significant, although the top reached to a height of nearly thirty meters. It looked to have been much taller at the time of its construction, but much of its edifice had crumbled since then.

The doorway at the base was narrow and not very high. Richard could see other rectangular openings at the bottom of the round structure that had probably once served as vantage points for archers. Higher up were the remnants of pillars, a reminder that they had at one time supported larger rooms.

When the two men entered the abandoned structure, the first feature they noticed was a staircase that wound its way up to the top. The steps, covered with boulders and debris, were difficult to climb. They labored to reach the top. Once there, they found nothing out of the ordinary, and certainly no trace of recent human visitation. Satisfied, they retreated back downstairs to look through the lower portion of the tower. There were so many stones and boulders strewn about that it would have taken great effort to remove all the rubble. It didn't seem worth the effort to search for an access to the basement.

"The ghosts haven't chosen a comfortable place to call home," quipped Franz. "If I had to perform the duties of a spirit after death, I would make sure that I at least had a comfortable sofa and my favorite pipe. I feel sorry for these spirits!"

"Then you can feel sorry for yourself as well," Richard commented.

"Why do you say that?"

"Because this place will substitute as your guardhouse for the next few days. You'll have to do without the usual creature comforts."

"I'm assuming it's part of my military duty," Franz said with a sigh. "As such, one can't be too choosy. Anyway, I'm not about to set up camp in the tower itself. If any ghosts actually come by, they'll come through that small entrance," he said, pointing to the narrow doorway. "To be completely honest with you, I'm looking forward to it. After all, I haven't had the privilege of meeting any ghosts before."

Richard knew that Franz was a brave, dependable soul who didn't put much stock in ghost stories, or even the devil, for that matter.

"Well, we'll see about that," his master said as they left the tower, heading for the clearing. "We'll go our separate ways for now. Look, the first drops of rain are starting to fall, and I suspect a storm isn't far off."

They parted company, each man absorbed with his own plans.

CHAPTER THIRTY-ONE

The Tower Ghost

Franz's destination lay in the houses of Thionville, in the not too far distance. While his servant hurried eastward, Richard headed west, back in the direction of the tower. The abandoned structure lay directly in his path back to the castle, making it the most obvious place of shelter from the coming storm.

Strong winds whipped through the trees, their tops crackling and straining back and forth under the pressure. A shrill, sharp moaning sound cut through the stillness. Suddenly, darkness enveloped the area, the only light coming from the odd flash of lightning. A massive thunderclap shook the ground as the clouds began pouring rain in broad sheets.

Fortunately for Richard, he was already in the vicinity of the ruins when the rain came. He hurried between the rubble, and was about to enter through the narrow opening, when a lightning flash illuminated another person seeking refuge from the downpour. He hesitated, on his guard, then relaxed when he saw it was Marion.

"Forgive me, gracious lady!" he managed to call. "I didn't realize someone else was in here." Once in the confines of the tower's darkness, they couldn't see each other.

"I too thought I was alone," she replied. "But you don't have to apologize. The forest is available to all."

"Even this structure, Mademoiselle?"

"Of course. Why shouldn't you seek shelter here, just as I did. Did you get wet?"

"Not enough to be worried about."

"I also managed to escape the deluge. The tower was close by."

Richard speculated that she had been visiting her mother's grave when the storm hit. How she must have loved her that her first priority upon returning was visiting her mother's final resting place.

"Did you come alone?" he asked.

"Yes," she answered. "I fear the downpour will last for a while. Perhaps we should get comfortable."

Richard's eyes finally adjusted to the darkness, and he noticed that she had removed her wrap and placed it on the nearby steps, sitting down. He remained standing, simply leaning against a pillar. Outside, it thundered ominously and the rain continued to pour. From time to time, lightning flashes illuminated the inside of the tower. Both refugees remained still, occupied with their own thoughts.

Finally, Marion broke the silence.

"It would seem we're destined to meet in stormy weather," she observed wryly. "Fortunately, this storm is nothing compared to the one we encountered on the Mosel."

What could he say? Unable to think of a proper response, he remained silent. She hesitated as well, not sure how to proceed.

"Why did you leave the dairy farm so quickly?" she said after a long pause.

"I knew you were out of danger and in good care," he replied. "I saw no reason to stay."

She noted that his words had been spoken with a peculiar tone. Rather than speculate on a reason, she continued on. "I haven't found the opportunity yet to express my gratitude. Please, Doctor, allow me to do so now."

She offered him her hand, a fine hand that shone even in darkness. He took her warm, soft fingers in his and felt a firm squeeze. Curiously, she didn't pull her hand back right away, but permitted him to reciprocate the action. It seemed to him as if a heavenly essence flowed from her hand into his, permeating his entire body. The stale air of the tower seemed suddenly to change into a refreshing fragrance of balsam. He felt a tingling in his hand and, although he fought the urge to linger, he squeezed her fingers again. This time, she withdrew her hand.

His thoughts roiled. *Is she upset with me?*

She cleared her throat. "Naturally, I inquired after you," she said softly.

No, there's no reproach in her voice, he concluded.

"I couldn't find out anything about you, though." she continued. "It occurred to me that you weren't totally unfamiliar with Dr. Bertrand, but he was unusually reserved about you. You can imagine my surprise today when I saw you at the castle, engaged no less as tutor to my stepbrother. Did you know who I was on the ship?"

This was an admission he couldn't avoid, and so he answered truthfully. "Yes," he said.

"Then why didn't you tell me we would be seeing each other again?"

"I didn't find a suitable opportunity," he offered, trying to mitigate his earlier omission.

"Perhaps," Marion allowed, undaunted. "Still, I'm glad to find you on the estate. I know you can't have an opinion about your new surroundings, since you've only been here a short time, but I ask that you overlook certain oddities, out of love for Alexandre, whose love you've already gained. He told me about your trials with real enthusiasm, and how you had to demonstrate your abilities in front of my grandfather. Incidentally, my grandfather admitted to me that you're an accomplished fencer, marksman, and a daredevil in the saddle. Therefore, I was perplexed when I... I—" She stopped in mid-sentence, reluctant to go on.

"Please, go on, Mademoiselle!" he encouraged.

"I was puzzled to find out that you were unfamiliar with something that most men are quite competent in."

"What would that be?"

"The game of billiards. Colonel Rallion spoke of it after lunch, insinuating that you were incompetent. Besides," she continued in a heightened voice, "won't you tell me why you ignored his insult?"

Had there been more light in the tower, she would have seen a painful expression come over his face. "I'd rather not say," he said.

"Why?" she asked quietly. "Are you afraid of him?"

Richard didn't respond right away. Instead, he walked toward the tower's entryway, exposed to the downpour, oblivious to the falling raindrops. Marion's intuition told her that he was trying to suppress some inward conviction. He stood motionless as the storm raged outside. Richard became completely soaked, yet didn't seem to pay any attention to it. As she gazed at him, Marion's perplexing look turned into one of concern.

She stood up and touched his arm. "Why don't you answer me?" she asked.

Now that she addressed him, he slowly turned around, allowing her hand to slip from his arm.

"Because your words have offended me more than the colonel's," he said. "Yet... Pah! I'm just a simple tutor, collecting his salary."

"You're mistaken, Dr. Müller! I had no intention of offending you," she quickly clarified. "You're the one who rescued me and my brother. Why would I want to embarrass you? Besides, neither one of us counts more than the other. It was providence that allowed me to stem from nobility. You, however, have attained your knowledge, accomplishments, and experience through hard work and diligence. My brother is to glean from your expertise. Tell me honestly, will this diminish or increase your worth in our small circle?"

The young woman had spoken convincingly. Richard sensed that it mattered to her whether or not he judged her in the wrong light. This realization lifted his spirits.

"I had no other basis for my question," she added, "other than that I would have liked to see you stand your ground against the colonel, like the man I came to know. When I found myself in danger, Rallion's only concern was for himself. When he puffed himself up and belittled you, the schoolmaster, in front of his employer, you chose to withdraw quietly. Doesn't that seem a little unusual?"

Richard saw that Marion was apologizing for giving him the wrong impression. She plainly affirmed that she would have preferred to see the colonel rebuffed for his thoughtless remarks. Through the unspoken sentiment, he found hope. He wanted to wrap his arms around her to thank her as lovers take comfort from each other in difficult circumstances.

"But Mademoiselle," he objected, "I could only have answered him with a weapon. Mere words wouldn't have been enough."

"Well, why didn't you use a weapon then?"

"Because no opponent has yet defeated me in a fight," he said, revealing the depth of his inner modesty and confidence.

She somehow knew he wasn't boasting. "That may be, but you shouldn't allow others to take advantage of your genial nature."

Richard walked up to her, his tone deathly serious. "Is it your intention that I kill your betrothed?"

Marion blushed at the question, but persisted. "So you forfeited your right to answer the colonel on my account?"

"That was the only reason."

"Yet it was completely unnecessary!" she exclaimed, slightly embarrassed. "Who told you he was my fiancé?"

"He proclaimed it openly on several occasions."

"Really? Well, just in case you haven't noticed, he doesn't appeal to me at all. I see no need for you to spare him on my account. My grandfather desires to bring us together, but I would never give my heart to a man I couldn't love or respect!"

Marion suddenly stopped, fearing she had said too much, yet Richard sensed she had spoken from her heart.

"I thank you for being so forthright, Mademoiselle!" he said, inwardly jubilant. "I know I have the right to defend my honor against the colonel, but could I have done so? After all, he is your grandfather's guest. I am merely his employee."

"It doesn't matter. Do you know my grandfather's penchants?"

"I haven't had the opportunity to learn that much about him."

"Well then, I should point out that he considers himself to be an ardent follower of fencing and marksmanship. His greatest pleasure comes from being a spectator of such events. Had you challenged Rallion, my grandpa wouldn't have criticized your actions. In fact, I'm convinced he would have assisted you by—"

A spectacular lightning flash illuminated the entire area and a crash of thunder seemingly directly overhead shook the old ruins, threatening to collapse further portions of the old wall.

Marion's hand flew to her open mouth in terror.

"Oh, my God!"

The flash outlined the nearby stone blocks, including a ghostly white shape that seemed to float toward them. Even when the intensity of the flash subsided, they saw the white figure glide closer, not in a rush as though trying to escape the rain, but in slow, measured steps. Whatever it was, it didn't seem to be confined by the natural world or subject to its meteorological forces.

Marion, who hadn't resumed her earlier place on the staircase, stood beside Richard, mesmerized by the apparition.

"It's my mother's ghost!" she whispered, drawing nearer to him. The closer the figure came, the more Marion pressed herself into the corner of the staircase, and against Richard, who evaluated the apparent ghost with mounting interest. The apparition had probably ventured in from the area of the grave. Although Richard didn't believe in ghosts, he couldn't suppress a sullen dread as the lifeless shape approached.

Marion had shown her resilient nature during the steamship's sinking, but now she pressed herself tighter and tighter against Richard, to the point that he put his arm around her. She hardly seemed to notice. When the spirit reached the entrance at the base of the tower, the poor girl wrapped both her arms around Richard. He could feel waves of tremors coursing through her as fear took its hold on her.

The apparition stopped under the doorway, then turned around to face the forest and raised both of its arms to heaven.

"*Allah il Allah!*" Liama called out in a deep, sonorous voice. "In the name of the all-merciful God! Praise and honor to the Lord, the Almighty, who reigns on judgment day. We want to serve only you, and entreat you to lead us on the paths of righteousness, the way reserved for those who rejoice in your mercy, and not in the way of those whom you despise, the way of the lost!"

The ghost allowed her arms to sink and she stepped back and continued the prayer. "It is Allah who directs the lightning and causes the rain to fall. The thunder proclaims his praise and the angels worship him in fear. He sends his retribution and destroys whom he will. *Allah il Allah, Allah akbar!*"

The figure climbed the steps without paying attention to the two earthly beings standing to the side of the staircase. One final lightning bolt flashed around them, almost as if in direct response to her proclamation. A moment later, a powerful thunderclap resounded, and then it was still.

The rain continued to fall for another minute, but then even that suddenly ceased. The clouds parted quickly and the brightness of the day returned. The apparition, however, had disappeared into the upper portion of the tower.

Still clinging to Richard, Marion stood transfixed in his embrace. He felt he could hold her like this for all eternity. He looked with concern into her face that had lost its color. Her eyes closed as her shudders subsided.

"Marion!" he whispered, trying to rouse her.

She stirred, responding to the sound of her name. Richard, intending to snap her out of her frightened state, realized too late that he had been careless. *How can I, a lowly schoolmaster, dare to address a noblewoman by her first name? What will she say?*

But it was too late to retract his plea. She opened her eyes slowly and looked into his. A deep redness spread over her pale complexion, and she released her embrace. She stepped aside so that he was forced to remove his arm.

"Where is she?" Marion whispered.

"Up there," he replied, pointing to the staircase.

"She might return. Please, let's leave this place."

He shook his head, still deep in thought. "No, let's stay and wait. Do you really think it was a ghost?"

"Yes," she answered, completely convinced. "It was my mother's ghost."

"What if you're wrong?"

"I'm sure of it!" she said firmly.

"Have you seen it before?"

"Never! But people from this district talk about it. It's no illusion."

She shivered at her own words, but Richard shook his head in contradiction. "Ghosts don't appear during the day," he argued. "Ghosts don't get wet. I saw her white robe, worn in Arabic fashion, and it absorbed the rain. Besides, spirits don't loudly proclaim the words of the Qu'ran."

"Her words stemmed from the Qu'ran?"

"Yes. She prayed the first verse of the Qu'ran, known as the Opening, then followed it up with the thirteenth verse, or the Thunder."

"She was a follower of Mohammed," admitted Marion, still shaking from the fright of having seen her mother's spirit. "I want to leave this place."

"And what if it wasn't a ghost?"

"Sir, I don't want to stay. I have to leave!"

"Please, just wait for a moment. I want to see where she went."

"For God's sake, no!" she pleaded. "I'm afraid to remain by myself. Don't leave me. I have to go home. I have to pray to God so that he will grant my mother's eternal rest. Please, let's go!"

Marion pulled him along, out into the wet forest. He looked back at the tower reluctantly, having no choice to but follow her. As they hurried between the boulders, she also looked back, pointing with fright at the pinnacle of the ruin.

The white apparition stood at the top, its arms outstretched and pointing to the east, symbolic of the location of Mecca. They heard the words of her prayer reverberate down to them, as if they were meant for the fleeing rainstorm that was rapidly passing to the east. Behind the apparition, the setting sun shone in the west, and above it a rainbow arced through the sky, displaying its brilliant colors.

Richard let his mouth hang open, amazed. He had witnessed the spectacle of the tower ghost. Its deepest mysteries, however, eluded him.

TRANSLATION NOTES

I have taken the utmost care to render the original German text into a coherent and legible English format. Some of the passages were difficult to translate in the way they were presented, whether because of the sentence structure or by their sheer length. Karl May seemed to enjoy enveloping his readers with a series of interwoven thoughts, all in the same paragraph, or plunging them deeper into the story through long sentences. You may read it in its entirety in German, all the while trying to catch your breath; but it just doesn't translate well into English.

In some cases, May employed old idioms or outdated sayings that I've coined as "Blücherisms." Although they heighten the dramatic moments, rendering the literal expressions into English would have modern readers shaking their heads. This was especially prevalent in the first book, *The Prussian Lieutenant*. In the second book, *The Marabout's Secret*, May placed more of an emphasis on drawing the reader into the Bedouin world in North Africa, and delighted in using Arabic language.

The final translation has to be faithful to the original, as much as possible, while maintaining an enjoyable read for anyone unfamiliar with the original German text. The editor affixed parentheses to outline where changes had to be made, and notes were created to explain the deviations. In some cases, a further explanation of a word or phrase was necessary.

1.1   Timbuktu
      The small town of Timbuktu derived its name after a Tuareg woman who dug a well, calling it 'Buktu's well'. Today it falls within the territory of Mali, about 15 kilometers north of the Niger River. It lies along an important trade route, linking the Sahara with various ancient kingdoms. It played a key role in the transport of gold, ivory, salt, and the trading of slaves. The inhabitants come from mostly Berber and Tuareg descent (from Wikipedia).

1.2   Tuareg
      The Tuareg, or Touareg, are a nomadic, transient people of the Western Sahara. Descendants of the Berber tribe, they facilitated trade on the great caravan routes, including the slave trade, linking

the northern coast of Africa with the southern cities. Although they strongly resisted French colonization in the 1800s, they were no match to French weaponry and military tactics and were therefore forced to concede to treaties with the ruling regime.

1.3 **Moor** or **Moar**
A Muslim people of North Africa. The Moors were a mix of Arab and Berber descendants who converted to Islam in the 8th century. The word Moor originated from the Greek word *Maurus*, meaning black or very dark. The Moors were skilled craftsmen, excelling in construction of mosques and palaces.

1.4 **Cerberus**
In Greek mythology, Cerberus was a mythical three-headed dog. Also called Kerberus, the Hound of Hades. It was grotesque in appearance, with a snake for a tail. Its head was covered with interlacing tiny snakes. Cerberus was the keeper of the gate of Hades, ensuring all those spirits confined there were unable to leave.

1.5 **Gérard**
Jules Gérard (1817-1864) was known as "the lion killer." He was a French officer who distinguished himself in various military campaigns in Algiers. One of his passions was hunting big game, especially lions.

2.1 **Sirius**
Sirius is one of the brightest stars in the southern hemisphere. It is not a single star, but a binary star system approximately 8.5 light years from Earth. Ancient mariners used it as an important reference point in navigation.

2.2 **"Hans im Glück."**
This is a reference to the Brothers Grimm fairy tale *Clever Hans*. It's the tale of a simple boy, Hans, who bargained away his possessions. At first, he started off with a lump of gold, bartering it for animals. By the end, he had a heavy grindstone. It was burdensome to carry the stone around with him, so he eventually rid himself of the burden, once again becoming happy.

3.1 **"Quid pro quo."**
Literal: "Something for something."
Translation: This is a Latin proverb. The implication here is that both parties obtain equal value in the exchange. Also referred to as "a favor for a favor."

4.1   **Tschibuk**
A long, ornate Turkish tobacco pipe. The large head could be made from clay or wood, with the stem displaying intricate carving.

4.2   **Hajji**
Hajji, or pilgrim, is an honorary title usually held by the followers of Muslim precepts. If the faithful pilgrim has completed a journey to Mecca or Medina, he may employ the term *hajji* by incorporating it into his name. It stems from the Arabic term *al-Hajj*, referring to a title. In some instances, the term *hajji* has been incorporated into family names, and is passed down from one generation to another. For example, Hajji Halef Omar.

4.3   **Dey**
The title *Dey* was given to the rulers of Algiers and Tunisia who reigned during the Ottoman Empire. The *Dey* governed three states, each one being administered by a trusted man of his choosing, called a *Bey*.

4.4   **Burnus**
A *burnus* was a long-hooded coat, often white in color. It covered the upper body and served as protection against wind and rain. It typically had no sleeves. A favorite garment of the Tuareg and Bedouin tribes.

       Turkos
4.5   A reference to local Turkish guides employed by the French regime. These men were skilled in warfare and proved to be exceptional guides to the military, not just in traversing the country, but also in dealing with customs and traditions.

4.6   **Chasseurs d'Afrique**
A light cavalry corps located in Algeria. They were first established in 1830 from French settlers and army recruits. They received adequate training and were the mounted version of the *Zouave* infantry. They became known as formidable warriors on horseback, not unlike the European Hussars.

4.7   **Fakihadschi**
An old term referring to a fruit merchant, specifically one dealing in dates and figs in an open market. The merchant often had an improvised stand set up in a local market where he could hawk his wares.

6.1   **Kuchenreutersche**
A black-powder firing pistol. Founded by Johann Kuchenreuter in the mid-1700s, the line of hand-crafted pistols that were renowned for their impeccable craftsmanship. The excellent reputation was continued with Bartholomaus Kuchenreuter (1782-1864), another highly skilled gunsmith, who specialized in black-powder pistols as well as long rifles. Some of the company's famous customers included the likes of Frederick the Great, Napoleon Bonaparte, and the Czar of Russia. As the production was limited to roughly 25 pairs of pistols per year, the cost of ownership was staggering and could only be afforded by nobility or the very wealthy.

6.2   **Jahennum** or **Gehenna**
A reference to hell. Muslim tradition indicates that there are seven levels of hell, commonly known as purgatory in the western world. It was not designated to be an eternal punishment for believers. A flaming hell was intended for unbelievers or infidels (Hindus, Sikhs, Jews, and Christians). Islamic paradise, known as the garden, or *Janna*, is a place of physical and spiritual bliss. The faithful are promised mansions and virgin companions, known as *Houris*. According to the Qu'ran, a person is placed at the appropriate level of *Jahennum*, each one according to his sins. The predominant belief is that Allah, the all-knowing and merciful god, will rescue the faithful after a time of purification. Infidels, however, aren't as fortunate; they are destined for a life of suffering.

6.3   **Giaur**
Giaur derives from the Turkish and refers to an infidel, or one without faith. The Arabic word *kafir* is a common Muslim term for an infidel. Although the word could imply that a person is devoid of faith, during the time of Karl May's writing (the 1880s), *giaur* was meant as an insult.

6.4   **Acacia trees** and **mimosa bushes**
The acacia tree sprouts yellow flowers, and affords the weary traveler shade from the burning sun. Because of its many thorns, however, it has to be approached with care. The commonly found mimosa bush, with its large clusters of star flowers, produces leaves that are sensitive to human touch.

6.5   **"Herr des Erdbebbens."**
Lord of the earthquake, Lord of thunder, or *Lord with the thick mane*, were just a few of the titles given to the mighty and revered lion. The

inhabitants of the desert knew his traits and considered themselves fortunate if they managed to escape by losing just a few cattle to this dangerous predator.

6.6	**Kuskus**

According to Wikipedia, Couscous (or Kuskus) is a type of pasta derived from the Maghreb people. It consists of fine granules made by rolling and shaping moistened semolina wheat and covering it with finely ground wheat flour.

7.1	**Schott Melhrir**

The Schott Melhrir is a large endomorphic, marshy saline lake in Western Algeria, and lies nearly entirely below sea level. It varies in size with the weather patterns, often reaching a width of 80 miles and extending into the Sahara.

7.2	**"Donner und Doria."**

Literally, it translates as "Thunder and Doria." This minced oath, or expletive, was taken from Schiller's story, *The Conspiracy of Fiesko to Genoa*, and could loosely be translated as "heaven and hell."

9.1	**Pompadour** or **Pompatour**

Named after Jeanne Antoinette Poisson, Marquise de Pompadour (1721-1745), companion of King Louis XV. The lady was more than a companion, and more like a mistress. The inference is that Napoleon would have drawn Margot Richemonte to his inner circle, keeping her as a mistress for himself.

10.1	**Effendi**

A Turkish title for "sir," often meaning lord or master. An implication can be drawn that the *effendi* addressed is an educated or well-to-do gentleman.

10.2	**Lion's eye teeth**

The eye teeth are spaced far enough apart as to enable the predator to sever the cervical vertebrae of its prey in a single bite. The bicuspid teeth are sharp and act like scissors in unison with the back teeth, the carnassials.

10.3	**Hamaïl**

A *hamaïl* was a small pouch or purse containing whole segments or fragments of the Qu'ran. A faithful Moslem would always carry the purse with him.

10.4   Atuscha

The *atuscha* was a unique form of transport for women. Originating in Persia, it was a cocoon-type enclosure, self-contained and strapped onto the back of a camel. This afforded the occupant a fairly comfortable means of travel, while remaining discreet enough to keep her away from prying eyes.

11.1   Bismarck

Otto Leopold von Bismarck (1815-1898), statesman and minister-President of Prussia (1862-1890). At the young age of 32, he was appointed to the Prussian legislature, and soon became known for his stinging rhetoric. He was a true diplomat, fostering unification between the loose German states and Prussia, forming a solidified new Germany. The Franco-Prussian war of 1870 proved to be a great success for Prussian forces, pushing back the French and capturing Napoleon III. Bismarck not only secured his appointment as imperial chancellor of the German empire, but his most important legacy was the unification of Germany. He also implemented the first health reforms and instituted old age pensions for retired citizens. He died of throat cancer in 1898.

11.2   Moltke

Helmuth Graf von Moltke (1800-1891). Under Bismarck's leadership, Moltke advanced to chief of staff of the Prussian army, a post he held for thirty years. Fluent in seven languages, including Turkish, he was known for being reserved rather than boastful, earning the nickname "Der große Schweiger" (The great silent man). He turned out to be one of the finest military strategists Germany ever had. He was instrumental in defeating Austria in the Austro-Prussian war of 1866, leading Bismarck appointing him to oversee the Prussian forces in the Franco-Prussian War of 1870. He won a resounding victory at the battle of Sedan, capturing Marshall MacMahon and Napoleon III at the same time.

12.1   "Verliebt noch weiter als bis zu den Ohren."

Literal: "To be in love past the ears."
Translation: The expression comes from an old German idiom that implied a man was not just attracted to a woman, but infatuated with her. The attraction was more than just "skin deep", or head over heels in love.

12.2   Terzerol

The name is of Italian origin, meaning "small gun." It was a small caliber, front loading pistol. Also referred to as a pocket pistol. Much like the American Derringer, it was a formidable weapon in close quarters.

17.1 **Castrum Deloris**
In Latin, *castrum deloris* signifies a castle of grief. It was an elevated structure over a bier, its size signifying the status and prestige of the deceased. It often consisted of a canopy and was complemented with candles, flowers, and small statues.

19.1 **Courtisane**
This is an older term for a lady plying her trade in the "oldest profession," a prostitute with an upper class clientele.

20.1 **Prometheus**
According to ancient Greek mythology, Prometheus, which literally means "forethought," was pivotal in human history. He is credited in folklore as the god who brought fire to mankind.

21.1 **Juno**
The daughter of Saturn, Juno was a goddess in Roman mythology. She was the patron goddess of Rome, often referred to as *Juno Regina*. Each March 1, a festival called *Matronalia* was held in her honor. Tradition held that the month of June was the most favorable time to get married.

21.2 **Vox Humana**
In Latin, this literally means "human voice." A short resonator reed in a pipe organ. It apparently parallels the human voice. *Vox humana* is intended to simulate the singing of a small choir or a soloist.

21.3 **"Da steckt er wieder die Teufel's Phanne heraus."**
Literal: "He's showing the devil's flag."
Translation: "There he goes again, showing his devil's face for all to see." This is an old idiom that depicts a man's radical facial transfiguration.

23.1 **Lorgnette**
A *lorgnette* was a fancy *pince-nez*, with a handle. These fancy spectacles were used primarily by society ladies as a fashion statement, although it wasn't uncommon for a gentleman to use one, too. It was originally invented by an Englishman, George Adams.

26.1 **"Bilde zu Sais."**
A picture of the veiled Isis, "Queen of the throne," the goddess of magic and healing. It was based on a poem written by Friedrich von Schiller (1759-1805), and is a reference to the shrine of Isis, located in

Egypt. Richemonte is drawing a parallel to Isis. It's a warning that anyone thinking of taking a look into his affairs is like someone looking under the veil of Isis; both acts will result in death.

26.2 **Pedagogic regimen**
Pedagogic, meaning upbringing. A sort of educational science. The ancient Greeks used this form of education when tutoring pupils. The master would take the young pupil "under his wings" and mold the curriculum to fit the needs of the young learner.

28.1 **Franctireur**
A *franctireur*, or *franc-tireur*, was a French partisan soldier, or one belonging to a faction of troops engaged in forays, skirmishes, and upheaval. In its simplest form, a *franctireur* was a civilian who voluntarily enlisted to aid France's cause in the French-Prussian War. At their worst, *franctireurs* were seen as opportunists or highwaymen, only concerned with their own gain.

What follows is an exclusive peak
from *Buried Secrets*, the next volume
in *The Hussar's Love* series.

CHAPTER ONE
A Persian Visitor

The city of Metz was a fortress without equal, having been chosen by Napoleon III to quarter his second division, and together with the Strasbourg, Besançon, and Chalons sur Marne belonged to the eastern military command, its headquarters located in Nancy. Metz, originally a German city stemming from the time of Lothar the Young, had once upon a time come into the possession of German King Ludwig, much like Austria had. Only through repeated scheming and subterfuge were the French finally successful in obtaining this strategic military outpost, solidifying their sovereignty through the West-Phalia peace initiative. For many years, the possession of Metz was a source of contention between Germany and France, and before the last word was spoken through cannon fire, the fortress was not only the main marshalling point for the French, but it also served as the place of deployment for countless hostilities, which Germany had no choice but to tolerate at the hands of its insatiable neighbor.

One of Metz's finest and largest hotels was *l'Hotel de Europe*, situated in the prettiest section of the city and conveniently located near the railway station. The hotel was frequented by all manner of distinguished guests who found that everything was provided for them upon arrival, as was customarily the case among people of both abundant wealth and high expectation. In the spring of 1870, the hotel's management was particularly favored among the upper class. The city was inundated with constant military traffic at this time, though the hotel proprietors knew better than to proclaim it openly. High-ranking officials came and went; no one knew where they came from or where they were going, not to mention the purpose of their comings and goings. Even though most were dressed in civilian clothing, the management and staff of *l'Hotel de Europe* were astute enough to realize that they were dealing with influential military men whose mere presence suggested the reality of important military matters in the works.

For several days now, an older, stately-looking gentleman occupied the best suite in the hotel. He had several of his own servants at his disposal and his suitcases still bore the insignia of his recent travels via railway, Paris and Nancy. The gentleman had come from the French capital, stopping along the way in Nancy before arriving in Metz to review the current state of military readiness. He simply referred to himself as Monsieur Maçon, but one bartender who served in one of the finest cafés claimed to know the recluse's true identity. According to the barkeep, Maçon was no commoner, but rather Count Jules Rallion, the proclaimed favorite of the emperor. In this assessment, the bartender was entirely correct. He had gleaned the information by closely monitoring Maçon's visits to the divisional commander, fortress commander, and other high-ranking men of the city who rendered unto him the respect of a man of distinction and nobility. He had even paid attention the previous evening when Rallion instructed his entourage to prepare themselves for an 11:30 a.m. departure from Metz. The count's plan was to arrive in Thionville at precisely 12:46 p.m. that afternoon.

Punctually at 9:00 o'clock, a young gentleman, likely another officer traveling incognito, inquired with the manager of the hotel if Monsieur Maçon was available to receive a visitor. The newcomer was politely welcomed. When asked for his name, he responded by way of a business card: *Bernard Lemarch, Squadron Commander.*

The proprietor had seen many such cards, and immediately understood what it actually meant. This newcomer, in fact, was a captain, and more specifically, a cavalry master. The pronouncement made, the bearer of the card was readily admitted into the spacious foyer.

Count Rallion received Captain Lemarch with courtesy, bidding him to take a seat and accept a cigarette.

"I happened to see a chalk drawing depicting a country scene hanging in the colonel's anteroom," began Rallion. "One drawn by your own hand, it would seem."

"It is one of my early works, sir," replied Lemarch modestly.

"A beginner's work, perhaps, but one that shows the promise of better things to come. I'm convinced you will be able to play the part of a scenic painter quite competently."

"Thank you. It shouldn't pose a problem."

"I'm glad to hear of it. Do you know who I am, Captain?"

Lemarch smiled at the irony of the question. "Do I have the honor of conversing with Monsieur Maçon?"

The gentleman nodded. "And how would you address me in different circumstances?" he asked.

"Under different circumstances, I would have the honor of speaking with Count Rallion." The captain bowed deeply.

"That's good," Rallion observed. "I see you have been informed. I too have been informed of your accomplishments and I'm satisfied you will render your country a valuable service. You might even receive some recognition from this, Captain. Even a commendation."

The captain's face lit up, leading him to make a quick reply. "I plan to make the most of this opportunity. I won't let you down. I'll prove to you that I'm capable and determined to carry out whatever service my country requires of me."

"Excellent! I take it you're proficient in the German language?"

"Completely. I was born near Strasbourg."

"Would you be able to pass yourself off as a German in Berlin?"

"I expect so," Lemarch said. "All I require are the necessary documents to carry it out."

"I will see to it that you will get them," Rallion assured him. "Now, here is what I need to discuss with you." The count reached for a new cigarette and lit it while assuming his most diplomatic face for Lemarch's benefit. "We in the government feel the necessity," he continued, "to consider the possibility of an imminent war with Germany. Unlike last time, we're not assuming we can just barge in blindly. The last German-Austrian battle was ample proof of the Prussians' far-reaching and well-executed wartime strategies. We'll have to take our time getting acquainted with the full circumstances. It stands to reason that the Prussians are shrewd enough to deduce our intentions and prudent enough to plan for contingencies. We need to be absolutely certain in these matters, and we need to ascertain the following: first, if they are aware of our plans, and second, what countermeasures they intend to carry out. Are you following me?"

"Completely, sir!"

"Of course, we couldn't place such a delicate assignment in the hands of the diplomatic corps. We require another, less obvious way, one which is more discreet. The mission must be given to a man who, aside from his vast military knowledge, possesses intelligence, discernment, and courage to outsmart the enemy. It's our intention to send such a man with the necessary documentation and recommendations to Berlin. He will be briefed in how to conduct himself. He will have money at his disposal, first to satisfy his personal needs in order for him to blend in, but then also for other, unexpected demands. This man must be clever, as well as tactful, and daring. Yet also prudent! His assignment won't be an easy one, but the rewards will outweigh the risks." Rallion paused, looking appraisingly at Lemarch. "You have been recommended to me, Captain. What is your response?"

Rallion detected no surprise in the captain's features. Of course, that was probably because Lemarch had probably already been briefed by his own superior.

When Lemarch gave his answer, it was as unequivocal as the one he had already given his superior. "I will embrace this opportunity to serve France with distinction! I give you my word that I will do anything and everything in my power to reach my goal in this assignment."

"That's what I expected to hear. Now, I have to point out that time is of the essence, so I can't spare you much time to arrange your affairs. Have you ever been to Berlin before?"

"No," Lemarch admitted softly, not wanting to disappoint. "I haven't."

"That's encouraging," Rallion said quickly, noting the slight surprise on the man's face. "You won't face the danger of being recognized." He glanced up at a clock. "I'm leaving on a train at eleven o'clock bound for Thionville. You will accompany me. Are you able to put your affairs in order and be available to travel on such short notice?"

"A soldier must always be ready to march!"

"Exactly! There's something I must see to there, and after its completion, I can supply you with further instructions. My business should take two days at the most, allowing you to travel to Berlin. Once there, your greatest priority will be to work your way into the higher circles. I have an address that may be of advantage to you."

Rallion pulled a notebook out of his pocket and began flipping through it. "I have heard of a most competent strategist, an officer who, despite his youth, has been entrusted with important assignments which he often takes home with him. If you were able to gain his confidence, even become his friend, you would end up in a position whereby you could catch a glimpse into some of his secret correspondence. No doubt, he would have no intention of speaking directly about his work, but a good cigar, even a few bottles of wine, have been known to loosen the most reluctant tongue. Perhaps this man has relatives, or a fine looking sister, whose trust and love you might be able to win." Finding the address in the book, he ripped out the page. "Finally, I want to share a piece of wisdom with you. A clever man understands how to use all things to his advantage. I trust that you are just such a clever man."

"I will say it again," replied the captain, "that I will do my best to win this man's confidence. May I learn his name?"

"His name is Richard von Löwenklau, a cavalry master just like you," Rallion answered, handing over the address. "But wait, there's one more thing you should know. He has a grandfather, a veteran from the old regime. His grandfather first served under Lutzöw, and then later under Blücher. It is rumored that he was wounded at *la Belle Alliance*. To this day, the old man speaks passionately about his accomplishments. I'm sure you know that the best way to win the approval of such people is to make them believe you're caught up in their romanticism. That's all that I need to tell you for now. You will be receiving further details in due course." With that, Rallion stood. "Are you equipped with a costume. After all, you'll have to look the part of an artist."

"I can procure one in a matter of minutes."

"And an easel?"

Lemarch couldn't suppress a smile. "To drag an easel from here to Berlin would be a bit cumbersome, even unnecessary, don't you think? In order to play the part of a painter, all I need to have are proper garments and a map folder. I can purchase the easel and other supplies in Berlin."

"Fine. I will entrust those minor details to you. For now, conclude your preparations quickly, because I expect you to be back here punctually at eleven o'clock. *Adieu!*"

Rallion shook the officer's hand with an air of indifference, as though he meant to say: *I'll allow you to shake my hand, but for God's sake don't make too much of it. Once you're gone, I'll be carefully washing this hand to remove any trace of such an ordinary man.*

The captain accepted the offered hand as one who is afforded a high honor. He left, bowing deeply with a flair that would have pleased even a duke, or prince. After all, despite the count's rank, he knew Rallion had more influence with the emperor than most of the egotistical ministers of the French government.

❧❀❧

While the 11:50 train stood ready to depart for Thionville, Rallion climbed into a second-class carriage, followed by a young man in tight grey pants, patent leather boots, decorated velvet jacket, wide-rimmed hat, and yellow gloves. He carried a voluminous folder under his arm, leaving little doubt as to his profession – a painter. Rallion had to look twice before recognizing Captain Lemarch in his new guise.

As they disembarked in Thionville, Rallion saw his old associate Captain Albin Richemonte, from Castle Ortry, waiting for them on the platform, ready to welcome his guests. Rallion patted the old man on the back in a friendly manner.

"Well, Captain," said Rallion, "I see by your timely arrival that you must have received my wire."

"Two hours ago, my good Count," replied Richemonte. "Naturally, I made arrangements to collect you myself."

"May I present Captain Lemarch, traveling as a painter to Berlin. I'm sure I don't have to tell an old vanguard like yourself in what capacity he goes there."

The old captain examined the young officer, baring his teeth as though he intended on snapping at all of Berlin. He nodded conspiratorially to the younger man.

"You're traveling as a painter, it seems. If you perform to our satisfaction, those Prussians will finally get the reward they deserved long ago."

"The captain will do his best, I'm convinced of it," Rallion replied in the young captain's stead. "Do you have a carriage waiting?"

"Two, actually. The second one is for your servants."

"Excellent. We should go then."

A short time later, two carriages meandered down the road toward Ortry. They had barely left the outskirts of Thionville when the coachman spotted an unusually dressed man walking on the road ahead of them. He wore Persian-style baggy pants, which were bound together under his knees, with sandals on his feet. He wore no socks, revealing his thin, brown calves. A red jacket, adorned with decorative tassels, covered his upper body. An old blue shawl was tied around his waist, containing all sorts of strange items that left observers shaking their heads as to their purpose. Underneath the open jacket, a grey shirt, which may have been white at one time, was visible. A large turban completed the ensemble.

The stranger carried a large leather sack over his shoulder, the contents seemingly moving about inside. He likely carried live items in it. The man's face was covered with a sizeable beard, augmented by two small piercing eyes.

The stranger stepped aside, allowing the approaching carriages to pass on by. His eyelids lifted slowly and his eyes looked ahead with indifference, but as soon as he glanced at the occupants in the first carriage, he came to life. His eyes transformed themselves into glowing coals, threatening to leave their sockets. But as quickly as he showed his displeasure, he composed himself again, leaning up against one of the roadside trees. As the first coach passed, he let out a high pitched whistling sound. Instantly, the horses reacted and reared up, refusing to move forward. The coachman used his whip and swore at the horses. Finally, he pleaded with them persuasively, all to no avail. The stranger fixed his gaze on the old captain.

"Hey, you," Richemonte admonished with a threatening gesture. "Don't you realize that you've made the horses skittish? Get out of the way!"

"Skittish?" asked the man in a deep, accented voice. "I've never made horses uncomfortable. I have a way of handling them. Who does this team belong to?"

"What business is that of yours, you vagabond? I'm telling you, if you fail to move, I'll get the coachman to run after you with his whip!"

"I'm not afraid!" replied the stranger calmly. "I'll only instruct the horses to obey your coachman after you tell me where you're headed."

Richemonte shrugged his shoulders, his scorn obvious to all. He ordered the coachman to continue the trip, but the man was unable to budge the team from their place.

"I can't do anything with them," the coachman lamented. "The devil seems to have got control over them. Either that or that fellow put a spell on them. I don't want to injure the horses, sir."

Until now, the count had sat quietly, observing the scene. Rallion turned to face the second coach occupied by his servants.

"Remove the fellow," he ordered, "so that the horses can't see him anymore."

The two servants climbed from their carriage and approached the stranger. They ordered him to depart, but when it became clear that he wasn't going to comply, they tried grabbing him, only to recoil in horror. The stranger had loosed his sack, allowing the heads of three speckled cobras to venture out. The creatures wrapped their tails around their master's neck, moving back and forth with lightning-like swiftness, defending him.

Rallion's servants hadn't been exposed to a cobra before, but recognized the reptiles immediately. They knew they were dealing with one of the most poisonous reptiles in the world. The men jumped back, not daring to confront the stranger again. The odd-looking man had somehow managed to tame the snakes, further demonstrating the rapport by caressing them gently.

"Anyone foolish enough to risk it, let him come!" he challenged. "All sorts of animals pay heed to my commands, even well-trained horses. These steeds won't move a muscle until I give them permission. So, where are these carriages headed?"

The gentlemen in the first coach considered it beneath them to respond, and yet realized he was untouchable. The coachman brought them out of their predicament. "We're headed to Ortry," he acknowledged.

"Fine. You may proceed," the stranger said. He let out an unusually low whistling sound. Almost immediately, the horses perked up and started moving forward again. Soon, they were in a near gallop, leaving the coachman struggling to maintain control. The stranger followed their progress until they disappeared from his sight.

Once they were out of sight, he faced eastward, his eyes shining with purpose. He sank to his knees and held his hands skyward.

"*Allah il Allah!*" he called out. "Your name is worthy and your might is unending. Praised be your name. I have finally found the first signs of Liama's trail. Liama, the daughter of our tents! I implore you and all your holy caliphs to free her. If she should no longer be alive, avenge her like no child of the desert has ever been avenged!"

When he had spoken to the Frenchmen, he had done so in broken French, but now alone, his prayer was in Arabic. Kneeling on the ground, surrounded by snakes, he had a most unusual, wild appearance. At last, he got up, replaced the snakes in his sack, and continued on his way, heading in the same direction as the carriages.

Shortly after, he arrived at a local inn in the next village. He found an old innkeeper at work and requested a refreshment. The innkeeper examined the odd-looking man with curiosity.

"No doubt you weren't born around here, in the north of France?" he asked.

"No," was the response. "I was born in the heat of the south."

"Then what are you doing here? What is your trade?"

"I am called Abu Hassan, the magician. I have studied magical things and all creatures are subject to me."

"Ah, a juggler," laughed the innkeeper. "Where do you plan to show off your skills?"

"At Ortry."

"Oh no, you won't get much business there!"

"Why not?"

"The workers at the ironworks, although perhaps inclined to watch the show, aren't permitted to mingle with strangers, and the occupants of the castle have seen many a magic trick."

"Abu Hassan is capable of more than any regular magician," replied the visitor proudly. "Who lives in the castle?"

"The Baron de Sainte-Marie."

Hassan shook his head, disappointed with the answer. "Who else?"

"His wife and their two children."

"How old is the baron?"

"Perhaps fifty years old."

Hassan again shook his head, but wasn't about to give up. "Doesn't a man live there, one who has a large, grey moustache?"

"Yes," the innkeeper answered. "The baron's father."

"What is his name?"

"Actually, that's an interesting question. You would think his name would be Sainte-Marie as well, but it's not. The baron was awarded his nobility just a few years ago and found himself the recipient of a new name at the emperor's bidding. The old man's name is Richemonte, but he's most commonly known as the old captain."

Hassan listened. His calculating eyes sought refuge under his eyelids. He strived to carry on indifferently. "Was he a former soldier?" he asked.

The innkeeper nodded. "He fought under the old emperor and even journeyed as far as Africa, spending time in Algiers."

"Did the old man have a wife?"

"Naturally, since the baron is his son."

"Was his wife French?"

"I should think so, but I didn't know them back then. The Sainte-Marie family have only been at Ortry for a few years. The old captain's wife must have died a long time ago."

Hassan paused, then asked the most important question on his mind. "Have you ever heard of a woman by the name of Liama?"

"Liama?" asked the innkeeper quickly. "That was the baron's first wife."

"The baron's wife? Was the baron also in Algiers?"

"That I don't know. But his first wife was called Liama. She was a heathen. Her grave lies deep in the forest near the old tower. Her daughter is still alive."

The stranger's eyes revealed a sudden flash of joy, but he managed to keep his emotions in check. "She left a daughter behind? What is her name?"

"Marion."

"Did she ever go by a different name?"

"Why would she have a different name? What a curious question..."

Both men conversed for some time longer. As they spoke, Hassan managed to find out everything the innkeeper and the townspeople knew about the baron's first wife. He even learned how Liama's ghost haunted the old tower.

Finally, it was time for him to leave. He paid for his drink and headed out into the street, shaking his head in wonder.

I've been looking for this old Richemonte, he thought to himself. *I'm sure that was him earlier in the carriage. I wasn't mistaken. Allah has finally guided my steps to success. But Liama, the noble daughter of the desert, is dead... I have to avenge her. But who is this Marion? Who is the Baron de Sainte-Marie? Who is the ghost that appears at the old tower? Mohammed, the prophet of believers, claims that a woman has no soul.* How can it be then that a woman's soul can appear after death? I'll have to go to Ortry and find out for myself. Once I've solved the mystery, I can go back to the sheik and tell him that the time for wrath has finally come.*

His eyes flamed up wildly as he contemplated the coming wrath. His mouth curved into scornful laughter. *Will Richemonte recognize me? Not likely. Grief has altered my appearance. And if he should learn my identity, I'm not afraid of him. Weren't they all afraid of my snakes? Allah has robbed them of understanding, so that they didn't even understand why their horses obeyed me. They were Arabian horses, from the desert, obeying their natural instincts. If the men want to challenge me, I'll show them my tricks and they'll fear my skill, perhaps taking me for Satan himself!*

---

*In the Qu'ran, the 7th *sura* states, "It is he who created you from a single soul and made its mate like nature, in order that he might dwell with her (in love)." In the *Hadith*, the sacred writings, women were viewed as 'unclean' creatures. They were not to exert any authority over a man, and were only allowed to talk when permitted to do so by their husbands. One caliph, Abd-A-Malik Ibn Marwan (685-705 A.D.) stated, "The end of a man's life is better than its beginning; his patience increases, his resistance to temptation is stronger, his trade is made perfect. But the end of a woman's life is worse than its beginning; her beauty vanishes, her womb grows barren and her morals deteriorate."

About the Author

Robert Stermscheg, born in Europe in 1956, was exposed to many wonderful writers – Edgar Rice Burroughs, Alexandre Dumas, and of course Karl May. He appreciated how they opened up a whole new world to our imaginations through their portrayal of life. His parents were of Austrian descent, and as a result of his father's occupation as an electrical engineer, he moved several times in his early childhood. His father kept a steady supply of books to broaden his son's education, including a repertoire of Karl May books.

The entire family moved to Canada in 1967, eventually settling in Manitoba. Robert was involved in chess, hockey, and flying, but always kept up his interest in the German language. His passion to share the works of Karl May, largely unknown in North America, resulted in the search for English translations. After retiring from a satisfying career with the Winnipeg Police Service in 2006, he had the opportunity to pursue his dream – translating one of Karl May's novels into English. His wife, Toni, embraced his dream and encouraged him in the writing process. She supported him in this new venture by being a proofreader.

In 2006, Robert embarked on his first book, *The Prussian Lieutenant*, based on an earlier work by Karl May. His first book was well-received, encouraging him to continue with the sequel, *The Marabout's Secret*. This second book shifts to the sands of the Sahara, pitting the young Lieutenant von Löwenklau against his family's nemesis, Captain Richemonte.

Robert resides in Winnipeg and is currently working on his third book, *Buried Secrets*.